The KING of the TREES
BOOK TWO

TORSILS IN TIME

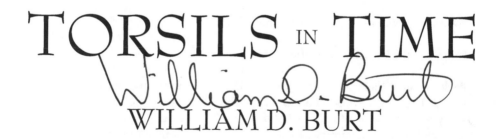

WILLIAM D. BURT

WINEPRESS WP PUBLISHING

Printed in the United States of America.

Packaged by WinePress Publishing, PO Box 428, Enumclaw, WA 98022. The views expressed or implied in this work do not necessarily reflect those of WinePress Publishing. Ultimate design, content, and editorial accuracy of this work is the responsibility of the author(s).

Verses marked NASB are taken from the New American Standard Bible, © 1960, 1963, 1968, 1971, 1972, 1973, 1975, 1977 by The Lockman Foundation. Used by permission.

Cover by Terri L. Lahr. Illustrations by Rebecca J. Burt and Terri L. Lahr. Llwcymraeg translations by Lyn Mererid.

ISBN 1-57921-368-5
Library of Congress Catalog Number: 2001087336

"For the word of God is living and active and sharper than any two-edged sword, and piercing as far as the division of soul and spirit, of both joints and marrow, and able to judge the thoughts and intentions of the heart. And there is no creature hidden from His sight, but all things are open and laid bare to the eyes of Him with whom we have to do."

—HEBREWS 4: 12–13 (NASB)

In loving memory of Erica Lahr-Auvil

CONTENTS

Prologue: Of Crowns & Quill Pens

Kraawwk! Kraawwk! Timothy son of Garth looked up to see an ill-favored, pink-headed bird perched in the tree above him. Eating his lunch of rye bread and cheese, he sat alone in the whispering wood, having no sisters, brothers or other playmates.

As usual, his father was somewhere between Beechtown and the Green Sea, poling his raft up the River Foamwater. A flaxen-haired boy of ten, Timothy wished Garth could spend more time with him, especially during the summer—a raftsman's busiest season. Timothy's mother Nora took in laundry, scrubbing the soiled tunics of the rollicking bargemen and raftsmen who stopped in Beechtown to test their landlegs.

Timothy whiled away many an idle June afternoon in the forests above Beechtown hunting squirrels and pheasants or spying on stoats and badgers, salamanders and snakes. Still hungry after his meager meal, he picked a few wild strawberries, popping the sweet, fragrant fruits into his mouth.

As the ruff-necked bird raucously croaked again, Timothy saw it was a vulture. The carrion eater was tugging and pecking at something, no doubt a poor dead thing stuck in the tree. Then Timothy's keen eye caught a metallic luster—perhaps the point of a huntsman's arrow lodged in a limb. He had often seen crows carry off coins and other shiny objects with which to brighten their drab, untidy nests—but never vultures. Failing to pilfer the pretty, the bird squawked and flew away.

Timothy smiled. Such a lot of fuss over a snippet of steel! Just then, a wind gust waded through the foliage, caressing the polished leaves into rustling curls and setting the "arrowhead" to twirling and flashing. Timothy wished he could view the mysterious object through a starglass, such as riverboat captains often used. He sighed and made a face. Owning a starglass was out of the question; one of those long tubes with their glass lenses would cost his father a month's wages. If he wanted to see what had so attracted the vulture, he'd have to climb the tree.

Ten minutes later, moss-grimed and well winded, Timothy had reached a gnarled limb halfway up the tortoiseshell trunk. Crawling out on the branch, he found a black satchel, its strap caught on a couple of crooked twigs. Sunlight glinted off a metal clasp securing a wide flap to the case's front.

Timothy gave a low whistle. Some wily highwayman—maybe Bartholomew the Bold himself—must have flung the satchel into this tree while fleeing a sheriff's posse, intending to retrieve his loot later. "Catcher, keeper, thief's a weeper," Timothy chortled. Whatever was inside, it now belonged to him.

Freeing the tangled strap, he hefted the grimy satchel, which looked as though it had hung in the tree for quite a spell. Though heavy, the case didn't rattle or clink the way a pouch of gold and jewels would. When the rusted catch refused to open, he looped the strap around his neck, wriggled back down the tree and set off for home, clutching the case to his chest.

After crossing the Beechtown bridge, he ducked into an alley to avoid notice—but not quickly enough. Someone had been waiting for him. "Hey! It's Garth the River-Rover's brat!" growled Baglot son of Baldwyn, the brash town bully. "I thought I told you never to show your ugly mug around here again!"

As Timothy broke into a run, Baglot and his gang gave chase, catcalling, "Tim-my boy, the tin-ker's son, watch him run, O what fun! Tim-my boy, the tin-ker's son, go hide in your hole by the waa-ter!" *Whizzz!* A stone sailed over Timothy's head. Another struck him in the thigh. He vaulted a fence and hopped into a drainage ditch, where he crouched among some cattails.

When the hoots and cries had died away, Timothy crept out of the ditch and limped along the riverbank to his parents' thatched hut. Beside it sat his father's ramshackle shed. Inside the shed, broken furniture, warped wagon wheels and pitted pieces of iron littered the floor. In his spare time, Garth repaired and sold cast-off odds and ends to help his family eke out a living.

After rubbing away his tears and catching his breath, Timothy set the satchel on Garth's workbench, noting a peculiar emblem embossed on the side. Arranged in a crowned "W," a gold circlet and four quill pens rested on an open-book design, like this:

Convinced the symbol must be the mark of royalty or nobility, Timothy pried open the latch with a chisel. As he raised the flap, a musty, furry smell escaped. "Papers?" he groaned. "All that work for a bunch of moldy papers!" Stomping out the door with the case, he was about to fling the whole lot into the river when he realized that the owner might pay a handsome price for the satchel's return. Besides, its contents might make interesting reading. Thanks to his grandmother's training, Timothy had already devoured all the books he could lay hands on, and his parents could ill afford to satisfy his demand for more.

After settling down on the riverbank, he removed all the stacks of parchments from the satchel. Then he upended and shook it. Only a frayed quill pen fell out, its hollow tip heavily scored as if by a knife or file. Squinting at the spidery script squiggling across the stiff, yellowed papers, Timothy read, "Be it hereby enacted by the power vested in me . . ."

Grappling with more flowery terms, he came upon the names, "King Rolin" and "Queen Marlis" penned in bold letters. His first hunch hadn't been far from the mark; it seemed he had discovered the records of a royal court. More references to the king and queen were sprinkled throughout the following pages.

Then he came to a thick sheaf of parchments bound with green and purple cords. Across the front, someone had scrawled the words, "Torsils in Time." Torsils? Timothy pictured pea-green lizards with powerful tails and long, forked, flickering tongues. Chewing on a river grass stem, he read further.

Torsils in Time
Part 1

MAE'R GOEDEN YN FYW

THE TREE LIVES

CHAPTER 1

THE BLACK PEARLS

Rolin, King of Lucambra whistled cheerily as he hurried down the familiar cobbled path along the bluffs above the Sea of El-marin. Just before entering a thick pine wood, he paused, thinking he'd heard footsteps. Putting a long wooden tube to his eye, he perused the empty trail behind him. Then he focused on a balcony high on the Tower of the Tree, where a bright-faced woman was waving a white kerchief.

"Goodbye, my queen," murmured Rolin, waving back. "I shan't be long!" Pocketing the starglass, he strode into the forest.

On this fine autumn morning, the sunlight was slanting through the treetops to caress red-capped *pogankas* sprouting on the forest floor. Ordinarily, Rolin would have tarried to admire the striking colors of those deadly mushrooms. However, he was anxious to take in the last day of Beechtown's annual fall market, where he hoped to meet his father, Gannon son of Hemmett.

Once among the poorest of Beechtown's hill folk, Gannon no longer made his living as a vendor at the spring and fall markets. Thanks to the rubies and emeralds his son had pocketed from the sorcerer Felgor's hoard, Gannon still lived very simply but much more comfortably. Peddling his prize honey and potatoes was now only a pleasant pastime.

Today, Rolin had shed his royal robes for the homespun jerkin and leggings of a Thalmosian hill dweller, the better to blend into the crowds of marketgoers. A floppy, broad-brimmed hat topped off the disguise, hiding his auburn hair.

At length Rolin came to a mossy-barked tree whose branches spread like many-jointed arms. "Is anybody home?" he called, tapping on the trunk. He heard only a rumbling rattle in reply. How trees snored—being noseless and all—was a mystery to Rolin. *Rattat-a-tat-tat,* he rapped again on the whorled bark.

"Umph, who's there?" croaked a creaky voice. Owing to the scent of amenthil blossoms, Lucambrians could converse with trees and other forest dwellers, a secret they jealously guarded from their Thalmosian neighbors.

"It's me, Rolin. Wake up!" Lately, Lightleaf had been dozing most of the day. After all, he was over four hundred years old.

"Forgive me, my lord," yawned the tree. "I was just enjoying the most marvelous dream: It was autumn, the poppies were blooming, and—"

"It *is* autumn, you silly torsil!" Rolin laughed. "You shouldn't be sleeping away such fine fall weather."

"Why can't a tree take a nap without all the neighbors complaining? Humph. I suppose you want passage."

"I do—if you don't mind, that is."

Lightleaf sighed. "I suppose not, but only if you promise not to disturb me again until my dream is finished."

"That could take months!" Rolin retorted. "I'll be gone all day, so you can dream away until I return." Climbing the tree, Rolin took care not to scuff off any bark. At the top, he looked back at the tower, its colorful flags and banners waving. Still higher, a griffin lazily circled in the sky. Any enemy with designs on Queen Marlis or the Hallowfast would first have to reckon with Ironwing.

Before climbing down, Rolin lightly rubbed his finger under one of the torsil's shiny leaves. The tree shivered, making a sound not unlike a sneeze.

"Whuff!" wheezed Lightleaf. "You know how I hate being tickled. Stop it at once, or I won't let you back into Lucambra!"

Rolin chuckled, knowing the tree was only bluffing. Like most torsils, Lightleaf could be touchy—even cantankerous. However, the tree had never refused him passage. It helped that Rolin always avoided breaking any of his friend's branches.

"Touch the top, then drop," he told himself, repeating the rhyme all Lucambrian children learned when they were old enough to climb trees. Though Thalmosian by birth, Rolin was half Lucambrian and had learned the first rule of torsil travel: If you didn't climb all the way to the top of a tree of passage before starting down again, you wouldn't go anywhere at all. You might as well have climbed a cherry or an alder for all your trouble.

After a moment's dizziness and tingling—the only side effects of making passage—Rolin alit on Thalmosian soil. Though he'd often traveled between the two worlds, the abrupt change of scenery was still unsettling. Gone were the bright-needled pines and high sandstone cliffs overlooking the Sea of El-marin. In their place stood a stolid fir forest marching down from the Tartellans' craggy, snow-clad peaks, now flushed pink with the dawn.

Rolin bade Lightleaf farewell and made off down the mountainside. Following paths known only to him and a few trusted Lucambrian scouts, he came at last to the River Foamwater.

Melting into the crowd crossing the new Beechtown bridge, Rolin fell in behind a boy and girl accompanying a lanky "Greencloak," as Lucambrians were called in Thalmos. He couldn't help overhearing their conversation.

"Thank you, Father, for letting me join you and Sylvie today," the boy bubbled, his mop of hazel hair bouncing with each step.

"I did promise you a visit to the market before your thirteenth birthday," sighed the long-legged man, whom Rolin recognized as a Lucambrian woodcarver named Gaflin son of Hargyll. Rolin guessed the lumpy bag he carried contained wooden bowls, cups, spoons and trinkets for sale. "Since it's the final day of the market, you might find some rare bargains, if you're lucky."

"Oh, I hope so," beamed the boy. "Say, what are all these yeg statues on the bridge? They're awfully ugly."

His sister rolled her eyes. "Oh, Arvin. Don't you know *any-thing?* King Rolin petrified those batwolves in the Battle of Beechtown. So many fell into the Foamwater that they dammed up the river and made this bridge."

"Lifelike, aren't they?" remarked Gaflin, running his fingers over a stone yeg's razor-edge teeth. "I'm glad we cleaned these cursed creatures out of Lucambra."

Arvin pointed out some snarling statues standing by a shop entrance. "Then why do people keep them by their doors?"

Gaflin snorted. "They're supposed to scare other yegs away. They don't, of course. Even the birds pay them no mind. See? There's a nest on that one."

Arvin gestured at two more statues flanking another doorway. "What about those? They don't look like the others."

"That's because they're man-made," his father replied. "When the Thalmosians ran out of whole petrified batwolves to guard their homes, they started carving their own. If you ask me, they're even uglier than the real thing."

Rolin grimaced. *Gargoyles,* the townspeople called their grotesque sculptures, evidently a corruption of the Lucambrian word, "yeggoroth."

"I only hope your starglass peddler won't drive you too hard a bargain," Gaflin was saying to Arvin. "Most of his kind are cheats and ne'er-do-wells. Have you enough gilders for the thing?"

The boy held up a leather sack. "I don't need any money to buy my starglass. I'll just trade for it."

"I'm sure any peddler would love to have one of your *frogs,*" sneered Sylvie. "Or did you steal Mother's rings to barter with?"

"They're not frogs or rings, and I didn't steal them; I found—" Arvin began. He broke off, the back of his neck flushing pink.

His fair-haired sister pawed at the pouch with greedy fingers. "So there *is* something valuable in this bag of yours! Come on, open it; I want to see what's inside."

Arvin pressed the sack to his chest. "Stay away from me!"

"I don't care what you've got in there," Gaflin said. "Just be sure to find me once you have your starglass. Remember: Not a word about the torsils! These potato eaters are a crafty lot."

Rolin chuckled. Since becoming king, he had encouraged his people to trade freely with the "potato eaters," who differed from Lucambrians mainly in their broader stature, more boisterous ways and eye color. (Lucambrians' eyes were a deep green.) Lucambrians also lived much longer than their neighbors.

Visiting Beechtown was not without its risks. Some nosy potato eater might trail a Greencloak back to a torsil, and that would be the end of tranquil Lucambra. A flood of Thalmosians would surely follow, unless the Lucambrians cut down all the torsils leading to their sister world—an unthinkable act.

"There he is!" cried Arvin, darting away. Curious to see how the boy would fare with the starglass peddler, Rolin followed. Like as not, a sadder and wiser Arvin would come away from the market empty-handed.

The wizened starglass peddler and his stall had been fixtures at the spring and fall markets longer than Rolin could remember. Nobody knew where the old codger lived, but everyone knew what he did: He sold the magical tubes, and nothing else. Not horses or hogs, baskets or beads, hammers or harnesses—just starglasses, and everybody wanted one.

As Rolin pushed his way through the milling marketgoers, he noticed a squat bulldog of a man talking to Arvin. "Whatcha got in yer pouch, boy?" The stranger reached for the sack.

Arvin recoiled from the man's hairy paw. "Nothing!"

Rolin wedged his body between Arvin and the pickpocket. "Begone, ruffian, or I'll have you thrown in irons!" he roared.

The thug brandished a long knife. "If it's trouble ye're wantin', I'll give ye plenty!" he snarled, showing a mouthful of broken, discoloured teeth.

Crack! Rolin's starglass struck the thief's hand, knocking the knife away. Muttering a stream of oaths, the man slunk off.

"Fawnk you, fine fur!" mumbled Arvin, whose bobbing head reminded Rolin of a spring-necked doll's. His bulging cheeks wobbled like a fat dowager's.

"What did you say?" Rolin asked.

The left bulge disappeared, only to bolster the right one. "I said, 'Thank you, kind sir!'"

Rolin burst into laughter at the sight of Arvin's lopsided face. "Whatever have you got in your mouth?"

"My pearlf," he replied with a guilty look. "I almoft fwallowed vem!" Rolin grinned in sudden understanding. Arvin had scooped the pouch's contents into his mouth, the better to hide them from the bulldog. Now where had the son of a Lucambrian woodcarver gotten a mouthful of pearls?

"Might ye be lookin' for one o' *these*?" quavered a dry, cobbly voice. There stood a shriveled prune of a man dressed in a baggy black jerkin and breeches, his beak-nosed, weathered face wreathed in a toothless grin. Loose pink skin ringed his scrawny neck in wrinkled folds. In his clawlike hands, he held a wooden starglass elaborately inlaid with silver stars and a gold moon.

"Yeth. Pleeth," Arvin lisped through his pearls.

Rolin frowned. The peddler looked different. For one thing, the starglass hawker he remembered had brown eyes, not these light-licking, coal-deep pits in a fawning, pockmarked face.

The old man must have noticed his gaze, for he winked and cackled, "I look just like the man in the moon, don't ye think? Ye can see for yerself through my starglasses. They're fifteen gilders this year." He nodded at the wheeled stall behind him, where rows of glittering starglasses stood at attention along worn wooden shelves. Seeing Arvin's despairing look, he hastened to add, "But for a young feller like you, I'll make 'er ten."

"Oi dot haf amy momey," Arvin mumbled, evidently trying to dislodge a pearl from under his tongue.

The peddler clenched his fists. "Er ye playin' games wi' me, boy? If ye er, I'll—" He broke off as Rolin shot him a stern glance.

Arvin shook his head until the pearls in his mouth rattled.

"Then give me yer money, an' stop makin' a dumb show!"

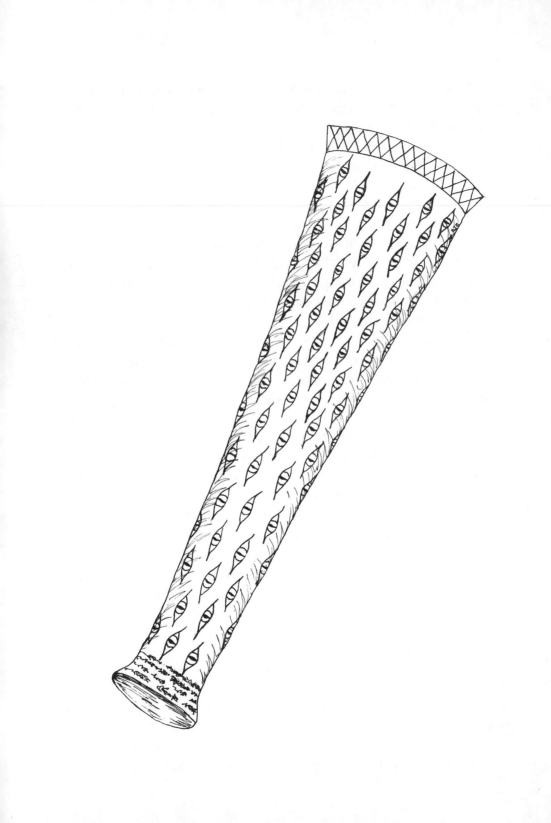

Grimacing, Arvin spat out five jet-black pearls into his cupped hands. At the sight of the marble-sized spheres, the peddler's eyes bulged. Then he gripped Arvin's arm with bony fingers.

"Come back here with me, boy," he hissed, drawing Arvin behind the display table. "Even if ye haven't the usual *fee,* those five will buy ye the best I got—this 'un here." Unlocking an oaken cupboard, the hawker drew out the most exquisite starglass Rolin had ever seen. Fully a foot longer than its fellows, it was encased in gleaming silver and embellished with intricate eye designs.

The peddler held up a leather canister with a sturdy strap. "Comes wi' its own case, too. Does it please yer fancy, young sir?" The old man licked his lips, his greedy gaze wavering between Arvin and Rolin.

"Yes, very much," Arvin said, putting the starglass to his eye.

The peddler thrust his hand in front of the eyepiece. "No! Ye mustn't look through it yet."

Scowling, Arvin lowered the tube. "Why not?"

"Ah, the *light* down here is poor so early in th' morning. Ye should wait awhile—say, an hour or so, until ye get home. The light'll be better then."

Arvin nodded and grudgingly slipped the starglass into its case. After dropping his payment into the peddler's outstretched palm, he left Rolin to puzzle over the five black pearls.

The rarest of all gems, black pearls were found only in the Elmarin's southern waters. Even one was worth a king's ransom—and Rolin had never seen such perfect specimens. They reminded him of the peddler's fathomless, ebony eyes.

Convinced the boy had gotten the worst of the bargain, Rolin feigned an interest in some wicker baskets while watching the starglass peddler out of the corner of his eye. Though curious shoppers were still crowding around, the old man swept up his wares and climbed into the cramped confines of the rambling, rickety stall. As soon as the hinged doors had scraped shut, Rolin ambled over to press his ear against the caravan's side.

The peddler's raspy voice carried through the thin wooden wall. "I'd nearly given up hope, my pretty pets! But we knew he'd come along one day, didn't we? Now we'll be free of this stinking town. No more selling starglasses to grubby, half-witted street urchins and bumbling country bumpkins! Since we've done *his* bidding, we'll be rid of him and his confounded riddle, too!

> Of all the fish that are in the sea,
> You must hook the one without the fee;
> For in its mouth, it carries the prize
> To purchase the power to mesmerize.

"I'd say we've found our 'fish,'" the starglass vendor chortled. "It won't be long before he takes the bait—and he'll be only the first of many. Let's hope he crosses over before using it."

Rolin heard a 'bang,' and a hatch flew open in the top of the stall. "Fly, fly, to the five corners of the sky!" the peddler cried. With strangled croaks and a flurry of wings, five coal-black ravens flew out to scatter over Beechtown.

CHAPTER 2

A MESSAGE FOR THE MAYOR

The peddler's words still ringing in his ears, Rolin hurried through the market to find Arvin. He caught up with the boy and his family just beyond the bridge.

"May I see it? You *said* I could." Sylvie was pawing at the silver starglass, her pert mouth twisted petulantly. With a sigh, Arvin handed her the tube, warning her not to look into it.

Gaflin frowned. "Why didn't you ask the fellow his name?"

Arvin shuffled his feet. "I'm sorry, Father. I was in a hurry to find the peddler and I just forgot."

"That's no excuse!" Gaflin scolded him. "You should never let a stranger's kindness go unrewarded."

"The boy's happiness is reward enough for me," Rolin broke in with a smile. Startled, the three turned toward him.

"It's the stranger!" Arvin cried. A hunted look came over him.

Gaflin bowed, his green hood flopping forward. "Thank you for rescuing my son, good sir. I should like to repay you for your trouble, but a poor woodcarver like myself has few means—"

"Do not fret yourself, Gaflin," said Rolin, doffing his hat. "Your gratitude belongs more to Gaelathane than to me."

Confusion and alarm spread across the woodcarver's bearded features as he took in Rolin's chestnut hair, green eyes and royal bearing. "You—you're . . ."

"King Rolin!" gasped the children. "It's King Rolin!"

Gaflin bowed again. "Forgive me, Sire. If only I had known . . ."

"I apologize for deceiving you. When visiting Thalmos, I usually dress as one of the hill folk. People here know me only as 'Rolin-the-beekeeper's-son,' and I prefer to keep it that way."

"As you wish, my lord," murmured Gaflin.

"I can also vouch for your son's honesty," Rolin went on. "He fairly paid for that starglass with—" *Don't tell them about the pearls,* Arvin's green eyes pleaded.

"With a goodly sum," Rolin ended lamely. "I'll speak to the mayor about that rascal who tried to rob your boy, too."

The woodcarver looked relieved. "Thank you, Sire. Forgive me, but I must be leaving. My wife Lepia will be worried, you see."

"Be at peace, son of Hargyll. I, too, must be on my way."

"Then please accept this gift as a token of my gratitude," said Gaflin. Taking a toy rocking horse out of his bag, he handed it to Rolin. "If ever you go fishing on the Mosswine, I'd be honored if you'd share a bowl of mushroom soup with our family."

"I'd be delighted. Until then, friends, go with Gaelathane!"

After helping his father serve the long lines of customers clamoring for a square of honeycomb or a sack of spuds, Rolin went to see the mayor. A maid let him in and took him down a musty hall to a dingy room that served as the mayor's study. An unwashed window admitted a little gray light that fell unflatteringly on the balding head of a fat man slumped behind an old maple desk. His mouth agape, the mayor was snoring.

Rolin coughed self-consciously, and His Honor's lolling head snapped upright. "Wha-who—?" he began, scrabbling backwards in his seat. "I'll call for him today! I promise! Oh, it's you, the beekeeper's boy." The mayor crumpled in on himself.

Bit by bit, Rolin coaxed an incredible tale out of the trembling dignitary. The night before, a brilliant light had awakened him out of a sound sleep. Thinking it was the moon, he had risen to shut the drapes. They were already closed.

"Fire!" was on his lips when a bearded figure with eyes like glowing sapphires stood before him. The mayor shrank back from the man's white-robed radiance.

As the stranger's words pierced his heart like burning arrows, the mayor grated his teeth. Why must he hire that *gadabout*? Surely there were other craftsmen equally capable—and more willing to show proper respect for his high office. Wilting under his visitor's unwavering gaze, he reluctantly nodded. He would call on Garth the River-Rover first thing in the morning.

"He must precisely follow the plans I will give you," commanded the personage. "When all is done, I shall return."

Then a large, gem-studded golden egg appeared in midair before the perspiring mayor. As the gleaming globe spun like a child's top, its jewels threw off beams of reddish light. Inscribed with a spiral of silvery letters, the lower half was diamond tipped, adding to the top-like effect.

"What is it?" the mayor asked. However, his visitor—and the vivid vision—had vanished, leaving him to ponder the unpleasant task before him until night welcomed the dawn.

———————— ⟳ ————————

The parchments dropped from Timothy's nerveless fingers. Whoever had written these words had known of his father's undeserved reputation in the town for shoddy work. Garth's unflinching honesty in a trade rife with fraud had earned him many enemies. Still, who would send the mayor of Beechtown to see a simple man of the river? For the second time in as many hours, Timothy fought the urge to hurl the leather satchel and all its contents into the river. Several months would pass before he dared read from the book again.

CHAPTER 3

MUSHROOMS AND MYSTERIES

Shortly after visiting the mayor, Rolin was hurrying up the path toward the Hallowfast. Marlis was waiting for him with arms akimbo. Clad in a simple green gown, the queen tossed her head and crinkled her small, sharp nose—a sure sign of displeasure. "So you like selling your father's potatoes better than helping me tidy up the Hallowfast, is that it?"

"You know how I hate brooms!" Rolin shot back, lightly kissing his wife. He loved the sweet smell of her silky, straw-yellow hair and the way it flowed over her shoulders like sunshine. "I've also been busy defending Beechtown from thieves and brigands."

Raising an eyebrow, Marlis held him at arm's length. "How dashing! But how did you escape them unscathed?"

"I'll tell you all about it inside." Rolin was closing the tower's stone door behind them when he felt something brush past. Yet, he saw nothing, and the guttering torches set in the walls cast no shadows save his and Marlis's. Mounting the stairway winding through the heart of the Hallowfast, the king and queen found their three children awaiting them in the throne room.

"Father!" cried the three as one, running up to twine themselves in Rolin's legs. "Did you bring us anything?"

"Not this time, children!" he laughed, patting their heads.

"What about me?" pouted Meghan, her blond hair framing a round face. "I'll be six tomorrow!"

"The day *after* tomorrow," her older sister Gwynneth corrected her with a stern look.

"You'll have lots of treats then," added Elwyn, the eldest.

"As it happens, I do have a present for you, Meghan," Rolin announced. He was pulling Gaflin's rocking horse from his pocket when something knocked it out of his grasp. The children all laughed as if he'd played a great trick.

Meghan kissed her father on the cheek. "Thank you, Papa!" Then she showed the toy to her admiring brother and sister.

Rolin flapped his hands at them. "Run along, now. Your mother and I need to speak—privately."

Rolling their eyes and making smacking noises with their lips, the children scurried from the room. As soon as they were gone, Rolin took his wife aside and whispered, "Something's wrong here. What is it?"

Marlis shook her head and drew him onto the balcony. "Odd things have been happening," she said in a low voice.

"What sort of things?"

Marlis knotted her long, slender fingers and glanced nervously about. "Whenever you're away, I sense someone watching me, listening, breathing. I hear laughter in the tower, too, and fluttery night sounds outside, even when no sorcs are about."

Rolin nodded, telling her of the blow he'd felt when handing Meghan the toy rocking horse. "I heard footsteps on the trail yesterday, too," he added.

Marlis blanched and gripped his arm. "Rolin, you don't suppose the Hallowfast is haunted, do you?"

Rolin forced a laugh. "Who would want to haunt this boring old place? Anyway, I don't believe in ghosts. There must be another explanation."

"Perhaps," sighed Marlis. "I only wish I knew what it was."

After that, the servants searched the tower from top to bottom but found nothing to account for the eerie noises echoing through its halls and stairways. The children refused to go to bed unless lamps were left burning in their rooms. Then the fall rains arrived, cooping up everyone for days on end. When a wan sun broke through the gray clouds one morning, it found King Rolin starting an oatmeal war at the family breakfast table.

"What is going on here?" a familiar voice boomed into the room. "Wasting perfectly good porridge again, I see."

"Grandfather Bembor!" squealed the children, aiming their oatmeal-heaped spoons at him.

"Truce! Truce!" cried the old man as he strode into the kitchen. "Who wants to go mushroom gathering with me today?" Now Lucambra's high chancellor, Marlis's grandfather had grown more stooped since Rolin had first met him, and his hair was a shade whiter. Yet his mind was as keen as ever and his eyes just as sharp— especially when it came to spotting mushrooms.

"Can we, Father? Please?" implored Elwyn. "There will be lots after this rain. I already saw some outside this morning."

Bembor produced a cluster of whitish, egg-shaped mushrooms. "I've found this fine clump of Inky Caps. They're still in their prime. They haven't even darkened yet."

Known as "Mop-on-a-stalk" among Thalmosians for its fluffy, upturned scales, the fungus dissolved into a black sludge if left to its own devices—hence the Lucambrian name, "Inky Cap." Despite its revolting appearance when overripe, the princely mushroom made a savory dish if prepared soon after picking.

"Very well," Rolin sighed. "The fresh air and sunshine will do you all good." Shouting for joy, the children danced around Bembor, their bright eyes snapping with excitement.

Bembor playfully poked Rolin in the chest with his staff. "What about you, my boy? I've never known you to pass up a mushroom hunt." No other Lucambrian was on such familiar terms with the king, save the queen and her brother, Scanlon. Rolin didn't mind; Bembor had become like a second father to him.

"I'd love to join you," he replied. "However, I've already promised Marlis a torsiling picnic today." Exploring as-yet-undiscovered torsil lands was his favorite sport.

Marlis smiled at him. "If it's all right, I'd like to make it a three-some and invite Scanlon, too. There's nothing he enjoys more than torsiling."

"Except picnics," Rolin teased her. Though thin as a whip, Marlis's younger brother was always eating. "He can come along, but only if he promises to leave my crown alone!" A few days earlier, the king's rascally chief deputy had smeared the royal crown inside with soot, which in turn left a black ring on the royal head. Rolin was not amused.

While Marlis bustled about collecting boots and baskets for Bembor and the children, Rolin searched out Windsong and Ironwing. He found the griffins resting under an amenthil tree in the King's Grove, their eagle's heads tucked under broad wings. Ordinarily, they would be chasing rabbits (or each other) on such a morning. However, the two had just returned from a matchmaking errand for Whitewing, king of the griffins, who had decided it was high time he had a mate. Unfortunately, none of the she-griffins they had found met with Whitewing's approval.

Ironwing glared at Rolin from under his wing. "What do *you* want? I'm already worn out with all this flying around. Whitewing can be impossible sometimes!"

"That's right," said Windsong. "'This one's too fat and that one's too skinny; go back and get me another!' I say, let him find his own mate."

"Since you're both so tired, you probably wouldn't enjoy a torsil hunt and a picnic," Rolin said, turning as if to leave.

Windsong fixed him with a large, inquisitive eye. "Picnic?"

Ironwing growled, "That means he's bringing *two-legged* fare—bread, butter, jam, roasted meat and the like—and he wants us to carry it for him."

Sorcs could be terribly stiff-necked, even at the best of times. Their feathers were easily ruffled, too. On this occasion, their insolent, indolent "lion side" was showing. "I'm sure the cook could spare us a few fresh rabbits," Rolin countered.

"Who is it that catches the cook his conies?" demanded Ironwing. "We sorcs, that's who! I'd just as soon sleep here."

Rolin recalled Bembor's advice: "Food and flattery are the keys to a griffin's heart. If one doesn't work, try the other." With a wounded air, he said, "Marlis, Scanlon and I simply wanted to take a little holiday with a couple of companions. As our dear friends and the finest fliers in the land, you two naturally came to mind." The temperamental beasts only yawned and preened their neck feathers.

Seeing that food and flattery had failed to move the sorcs, Rolin began stroking Windsong's back. With a rumbling purr, the griffin rolled over, exposing his tawny belly fur to be scratched. When the royal scribe's eyes were half-closed with ecstasy, the king re-marked, "Of course, if you're not interested in joining us, I'm sure I can find a couple of other sorcs—"

"*Other sorcs?*" the griffins screeched. "*What* other sorcs?"

Windsong fell over himself getting up. "I know of a secluded torsil grove not far from here," he chittered. "We call it the 'torsil dell.' It's impossible to reach on foot and so icy most of the year that even sorcs rarely fly there."

"Then I'll see you at the tower in an hour," Rolin said, patting Windsong on the flank. Though sorcs were notorious for biting first and asking questions later, the king's personal mount was ac-customed to such undignified gestures.

Ironwing heaved himself off the ground with a throaty moan. "Oh, have it your way. I'll go, too. It must be my lot in life to be a pack animal."

Back at the Hallowfast, Rolin found Scanlon waiting for him in the throne room. The two embraced with the greeting, "May Gaelathane be with you."

Nearly as tall as the king and only a year younger, Scanlon was outfitted in the green leggings, tunic and cloak of a Lucambrian scout. A feathered cap sat jauntily over his closely cropped dark hair. Similarly garbed, though without the cap, Rolin wore a gold *soros* medallion around his neck as the sole mark of his royalty. Both men carried a shining, glassy lightstaff taken from the Tree.

"I'll bet you my cap I'll be the first to find an unclimbed torsil!" boasted Scanlon. Before Rolin could explain that no two-legs had likely ever visited the torsil dell, let alone climbed its trees, Marlis came up behind him and threw her arms around his neck.

"What's this?" she cried in mock outrage, pointing over Rolin's shoulder at Scanlon. "A churlish vagabond, I ween, who has presumed to make a wager with the king. Shall I call the royal guard to throw out this impudent knave?"

Rolin slapped Scanlon on the back. "He *is* the royal guard! As for your dare, dear fellow, I accept. Now if you both are ready, new torsil worlds await!" Climbing a ladder through a trap door in the ceiling, the three emerged in an open pavilion at the Hallowfast's pinnacle. Here in the *sorcathel*, daring griffin riders once met their mounts before flying off to engage the enemy.

Just then, Windsong and Ironwing arrived with a flurry of wings. Ironwing padded over to nuzzle against Scanlon's chest. Not even Rolin could command such affection from his brother-in-law's personal mount, who had a well-deserved reputation for ferocity both on the battlefield and off.

"You've brought the victuals?" asked Windsong pointedly.

Marlis held up an ample wicker basket. "From apples to venison, it's all here."

"Then let's be off!" said Rolin. He and Marlis sat astride Windsong, while Scanlon hopped onto Ironwing. The griffins trotted up to the tower's ramparts and leapt into space.

———————— ⌣╫◉ ————————

While Timothy slept in his riverside hut, Beechtown's mayor stewed in the cramped, gloomy cubicle he called his study. "No one can push me around like this!" he fumed. "Why should I pay for this job?" He'd be giving up better than half his fortune: Two gold bars, his five largest rubies and the magnificent, flawless diamond he'd saved for his youngest daughter's dowry. If it weren't for the parchments he'd found on his desk that morning, he would have written it all off as a bad dream.

His gaze strayed to a loose brick in the plastered wall beside him. Behind it lay the bag of gold and jewels the Greencloaks had given him several years earlier. The mayor had promised to use those riches for rebuilding the dragon-ravaged town, but over time, he'd convinced himself that the bag's contents belonged exclusively to Beechtown's leading citizen—him.

After railing at the empty air until his breath gave out, the pudgy man paused, and a sly smile creased his oily face. Though nothing had been mentioned about compensation, surely he could expect a generous reward for delivering the jeweled piece. On the other hand, if Garth failed to follow through, the mayor could rightfully reclaim his treasures. Either way, he had nothing to lose. What still puzzled him was how the shining visitor had known about his secret hoard.

CHAPTER 4

KING ARVIN

R olin's stomach flip-flopped as Windsong dropped through the air. "Ooooooh," cried Marlis from behind him. Then the griffins caught the wind under their wings and soared over the Hallowfast. Rolin and Scanlon whooped and waved their lightstaffs.

The sorcs wheeled and headed southeast toward the coastal mountains, known as the Brynnmors. As they threaded their way through the foothills, Rolin recognized the river valley they were following. "Isn't that the Mosswine below us?" he asked Marlis.

"I think so," she answered. "It's got that ear-shaped bend."

Rolin noticed not only the squiggly loop in the river but also a telltale tendril of smoke wisping through the trees, reminding him that Gaflin's family lived near the Mosswine. At his urging, the griffins dropped lower, spiraling toward the smoke plume. Windsong landed beside a smoldering campfire with a rusted iron kettle nestled in its coals.

"Why, look at this," Marlis remarked. "Somebody's supper is all spoilt. It's been cooked to a crisp." Using a stick, she poked at a charred, smoking lump stuck in the bottom of the glowing pot.

Scanlon sauntered up. "I smell fish. Is there any left for me?"

Rolin and Marlis laughed. "Help yourself," Rolin said, gesturing at the ruined pot.

Scanlon looked inside and wrinkled his nose. "Ugh! Someone forgot to mind the stew." Cupping his hands around his mouth, he called, "Is anybody here?" His voice echoed and re-echoed through the surrounding woods.

Marlis pointed to a thick-limbed fir standing nearby. "That looks like somebody's home tree. There's something wrapped around its trunk about halfway up."

"I see it, too," Rolin said. "It must be a treehouse!"

"There's a rope hanging from it," added Scanlon. "Let's see if anyone's home." Hurrying to the fir, the three shinnied up the nettle-fiber rope dangling down the tree's side. The line passed through an open hatch in the bottom of the rustic treehouse, which was built of stout sticks lashed together with basswood-bark twine. The walls and ceiling were adorned with lifelike wooden replicas of plants and animals.

"These carvings look like Gaflin's work," Rolin remarked.

"You know who lives here?" asked Scanlon in surprise.

"I might," Rolin said. "We met at the last fall market."

Marlis looked up from a fish carving. "Then where is he?"

"*Inside,*" rumbled a sad, deep voice.

The torsil hunters stared about the treehouse and out the westward-facing window. They were alone. "Who are you?" Rolin asked.

"It is I, Graylimb the fir."

After introducing himself and his companions, Rolin asked the tree, "Do you mean Gaflin and his family are inside your trunk?" Lucambrians often made cozy homes within hollow oaks, maples and firs, where they were safe from enemies on the ground.

"Oh, no," said Graylimb indignantly. "I'm as solid as stone from top to bottom. Your friends gazed *inside,* and that's where they are now. I can't get them out, either."

Inside. The word took Rolin back to a cell deep in the dragon's mountain, where his sister-in-law, Mycena, had found him languishing. Though Mycena had been referring to Felgor's fortress, *inside* was more than just a place. It was also a hopeless state of separation from home, friends and Gaelathane Himself.

Uneasy, Rolin glanced at Marlis. Was Graylimb saying that the woodcarver's family was being held prisoner in Felgor's dungeons? That was impossible. Mt. Golgunthor had caved in on itself over a decade earlier.

"Where is 'inside'?" he asked.

"Come up higher, and I will tell you," said the tree. Instructing Marlis and Scanlon to wait for him, Rolin wriggled through the window and grasped an overhanging branch. Then he climbed to the top of the tree, where he was surprised to find Arvin's starglass hanging in its case. The starglass was making an odd chiming noise. He was just reaching out to take it when Graylimb said, "You mustn't touch that."

A little miffed, Rolin withdrew his hand. "Why not?"

"It will only bring you death," Graylimb gruffly replied.

"Nonsense," Rolin retorted. He slid the starglass out of its holder and the music ceased. Glinting in the morning sun, the stylized eyes engraved on the silver casing caught and held his gaze, following him whichever way he held the tube. Bold words were etched at one end in a cryptic script. He was putting the starglass to his eye when the fir spoke again.

"Do not look into it. You will only see *inside*."

Rolin lowered his arm. What was the tree babbling about? "All right, but you promised to tell me what happened to the people who lived here."

"So I did. Young Arvin spent hours sitting where you are, just staring through that hollow-branch thing. His mother and father told me they were afraid he had the *sickness*, he was becoming so thin and sallow."

Rolin shivered. Nowadays, the dreaded *sickness* was only a distant memory. Formerly, the sole remedy was to transplant and cultivate a wild tree seedling, making it one's "life tree" (or *sythan-ar*, in the Lucambrian language). A slow, wasting death awaited those who lost a life tree to disease or dragon fire. Rolin's mother and grandmother had so perished when their life trees had fallen to wind and ax in the hills above Beechtown.

Since Rolin's return from the Isle of Luralin, the sickness had claimed few lives. Lucambrians now had plenty of the Tree's seeds to plant as sythan-ars. After their first few years, these seedlings were impervious to ax and fire, though dragon raids were no longer a threat; the serpent Gorgorunth was long dead.

"The boy used to tell me all he'd seen and done in the wide world," Graylimb wistfully went on. "Lately, though, he'd become downright rude, carrying on as if he were the only tree in the forest. He even made up a song about himself:

> One day I'll wear a crested crown,
> And all will tremble when I frown.
> My robes will be of richest hue,
> As is the royal monarch's due.
>
> In gilded chariot I'll ride,
> My lovely queen to stand beside,
> And all shall bow before my face,
> Or torsil exile they shall taste!
>
> 'Your Majesty, Your Grace,' they'll say,
> 'We pray thee, smile on us today.'
> But like a callous, cruel god,
> I'll spurn them with a regal nod.
>
> From cups of gold I'll drink my milk,
> My servants clad in finest silk;
> With faithful warriors, fierce and brave,
> I'll soon make every world my slave.
>
> No richer king will ever reign;
> My wealth and might will never wane;
> All rule will rest beneath the thumb
> Of Arvin, King of Torsildom!

"'King of Torsildom,' indeed!" Rolin snorted. That lofty title was Gaelathane's alone, though some Lucambrians had revived the ancient custom of "torsil-claiming." By hanging one's clan colors in the top of an unexplored torsil, one could lay claim to the world that lay beyond. As for "torsil exile"—cutting down a passage-tree to strand a climber on the other side—no true follower of Gaelathane would wish such a fate on his worst enemy.

Rolin polished the starglass with his sleeve. "Every boy fancies himself a king at one time or another," he told the fir. "He'll grow out of it soon enough, as we two-legs say."

"You would know better than I," grunted Graylimb. "As we trees say, 'No slender, shaded sapling ever stood, but wished to be the tallest in the wood.' He seemed quite serious to me." The fir's deep voice dropped to a rustle. "He talked of destroying all the trees in the King's Grove with *ashtag* venom, so that 'a pure-blood can sit on the throne, not that half-breed.'"

Rolin recoiled at the treasonous words. The hideous ashtags and their caustic sap had once poisoned most of Lucambra before Gaelathane's blood had rid the land of them. If Arvin somehow slew Spirelight and the other sythan-ars in the King's Grove, the entire royal family would perish. His suspicions aroused, Rolin asked, "Did the boy tell you how he purchased his starglass?"

"Now that you mention it, he said he had bought his 'prize' with five black pearls he'd found in the dragon's mountain."

The dragon's mountain? A long-dormant memory stirred. Shortly after Felgor's defeat, a small boy named Arvin had become lost in the citadel's dark, labyrinthine tunnels. Rolin relaxed. The pearls weren't stolen after all. Instead, Arvin must have come upon part of Felgor's ill-gotten loot.

Rolin planted his eye against the starglass's deeply recessed eyepiece. At first he saw only darkness. Then a bright dot appeared, bursting into a pinwheel of iridescent hues, like an oily film shimmering on a quiet pool. The colors spun faster, exploding in riotous eruptions of reds, blues, yellows and greens.

Puzzled, Rolin looked up. The starglass was pointed at a birch tree, as plain as plain could be. He fitted his eye back against the tube. This time he was gazing at a colorful crowd of people. Adoring subjects from many torsil lands were paying homage to a figure dressed in royal raiment, crowned head held high. Rolin's eyes widened. This noble king was an older version of himself!

The sweat-slick starglass trembled in his hands. Surely it was a trick of the light or some cheap illusion. No, there he was again, King of Torsildom, regally smiling and waving. How happy he seemed, so commanding, so confident, so—

"So what did you see?" asked Graylimb.

"N-nothing," Rolin replied, his heart racing. Dare he look into the tube again? Could it actually reveal his future—or make all his wishes come true?

Graylimb muttered, "Lies it will show you, only lies. Do not believe them. Arvin believed and is no more."

"What about Sylvie and Gaflin and Lepia? Where are they?"

"They also believed the lie and are *inside*."

Rolin rapped on the tree. It sounded solid enough, though the fir might have gone soft at the core. As trees decayed, their thoughts often grew muddled. That might explain Graylimb's ramblings. If anything was living inside the fir, it was termites! After sliding the starglass back into its case, Rolin looped the strap around his wrist and rejoined Marlis and Scanlon.

"There you are!" Scanlon said. "Any sign of your friends?"

Rolin shook his head. "They could be anywhere. I only know they're not holed up inside this tree."

"I wouldn't worry if I were you," said Scanlon. "I'll wager they all left on a torsiling expedition, just as we're about to."

"You're probably right," said Rolin, much relieved. Yet, if the foursome were romping through the fragrant meadows of some pleasant world, why hadn't Graylimb said so in the first place?

Marlis stared at the starglass case. "What's that?"

"It's my—er, *Arvin's* starglass. I found it in the top of the tree."

"May we see it?"

"I suppose so." As Rolin pulled the starglass from its sheath, Marlis's hands flew to her mouth.

"It's lovely! Let me have a look through it, won't you?"

Rolin slammed the starglass back into its case. "No! It . . . doesn't work properly. Out in the weather too long, I imagine." Blushing, he brushed a hand across his face. *What's the matter with me? I've never lied to Marlis before.*

Frosty-eyed, the queen quoted one of Bembor's favorite sayings: "'What you grip is sure to slip, but once you share, you'll have more and to spare.'"

"I hope that first part doesn't apply to climbing ropes," said Scanlon. "It's a long way to the ground!"

With that, the three slid down the rope to the bottom of the tree. As Rolin started toward Windsong, Marlis tugged on his cloak and pointed at his arm. "Haven't you forgotten something?"

Rolin looked down to see the starglass dangling from his wrist. "I guess I have," he said sheepishly. "I'll just leave it here." He propped the case against Graylimb's trunk. However, he couldn't shake the nagging feeling that he ought to have heeded the fir's warning and let the starglass alone.

———————————————

"Father, has the mayor spoken to you lately?" Timothy asked. Garth was in his workshop fitting a red-hot iron rim onto a wooden wagon wheel. He looked up in surprise.

"Why, yes. How did you know? Chased me down in his carriage last week. Nearly ran me over, he did."

"What did he want?" Timothy held his breath.

Garth chuckled. "For once, he wasn't after me to spruce up my 'eyesore.' Turns out he wants me to make him some kind of fancy bauble. Said he'd send the plans and materials over soon. He even promised me three hundred gilders for the job."

"Three hundred gilders!" Timothy gasped. That was more money than his father ordinarily made in a whole year.

"Yep, can you feature that? The stingy varmint half-gagged on the price. Maybe he's hoping I'll use the money to whitewash this shed. It could use a new coat." Garth poured water over the wheel, and steam spurted off the hot iron hoop.

CHAPTER 5

THE TORSIL DELL

S o this is where the Mosswine begins!" Marlis exclaimed. She and Rolin were standing beside a clear, rushing river, breathing deeply of the bracing, pine-drenched mountain air that poured through their veins like a pure and unpolluted stream. Windsong had been right: This ravine *was* secluded—and a perfect spot for seeking out unexplored torsil worlds.

Ironwing jabbed his beak across the dark water toward a grove of crooked, shiny-leafed trees. "There are your torsils. Get on, and we'll take you across." After flying to the opposite side, the sorcs curled up for a nap while the menfolk helped Marlis lay out the picnic lunch on a linen cloth.

"Doesn't this look delicious?" she gushed. The royal cook had prepared a sumptuous feast: Creamy beechnut butter to slather on cattail-pollen bread; thick, golden honey from Rolin's own hives; rich oatmeal scones; white and yellow Thalmosian cheeses; and delicate pastries filled with fruits, nuts and mushrooms.

"Let's bless the food before it gets cold," Scanlon suggested.

The three joined hands and bowed their heads. "Dear Gaelathane, we thank You for these gifts but most of all for Your sacrifice on our behalf," Rolin prayed. "Protect us and direct us as we seek to serve You in the uncharted torsil worlds beyond these trees. May our lives reflect Your glory and the glory of Waganupa, the Tree of Life. *Mae'r Goeden yn fyw!*" The Tree lives!

"Mae'r Goeden yn fyw!" echoed Scanlon and Marlis. Then they grabbed their knives and forks and fell to.

Smelling food, the griffins awoke, shook themselves like wet cats and sauntered over to eye the victuals disdainfully. "Where are the conies?" Windsong demanded. It turned out that in all the last-minute preparations, the cook had neglected to pack the sorcs any fresh meat. As Ironwing had so peevishly predicted, the picnic cloth was spread with food unfit for griffins.

"I suppose we'll just have to *catch* something, since we lowly *beasts of burden* aren't worthy to eat with the likes of royalty," Ironwing huffed, glowering at Rolin. Then he and Windsong flew off in search of dinner.

As the griffins disappeared above the trees, Rolin sighed, "There they go like a couple of mad hornets. I wish they weren't so sensitive. You'd think we had purposely left out those rabbits."

Scanlon dug into a meat pie. "They'll find a couple of gophers or some nice, fat groundhogs and forget all about us and our picnic. You'll see. Sorcs are that way. Ready to tear off your head one minute and begging you to scratch their bellies the next. We'd better warn the cook to avoid those two until they cool off."

"I suppose you're right," said Rolin. "It's a shame they can't eat with us. I wish them good hunting."

Marlis grimaced. "If they do catch something, I hope they don't bring it back here. Their table manners are atrocious."

By late afternoon, Rolin was polishing off his last few bites of berry pie, washed down with icy river water. Comfortably full, he brought out his flute and played some Lucambrian melodies he'd learned from his friend Opio. Scanlon sat against a torsil tree, picking his teeth. "That was wonderful!" he sighed. "Everything tastes better in this fresh mountain air. Now I'm ready for a nap."

Marlis threw him a disapproving look as she shook the crumbs out of the picnic cloth. "Not until we've climbed a torsil or two. That's why we came here, you know."

"Just give me a few minutes' shuteye," Scanlon mumbled. He added under his breath, "Worst job in the kingdom, being the queen's brother." Marlis playfully kicked him.

Rolin grinned. "Leave him alone. If he wants to lose his bet with me, let him!" After pocketing his flute, he led Marlis into the sun-dappled torsil grove. As they strolled along, Marlis sang:

Now we go a-torsiling
Among the trees so fair,
The name of Gaelathane to sing,
His wondrous works declare.

O, what joy fills my soul,
As the ringing praises roll,
To the One Whose blood has bought
All torsil kingdoms everywhere,
To the Lord of torsil kingdoms everywhere.

Sizing up the torsils, Rolin said, "These trees look ancient."

"We are," creaked a chorus of breathy voices. "What's more, we don't like strangers. Who are you?"

Rolin wasn't put off by this unfriendly reception. "I am Rolin son of Gannon, king of Lucambra, and this is Queen Marlis."

A muttering sigh ruffled through the grove. "We recognize no king but the One Who made us. Are you He?"

"I am not," answered Rolin. "However, He is my king also."

More whispers. "Why have you come to the Valley of Wherren and Therren?"

"We mean you no harm, good trees," Rolin assured them. "We came here seeking new worlds to explore. The King of the Trees Himself commanded us to proclaim the good news of His cleansing death and new life to all torsil lands."

"Then we bless you in the King's name. Go now to Father Thickbark. He will take you from *herren* to *therren*."

Wondering at the trees' strange words, the two ventured farther into the grove, their feet crunching on fallen leaves and twigs.

Twice Rolin looked back, thinking he'd heard other feet following. At length they came to a sprawling torsil, its lichen-draped limbs shading a thicket of its own seedlings. With deeply fissured, tortoiseshell bark, "Thickbark" lived up to his name. Rolin tapped the torsil's trunk with his staff. *Thunk! Thunk!*

"Eh? Whaaaat are youuuuu?" the old tree mumbled sleepily.

"What are we?" Rolin repeated, glancing at Marlis.

"Yessss. Are you bearrrrsss?"

"We are two-legs," Marlis explained. "Our bark is thin and smooth, and we go about on two, er, *limbs*. If you'll let us climb you, we'll be very careful not to injure your leaves or branches."

The torsil pondered her words. "Then youuuuu are of Gaaaelathane's kind." The tree's leaves rustled. "I am verrry glad you are not bearrrrsss. They love to tearrrr my barrrrk! Wherrrrrren are youuuuu frrrrrommm, two-legs?"

"We live on the sea plain below this valley," Rolin replied.

Thickbark chuckled. "Below our valley? Ho! Ho! Ho! I liiiiike your two-legged wiiiiit. Nooooo one has made meeee laugh like thaaaaat in maaaany summmmerrrs. Nothing lies outside the Valley of Wherrrren and Therrrren. There is only thissss side of the riiiiver and that, the hiiiigher grrrround and the lowwwer."

Not wishing to dispute the quaint old torsil's geography, Rolin and Marlis asked, "Then we may climb you?"

"Youuuu mayyyy. I hope youuuu enjoyyyy therrrrrren."

Rolin whispered to Marlis, "Do you think he talks that way because he's past granting passage?" With age, torsils sometimes lost their ability to open and close the gates between worlds.

"Shush!" Marlis scolded him. "You don't want to offend the tree, do you? Now stop being such a fussbudget and help me up."

With a sigh, Rolin made a stirrup with his hands for Marlis's foot and hoisted her into the torsil. They had just reached Thickbark's dying crown when Rolin heard a fluttering sound and smelled an acrid stench. As he and Marlis descended, the stink grew stronger. Lucambra was just fading from sight when a giant hand flung the king and queen into oblivion.

It was a banner day when one of the mayor's liveried messengers rode up to Timothy's cottage and handed Garth a heavy leather bag. "You'll be paid when the work is completed, churl," the servant said. "The instructions are inside." Then he and his retinue reined their horses around and galloped off.

Only when Garth and Timothy had bolted the workshop's door behind them did they open the sack. Inside were an enormous diamond, five rubies and two glossy gold ingots. Garth's eyes grew as round as one of his wagon wheels. "All this, just for a trinket to trim the mayor's wassail tree in December?"

In the sack they also found a couple of rolled-up parchments, a lock and an intricate brass key. After examining one of the parchments, Garth rubbed his chin. "This is a far cry from knocking together a common bar stool. Still, it's a manageable job. Why anyone would want to lock this thing is beyond me."

Chapter 6.

SILVERQUICK

"I still don't understand how you could have lost the king and queen," growled Bembor. "Tell me again exactly what happened." He and Scanlon were standing in the sorcathel, buffeted by fierce, wintry winds. A pale sun was sinking into the Sea of El-marin, its last rays lighting up the tower.

Scanlon groaned. He and Bembor had gone over those events countless times in the past month. "It was supposed to be a torsiling picnic," he began. "When I awoke after lunch, Rolin and Marlis had already disappeared into the trees . . ."

Click-click. Scanlon jerked awake. What was that? *Clicketty-click.* There it was again: A sharp sound near the water, like the rattle of river rocks—or a big cat's claws on stone. Yet, the sorcs were nowhere in sight and it was not like them to play hide-and-seek. As still as a yeg statue, Scanlon crouched behind a tree.

When the sound had died away, he crept down to the riverbank. Only a few red-winged blackbirds were twittering among the whispering willows and rushes. Then he noticed fresh footprints in the sand. Much too large for yegs, the deep, five-toed tracks snaked away from the river and toward the woods.

Scanlon broke out in a cold sweat. Praying he was not too late, he raced into the forest, heedless of the leaves and branches crackling underfoot. The tracks led him to the foot of an ancient torsil. Rolin and Marlis were just climbing out of its droopy crown when—*Ka-whoom!*—a noise like ten thunderclaps stripped Scanlon's world of all light and sense.

When the king's chief deputy came to, he was draped over a torsil limb. Ears ringing, dazed and plastered from head to toe with ashes, dirt and pulverized bark, he clambered out of the now-leaf-less tree. A scene of utter devastation greeted him.

For some distance around, all the trees had been broken off or uprooted. A smoking crater gaped where Rolin and Marlis's torsil had stood. Had a lightning bolt blasted the tree? If so, it had struck out of a cloudless sky. A pungent, sulfurous haze hovered over the ruined forest.

Pawing through smoldering heaps of splintered wood, Scanlon found no trace of the king and queen. In hopes they had been thrown clear, he widened his search, all the while calling out their names. There was no answer. When the griffins returned, they flew over the area but saw no signs of the pair, either.

After Scanlon had finished his tale, Bembor stroked his beard and remarked, "Since you found no bodies, we can be reasonably certain they survived."

"They might have made passage to the other side and are looking for a way back," Scanlon ventured.

"If they didn't . . ."

Scanlon understood. If Rolin and Marlis had been mid-passage when their torsil was destroyed, they had either perished or were trapped in *Limbo,* that light-devouring, sound-snatching nether world where careless climbers fell forever into the void.

Changing the topic, Scanlon asked, "What could have demolished their torsil?"

Bembor sighed, his breath billowing whitely in the frosty fall air. "I don't know, but I have my suspicions. You saw the tunnels in Felgor's fortress before they collapsed, my boy; how do you suppose they were made?"

Scanlon shrugged. "Stoneworms must have bored the bigger passages and Felgor's slave labor later connected them."

Bembor shook his head. "Stoneworms detest dragons. Besides, Mt. Golgunthor is solid granite, too tough for most mining tools."

"Then what did make those tunnels?"

With a broad wink, Bembor tapped a finger on his temple. "Dragon's breath." Seeing Scanlon's puzzled look, he added, "Not a real dragon's breath. That's only what we called it. When I was a lad and there were fewer yegs about, I sometimes spied on the tunnel-delving works. Every so often, I'd see a puff of smoke and *BOOM!*—a piece of the mountain would come crashing down."

Scanlon gasped. "That's just what I heard, too! What was it?"

"No one knows. Felgor tried using it against our people once or twice, but the sorcery killed more of his warriors than of ours. It makes a tremendous 'bang' and leaves a telltale sulfur stink, just like the breath of a dragon. That reminds me; those tracks you saw sound suspiciously like a dragon's."

"How can that be? The sorcerer and his serpent are dead!"

Bembor pursed his lips. "Perhaps, and perhaps not. Even if Felgor and his egg perished in his life tree, I'm sure his henchmen were behind your 'accident.' For now, we must entrust Rolin and Marlis to Gaelathane's faithful care."

Scanlon struck the battlements with his walking stick, snapping it in two. "I won't sit idly by while they're in distress!"

Bembor laid a gnarled hand on Scanlon's shoulder. "Why, what would you do? Even if you climbed all the torsils in Lucambra, I doubt you would find the right one. If the king and queen are between worlds, only Gaelathane can help them now."

"I'll storm the gates of Limbo if I must! I'm going back to the torsil dell tomorrow 'ar doriad gwawr'—at daybreak—to pick up Rolin and Marlis's trail, if there's anything left of it."

"Then go with Gaelathane, dear boy," Bembor murmured. "May He not bereave me of you as well."

Long ere dawn had gilded the Hallowfast, Scanlon was flying on Ironwing high above the fog-shrouded Brynnmors. A feeble, frost-rimmed sun was just rising when the griffin glided into the hidden valley known as the torsil dell.

Winter was nipping hard on the heels of autumn in that lofty, lonely canyon. Its swift river was locked in ice more than half the year, and the ground was frozen solid even longer. As Scanlon dismounted, a thick blanket of hoarfrost spears crunched beneath his feet. Ice rimed the rocks on the riverbank.

"I still can't see the reason for coming up here before breakfast," grumbled Ironwing. Like most sorcs, he disliked rising early. "Not even the wind is awake at this hour of the morning."

"As I've already told you, the days are short and the light is poor down here. If we're to find the king and queen, we must speak with these torsils before tree sleep sets in for the winter."

"I'd settle for *sorc* sleep," Ironwing growled. Nonetheless, he followed Scanlon into the torsil grove, where the frost-bitten trees were all but bare.

"Hallo!" called Scanlon, scuffling through windrows of fallen leaves. "Is anyone here still awake?" He rapped on a torsil trunk with his blowpipe—*Knock! Knock!*—but the sound only echoed back emptily from rocks and trees.

"I could have told you it was too late," sniffed Ironwing. "Anything with half a stone's sense has already left this place or is curled up in a cave or hollow tree somewhere. If we had any sense, we'd leave for home now, too. We might just arrive in time for breakfast." The griffin clicked his beak.

"Oh, bother breakfast," Scanlon snapped, missing his warm bed and chestnut cakes. "Rolin and Marlis are depending on us." He bowed his head. "Gaelathane, You see the fix we're in. We've nowhere to turn except to You. Please show us which way the king and queen have gone. *Mae'r Goeden yn fyw!*"

At that very moment, a silvery voice spoke up. "Who's there?"

"Servants of Gaelathane and of the king," Scanlon called back, peering through the forest. "Who are you?"

"Don't answer him, Sliverstick," grated another voice. "He's come to make more mischief among us. Remember what happened to Thickbark! Two-legs can't be trusted."

"We only want help in finding our friends," Scanlon pleaded.

"You'll have no help from us, two-legs!" sniped a third tree. "'Torsils for torsils, and 'legs for 'legs,' we say. Go back to your den and leave us be."

"Don't mind them," the first voice said. "They're just jealous because they can't move about the way your kind can. You are welcome in the Valley of Wherren and Therren. Maybe I can help you find your friends."

"Er, thank you," Scanlon said, puzzling over the place-name.

A mournful sigh moaned through the grove. "Pay no attention to her, two-legs," the torsils muttered. "She can tell you nothing."

Over the other trees' objections, Scanlon and his sullen mount soon found "Sliverstick" at the river's edge, her scarlet leaves still clinging to frozen limbs. With bowed trunk, she had borne the biting winds and deep snows of many a bitter winter. Yet, her sweet voice belied the years of suffering.

Scanlon rubbed a frosted leaf. "Your name is 'Sliverstick'?"

"Oh, no," tittered the tree. "I'm only called that because of my spindly shape. 'Silverquick' is my real name. When I was a mere sapling, the King Himself told me, 'Little tree, I dub thee Silverquick, for your speech shall run as swift and pure as quicksilver. Though you are not to be a tall torsil, one day you will help Me save this land!' Thus I have bided the ice and snows of winter, the spring floods and summer droughts to serve my King."

"Then we are doubly pleased to make your acquaintance," said Scanlon. "Your name befits you well. As for us, we are looking for our king and queen, who disappeared when the torsil they were climbing met an untimely end."

"Ah, yes. Thickbark, the first of all trees of passage in this place. His heart was as true as his bark was thick. You say your friends were a king and queen? King and queen of *what*, if you don't mind my asking?"

"Of Lucambra," Scanlon said, warming the torsil's branches with his hands.

"Where is that? On the other side of our river?"

Scanlon exchanged surprised glances with Ironwing, who made a sound halfway between a yawn and an amused purr. Evidently, the torsil dell was so isolated that the trees sheltering in it knew nothing of the outside world.

"Lucambra lies both inside and all around this valley," Scanlon explained. "It reaches from the Sea of El-marin in the west to the Mountains of the Moon in the east; south past the Willowahs and north into the Forlorn Fens." When a dismayed murmur rippled through the wood, he hastily added, "Our king and queen rule their realm justly and wisely and permit no wanton tree cutting."

Silverquick's few leaves rustled. "Then they are truly worthy of our love and loyalty."

Impatient, Ironwing asked, "Do you have any idea where Thickbark might have taken our friends?"

"From *wherren* to *therren*, of course."

Tiring of tree riddles, the sorc testily demanded, "Where might that be? Beyond the Sea of El-marin?"

"It all depends upon wherren you start."

Scanlon tried another tack. "Could you take us from 'wherren' to 'therren,' good torsil?"

"Yes, but you might not find your friends that way. Your wherren is different than theirs, and I cannot take you to Thickbark's therren. If you do climb me, you'll see wherren you will be!" Ironwing groaned and buried his head beneath his front paws.

"Very well," said Scanlon. "I accept your invitation to visit the land of therren—or wherren. My four-legged friend will stand guard until I return." Then he told Ironwing, "Don't let anyone come between you and this tree while I'm gone."

"Don't worry," grunted the griffin. "If so much as a bird alights here, I'll give it twenty-one good reasons to move along!" He gnashed his scimitar beak and bared all twenty of his curving, needle-sharp claws, leaving no doubt as to his meaning.

Scanlon scratched Ironwing's head. "Thank you, dear griffin."

"Just don't leave me here too long," retorted the sorc as he curled up beneath Silverquick. "I'm hungry, and I don't want to come searching for you!"

After promising he would only have a quick look around the other side, Scanlon strapped on his blowpipe, shinnied to the top of Silverquick's trunk and slid down into the next world.

———————— ～☀️◎ ————————

"Father, might we have a real wassail tree this year?" Timothy asked as Garth hammered a lump of gold into a sheet. The wassails were a wonder—and impossible to cut except when very young. "Wag"-something-or-other the Greencloaks called the shining evergreens they had planted in honor of their creator-king, but most people knew them as "wassails." Those who could afford one decked it with candy and colorful baubles to help pass December's dark, dreary days. Poorer folk made do with a fir or pine trimmed with candles, which often started fires.

Garth held the shimmering gold sheet up to the light. "That we shall, my boy, that we shall. We'll have the finest wassail in all of Beechtown!"

CHAPTER 7

LIMBO

A s I am, so you shall be also, *river scum!*" The spiteful slur resounded in Rolin's ears as he spun round and round, falling into a lightless, fathomless pit.

As the absolute terror of unbeing seized him, Rolin reached in vain toward a shrinking spot of light in the suffocating blackness. Instinctively he knew that if that portal vanished, all hope of rescue would vanish with it.

"Marlis!" he screamed into the soundless void. Faster he whirled in a twisting vortex that was sucking him deeper into nowhere. Like a drowning swimmer entangled in slimy seaweed, he flailed toward the dwindling pearl of light.

"Gaelathane!" he cried. "Save us!"

"Fear not," came the Creator's calm, reassuring voice. "I am still with you. Trust Me and use your staff." His staff! Unsheathing it, Rolin aimed the bravely glowing wand at the portal.

Instantly, a brilliant beam shot through the nether hole, widening it. Light flooded the vortex, which convulsively vomited Rolin out through the portal.

"Ugh!" he grunted, falling face first onto hard dirt. He had scarcely caught his breath when something landed on his back, knocking the wind out of him again. Gasping, he crawled out from under the weight and rolled over. He was lying at the bottom of a deep depression filled with an acrid, yellowish smoke. A thin, cold rain was falling, pooling in the bottom of the pit. Marlis was nowhere to be seen.

Then he heard his wife's frantic voice: "Rolin, where are you?"

"I'm over here," he called back.

Silence. Then came the fear-thick words, "What are those?"

Now Rolin saw them, too: Brown, snaky things hanging out of the pit's raw walls. He drew back. There was no telling what savage creatures might inhabit this strange world. Then as the choking haze cleared, he recognized the "snakes."

"Those ropy things are only roots," he said. "See the fresh sap dripping from their frayed ends? Now, where are you? I hear you talking, but I don't see you."

"I'm right here, and I can't see you, either!"

Rolin jumped at the loudness of the queen's frantic reply. Thinking she must have fallen into a hole, he staggered to his feet and headed toward the sound of her voice. All at once, he stumbled and sprawled headlong into a puddle of water.

"Ow! What was that?" squealed Marlis. "Rolin, where *are* you?"

"I'm coming, I'm coming," he sighed, picking himself up. As he began feeling his way back, another unseen obstacle tripped him up. Throwing out a hand to catch himself, he grasped a nest of warm, fleshy tentacles.

Marlis screamed, "Help! Rolin! Something's got my hand!"

"Aiiii!" he yelled, yanking his own hand away as if he'd touched a hot stove. However, his hand was gone. The *thing* had taken it! Horror-stricken, he scooted backward across the dirt, jabbering, "My hand! My hand! My hand!"

By then, Marlis was crying hysterically. "Please, Rolin, do something! If this is another of your silly tricks . . ."

Rolin stopped short. If he had just lost a hand, where was the pain, and why could he still feel his fingers? He picked up a stone, though he couldn't see the hand that held it. His arm was gone, too. Both arms, feet, legs—his whole body—all had vanished. Rolin began to shake. *He couldn't see his own nose.*

"It's me!" he blurted out. "I'm the one who grabbed you." He found his wife's tear-moist face and ran his fingers through her hair, the way he often did when they were alone together.

"It's really you!" Marlis wept. "Why can't I see—" She gave a strangled gasp. "What's happened to me? I can't see myself!"

Rolin fought off a paralyzing surge of panic. "I know. I can't see me, either." Taking a shuddering breath, he closed his eyes. He could see right through his transparent eyelids! Bembor had never mentioned *this* as a hazard of torsil travel.

"We're invisible," he said, trembling at the finality of the word. "Only Gaelathane knows why. Maybe we left our real bodies behind in that black tunnel."

Marlis clutched at him. "How do we get them back?"

Rolin shook his head before realizing the unseen gesture was wasted. "I can't tell you that, either. I'm just thankful we're together, alive and unhurt. You are all right, aren't you, my love?" Feeling her head bob, he fiercely embraced her, reassured that she was still there.

Marlis whimpered, "What if we're really . . . dead?"

Rolin jerked as if struck with a lash. Dead? He hadn't considered that dreadful possibility. However, if they had died, why did their bodies feel so solid?

"I think—I'm sure we're still alive," he waffled. "Something must have changed us while we were in—where *were* we?"

"In Limbo, I think," said Marlis. "It's a place that's not a place. Torsil climbers end up there if their tree blows over in a storm or gets struck by lightning while they're making passage. Maybe that's what happened to Thickbark."

"If it was lightning, the tree must have taken a direct hit," Rolin declared. "Anyhow, we've got to get out and find a Lucambra torsil, if we're not already there. This place smells awful."

Helping Marlis to her feet, he stumbled over her again, creating an invisible tangle of arms and legs. Struck with the absurdity of their predicament, the two collapsed in fits of laughter, which only made matters worse. Warm tears flowed down Rolin's invisible face and dripped visibly off his chin.

"Gh-*urk*-osts c-*urk*-an't cry, can-*urk*-they?" he hiccuped.

Marlis giggled, "Or hiccup or hurt themselves, either."

Hurt themselves? Rolin pinched his invisible lip and immediately regretted it. He had another thought. "You know, we can't be dead. Otherwise, we'd already be in Gaelessa!"

Marlis let out a pent-up sigh of relief. "You're right! How silly of me. If we had died, Gaelathane wouldn't leave us here. Besides, I'm still breathing. Everyone knows spirits don't need air."

Rolin felt Marlis's lips brush his cheek and attempted to return her groping kiss. He spat out a mouthful of invisible hair. "Maybe this . . . this *seethroughedness* will wear off in time, like the tingling that comes with torsil travel," he speculated.

"Or else everyone in this world is invisible, and once we return home, we'll become visible again," Marlis suggested.

Rolin flicked raindrops off his nose. "In the meantime, we'd best get out of this crater and find someplace warmer and drier."

Using the dangling roots as handholds, the king and queen hauled themselves out of the hole and collapsed on level ground. Rolin grunted as Marlis's hand smacked him wetly in the face. "I wonder what world this is," she panted.

Rolin gaped at the flat squiggles Marlis's body made in the mud. "Who knows? We could have landed almost anywhere."

"Wherever we are, it can't possibly be worse than Limbo."

Spying a wide sweep of fallen trees fanning out from the pit, Rolin croaked, "I wouldn't be too sure of that." Thousands of ebony ashtags had been knocked down like so many matchsticks or shattered into black, stony shards.

"Oh, noooo," Marlis wailed. "Not the black trees! What do you suppose happened to them?"

"Lightning couldn't have smashed so many," said Rolin, shaking his head in disbelief. "This smells of sorcery."

Marlis gripped his arm. "'As I am, so you shall be also . . .'"

"You heard him, too? I was hoping I'd imagined it. The fiend loosed fire and brimstone on Thickbark just to kill us, and he didn't care how many of his own trees he demolished doing it."

"He wasn't trying to kill us," whispered Marlis.

"Why else would he have blasted Thickbark to bits?"

"Don't you understand? Felgor wanted to imprison us forever in Limbo and make us like himself: Invisible!"

———————— ✳ ————————

"It's marvelous, Father!" Timothy breathed. The melon-sized, jeweled sphere of gold sparkled in the sunlight seeping through cracks in the workshop's walls. Timothy was reminded of the glass floats Garth sometimes brought home from his river trips. "Why are the rubies all out of line?"

Garth was polishing the globe to a mirror finish. "I followed the mayor's plans to the letter, and this is how it turned out."

"What's it for?"

"I don't rightly know. Probably to hold His Honor's gilders." Garth snorted. "Now the old skinflint can lock up all his money in one pretty package and hang it on his tree. It would take a stout limb to support the thing, I daresay."

"Maybe it's supposed to be one of those spiky club-things."

Garth chuckled. "With these jutting jewels, it does look a little like a mace, though who would want to dent heads with such a fine piece of work?"

"Not me!" Timothy said. "What's this writing on the side?"

"A poem, I gather. I copied it from one of the parchments."

Timothy squinted at the strange words engraved in the gleaming gold. "I never knew the mayor liked poetry."

CHAPTER 8

ARLAN SON OF WILLIAM

I wish we'd gone mushroom picking instead of picnicking," Marlis moaned. "Then we'd still be perfectly visible. We could die here and no one would ever see our bodies!"

"We're not going to die," Rolin said. "Gaelathane will help us find a Lucambra torsil, if not in this world, then in another."

"Even if we could return home, who would welcome an invisible king and queen? They'd all think we were ghosts."

Rolin wasn't listening. With a sinking feeling, he was patting the pockets of his invisible garments. "I must have lost my lightstaff in Limbo," he groaned. "Do you still have yours?"

"Oh, no!" Marlis gasped. "I've lost mine, too. Now isn't this a fine kettle of stew. No lightstaffs, no shelter, no food or fresh water—and we can't see ourselves or each other."

"Well, there's no point in staying here," Rolin said. Hand in hand, he and Marlis left the belt of fire-blasted ashtags and entered gloomy groves of standing black trees. No birds or other wild creatures greeted them, and the ground was bare of undergrowth. A sickly-sweet odor hung in the heavy air.

"Brrr! These trees are too quiet," Marlis remarked. Left to themselves, ashtags ordinarily kept up an incessant muttering, cursing the light, cursing each other, cursing Gaelathane. Now, however, the dismal wood was as still as death.

All at once, shrieks and shouts shattered the silence. Gripping hands to keep from losing each other, Rolin and Marlis raced toward the commotion. Just beyond two enormous ashtags, they came upon a well-trodden trail. Rolin's heart skipped a beat.

"Someone must have made this!" he exclaimed.

"Someone or some*thing*," countered Marlis, tugging Rolin toward the noises. "I just hope they're friendly. Hurry—this way!" The two were rounding a bend when Marlis screamed. There on the path writhed a grunting, groaning nightmare.

"Why, it's a person!" Rolin cried, rushing toward the fallen figure. Tangled in a tracery of blood-laced, ghostly white threads were a man's head, torso and limbs. A longbow lay beneath him.

The bearded stranger's head was lolling from side to side. "Git 'em off me," he moaned. When the stubborn strings stung his fingers like fire, Rolin cut them away with his knife. The man's blue eyes fluttered open, staring sightlessly before settling on the slashing knife. "Arghh!" he gurgled and tried to wriggle away.

"Stop thrashing about!" Rolin said. "You're making it harder for me to free you, and I don't want to hurt you."

"Wh-where are ye?" the terrified stranger croaked, his eyes rolling in their sockets.

In his haste to help the man, Rolin had forgotten his invisibility. "I'm right here in front of you," he said. "You just can't see me, that's all. What's your name?"

"Ar-Arlan son of William. Who are ye?"

"Rolin son of Gannon—and please hold still."

Once freed from the stinging strings, Arlan still looked more dead than alive. Rolin carried the stricken man up a bushy knoll rising above the ashtags and laid him on a bed of withered grass.

"Rolin! Rolin, where are you?" Marlis's plaintive cries echoed among the squat, stony trees surrounding the hill.

"I'm up here!" Rolin shouted back. He kept calling out until Marlis bumped into him and her moist face pressed against his.

"I thought something simply awful had happened to you," she sobbed. "Please don't ever leave me like that again!"

Rolin stroked her face. "Forgive me, dear one. I wasn't deserting you. When we came upon this poor fellow lying in the path, I knew Gaelathane wanted me to help him. He's in a bad way."

Through rents in his ragged tunic, Arlan's lacerated skin glared an angry, blotchy purple. Shorter and stockier than Rolin, brown-haired and broad-faced, Arlan appeared fewer than forty summers old. His glazed eyes roamed over the space where Rolin and Marlis stood, finding nothing to focus on.

Rolin cleared his throat. "Arlan, I'd like you to meet my wife, Marlis. You can't see her, but she's standing right beside me."

Arlan wheezed, "Wife? Ye have a *wife?*"

"Of course," Rolin laughed. "And children, too. Don't you?"

"I've a wife, Elena, an' two young 'uns," said Arlan in a husky whisper. "What's yer wife look like?"

Realizing with a pang that he was already forgetting Marlis's features, Rolin said, "She has blond hair, green eyes and a bright smile. I can't tell you what she's wearing, because we're also invisible to each other."

"Were ye always that way?"

"No," Marlis said. "It happened when we were stranded here."

Arlan's gaze shifted between the two disembodied voices. Then he groaned and closed his eyes, gulping air like a beached fish.

"What did this to you?" Rolin asked.

"Strykkies." The word rolled off Arlan's tongue like a curse. "It's only a matter o' time till th' poison . . ." His voice trailed off.

Poison! Rolin winced at the word. Was there an antidote? Maybe Marlis knew what "strykkies" were. All of a sudden, Arlan's eyelids flew open. Judging from the man's frog-eyed expression, the queen had placed her hands on his head.

"Gaelathane, we don't understand what's wrong with Arlan, but You do," she prayed. "Please heal him so that he can return to his family and learn of Your love. Thank You. *Mae'r Goeden yn fyw!*" Arlan's breathing became more regular, his eyes closed again and he drifted into a deep sleep.

"Who is it?" the mayor quavered, pulling the bedclothes around him. He'd been dreaming of the gleaming, golden prize that Garth would soon deliver when a bright light had flooded the room. His visitor was back. "I'll have it ready tomorrow. I promise!" he cried. If only Garth would work a little faster!

"Do not be afraid," the intruder replied. "I know it is nearly finished, and I am pleased. However, you have misjudged its purpose. The chest is not intended to hold this world's wealth."

"What do you mean?"

The man answered the mayor's question with another: "Why have you held back the blessing of a gift that could help others?" His words carried a note of sadness and disappointment, not anger. The look in those sorrowful eyes penetrated the mayor's flinty, selfish heart, softening and breaking it. The little man's face flushed with shame and tears rolled down his cheeks.

"I—I'm sorry," he stammered. "What must I do?" After the stranger told him, the mayor's jaw dropped. Give away the rest of his treasure, every last gem and gold bar—and pay the River-Rover double his wages? "What of the chest?" he asked. Perhaps he'd be allowed to keep that. He blanched at the answer.

It would have made such a fine money box.

CHAPTER 9

STRYKKIES

arlis and Rolin kept vigil over their feverish patient until evening, when he stirred and awoke. "Hullo?" he called, his unfocused eyes roving aimlessly.

"We're right here," replied Rolin. "How are you feeling?"

"Better." He seemed embarrassed. "I ain't properly thanked ye fer savin' my life. I don't know why ye did it, but I would've died if ye hadn't come along. It was right neighborly of ye."

"Never mind that," said Rolin, laying his hand on Arlan's forehead. It was cool. "If you're well enough to walk, we should get you home. Where do you live?"

"North o' here. 'Tain't far." He tried to get up, but his legs gave way and he collapsed to the ground in an undignified heap.

Marlis fussed over him. "You'll never make it alone. We'd better help you—if you'll trust us, that is. Here's my hand."

With a resigned nod, Arlan lifted his arm. Then he drew it back again. "Wait—I dropped my bow in th' woods. We cain't leave without it." When Rolin suggested they go back for it later, Arlan's shocked stare stabbed the air. "Later? Without a bow and arrows, how do ye expect to git through th' strykkies?"

"Just exactly what are 'strykkies'?" Rolin burst out.

"Ye really don't know? How'd ye manage to git this far—oh, yes, I fergot." Arlan's mouth twitched at the corners and he chuckled, "It's a lucky thing ye're invisible!"

"Lucky?" the king and queen chorused indignantly. "Why?"

"Never ye mind. I'll explain later. Jest fetch my bow. The daylight's about gone, and believe me, ye don't want to be caught in these parts after sundown."

By the time Rolin returned with the bow, dusk was stealing out of the ashtags and into the hills. Supported by Rolin and Marlis, Arlan limped down the knoll. They hadn't gone far when Arlan signaled a stop.

"They're all around us," he murmured.

Rolin glanced about, seeing nothing but black trees. "*What's* all around us?" he asked.

"Strykkies. Death lilies." Arlan pointed out a hulking ashtag, its gnarled limbs festooned with pallid, luminous disks resembling the unblinking bug-eyes of a gaggle of gorks. Their wan light reminded Rolin of *moonwood*, the fungus-infected wood that Lucambrians used for lighting caves and tunnels.

Marlis picked up a dead ashtag branch. "They do look like trumpet lilies, only paler. I think I'll knock one down—"

"No!" Arlan cried, but Marlis had already hurled the branch at the nearest flower. *Strikka-strikka* went the strykkies, and the limb fell short in a flurry of ghostly streamers. Running over, Rolin found the stick enmeshed in the same sticky, white threads he'd cut away from Arlan's body.

"Don't touch it," Arlan warned. "Each o' them threads is tipped with a tiny, poison dart. That's th' most dangerous part. When a strykkie senses something moving, it shoots out these strings, snaring an' paralyzing its prey. I've seen a deer die within minutes o' wandering into a strykkie patch."

Rolin trembled, recalling how the strykkie strings had nearly mummified Arlan's body. "You're saying that when I first found you, the strykkies didn't attack me because I'm invisible?"

Arlan nodded. "They'd also used up their darts on me, leaving none fer ye. They don't hold back even after their prey is down."

"How awful!" Marlis murmured. "How on earth do they eat?"

"Through the threads. It takes a long time, and there ain't much left afterwards 'cept fer bones. Th' snarks clean those up."

Rolin stifled a groan. Snarks. Another curious local term. "Pray tell us, what exactly are 'snarks'?"

"That's these dratted tar trees. The snarks and the strykkies live together in a right clever arrangement. Th' strykkies kin strike farther and faster, but the snarks kin squeeze th' life out of a body, snakelike. They also keep things cool and shady underneath, the way th' death lilies like it:

> Where the silent shadows slink,
> Beyond the snarks' black brink,
> Beware the strykkies' strident call,
> For there the deadly darts will fall.

"Travelin' through these parts gits harder every year," he added. "Whenever we blaze a new trail through here, strykkies start croppin' up along it. Them little seeds of theirs spread fast."

"How did you fall afoul of the flowers today?" Rolin asked.

Arlan grimaced. "I was in sech a hurry that I brought only three arrows with me. I shoulda known better. Most times, it takes eight or ten shots to reach th' river."

"What good are arrows against strykkies?" asked Marlis.

Arlan coaxed a lopsided smile out of his swollen face. "Plenty. We use 'em to draw the flowers' fire. Tyin' a tassel on the back o' the arrow really sets off the strykkies, 'specially in summer. They ain't so touchy in th' winter."

"Once they've shot off their stingers, then it's safe to pass?" Marlis asked with an eager intensity in her voice.

Arlan nodded. "Leastways, until they grow more darts. Of course, ye two don't have to worry about the strykkies, bein' invisible and all. Ye could walk right by 'em and they wouldn't even twitch." He grinned. "That reminds me: Before it gits any darker, ye should run up to my cave and bring me back more arrows so's I kin finish clearing this path."

"Hmph! I can do better than that," snorted Marlis. *Rrrrippp!* A long strip of green cloak fabric appeared in midair and flew down the trail, twirling and flapping like a kite's tail.

"Stop! Come back!" Rolin cried. However, it was too late.

"Mae'r Goeden yn fyw!" Marlis's voice rang out among the inky trunks. *Thrrrip! Brrrrip!* Like streamers at a parade, thousands of lethal threads arced across the path. The crackling fusillade followed Marlis through the woods.

"She's making too much noise," Rolin groaned. "If the strykkies don't get her, the ashtags, er, *snarks* will."

Arlan threw a sharp glance in his direction. "She'll be all right. Spunky woman, that 'un. As fer th' snarks, they let the strykkies do their dirty work for 'em."

Presently, the cloth strip came sailing back like a victory banner, white with threads and dripping with poison. "The strykkies took the bait! I didn't get hit once," Marlis crowed as the decoy fluttered to the ground.

Rolin hugged her, just to be sure she was unhurt. "Please warn me before you do something like that again!" he whispered.

"How far did ye run?" Arlan asked, staring at the "bait."

"Until the strykkies ended, beyond that rise just ahead."

Arlan grunted approvingly. "That'll do. I won't be needing them arrows after all. Now I can use 'em fer hunting game!"

Leaning on Rolin's and Marlis's unseen shoulders, Arlan hobbled down the trail, his numerous strykkie wounds still oozing blood. Rolin hoped none of the lilies had been napping when Marlis had run the gauntlet. Arlan would make an inviting and easy target for the flowers hanging over the path—and his invisible escorts would be caught in the line of fire.

Just when dusk was devouring the trail, the trees thinned out and a pink sunset peeped through. Stepping onto a grassy verge, Rolin and Marlis smelled the tangy scent of evergreens and heard the welcome murmur of tree speech. They had escaped the snarks and strykkies.

Dawn was breaking over Beechtown, but the mayor's visitor wasn't finished with him yet. A scroll of purest white materialized in his scarred hand. Lines and letters appeared on the sheet, which floated across the room to land in the mayor's lap. "The key must go there," he commanded. "Once the chest is locked, it must not be opened again 'until he comes who holds the key.'"

CHAPTER 10

GHOST OF HOLLOW, GHOST OF CAVE

Rolin and Marlis were gasping with the strain of half-carrying Arlan when they came to a hill covered with leggy vine maples. "Here we are," Arlan said. As he shrugged off his invisible helpers, a tall, rawboned woman emerged from the bushes. Brandishing a heavy club, she raked Arlan with a squinty gaze before grabbing him by the wrist.

"Where've you been?" she hissed. "I've been worried sick over you! It's long past sunset; I thought you were gone for good."

"I know, Elena, I know," sighed Arlan. Staggering after his wife, he tripped and fell heavily against her.

"You're hurt!" she cried. Dropping the club, she wrapped her long arms around her husband and dragged him through a door hidden in the brushy hillside. Rolin and Marlis squeaked in after them, entering a dingy, dimly lit cave. Rolin had the uncanny feeling he'd been there before—but when?

Seating Arlan in a chair next to an ancient iron stove, Elena pored over his wounds by the light of a sputtering candle. Her fingers cast quick, spidery shadows on the cavern's walls. On removing his tattered tunic, she gasped. The strykkies' darts and stinging strings had seared scores of puckered pockmarks and bright red welts into his neck, chest and shoulders.

"Mercy me! What in the name of Peton happened to you? Did you bumble into a bees' nest or a strykkie patch—or both?"

"Strykkies. Ran out of arrows," Arlan groaned. He threw a quick, furtive glance around the cave. "Is anyone here?"

Rolin tapped the man's shoulder, making him jump. "Twitchy tonight, aren't you?" said Elena tartly as she lit an oil lamp from the candle. "If it's the children you're asking for, they're already a-bed, as you should be, too! All this comes of staying out after dark. Now, where did I put those tweezers?" She poked about in a pigeonhole behind the stove. "Ah, here they are."

"Never mind th' tweezers," grunted Arlan. "I'll be all right. Ye must meet my friends. They're around here somewhere."

Elena brushed some stringy wisps of moist, mousy hair out of her eyes. "Friends? What friends? You know as well as I do that we're the last. Besides, I didn't see anybody else with you."

"That's because ye cain't see 'em. They're invisible. One was standing right beside me and touched my shoulder."

Staring warily at her husband, Elena bolted the door. Then she searched the shadowy cave with her smoky lamp. Rolin and Marlis took care to stay out of her way. "Nothing—just as I thought," she muttered. "That strykkie poison's plumb addled his wits." She dipped a rag in a bucket of dirty water and slapped it on Arlan's forehead. "You'll feel better after I pull out those darts."

Arlan knocked the rag away. "I'm fine," he snarled. "Don't worry about me; git some fresh water fer our guests, won't ye?"

Elena glared. "All right, then. Since you're so all-fired set on playing host to ghosts tonight, why don't you invite them in?"

Rolin let out a short, dry cough. "Um, we're already here."

Snatching up her long skirts, Elena shrieked, "You ghosts leave my cave this instant!" Then she began in a high, cracking voice:

Ghost of hollow, ghost of cave,
Hear me now; you must behave!
No matter how you met your doom,
You cannot come into my room.

You mustn't groan, you mustn't chatter;
Don't even think to make a clatter!
You mustn't make your home with us,
Or I shall raise an awful fuss.

I'll scream and cry and howl and gibber,
And make your bloodless lips to quiver,
I'll bare my teeth and bite the air;
You've never had such a frightful scare!

So get thee hence from here, old haunt,
And find another place to flaunt
Your ghastly wails and your ghostly wiles
Where your hosts will shiver at your spooky smiles!

"There," she sighed. "That should do it. My mother's rhyme works every time." Much to Elena's dismay, Rolin and Marlis burst into peals of uproarious laughter.

"Your incantation may work on ghosts but not on us," Rolin chuckled. "You've nothing to fear; we're not here to harm you."

"That's right," Marlis said. "We're not ghosts or ghouls, haunts or hobgoblins. Besides, such things don't exist."

"I don't care *what* you are; just get out of my home!" Elena cried. Grabbing a stack of plates from the table beside her, she began flinging them helter-skelter across the cave. Most went wide of the mark, but one glanced off Rolin's head.

"Ow!" he exclaimed, falling backward and tipping over a chair.

"Elena!" growled Arlan. "Stop that at once—ye're hurting them!" White-faced, Elena stiffly swept up the broken plates and set the chair upright, all the while glancing nervously about.

"That's better," her husband said. "Now, let's show our guests some proper Peton hospitality. Bring 'em some o' that bread ye baked today and a spot of yer jam. *I'll* fill the bucket from th' spring." Picking up the wooden pail, Arlan disappeared outside while Elena went to a set of shelves sagging along one wall.

As soon as her back was turned, two small heads popped out from behind some threadbare blankets strung across the rear of the cave. They ducked back inside when Elena returned with a couple of fragrant loaves and a jar of thick, purplish jam.

"Real bread and raspberry jam!" whispered Marlis to Rolin. "Maybe this won't be such a bad world after all. I'm famished!"

Elena spoke to the blankets. "You two may as well come out. If it's ghosts we've got, you can't hide from them. They'll find you wherever you are. You can thank your father for letting them in."

Shyly, a tow-headed girl and boy clad in nightclothes crept out. Bobbing and blinking, both looked right through Rolin with hazel eyes. "I don't see any ghosts," the boy pouted.

Just then, Arlan stumbled through the door. Setting down the filled water pail, he collapsed into his chair. "These are my children," he said with a weary wave toward them. "Bronwen and Evan, meet Rolin and Marlis. They saved me from the strykkies."

Elena's eyebrows jumped. "Is that so? I'd like to know how—"

"I'm seven; Bronwen's nine," said Evan, drawing himself up.

"Mother, who is Father talking to?" asked Bronwen.

Elena clenched her narrow jaw but failed to stop her lips from trembling. "I don't know. He tangled with some strykkies today, you see, and now he's not himself. Let's just try to humor him, shall we? I'm sure he'll be much better in the morning."

"Ain't nothin' wrong with me that a cellarful of Peton's best beer wouldn't cure," muttered Arlan.

"It's very nice to meet you, Evan and Bronwen," said Marlis.

"Ooooh," the children gasped, their eyes and mouths making circles. Clinging to each other, they hurriedly backed away from the table and entangled themselves in the hanging blankets. "Ghosts!" they shrieked. "Help! The ghosts have got us!"

"Ye mustn't be afraid of Rolin and Marlis," Arlan told them as he pulled the blankets away. "They're people jest like us, only ye can't see 'em. Harmless as doves, too."

"Why can't we see them?" asked Evan, staring through the spot where Rolin and Marlis were standing with arms entwined.

"Enough jabberin' fer now," said Arlan gruffly. "Let's all have some bread and jam before bed." He cocked his head toward a couple of chairs. "You two kin sit there—if ye like, that is."

Rolin eased himself into one of the rickety, rush-bottomed affairs, noticing the seat beside him sag. Holding his wife's hand, he murmured a quick prayer to Gaelathane in gratitude for the food. Then he plunged his knife into the larger of the loaves.

Elena let out a strangled cry as the dancing blade sliced off several thick slabs of bread and slathered globs of jam over them from the upended jar. Then the floating pieces of jam-smothered bread vanished bite by half-moon bite.

"Mmmm, this is good. Don't you want some?" Marlis asked her hosts, whose faces were frozen in slack-jawed astonishment.

"Er, well, of course," murmured Elena. Using only her fingertips, the gaunt woman plucked a slice of bread and jam from Marlis's invisible hand. Then she sniffed it with wrinkled nose before taking a tentative nibble.

Marlis's laugh tinkled into the cave. "Invisibility isn't catching like some sort of disease, you know. If anything, we were hoping your visibility would rub off on us!"

"Jest like I told ye, Elena," Arlan remarked as he made himself a jam-and-bread sandwich. "They ain't haunts. Who ever heard of ghosts with an appetite, or ones ye kin hit with a plate?"

"Maybe they're like worggles, only with see-through bodies," Bronwen suggested as she sliced some bread for herself and Evan. Her brother managed to smear jam on himself and his sister.

"We're certainly not," said Rolin stoutly, wondering what "worggles" were. He wished Arlan and his family wouldn't speak of him and Marlis as if they were recently deceased relatives.

"Worggles? What are those?" Marlis asked, licking off the knife. Bronwen and Evan stopped eating to watch in wide-eyed wonder.

Hands hitched on hips, Elena sneered, "You've never heard of worggles? Where are you from, anyway—across the mountains?"

"Maybe they have different names fer 'em where they live," Arlan cut in. "Rolin called the snarks 'afgars.'"

"Ashtags," Rolin corrected him.

With clawed fingers, Bronwen pounced on her brother, crying, "The worggles are after you!" The two wrestled on a frayed brown rug covering the cavern floor like a big mud puddle.

"You won't get me!" hooted Evan. He dove behind the stove to escape Bronwen's clutches. She stuck out her tongue at him.

"The worggles come out of the woods at night," Elena explained. "That's why we don't go outside after dark, especially not alone." She glared daggers at her husband.

"What happens if you do?" asked Marlis.

Elena shrugged. "You don't come back. *Peton* takes you."

"Father, tell us again about old Peton town," begged Bronwen.

From the stove, Evan chimed in, "Yes, please do."

Arlan settled into his chair. "In Peton's prime, ships o' silver plied the river, and her streets shone o' gold. That was in the olden days when the trees were green as grass and men walked freely through the forest without fear o' worggles:

Peton town, O Peton town,
A place of riches and renown;
Of all the land the chiefest crown,
Until its houses tumbled down,
Was Peton town, high Peton town.

Its eyes of glass and streets of gold,
Where silver, brass and bronze were sold;
With wealth and splendor still untold,
No other sight would I behold,
Than Peton town, grand Peton town.

The mountains over, the river under,
Flowing full to falls a-thunder,
Till the bridge was split asunder;
Now who shall profit from the plunder
Of Peton town, proud Peton town?

Alas, the place was slowly strangled,
All her beauty maimed and mangled,
Beneath the tar trees' twisted tangles;
Moss grows where merchants wrangled
In Peton town, poor Peton town.

"What were the 'eyes of glass,' Father?" asked the children.

Arlan stroked his moustache. "Legend has it the Petonians lived in homes o' wood and brick with lots of glass windows."

"How silly," Bronwen said. "Who would want windows the worggles could look through? No wonder all the people died out."

"Th' land was safer before the snarks and strykkies moved in," Arlan reminded her, wincing as his wife yanked out a strykkie dart with her rusty pair of tweezers. Elena clucked her tongue.

"How did the snarks get here in the first place?" asked Rolin.

Arlan groaned as another dart came out. "As th' story goes, the first snarks were planted in Peton years ago by *grennocks*."

"May they be cursed forever," the children solemnly intoned.

"Why would anyone do such a thing?" Marlis asked in disgust.

"How should we know?" replied Elena, rubbing oil into Arlan's wounds. "That was then, and this is now." She cast a stern glance at Bronwen and Evan. "Remember how Grandfather William perished in a strykkie patch while searching for a sheep? Your father nearly met the same end today. Never forget what we've taught you about the black forests:

The strykkies sting, the strykkies snare,
Awaiting in their woodsome lair;
The snarks will grip, the snarks will grasp;
Their fearsome fingers hold you fast!

The snarks will trip, the snarks will trap
Unwary ones, and round them wrap
Their wicked, warty, fleshless fronds
That bind the arms like bars of bronze!

So go not near their darkened dens,
Nor tarry in those marshy fens,
Where strykkies hang with poisoned fang,
To strike the mark—and strike again!

Wagging her finger, Elena added, "Next time, there may not be any *invisibles* on hand to save your father—or you."

"An 'invisible,' am I?" Marlis sputtered. "How would *they* like to be called 'visibles'? My name is Marlis, and I won't answer to anything else!" Evan snickered and licked his knife.

"Marlis, what do you look like?" asked Bronwen, facing the wrong direction. The other visibles followed her gaze.

Marlis tapped the table. "I'm over here. Let's see. My hair is a shade darker than yours and I'm a few inches taller. You remind me of my daughter, Gwynneth. She's about your age."

"Really?" Bronwen blushed. "How do you know—?"

"She's completely visible, just as Rolin and I were until today," Marlis said. "We're hoping to change back very soon."

"What about Rolin?" asked Evan in his little-boy voice.

A long silence followed. Then teardrops spattered on the table and floor as Marlis's fingers explored Rolin's face. *It's happening to her, too,* he thought. *She can't remember what I look like.*

With a catch in her sweet-cream voice, Marlis said, "He's got hair the color of dark clover honey, green eyes, a cute nose, fine white teeth and summer's nut-brown skin."

Rolin wondered whether his tan would fade now that he was invisible. He dreaded becoming pasty-faced like Elena, who no doubt spent her days cooped up in the cave with her children.

"Where is *your* cave?" Evan asked, his eyes focusing past Rolin.

"It's very far away, over mountain, marsh and moor," Rolin said wistfully. *As near as a torsil, as distant as the moon.*

Elena's eyes narrowed. "If it's so far off, how did you two get through all the snarks in the first place?"

Arlan's puffy face reddened. "Since they're invisible, the strykkies wouldn't bother 'em. That's more than I kin say fer ye."

Ignoring her husband's pointed rebuke, Elena folded her arms and said, "Even so, you'll never convince me that they showed up on our doorstep by happenstance. It's all too pat."

"Of course they didn't; I brought 'em here," retorted Arlan.

"That's not what I meant!" Elena flared, her eyes flashing. "You know very well we haven't seen strangers in these parts for years, much less *invisible* ones. This all strikes me as very odd."

"Odd or not, if they hadn't come along when they did, I'd be dead now," Arlan growled. With that, he related how Rolin and Marlis had rescued him from the strykkies. "Them two could've passed by and left me to die, but they didn't. They could have robbed or killed us, but they haven't. Jest because we cain't see 'em doesn't mean they're fixin' to do us harm."

Elena stared through Rolin, her eyes wet with tears. "Whoever or whatever you are, I thank you for saving my husband's life."

Rolin's face burned. He blushed easily, making him the frequent target of lighthearted teasing and pranks around the royal household. Glad of his invisibility, he replied, "There's no need for thanks. We should be thanking *you* for taking us into your home, sight unseen, so to speak." He paused. "However, you are right, Elena. We didn't come here by accident."

Garth stood several minutes outside the mayor's door before rapping on it. He felt like a lamb about to enter a lion's den.

"Come in, come in," called a curt voice through the heavy door. Turning the knob, Garth stepped into the mayor's study. His Eminence sat behind a desk, ample bulk crammed into a protesting chair. A dingy window behind him let in a little rain-dampened light, relieving the gloominess of the drab chamber.

"Why, it's Garth the River-Rover," the mayor sneered. "Do you have it, or have you come to make excuses for botching the job?"

Wordlessly placing his bag on the desk, Garth removed the golden sphere. The mayor gasped and jumped up, jowls quivering. He looked at Garth, then at the ball, as if to say, "How could a rough-hewn river raftsman craft such a thing of beauty?"

CHAPTER 11

THE KEEPER OF THE CHEST

Elena shot a smug look at her husband. "You see? Even *he* admits they're up to something. I knew it all along."

"Hold on, now; I didn't say we came here on purpose," Rolin said. "On the contrary, we were *sent*."

Elena's eyes bored into Rolin's. "Sent? By whom?"

"The King of the Trees," Marlis answered.

Arlan leaned forward, curiosity and fear mingled in his face. "Th' King o' the Trees? Who's that, and what's He want with us?"

"He is Who He is, and He only desires your devotion," Rolin replied. His mind ranged back to his coronation day, when Gaelathane had told him he was to be ". . . the first of My emissaries to all torsil worlds, proclaiming My freedom to those who have long lain in darkness . . ." The visibles needed that freedom.

Marlis declared, "He sent us here not only to rescue Arlan, but also to befriend your whole family. We truly wish to become your friends, if you'll let us, that is." Elena looked doubtful.

Tears shone in Bronwen's eyes as she clapped her hands. "Before I go to sleep at night, I always ask the One Who made the moon and stars to send us some new friends. Now at last He has!"

Elena glared at her. "What a silly notion! Don't talk such rubbish. The moon and stars just *are*. Nobody put them there."

"But Mother, don't you suppose *someone* made the sky, the sun, the rivers, the earth—and us? Don't you think He listens when we talk to Him? I think He does." Bronwen turned blindly toward Rolin and Marlis. "Do you know His name?"

"Yes, we do," Marlis said. "He is called Gaelathane, the King of the Trees, and He did make the sky, the sun, stars and moon, the rivers, the earth and you as well."

Elena kneaded some breadcrumbs into a ball and popped it in her mouth. "What about the snarks? Did He make them, too?"

Rolin swallowed. "No, those trees are the works of Felgor, Gaelathane's enemy—and ours. They are the gates to his kingdom, an awful place of darkness and torment."

"A likely story," Elena sniffed. "Tree gates. Do they come equipped with hinges and locks and keys?" Evan sniggered.

"Where *is* Gaelathane?" Bronwen asked.

"He's here. He's everywhere," Marlis said. "When we call upon Him, He comes to our aid. He's our closest friend."

Evan's finger poked the air. "Is Gael'thane invis'ble, too?"

"Yes," replied Marlis. "However, He's not like us. He can appear and disappear whenever He wishes, wherever He wishes—and He can never die. He lives in a deathless land, too."

Arlan glanced about uneasily, as if fearing a third invisible might be lurking in the cave. He sidled over to the door and braced it shut with a board. Then he sat with his back to the wall.

"Hmph. The King of the Trees, you say," snorted Elena as she briskly cleared away the jam jar and plates. "Someone so high and mighty wouldn't be interested in the likes of *us*."

"Oh, but He is very interested in you!" Marlis assured her.

"Then why hasn't He done away with the snarks, the strykkies and the worggles? If your Gaelathane really cared about us, He'd make sure we had enough to eat!" Covering her face with her hands, Elena burst into tears. For the first time, Rolin noticed telltale hunger hollows in the children's wan cheeks.

Arlan fidgeted. "We ain't starvin', Wife. I try my best to put food on th' table, but times are hard. At least we have our cave."

"I know you're doing your best," Elena wept. "But what will happen when the snarks take over our mountain and the animals leave? What will we eat then? Snark roots?"

Marlis's chair scooted back. Then Elena's bony frame stiffened before she relaxed again and sagged into Marlis's invisible arms. "I—I'm sorry," she sobbed. "I don't mean to be unkind. It's just been so lonely here. The others have all died or gone away."

"There now, it's all right," Marlis crooned. "What others?"

"*Everybody.* Our neighbors, friends, relatives. We're the only ones who didn't have the sense to leave this place in time."

"You poor thing," Marlis said. "You might not believe it, but Gaelathane did send Rolin and me here in answer to Bronwen's prayers. He can restore your land, but He won't start with the snarks or the strykkies—He will begin with you."

"With us?" Arlan echoed. "We don't have much, y' know."

"He just wants your hearts," said Rolin. Then he told the tale of the King of the Trees and how He had suffered, died and risen to renew all creation and open Gaelessa to His children. When Rolin had finished, no one spoke for several minutes.

Elena broke the awkward silence. "I'm sure your Gaelathane is a fine king, but we can manage quite well without Him."

"The wife's right," Arlan said, yawning. "Even if this feller did die fer us, we ain't one whit the better off for it. Let Him find us a new home. Maybe then we'd believe in Him."

"Ask Him to help you," Marlis urged him. "He'll be more than willing to answer, though perhaps not in the way you expect."

"All right, then," said Arlan. "I'll do jest that." He bowed his head. "Gaelathane, if Ye're there, show us a better place to live."

Rolin and Marlis reverently added, "The Tree lives!"

Much to the visibles' disappointment, nothing unusual happened. To distract them, Rolin suggested, "Why don't you move away from the snarks? They can't be everywhere, after all."

Arlan shook his head. "Years ago, most of the valley folk did pack up and leave. We ain't heard from any of 'em since. Fer us, it's too late to move now. If ye look outside tomorrow morning, ye'll find snark sprouts jest down th' hill apiece."

"That's right," said Elena glumly. "We're trapped here, and we'll just have to make the best of it. Isn't that so, children." Bronwen and Evan nodded woodenly. Their mother raised one eyebrow at Arlan and tilted her head toward the floor. "Besides, if we left, what would we do with *it?*" Arlan didn't answer.

Bronwen jumped up. "Father, you promised you'd take it out last night, remember? Can we see it now instead?"

"Shush, child!" said Elena. "There are strangers here tonight."

Evan stuck out his lip. "Rolin an' Marlis aren't strangers."

"They aren't family, either," Elena shot back. "You know the rules: The thing is for our eyes only. It's always been that way."

Arlan chewed his thumb. "Maybe after our guests are gone."

"But you *pro*mised!" the children wailed. "Pleaassse?"

"Very well," Arlan sighed. "I'm a man o' my word. Ye kin have yer look—but then it's straight to bed for ye both."

Elena's work-worn hands fluttered to her mouth. "You can't! No Keeper has ever done such a thing! What if the invisibles—?"

"Don't tell me what I can or cain't do!" growled Arlan. "Nobody here's going to steal the thing. If'n they did, where would they take it? To Peton? Ain't nobody but us fer miles around."

Elena sulked and scowled while Arlan poured water into a basin and washed up. Then he dried his hands on a piece of linen.

"What's he doing?" asked Marlis.

"Hand washing always precedes the Ritual," Elena said.

"Father is 'Keeper of the Chest,'" boasted Bronwen.

"Keeper of the *what?*" Rolin asked.

"Just watch." Elena pointed at Arlan, who was throwing back a corner of the rug. With Evan's help, he wrestled a thick stone slab out of the floor. Then he reached into the opening beneath and drew out a spherical, cloth-covered object, which he placed ever-so-delicately on the table.

Holding hands, the visibles stood and chanted in unison, "The ball has been, the ball will be, until he comes who holds the key."

"This chest was my father's and his father's before him," Arlan intoned. "It has remained in my family for generations beyond reckoning. When I am gone, it will pass to my son, Evan." Then with a flourish, he pulled off the cloth.

Rolin and Marlis gasped. Before them sat a splendid golden ball. A brass lock and a sturdy hinge joined its upper and lower halves. Jutting from its top was a colossal diamond surrounded by fat, crimson rubies. Not even the dragon's hoard beneath Mt. Golgunthor had boasted such a wonder.

"What's inside it? More gems and gold?" asked Rolin, hoping his question wasn't out of order.

"That's the mystery," Elena said. "We only know it doesn't rattle when shaken. The children discovered that fact." She glanced disapprovingly at Bronwen and Evan.

"Then it's never been opened?" Marlis asked.

Arlan shook his head. "We don't have th' key. If we could cipher this riddle, maybe we could find it." He pointed out a line of neatly engraved letters winding around the diamond like a coiled top string. "Here's how it goes:

> With diamond eye I'll pierce the sky,
> To strike the strangling trees on high;
> On rays of light I shall ascend,
> To realms of wonder without end.
>
> With ruby light I'll rend the night,
> And set your fiercest foes to flight;
> Where greedy seed has taken root,
> I'll sear the twig and scorch the shoot.
>
> For me to doom each viper's den,
> You must return to where and when;
> And set me on the selfsame site,
> Where five black ravens once took flight.
>
> In time, the unseen hand will turn
> The key unlocking this simple urn;
> He'll find it lying firmly wedged
> Above the door, upon a ledge.

But now I wait with empty womb,
For Him to fill this golden room;
The ball within the ball will nest;
When once I'm closed, He'll do the rest.

When Arlan had finished, Elena said, "We've studied those words backwards and forwards, and we still don't know what they mean. The 'strangling trees' must be the snarks, but how the 'diamond eye' is supposed to 'pierce the sky' is more than any of us can fathom. If there's reason to this rhyme, we can't see it."

"That's because Gaelathane's hand is in these verses."

The visibles turned toward Marlis in surprise. "How do ye know? Did He tell ye He wrote them?" Arlan asked.

"After you've followed Him for a while, you learn to recognize these things," she replied. "If we want His help with your poem,

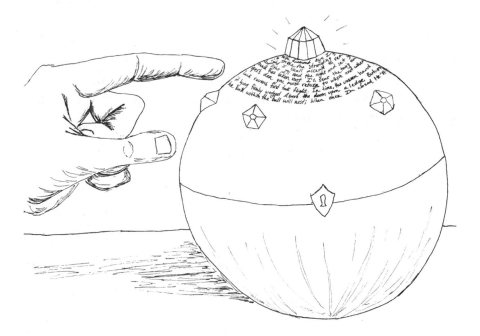

we need only ask like this: 'Gaelathane, whether this is Your riddle or not, please show us the meaning.' The Tree lives!"

Arlan and Elena cringed, as if expecting a lightning bolt to strike the ball. The lamp flame didn't even flicker.

"Thank ye fer tryin' to help us," said Arlan patiently. "To my mind, our chest was meant to be opened long ago. Whatever's inside cain't be much use to us now, anyhow." He returned the ball to its cubbyhole and replaced the stone that concealed it.

"Off to bed now, children," Elena said, shooing them along.

Wishing the invisibles good-night, Evan and Bronwen retired behind their blanket. Next, it was Rolin and Marlis's turn. Over their objections, Elena ushered them into one of the cave's back corners, where a goose down comforter lay draped over a shapeless mattress. "Can't have invisible guests lying in the middle of the floor," Elena declared. "We might trip over you in the night."

The comforter flew back and a furrow appeared on the mattress. "My, this is soft," Marlis said. "I could lie here for a week!"

Elena retreated to the other side of the blanket, muttering, "Invisibles! Whatever will we do with them?"

After Elena had left, Rolin and Marlis heard muffled snatches of conversation from the children's side of the cave: "Maybe the 'visibles will take us to live with them." "Do you think they wear clothes?" "I wonder if they can see *through* things, like walls," and so on. Presently, the whispers gave way to blissful snores.

---------------- ⚬⚭⚬ ----------------

The rumpled mayor turned his back on Garth and took something from his pocket. Coins clinked. When he faced round again, the mayor counted out six, hundred-gilder coins into Garth's palm, all the while grinding his teeth.

"In payment for your work, and a fine job, too," he rasped, biting off each word. "I trust you'll use this to clean up that dump of yours. It's an eyesore and a blight on the town."

Six hundred gilders! It was twice what he'd been promised. "Thank you, sir. Yes, I might do just that." Garth turned to leave, hoping to reach the door before the mayor changed his mind and demanded some of his gilders back.

"Wait." Looking for all the world as if he had just lost his closest friend, the pudgy little man locked the chest and shoved it across the table toward its maker. From a drawer he then removed a scrap of parchment that glowed with a brightness all its own. He handed Garth the key and the paper with the somber words, "You are now the Keeper of the Chest."

CHAPTER 12

WORGGLES AND WIFFLES

H aunted by the cave's familiarity, Rolin tossed and turned on the straw-stuffed mattress. When he fell into a fitful slumber, he was no closer to unraveling the place's secrets than when he had first stepped inside.

Towards morning, he heard snuffling, shuffling sounds outside. Rising quietly so as not to disturb Marlis, he slipped out the door to crouch among the vine maples. Twin, foggy wisps curled from his unseen nostrils in the cool dawn's twilight. What he saw gave him reason to thank Gaelathane for his invisibility.

Not a stone's throw away, seven ungainly creatures were sniffing about, scratching and digging among the rocks. *Gorks.* There was no mistaking those grotesque, wrinkled snouts; lolling, bulbous heads; pointed ears, spindly arms and bulgy eyes. As the sun's first rays struck them, the gangling gorks loped off to their lightless lairs in the snark woods.

After returning to bed, Rolin found sleep impossible. Why were the gorks lurking about Arlan's cave? What were they doing in this world in the first place? It was no wonder the visibles rarely ventured outside after dark!

At last, Rolin heard his hosts stirring, their shapes casting shifting shadows on the blanket partition. He woke Marlis and peeked with her through holes in the moth-eaten fabric. Arlan and his family were seated at the table, which was set with six steaming bowls. The visibles stared expectantly back at them.

Marlis gripped Rolin's arm. "They can see us! My hair must look a fright." For one ecstatic, heart-stopping instant, Rolin, too, thought they had become visible. But he still couldn't see Marlis.

"No, they've only noticed our blanket moving," he told her. As the pair brushed aside their privacy curtain, Bronwen and Evan greeted them. "Good morning, Aunt Marlis and Uncle Rolin!"

"Good morning to you," they returned politely. Marlis murmured, "The poor dears haven't any real aunts or uncles left."

Rolin said, "I hope we haven't kept you waiting."

"Not at all," Arlan boomed. "Have yerselfs a seat an' dig in."

Easing into their chairs, the invisibles thanked Gaelathane for the mysterious mounds of brown, pasty mush bubbling in their bowls. Then they started eating, ignoring the visibles' goggling stares at their two floating spoons.

Rolin's first bite of porridge missed his invisible mouth. Warm gruel dribbled down his chin. He gagged on his second bite. The disgusting stuff tasted worse than dandelion root! Yet, the visibles were shoveling theirs down with gusto. Marlis was making choking sounds. Then her spoon plopped back into her bowl.

"Do you like it?" asked Elena with an anxious smile. "It's acorn mush, prepared with my own special recipe." *Acorn mush!* Rolin and Marlis groaned. No wonder it was so revolting. You could boil acorns for days and still not wash out all the bitterness. Rolin was glad his hosts couldn't see the horrible faces he was making.

"It's . . . quite good," he lamely lied, prompting Elena to ladle out all-too-generous second helpings. Marlis stomped on his foot and "accidentally" overturned her bowl. While holding his nose, Rolin forced a few more mealy lumps down his throat. Then he dumped the rest into his cloak pocket, where the congealing gruel became invisible.

The king and queen then privately settled on a simple code for communicating when the visibles were present: One hand-squeeze meant "Yes" or "All right;" two meant "No," "Don't," or at mealtimes, "Yes-I-know-it-tastes-bad, but-eat-it-anyway-without-making-a-fuss." Three squeezes warned, "Look out!"

After Bronwen had whisked away the dishes, the grownups stayed at the table to discuss their day's plans. The invisibles remained seated out of courtesy to their hosts, who preferred them to stay in one spot during conversations. Several times that morning, Rolin had caught Elena speaking to an empty chair!

"I need to go a-gleanin' today," Arlan told his wife. With a glance at the invisibles' places, he added, "Ye're welcome to join us if ye want. We could use yer help."

"Gleaning?" cried Evan. "Yes, Papa, let's!" At his mother's stern look, he went back to scrubbing the breakfast bowls with a chunk of rough pumice that was scraping his hands raw.

"Do you mean foraging for berries, roots and mushrooms?" Marlis asked. "I'd like nothing better."

Elena screwed up her face scornfully. "Foraging? Oh my, no. We go down to Peton to dig for plates, pots and pans—"

"And porcelain dolls," Bronwen said with a longing look.

"And whistles," put in Evan, blowing on an imaginary one.

"Or anything *practical*," Arlan hinted with a frown at his children. "There ain't much left to salvage in th' ruins after all these years o' being picked over. Still, we find something useful every now and again: An ax, a spoon or a few rusty nails."

Bronwen yanked on her father's sleeve. "May Evan and I go with you? I promise we won't get in the way."

Arlan grinned. "Why not? When it comes to gleaning, my children's eyes are sharper than mine."

"Can Mother come along, too?" Evan asked.

Arlan shook his head. "She'll need to stay here to guard the cave. So, what do ye think, friends? Will ye be comin' with us?"

"Marlis and I would love to join you," Rolin replied. "We'll try to stay out of the way, too. When do we leave?"

"As soon as possible. We'll want to git there in time to scavenge fer several hours and still arrive home 'fore dark."

"Is Peton safe?" asked Rolin. Then he described the creatures he'd seen snooping around the cave at dawn. Beside him, Marlis whispered, "*Gorks!*"

Arlan's eyebrows beetled. "Worggles! They must've smelled ye. If we don't rub grass on our clothes to cover up th' man scent, they kin snuffle us out from miles away. They don't usually bother us during th' daytime, though. The sun hurts their eyes. Now, let's git our gleanin' gear together."

With that, the children pulled bundles of coarse cloth bags from under the table. Evan tossed a sack to his father and two more at the invisibles' chairs. Rolin caught his, but with a *flippety-flap*, Marlis's wrapped itself into a floating turban.

"Mmph," Marlis mumbled through the turban.

Elena scolded Evan. "You mustn't throw things at people without warning them first. You might put an eye out!"

Evan hung his head. "I'm sorry, Aunt Marlis. I didn't know you weren't looking. Are you hurt?"

The burlap rolled into a ball that dropped onto the table. "Not a bit," Marlis said with a laugh. "I'm just embarrassed, that's all. I never was a very good catch. What are these, anyway?"

"Our basswood-bark gleaning bags," replied Bronwen proudly.

"Do you happen to have any basswood rope lying about?" Marlis asked. Elena searched the cave and came up with a piece of stout twine she used as a clothesline. Marlis wound up the rope and dropped it into her pocket, where it vanished.

After Arlan had collected his bow and arrows, the gleaners bade Elena farewell and trooped outside. A fine morning awaited, windless and fair, with a crisp hint of winter in the rain-freshened air. A mournful hush hung over the hill, as if the trees knew the snarks would soon overrun them from below.

As Arlan had warned, clumps of snark sprouts turned up near the cave. Resembling thick, black iron pokers thrusting through the moist earth, the sprouts became taller and more numerous the farther the five hiked down the hillside.

At length, they came to the eaves of the snark wood, looming like a solid bank of dark thunderclouds. The squat trees gripped the bare earth with stony, black-knuckled roots. Nothing green grew beneath their deep shade.

"This is the way to Peton," Arlan announced. Twin lines of whitish stones wound among the trees, marking a faint path. Fouled with the snarks' black, dripping poison, most of the rocks had lost their natural luster. Rolin wished he had brought some moonwood with him, the better to see by.

"Hold on," said Marlis. Grass rustled. Then several tall fireweeds uprooted themselves in a shower of dirt and stones. Next, Elena's balled-up clothesline unraveled into the air. One end whipped around the fireweeds, binding them into a bundle. *Whish! Whish!* Tethered by the rope, the long-stemmed weeds whirled over Marlis's unseen head, shedding white, downy seeds.

"This will do nicely," she declared. "I'll call it my 'wiffle decoy.'" The fireweed sheaf sailed down the trail to the accompaniment of Marlis's light footfalls.

"Come back! Ye haven't got a chance!" Arlan shouted, but the strykkies' death chant had begun: *Whizz! Zinggg! Speeewww!*

"The Tree lives!" Marlis cried. Then all was quiet again.

"I hope she makes it," said Arlan. "It's a long way to Peton, and there's more than strykkies in them woods."

Rolin shuddered. If Marlis slowed or stopped, a volley of death-lily darts might find flesh instead of fireweeds.

Arlan ventured a few feet down the trail, now strewn with confetti-like threads. Picking up a stone, he tossed it into the forest. The spent strykkies were silent. "Come on in; it's safe now," he called back. Then Rolin, Evan and Bronwen plunged into the woods, following Arlan down the dusky path.

Timothy and his father stood in their workshop staring at the golden ball sitting on the workbench. It seemed larger than before. Timothy rubbed his eyes. The ball was still there, resplendent with gold and gems. "Tell me again what the mayor said."

"'You are now the Keeper of the Chest,' as I recollect."

"Why would the mayor pay you to make it and then give it back to you?" Timothy asked. "That makes no sense."

"I don't understand it, either," Garth sighed, lovingly stroking the polished gold. Then his eyes hardened. "Maybe he'll accuse me of stealing it. I wouldn't put it past him, the scoundrel!"

"Did he tell you what the chest was for?" asked Timothy.

"He said a man had ordered it made. When I asked him who it was, a queer look came over his face and he said, 'I don't know his name and I never want to see him again as long as I live.'"

CHAPTER 13

DOWN, DOWN TO PETON TOWN

That Marlis must be quick on her feet," said Arlan. "I thought we'd a-found her by now. Eh, what's this?" He bent over an oblong, white cocoon lying in the path. Fireweed stalks protruded from one end of the sticky bundle.

"Why, it's Marlis's wiffle decoy!" Rolin exclaimed. "The weight of all those darts and threads must have broken the line."

Kicking at the mummified decoy, Arlan said, "This thing looks like a young worggle that blundered into a strykkie patch. Now that Marlis has lost her lure, she could be in trouble. We'd better—" A shrill cry from above interrupted him.

"It's a willy-willy," exclaimed Bronwen. "Look—up there." She pointed at a reddish-green bird perched in a snark beside the path. The bird squawked again and flew off, its banded wings making a whistling "willa-willa" sound.

"I didn't think any birds lived among the snarks," said Rolin.

"Only the willy-willies do," said Arlan. "They sip nectar from strykkie flowers with their long tongues—and they eat other things, too. We've got to hurry!"

Trotting along behind the visibles, Rolin noticed more of the screeching birds circling over the forest just ahead. He stopped dead in his tracks. A mammoth, shaggy beast with a wedge-shaped head and beady, black eyes was shambling toward them.

"A *skraal*—don't move!" Arlan hissed. The bear-like creature nosed the dirt with guttural grunts. A pink tongue darted out of its fanged jaws, flickering at a white-headed snake on the trail.

Then Rolin realized the "snake" was actually Marlis's decoy rope. Its "head" was a white, sticky blob of carnivorous strykkie strands. There was no sign of Marlis.

Suddenly, the skraal lifted its head and sniffed the air sharply. *Whoof!* Rearing up on powerful hind legs, the hulking beast bellowed, swatting the treetops with foot-long claws.

"It ain't after us," said Arlan. "It wants th' strykkie threads."

Sure enough, the skraal dropped onto all fours and began licking Marlis's rope again. All at once, it snuffled suspiciously and lumbered down the path, trailing a long, hairy tail.

At the rope's other end, the skraal lowered its head and flicked out its tongue. Then came a sneeze—*Achoo!* Startled, the beast lunged backward and let out another infuriated bellow. Then it snorted like a bull and charged.

Twang. Arlan's bow sang once, then again, and the shaggy monster stopped mid-stride, rumbled and crumpled to the earth.

Arlan ran up to the twitching beast. "It's dead!" he called.

Rolin rushed past him to the rope's far end, where he heard weeping. Kneeling, he wrapped his arms around empty space and found Marlis's heaving shoulders.

"It's all right," he said. "Thanks to Arlan, the beast is dead."

"That thing almost killed me," she sobbed into his tunic.

"Are you hurt?" he asked, wiping the tears from her cheeks.

She shook her head in his hands and pulled him closer. "When the creature sniffed me, I curled into a ball, the way Grandfather Bembor taught me to do if I was cornered by a bear. I couldn't help sneezing when its tongue tickled my face. Ugh!"

When Marlis had recovered from her shock, she and Rolin joined the others, who were gathered at the skraal's carcass. Two feathered shafts jutted from the beast's hairy side.

"Thank you for saving my life," Marlis told Arlan.

He shrugged. "It's th' least I could do after ye saved mine."

"How did you know she was in danger?" asked Rolin.

"The willy-willies," Arlan replied, cutting into the skraal with a sliver of black volcanic glass. "They pick over whatever the skraals leave behind. How'd ye git th' critter so riled up, Marlis?"

"I didn't do anything! Since I saw no strykkies here, I stopped to clean my rope. That's when this beast came out of the woods."

Arlan spat. "Th' only place more dangerous than a strykkie patch is one without 'em. It's a sure sign ye're in skraal territory. When they can't find meat, they'll wave their paws in front of a death lily to set it off and then lick the strings off their claws before eating th' flower. The darts cain't pierce their tough hides. Skraals usually don't attack people—unless ye threaten their young or disturb 'em while they're feeding. This one must have smelled that mess o' strykkie threads on yer decoy rope."

"So it thought I was trying to steal its dinner."

Arlan shrugged again. "It was fer th' best." He held up a brownish strip of skraal skin. "Ye need a fresh lure, don't ye? This'll do till we git to Peton. We'll stop here on our way back to butcher the carcass. Elena will be glad o' the meat."

"You're going to eat it?" Marlis gasped. The children smirked.

"Yes, Ma'am," replied Arlan with a toothy grin. "A nice, fat skraal like this 'un will make pretty fair eating."

After that, Marlis didn't run so far ahead of the others with her furry decoy, in case she tangled with more denizens of the dark snark woods. When the black forest finally ended, Rolin and the visibles followed Marlis's lure through a grassy willow thicket to the sandy banks of a broad river.

"This is more like it!" sighed a voice at the river's edge. Seeing two splashy dimples in the water, Rolin gathered that his wife was cooling her feet in the current.

"Git out of th' water!" Arlan roared. Sweeping his arms forward and up, he hauled Marlis's invisible form onto the bank, where she spittered and sputtered and kicked sand. Arlan wisely retreated to the safety of the willow thicket.

"Can't a woman bathe her sweaty feet in peace?" Marlis fumed. "Just because he rescued me from that *bear thing* doesn't mean he can manhandle me. I wasn't going to fall into the water."

"Maybe it was an honest mistake," Rolin said. "After all, Arlan knows his world better than we do. He wouldn't act rudely just to spite you. I'm sure he had his reasons for pulling you out."

"Then they'd better be good ones!" Marlis's footprints marched through the soft sand up to Arlan. "What was the big idea, grabbing me like that?" she yelled at him.

Arlan shot straight into the air. "Water ain't safe," he grated, turning red. Then he muttered under his breath, "Techy women."

Bronwen followed Marlis's tracks back to the river. "Father was only trying to protect you from the—" she began, when she caught a warning glance from Arlan.

Straggling upriver, the gleaners found a fir with two ropes wrapped around its robust trunk, one above the other. Their free ends extended over the river to an ash on the opposite side.

The bottom rope quivered as Marlis tugged on it. "We're crossing the river on *this?* Are you sure it will hold our weight?"

"Don't worry; these ropes are stronger than they look," Arlan assured her. He hoisted himself onto the lower cable, where he teetered like a tightrope walker. Sliding forward a few feet, he called back, "Jest watch yer step in th' middle, where it's slicker. Whatever ye do, *don't look down!*"

In a matter of moments, Arlan had made his way across the river, followed by the children, who scampered over the flimsy bridge without a misstep. Next, it was Rolin's turn. He inched along, steadying himself with the top cable. Halfway across, the lower line sagged perilously close to the black, oily water.

Though the footrope had hardly jiggled when the visibles crossed, it now swayed and swung with Rolin's every step. After slipping once and receiving a nasty rope burn, he waddled the rest of the way to the opposite shore.

"Whew!" he groaned, climbing down beside his friends. "You made it look so easy. Isn't there another way across this river?"

Before Arlan could answer, the ropes bobbed as Marlis stepped onto the bridge. She made good progress as far as the middle, when the footrope started swinging wildly. Rolin winced.

"She's losin' her nerve," Arlan groaned.

"Keep going! Don't stop!" shouted Bronwen and Evan.

Marlis cried out. Then the top line went slack and the bottom one rebounded sharply. *Splash!* The whiplashing lower cable suddenly went taut again—sideways.

"Rolin, help!" Marlis's frantic voice echoed over the water. "I can't hold on; the rope's too slippery!"

Even as Marlis hit the water, Arlan was racing across the bridge toward her. Following close behind, Rolin spotted the ripple-ringed hole his wife's form made in the water—and a swirling, gurgling *something* a few yards beyond her.

Arlan leaned over the ripples and whispered, "Take my hand."

"Ow!" cried Marlis. "You're stepping on my fingers!" Arlan jumped aside. Another dark swirl licked the water closer to the rope. Grasping the top cable with one hand and Marlis with the other, the men hauled her partway out of the water. Just then, a sleek, olive-black hump broke the river's surface.

"Pull!" Arlan shouted hoarsely. With a final, desperate heave, the two dragged a flailing Marlis onto the rope, where she dripped like an invisible drowned rat.

"Don't move!" Arlan hissed through clenched teeth.

"Why? What's wrong?" gasped Marlis.

Arlan crouched low on the rope. "*Eelomar.* It cain't see ye, but it kin see me—and them wobblin' ropes'll give ye away, too."

"What's an eel—" Rolin started to ask, when a gigantic, reptilian head on a sinuous neck burst through the water. A lidless, jet-black eye stared down and through him. Then the hideous jaws yawned, revealing rows of needle teeth.

"Run!" Arlan screamed. Falling over one another, the three scrambled pell-mell along the makeshift bridge. The beast kept pace with them. Then it surged ahead.

"It's trying to cut us off!" cried Rolin as the eelomar brought its head slashing down on the ropes in front of its fleeing victims. The cables cracked and hummed like giant bowstrings. Then the powerful jaws snapped shut, threatening to sever the lines.

Zing! Zing! Something like strykkie darts struck the beast's sinewy throat. With a deafening screech, the creature jerked its head backward. Thrashing the water to a bloody foam, the eelomar sank beneath the roiling river.

Somehow, Arlan, Marlis and Rolin gained the opposite shore, where they collapsed in a heap. Rolin murmured, "Thank You for protecting us, Gaelathane."

"Father! Father! Are you all right?" cried Evan and Bronwen, rushing to his side. Arlan could only nod, his chest heaving with ragged, rasping gasps.

"What happened to it?" he panted after catching his breath.

"I shot it," Bronwen said, her eyes shining. Then she showed her father the bow he'd left on the bank. "I used your last two arrows, though. I hope you don't mind."

Arlan embraced his daughter. "Mind? O' course not! I've got other arrows. Ye saved our lives, girl!" To Rolin and Marlis he said, "I'm sorry fer not warning ye about the eelomars. They usually lie low during high water, and I didn't want to scare ye. I shouldn't have let ye walk the rope alone."

"It's my fault, too. I shouldn't have looked down," replied Marlis, wringing a visible stream of water out of her hair.

"How did that eel-a-thing know Marlis was out there if it couldn't see her?" Rolin asked.

"Eelomars will strike at any sound or movement in th' water," Arlan explained. He found a stick of driftwood and tossed it into the river. There was a sudden eddy, and *gloop!*—the stick was gone. "Ye see? I've known eelomars to bite the bridge when only the wind was hummin' through th' ropes."

"So that's why you dragged me out of the river when I was cooling my feet in the water," Marlis said sheepishly.

"Yep. Eelomars like to hide along th' riverbanks, lyin' in wait fer unwary animals coming down to drink. A good-sized eelomar kin swallow a skraal whole. Ye wouldn't make a mouthful."

"I want to go home," Marlis whimpered.

"Cheer up," said Arlan, forcing a grin. "Ye'll git used to it."

Sniffling, Marlis muttered, "I don't plan to stay in this horrible place long enough to 'git used to it.'"

"With those arrows in its neck, will the eelomar still come after us if we go back across the bridge?" Rolin asked.

Arlan snorted. "It takes more than a couple o' arrows to kill an eelomar. Besides, they hunt in pairs. We'd better move along now—if ye're able, that is."

Following the visibles downriver along a stony path, Rolin and Marlis found two dead limbs to use as walking sticks, which strode down the trail like a pair of riderless stilts. The children skipped ahead, stopping to gather thistle fluff and scatter handfuls of the tiny white parasols to the wandering winds.

At length, the path left the riverbank to meander through a hummocky field littered with bricks and weathered granite blocks, as if giants had once staged a pitching party there. Among them lay a massive slab of reddish marble whose cracked face announced in timeworn letters, "Peton."

"So that's where the place got its name," Marlis said.

To Rolin, the sign said, *Don't you recognize me?* He shook his head. From every angle, the letters spelled out "Peton," the name

of a long-dead town. Sensing that Marlis had left him to join the others, he rushed forward and ran right into her.

"Do try to be more careful!" she chided him. "I've already had quite enough falls and close calls for one day, thank you."

"I'm sorry! I couldn't see you, dear. Did you hurt yourself?"

"Not really. I just scraped my leg on this rock." The offending object was plainly visible through Marlis's body. Of a lighter color than its neighbors, the stone exhibited facial markings on its underside. Rolin rolled the stone over with his foot and gasped. Then Marlis's piercing shriek brought Arlan on the run.

"What's wrong?" he cried. "Did a snake bite ye?"

"No, nothing like that," said Rolin shakily. "We've just found a sculptured rock. Do you have any idea what it is?" He tapped the stone with his walking stick.

"There's rafts o' them things in these ruins. They're uglier than a skraal's snout, don't ye think? Now let's git to work. We won't have much time here as it is."

After Arlan had left, Rolin and Marlis stood staring at the stone, their fingers entwined. Though the carving was badly eroded, there was no mistaking the snarling features of a yeg.

"What a lovely wassail!" cried Timothy's mother, Nora, clasping laundry-worn hands over her heart. "I've never seen a tree shine so, and without candles, too. Wherever did you get it?"

"We bought it from a woodcutter at the market," said Timothy, kneeling with his father beside the sapling. Its light-bearing branches lit up the cozy cottage like a dozen oil lamps.

Garth braced the trunk in place with some bricks. "Rare as hens' teeth they are. This was the last one." He shook the tree, showering the room with snowflakes. That gave Timothy an idea.

He dashed outside, slogging through the season's first snow to Garth's workshop, where he found the gold chest under the workbench. After bringing it into the house, he tied a length of twine around the ball and stood on a stool to hang it from the top of the tree, which bowed under the weight. Everyone clapped as the golden orb gleamed in the wassail light. Timothy's mother even strung her harp and played some merry melodies.

"If only the mayor could see us now," she purred.

CHAPTER 14

GLEANINGS AND GARGOYLES

Marlis groaned. "So there are yegs here after all!"

"Or *were*," Rolin corrected her. "We haven't seen a live one yet. If we're lucky, we never will."

"This looks too real for a statue," Marlis pointed out.

"But too old to be petrified. We've had our lightstaffs only a few years, and this thing must be over a hundred, if it's a day. Maybe the yegs that lived here died out long ago, and all that's left are these decaying sculptures."

Marlis snorted. "Died out? From what? Nothing can kill them."

Rolin gave the yeg carving another kick. "How should I know?"

"Hey, over here—we've found something!"

Rolin and Marlis broke off their discussion and climbed through the rubble toward the sound of Arlan's voice. They found the visibles standing beside a shallow excavation with a small opening at its bottom. Evan was tossing rocks into it.

"We've unearthed a cellar!" shouted Bronwen, waving at the invisibles as their walking sticks pranced into view.

"Most people pick through th' surface rubbish," Arlan explained. "To find anything o' real value, ye must dig deeper, into th' cellars, where th' old Petonians kept their tools and the like."

"Isn't it dangerous poking about in these rocks?" asked Marlis.

With a grim glance skyward, Arlan said, "We're better off underground with th' snakes and scorpions than out here."

Rolin gulped. Could those deadly pests sense invisible prey? He'd seen snakes strike at burning sticks, as if they caught their quarry by heat, not by sight. As the visibles slipped and slid down into the pit, he asked, "What about us? How can we help?"

"Jest keep a lookout," Arlan shouted up to him.

"Keep a lookout for what?" Marlis asked.

"Grakkles!" Evan hollered back, pointing overhead. Then he vanished into the hole. Looking up at the serene sky, Rolin realized he wouldn't know a grakkle from a grasshopper.

Marlis plopped down on a pile of rock, touching off a small avalanche. "Grakkles. What are those? Flying sea serpents?"

"Who knows? Whatever they are, our invisibility should protect us from them, as long as we don't wave our sticks about."

"Invisible or not, I don't like sitting out in the open like a couple of stuffed partridges," said Marlis. Still grumbling, she took refuge behind a rotting heap of stone.

With one eye on the lookout for grakkles and the other for falling rocks, Rolin piled some stones in a circle around Marlis's sentry post. "This wall should give us some protection from anything wanting to make a meal of us," he said. The bulwark was nearly finished when Marlis cried out, "Rolin! Look!"

"What! Where?" Rolin stared wildly at the empty sky.

With her walking stick, Marlis prodded a hideous face leering out from one of the stones. Unlike the carving she had stumbled over earlier, this one was a crude yeg caricature, a grotesque, goat-faced creature with a mocking mouth, forked tongue, slanted eyes, a jutting brow and curving horns.

"*That's* no yeg," Marlis declared. "Yegs don't have horns."

"Wait—I've seen stone scarecrows like this before, in Beechtown," Rolin said. "The townspeople make them to frighten away the batwolves. They're called 'gargoyles.'"

"The ones in Beechtown don't have horns," Marlis said.

"What does it matter? If batwolves once lived in this world, the Petonians still might have carved these things to scare them off."

"Then where are the yegs now? If what you're saying is true, this place should still be swarming with them like flies in a Thalmosian slaughterhouse. I haven't even seen any bats."

"Rolin, Marlis—look what we found!" Evan, Bronwen and Arlan were scrambling out of the crater, dragging their gleaning bags behind them. The two would-be sentries slid down to meet them.

Evan held up a fistful of rusty iron spikes. "Nails for arrowheads! I found some marbles, too." One by one, he gingerly picked three colored glass globes out of his bag and squinted through them like a jeweler examining fine diamonds.

"Very pretty," said Marlis.

"Here's what I gleaned." Bronwen opened a dusty leather pouch and shook out an assortment of bone and metal needles.

However, the prize of the day was Arlan's find, a metal contraption equipped with a crank and hopper. "Elena's always wanted a gristmill," he said, beaming. "Now she can make acorn bread as light as cake." Rolin bit his tongue. Ground coarse as sand or fine as flour, acorns were still acorns.

"It's awfully heavy, Papa, and you'll need to carry it over the river," Bronwen said. "It might get broken on the way, too."

Arlan scowled at her. "By Peton's stones, I'll git it home in one piece if I have to tie that eelomar in knots!"

Rolin touched Arlan's arm. "Speaking of eelomars, you haven't answered my question yet: Must we still use the rope bridge, or can we cross the river somewhere else on the way home?"

"It's th' ropes or nothing," replied Arlan heavily. "Years ago, we used Peton's dam as a bridge until th' middle washed away."

"May we have a look at it?" Rolin asked, thinking that a washed-out bridge sounded safer than a flimsy rope span strung over eelomar-infested waters.

"Can we, Father?" Bronwen chimed in.

Arlan shrugged. "I s'ppose so. Cain't hurt, anyhow. Follow me."

Rolin soon regretted his request. He and Marlis tripped over half-buried bricks and gashed themselves on sharp stones trying to keep up with the visibles, who leapt among the jumbled blocks like spry mountain goats.

Cutting across a snark-overgrown street, the five reached the riverbank, where a flat-topped dam restrained the rain-swollen river. Black waters surged through a ragged gap in the middle, throwing up sheets of foam and spray. The banks upstream bore no marks of flooding. Downstream, however, the raw-edged channel was deep and wide, as if gouged out with a giant scoop.

"Ain't this somethin'?" Arlan shouted over the water's roar. "It's jest a bunch o' busted-up boulders. No wonder th' blasted thing failed. We tried to repair the breach, but it was too large. Prob'ly jest as well we didn't."

"Why is that?" Marlis shouted back.

"Too dangerous. When this was th' main river crossing, eelomars gathered here thick as snakes, jest waitin' fer some careless skraal or deer to slip an' fall off."

"Can we walk out a little ways?" Rolin asked.

"Jest don't go too far. I don't fancy fishin' ye slippery invisibles out of th' drink again!"

Hand in hand, Rolin and Marlis ventured along the causeway, clouds of silvery spray swirling up and over them. "This is far enough," said Marlis, tugging at Rolin's arm. "I don't want one of those eelomar things to spot us and climb up here."

"Have you forgotten we're still invisible?" Rolin retorted. "As long as we don't throw any rocks in the water, the eelomars won't know we're here. They can't climb, either, unless—" He picked up a small, tapering object. "Doesn't this look just like a tooth?"

"It certainly does, but not an eelomar's," said Marlis. A handful of grit, sand and gravel floated into the air. The finer grains trickled through Marlis's invisible fingers, leaving two stones that resembled parts of a pointed ear and a stubby nose.

"Why, here's a yeg snout, and this other piece is an ear!" Marlis cried. She and Rolin sifted through more of the rocks, finding yeg claws, yeg tails and yeg jaws mixed with the gravel.

"This is a regular gargoyle graveyard," Rolin quipped. "The Petonians must have used the river as a dumping ground for their castoff statuary, not to mention their other rubbish."

"Then they made an awful lot of gargoyles back in those days," Marlis remarked. "Whatever for, do you suppose?"

Leaving that question unanswered, the two returned to the riverbank, where they found Arlan and his children talking in low tones among themselves.

"I don't know what we'll do," Arlan was saying glumly. "I've run out of arrows, and we've scared off what little game still lives down here. I wish I'd brought some skraal meat with me."

"We can't go back without *something*," Bronwen protested.

"Maybe the 'visibles can help us," Evan suggested. "They could sneak up on a 'coon or a marmot and club it to death before—"

The visibles all jumped as Rolin scuffled his feet. "After killing that skraal, you shouldn't need any more meat for awhile," he reminded them. Marlis murmured her agreement.

Arlan's eyes slid through Rolin's. "Meat ain't the problem."

The gleaners made their way back upriver, keeping to the bank rather than returning to Peton's debris-choked streets and alleys. When they reached the rope span, Arlan growled, "That eelomar's still alive out there, waitin' fer us. I kin feel it."

"Let's spend the night here," Marlis ventured. "We can cross the bridge first thing in the morning and be home by lunch."

"We might even catch the eelomars napping," agreed Rolin.

"No!" Arlan snapped. "We cain't stay the night on this side o' the river, 'specially with a full moon, and that's that."

"Why not?" Marlis asked. "There aren't many snarks here, and no strykkies. We could build a fire to frighten away any stray worggles. I'm sure we would be perfectly safe."

Arlan glared at the empty air. "Peton's no safe place fer us after dusk. My grandfather once came this way under a full moon. When he returned home, his hair was as white as—"

"Father, what's that?" Bronwen was pointing at a fluffy ball of pure white nestled in the grass by the riverbank.

"Looks to me like a rabbit," said Arlan, scratching his head. "I ain't never seen a *white* one before, though. I'd swear it warn't there a minute ago. And me without any arrows!"

"Let the poor thing alone," said Marlis. "You have enough skraal meat to last you a month as it is."

"Ye don't understand! We need that rabbit to cross th' bridge."

"That's silly," Marlis said. "We got to this side without it, didn't we?"

Arlan kicked some river rocks. "Well, without it, we *cain't git back!* Now be quiet; I don't want to scare it off."

Crouching unruffled beside a tuft of grass, the hare twitched its long ears as if taking in every word of the heated conversation. Its dark eyes bored seeingly into Rolin's.

It's all right, they seemed to say. *You mustn't be afraid for me.*

"Don't jest stand there; hit it with a rock!" Arlan told his son.

"It's awfully far," Evan said. "Anyway, I left my sling at home."

"Then git closer!"

Evan picked up a rock and shuffled toward the rabbit. Then he drew back his arm and hurled the stone, which fell inches short of the mound of snowy fur. Evan paled.

"Drat!" Arlan swore under his breath. Yet, the hare continued gazing calmly back at its would-be assassins as if amused at their crude attempts to kill it.

Arming himself with another rock, Evan took aim again. This time, the stone struck home. Blood spurted from the hare's head, and the animal pitched over in the grass.

"You brutes!" Marlis cried. "Why did you have to kill it? That rabbit never did anything to you! It hasn't got enough meat to—"

"Quiet!" Arlan bristled. "The eelomars ain't deaf, ye know."

Evan presented the dead rabbit to his father. "Will this do?"

"I believe it will, Son," Arlan replied, stroking the animal's soft, crimson-spattered fur. Its head lolled limply in his arms, its eyes filming over. "If we'd had time, I'd skin it. Your mother could have stitched a fine pair of slippers from this 'un." He hefted the hare by its hind legs. "Now ye and Bronwen git yerselves across the bridge. I'll follow with the invisibles." He thrust out the rabbit stiffly. "Hold this, will ye, Rolin? My hands are full."

Rolin took the still-warm hare. "What should I do with it?"

"If an eelomar comes after us, throw it into th' river as far away from th' bridge an' th' beastie as ye can."

As before, Bronwen and Evan scurried across the rope like mice up a ship's hawser. The river below the bridge remained undisturbed. Rolin and Marlis were the next to mount the span, clinging to one another to prevent further mishaps. Clutching the gristmill under his arm, Arlan brought up the rear.

All went well until Rolin spotted a telltale wave streaking toward the bridge. Mustering all his strength, he swung the rabbit around and let it fly downriver in a white blur. *Splash!* The ominous ripples reversed course and headed toward the hare.

"Hurry!" Arlan cried. Needing no urging, Rolin and Marlis bounded along the rope like a couple of squirrels on a clothesline, Arlan at their heels. By the time they had reached the other shore, the river's oily surface was as placid as before.

"*Now* do ye understand what th' rabbit was fer?" Arlan panted.

"Yes," said Marlis. "I only wish there were some other way."

"So do I," said Arlan with a sigh. "So do I."

The next morning, Timothy awoke to find his world swaddled in snow—and the gold ball missing from its prominent place at the wassail's top. After a lengthy search, he and his father found the chest tucked back under the workshop bench.

While Garth examined the ball, Timothy suggested, "If it's not for trimming the tree, maybe it's meant to hold something."

"Perhaps, but that's not for us to decide," Garth replied. "The terms of the agreement are clear, and I intend to honor them. Our family will guard this thing until it's ready to be opened."

"When will that be?"

Garth stroked his stubbly chin. "I can't rightly say."

Timothy pouted. "May we sell it, then? We would be rich!"

Garth shot him a horrified look. "Weren't you listening the day I brought it home? We're to protect the chest, not auction it off to the highest bidder."

It seemed the mayor had gotten the best of them after all.

CHAPTER 15

Magic Sacks and Melon Heads

Since Marlis had disarmed the strykkies on her first pass through the snark wood, the gleaners safely retraced their steps to find the slain skraal still lying on the path. Rolin had just finished helping Arlan skin and cut up the carcass when Marlis remarked to him, "Have you noticed how the snarks haven't said a word to us since we arrived in this place?"

Rolin crammed a gleaning bag full of skraal meat. "Why, you're right! I'd almost forgotten they could speak."

"Maybe these trees can't," Marlis mused.

Arlan threw the smelly skraal hide over his shoulder. "All set? Home and dinner await, so let's be off!" Having eaten little since breakfast, the travelers hurried up the trail toward the setting sun, each lugging one or more sacks. The procession was nearing the limit of the snark wood when Rolin and Marlis heard voices.

"You-know-who said we shouldn't bother with the likes o' these pitiful two-legs, but 'e said nuthin' about magic sacks!" It was snark speech, deep, coarse and dripping with venom.

"Aye, Tarlimb," rumbled another. "This place is in 'is pocket, 'e said. Maybe 'is pocket's got a 'ole in it!" The trees guffawed.

"What shall we do?" whispered Marlis.

"Just keep walking and pretend you don't understand them!" Rolin hissed. As Marlis's bag forged ahead, Tarlimb spoke again.

"What say we find out what's in them sacks, eh, Wormroot?"

"Nar. It's just skraal, and we'll get the leftovers, anyways. Stones and bones, it's been a hunnert summers since I've had skraal marrow. They're crafty beasts."

"All the same, *he'll* have our bark if we let this bewitchery slip through. I've seen what 'e can do to a tree that don't suit 'im!"

"Then raise the alarm if you like," said Wormroot. "I'm too old for that sort o' thing. Let the *stingers* get 'em, I say. Then we'll have ourselfs a taste o' two-legs to go with the skraal."

Rolin and Marlis scurried up the trail, hoping the trees were only making idle threats. They were wrong. The snarks began to stir, creating a creaking and a clattering that swiftly spread through the dark forest like ripples on a placid pond.

"RUN!" cried the pair as they caught up with the others.

"What's gotten into them invisibles this time?" muttered Arlan.

Rolin pulled on his arm. "Hurry! The snarks are after us!"

"Ye're daft!" Arlan retorted. Then the light failed. Inky creepers were slithering down from above, weaving a tangled web around their hapless victims. Sticky, stinging snark seeds peppered them from all sides.

Their sacks bouncing on their backs, the gleaners dashed toward the fading twilight at the path's end. The last few feet were touch and go, but everyone managed to wriggle through the thickening tangle of tendrils into the open air.

"Peton alive, I never seen snarks carry on so!" Arlan exclaimed.

Rolin and Marlis exchanged warning squeezes. "Maybe they're upset we didn't leave them more skraal meat," Rolin quipped.

"We did pick the bones as clean as a hound's tooth," Arlan agreed, not realizing Rolin was jesting.

Shouldering their bags, the weary hikers trudged up the mountainside. They had just entered an osoberry thicket when Arlan put up his hand. "Something ain't right," he said. "Th' forest's too quiet. I'd better go on alone—"

"Let *me* do the spying, since I can't be seen," said Rolin firmly.

As stealthily as a cougar stalking a deer, Rolin stole through the woods. At last he saw them: Eight gangly gorks skulking around the visibles' cave, all armed with long spears. *Thump! Thump! Thump!* Several of the pallid creatures were hammering on something behind the vine maples. The door! They had found the door! With their blank, bulging eyes, could they see him despite his invisibility? Rolin shrank behind a thick fir trunk.

Fortunately, the gorks weren't watching for invisible spies. Having seen an eyeful, Rolin scuttled back into the brush, practically bowling over Marlis and the visibles.

"Ye're a clumsy one!" Arlan growled. "Did ye find anything?"

"Worggles—eight of them—outside your cave."

"Worggles!" gasped Bronwen. "What are *they* doing here?"

"Breaking down your door, if I'm not mistaken," Rolin replied.

Arlan drove a fist into his palm. "I knew I shouldn't have left Elena alone! She cain't hold off eight worggles by herself, and I've got only the two arrows I saved from the skraal."

"Are worggles immune to strykkie darts?" Rolin asked.

"Naw, but th' filthy critters have a way o' movin' through th' woods—more like swimming than walking—that don't set off the flowers. *Gallumping*, we call it. Why do ye ask?"

"I think I have a way to solve your worggle problem, if you want to use those arrows," Rolin said. Then he outlined his plan.

With a wicked gleam in his eye, Arlan ran his thumb along the keen edge of an arrowhead. "Now we'll spill some worggle blood and send the rest packing! It's about time we stood up to them."

"Just don't shoot until we've done our part, or you'll spoil it all," Rolin told him. Then he and Marlis quietly led their friends within sight of the cave. As the visibles took up positions behind some large cedars, Marlis and Rolin approached the cave from downwind. They could clearly see some worggles pounding on the door with heavy stones. Rolin touched Marlis's leg.

"Ready with the rocks; on the count of three: One, two, three!"

The worggles stopped what they were doing as a hail of stones pelted them from out of nowhere. "Melon heads! Melon heads!" Rolin and Marlis taunted, flinging their insults from just out of spear range. Howling with rage, five of the creatures charged to-ward the invisible voices, leaving three to guard the door.

"Bug eyes! Jug eyes!" the two jeered as they retreated down the hill and into the snark wood. Staying just ahead of the worggles, the invisibles kept calling out rude and unflattering names. By the time the creatures realized they had been lured into a thriving strykkie patch, it was too late to "gallump."

Whicker-whicker! Volley after withering volley of whistling strykkie strings raked the worggles' ranks. Soon, five long, white cocoons lay motionless on the ground beside five spears. Rolin and Marlis traded congratulatory hand squeezes.

Back at the cave, they found two of the guards lying dead, pierced with Arlan's arrows. The third worggle was barricaded be-hind some boulders in front of the door.

"Durned invisibles," Arlan was saying. "Never around when ye need 'em, and when they are, ye can't tell what they're up to."

Rolin was crafting a fitting retort when he noticed the visibles' door slowly opening behind the besieged worggle. Finding a short stick, he crept up and waved it in front of the worggle's face. Mes-merized, the goggling creature never saw the hand reaching through the door; never saw the heavy skillet the hand was wielding. It saw only stars.

———————————— ❦ ————————————

"I still don't see why we can't open the chest," Timothy grumbled. "Surely a peek inside wouldn't hurt."

"Maybe not, but when the mayor locked this thing, it was as empty as your mother's coin purse after market day," Garth replied. "Anyway, he said it's not for us to open."

Timothy stared at his father. "Then who can open it?"

"He who has the key and understands the words at the top."

"Well, we have the key."

"Not for long." Fishing a scrap of paper from his pocket, Garth handed it to Timothy. "You're to find the place marked on this map and leave the key there. Don't dawdle on the way, either."

"Leave it there?" Timothy echoed, unable to believe his ears.

"That's right. Leave it there."

CHAPTER 16

THE UNSEEN HAND

Well done, m' dear!" Arlan told his wife. "That worggle never knew what hit it." Seated around the table, the invisibles and their newfound friends were feasting on roast skraal. Though a trifle strong, the meat was far more palatable than acorn gruel.

"It was nothing," replied Elena modestly. "I wasn't about to let those worggles knock down my door without a fight, and a skillet was all I had at hand. I'm sorry there wasn't time to save the acorn patties; they would have gone so nicely with the skraal."

Rolin grinned invisibly. Much to his and Marlis's relief, the patties in question had gone flying when Elena flattened the gork.

"That's quite all right," Marlis assured her. "If you're going to whack a worggle, you can't always wait for an empty pan."

"No worggles will dare come around *here* again!" Evan crowed.

Arlan cleared his throat. "I'm afeared we ain't seen the last o' them. There's lots more where those came from, and they're bound to come sniffin' after their friends, if not our food. We cain't stay here much longer."

"Where will we go?" wailed Elena. "This is the only real home we've ever known! The children were born here; everything we own is within these walls. If we leave, we'll be fair game for the worggles and grakkles and everything else out there!"

"We'll be fair game if we stay put," Arlan retorted.

Tears streaked Elena's face. "It's such a hard time of the year to move. I just hope we can find another cave as nice as this one."

"Where there aren't any worggles," said Bronwen wistfully.

"Or strykkies," added Evan.

Marlis's cup rose and tipped back, dribbling water into her invisible mouth. "Rolin and I might know of such a place."

Elena's face softened ever so slightly. "You do?"

"It's near our home, and—" Rolin squeezed her hand twice.

Arlan leaned intently across the table toward Marlis's chair. "I thought ye said there are snarks where ye live, too."

"There used to be," Rolin put in. "All of them are gone now."

"How would we git to—what's yer town called?" asked Arlan.

Rolin tossed out the first name that came to mind. "Beechtown. It's a long journey from here, but with Gaelathane's help we'll find our way back."

"Is Beechtown a *nice* place to live?" asked Evan.

"Very nice," said Rolin, recalling his carefree boyhood days spent roaming the hills above the town. Homesickness squeezed the air out of his chest and choked his throat.

"Then I propose a toast," Arlan boomed, hoisting his water mug in a brawny fist. "To Beechtown!"

"To Beechtown!" echoed Elena.

"To Beechtown!" cried Evan and Bronwen, raising their own brimming cups and sloshing water over the table.

Half-heartedly lifting his cup, Rolin mumbled, "To Beechtown."

"To Beechtown!" Marlis sang out. All six mugs met over the table with a *clunk*. More water spilled.

Elena cleared her throat. "Let us not forget our guests."

"Yes, to our guests and to their unseen hands that'll lead us to our new home!" Arlan boisterously chimed in.

"Urggh," Bronwen gurgled. Breaking into a coughing fit, she spewed water across the table, showering Rolin and Marlis.

"Goodness gracious, girl, what's gotten into you?" Elena exclaimed, jumping up to pat her gasping daughter on the back.

". . . urrk . . . hands . . . urrk . . ." sputtered Bronwen.

Arlan mopped up with a rag. "What's she tryin' to say?"

"Something about *hands*," replied Elena. Glancing squinty-eyed at Rolin's and Marlis's chairs, she demanded, "Did either of you touch her? We don't hold with practical jokes around here."

"We did nothing of the sort!" retorted Marlis indignantly. "She just swallowed too much water, that's all."

"What . . . Papa said . . ." Bronwen choked out. "'Unseen hands,' just like the poem on the chest!"

"I believe she's right!" Arlan declared. He and Evan kicked back the carpet, lifted out the loose stone block and removed the gleaming chest. Then they set it on the table. Everyone crowded around the golden orb to find the third stanza:

In time, the unseen hand will turn
The key unlocking this simple urn;
He'll find it lying firmly wedged
Above the door, upon a ledge.

"It's right there, as plain as day," Elena murmured. "Still, how can our invisibles open this chest without the key? You two don't happen to have it, do you?"

"Of course we don't. Otherwise we would have given it to you," Rolin assured her. "It's certainly no use to us."

Elena smiled smugly, as if she had solved the riddle. "Just as I thought. They don't have the key, so they can't open the chest."

"No, no!" Bronwen stamped her foot. "Don't you understand? 'He' must mean Rolin. He's going to *find* the key. Then he'll unlock the ball with it. You'll see."

Arlan and Elena stared at her in stunned silence. Then they laughed until their faces turned blister-red and the tears streamed down their cheeks.

With arms akimbo, Bronwen glared at her parents. "What's so funny?" she demanded.

"Forgive us," Arlan gasped. "It's jest that Rolin's never been here before. How would he know where th' key's hidden?"

"Your father's right, dear," said Elena. "Generations of Keepers have searched in vain for that key. You can't expect a complete stranger—and an invisible one at that—to succeed where so many others have failed."

Marlis bristled. "What's invisibility got to do with it?"

"Maybe the key is 'visible, like they are," suggested Evan.

"Don't be such a thick-headed worggle," Bronwen said. "It's the *hand* that's 'unseen,' not the key."

"If you don't mind my asking, where have you looked for it?" asked Rolin. "Maybe Marlis and I can help."

Elena smiled condescendingly at Rolin's tipped-back chair. "No, you can't. We've looked everywhere," she said with a grand sweep of her arms about the room. "In Peton, under Peton and around Peton. On this side of the river and on that. Everywhere."

"You've searched this cave, too?" Rolin asked.

With a withering look, Elena retorted, "Why look here? Peton's where the first Keeper fashioned the chest, and that's where the key still lies, or I'm not a Keeper's wife."

"Ain't nobody lived in our cave afore us, except fer bears," added Arlan with a knowing nod.

"So you've looked above the door, just to be sure," Marlis said.

"Of course," replied Arlan with a wounded air. "Elena dusts up there at least once a week, don't ye, dear?"

Her face flushed with annoyance, Elena huffed, "Just because we live in a cave doesn't mean I can't keep house! If there was a key over the door, I would have found it, and that's a fact."

Rolin's own cheeks burned. "Then you haven't really *searched* there, have you? What harm could there be in looking?"

Scowling, Arlan took the oil lamp and went to the door. Holding the lamp high, he swept the length of the crude lintel with his hand, dislodging grit that rained down on his face.

"Blast!" he grunted, shaking his head and blinking his eyes. "Ain't nothin' up there, jest like I told ye. That key's buried in Peton somewhere under mountains o' rubble."

"May I?" asked Rolin. Taking the lamp, he placed his chair some ten feet back from the door. Then he helped Marlis onto the chair and handed her the lantern.

"What's this for?" she asked.

"Just shine it over the door," he instructed her. "If you notice anything unusual, tell me where to look."

While Marlis held up the lamp, Rolin felt along the ledge. Each movement of his hand raised puffs of dust. Still, no key.

"Thinks he can do better than me, does he?" Arlan muttered.

"Do you see anything?" Rolin called out.

"Not yet," answered Marlis. Then at the urging of Rolin's prying fingers, a pebble popped out of a cleft in the wall above the ledge and clattered to the floor.

"Wait," Marlis cautioned. "I do see something up there."

"What do you see?" the visibles cried with newfound curiosity.

"Go back a bit," Marlis said. "A hair to your right. No, that's too far. Yes! Right there in that crack behind some cobwebs."

Looking through his hand into the chink, Rolin saw a gleam. His fingers closed around something smooth, cold and hard. As he pulled, the object slid free with a rasping squeak. Slicker than eelskin, it squirted out of his grasp, glinting as it spun end over end through the air. *Clink*, it struck the stone floor. In the cave's confines, the sharp, metallic sound rang out like clashing swords.

"What is it? What is it?" twittered the children. Rolin dropped to his hands and knees to retrieve the thing. It was a brass key.

"All this trouble for a silly old key," Timothy grumbled to himself. Goodness knows there were crannies a-plenty in his cottage, enough to hide a hundred such keys. Instead, his father had sent him tramping through the snowy woods to find the spot marked on the sketchy map. More than once he'd been tempted to toss the piece of brass into the nearby stream. Only the prospect of facing his father with the truth kept the key in his pocket. He consulted the scrap of paper again:

In a dingle at the mark,
Waits a mantle in the dark;
Place the key above the mouth,
Where the crack is pointing south.

"What's a 'mantle,' and how do I find its 'mouth'?" he said, blowing on his cold-numbed fingers and wiggling his frozen toes. Coming upon a bubbling spring in a sheltered dell—the "dingle" described in the poem—he set out to find the hill pictured on the parchment. He soon spotted its glistening, snow-covered flanks. According to the pointing hand on the map, he was supposed to leave the key somewhere by the hillock. On reaching its base, however, he found only a thicket of contorted vine maples.

Then he noticed a shadow in the crusted snow under the maples. Probing the spot with a long stick, he felt emptiness instead of snow and rocks. Wriggling between the maple trunks, he found a drafty hole and poked his head inside.

Waits a mantle in the dark. It was dark, all right. Dark enough to hide a bear or a mountain lion—or a "mantle." He threw several stones into the hole, hoping to frighten away any hungry animals lurking within. Then he crabbed around to ease himself through the opening, legs first.

Scooting backward on a skiff of drifting snow, he tumbled into a dark, dank cave. Though the air was warmer inside, he shivered. Was this where the key belonged? Perhaps he should leave it on the rough rock floor. Next spring, he could return to explore the cave more thoroughly with one of the candles that stood over the brick fireplace in his ramshackle shanty—on the mantle.

"Place the key above the mouth, where the crack is pointing south," he repeated. As he groped above the entrance's "mouth," he felt a rock ridge jutting from the wall. So there was a mantle! Reaching still higher, he found a crack running down the wall, veering south where it met the ledge. After digging the oil-coated key out of his pocket, he jammed it into the crevice.

Chapter 17

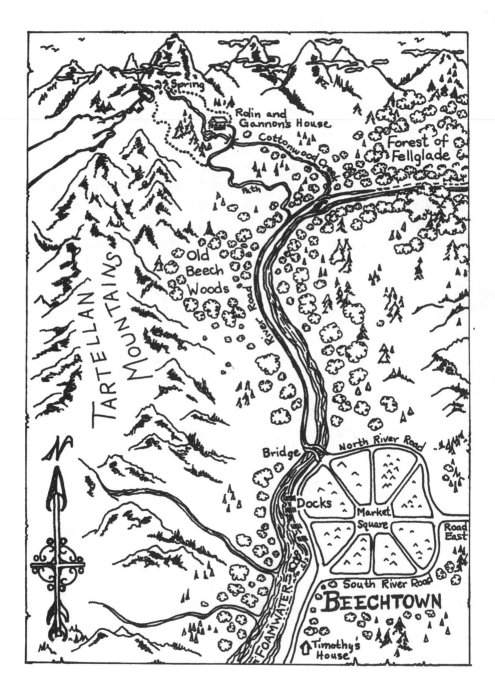

STONES ALIVE

Arlan's eyes grew as wide as a worggle's. "It's th' key!"

"It's *a* key, you mean," scoffed Elena. "It can't possibly be the right one."

"Let's find out," Rolin said. The key in his hand made a beeline for the golden chest, paused at the keyhole and slipped in.

"It fits! It fits!" squealed the children.

"That doesn't mean a thing," Elena sniffed. Rolin could feel all eyes riveted on the key as he turned it in the lock. *Snick.* Elena gasped and fainted dead away.

"Open it! Open it!" cried Evan and Bronwen, their hands dancing around the ball. "We want to see the treasure!"

"Hold on," Rolin said. "Let's wait until your mother wakes up."

Arlan sprinkled some water on Elena's face and she groggily came around. Then he pushed the globe toward Rolin. "Well, go ahead, open it. No use putting it off any longer."

Not wishing to be accused of filching whatever the ball might contain, Rolin pushed the chest back. "I believe that honor is the Keeper's and the Keeper's alone," he said gently.

Arlan placed his hands on the sphere's domed top and recited, "The ball has been, the ball will be, until he comes who holds the key." Then he lifted the lid. The cave grew as still as a tomb. Apart from the very tips of the diamond and rubies protruding through the top's polished half-shell, the ball was—

"Empty." The chalk-white Keeper's wife croaked the word as a curse. "We're too late. Someone else already opened it."

"I doubt it," said Rolin. "If we weren't the first to unlock this chest, then why was the key still hidden above the door? Besides, gold coins or precious stones would have marred the metal inside. There wasn't a thing in there to begin with."

Arlan glanced at his wife. "He's got a point."

Bronwen read from the poem's fourth stanza. "'But now I wait with empty womb.' Maybe the 'I' is the chest itself speaking."

"Then what's it waitin' fer?" puzzled Arlan.

"To be 'filled,'" Rolin said. "What else could 'this golden room' refer to, if not the inside of the ball?"

Covering her face, Elena wept. "All my life I've been dreaming of this day, and now it turns out our chest is as bare as a bone!"

Arlan put his arm around Elena's sagging shoulders. "Don't take it so hard, Wife. We'll figger out the rest of th' riddle. It's only a matter o' time." One side of his mouth turned up in a quirky smile. "We could've lived th' rest of our lives in this cave without ever knowin' the key was here. How did ye two find it?"

Rolin chuckled dryly. "Since we don't cast any shadows, we had better light to see by. I almost missed the key as it was."

"Who do y' suppose put it there in th' first place?"

"Only Gaelathane would know that," Rolin replied, locking the chest. He handed the key to Elena, who threaded it on a buckskin thong and gave it to her husband to hang around his neck.

After placing the chest in its nook beneath the floor, the Keeper said, "Ain't nothin' more we kin do here tonight. We'd best be off to bed. We'll all feel better after a good night's rest."

"As long as we don't have acorn gruel for breakfast," muttered Marlis as she followed Rolin behind their blanket partition.

Buoyed by his discovery of the key, Rolin couldn't sleep. He had just dozed off when a chill, damp draft shocked him awake. Bed, blankets, Marlis and cave had all disappeared. Instead, he was standing on the Peton side of the washed-out stone bridge. The pocked, jaundiced face of a full moon loomed over the deserted town. Its silvery light cast sharp shadows among the watchful ruins and shone shadowless through Rolin's body.

All at once, Rolin heard a *tap*. Moving only his eyes, he searched for the source of the sound. There it was again, a crisp, hard *click*, as of rocks knocking together. Still he saw no movement. The causeway stones lay silent before him, locked in their dreamless, seamless moon sleep.

Ripple-rap-tap-rattle. Rolin backed away from the bridge. Something was stirring out there. Pebbles were rolling and hopping toward one other, forming larger masses where they met. The swelling rock mounds took on sinister shapes, like malignant mushrooms springing up after a summer's rain. Soon, the entire dam resembled a kicked-over anthill. Rocks and sand boiled in the river, whipping it into a foaming fury. Stones even sprang out of the water and onto the bridge.

Crickety-crack. Rickety-rack. The tumbledown town also teemed with black, twitching bumps, now sprouting eyes and ears, wings, feet and tails. Then a hail of dagger teeth rattled into grinning jaws. Sinewy legs quivered, straining to break free of the stones beneath. Rolin crammed a fist in his mouth to keep from crying out and bit down till his knuckles bled.

Suddenly, the dam flew apart in a flapping flurry of yammering yegs and grinning gargoyles. Others erupted from the river, whose pent-up waters rushed forward with a roar, scouring away everything in their path.

Not all the stone creatures took to the air, however. Some of them surrounded Rolin and closed in, glaring at him with malicious, mocking eyes. For the second time in as many days, Rolin experienced the naked helplessness of being *seen*.

Just as the slavering, black-winged beasts poised to spring, the scene changed. Rolin found himself in a stony, moonlit field where menacing shapes swooped and soared overhead. Then he saw the stone slab proclaiming "PETON" to all passers-by. Before his eyes, the "P" in "PETON" began glowing like a hot coal. The bottom of the "P"-loop bulged, lengthened and doubled back to rejoin the fire letter's main stem. "B," it now read.

The liquid flames passed over the "E" to etch another "E" in blazing lines. Then a curving "C" joined its neighbors, followed by two vertical bars with a crossbar between them. Finally, the fiery ink traced a "W."

Rolin's eyes flew open and he jerked bolt upright in bed. Now he knew where he was. One by one, the flaming letters had transformed "PETON" into "BEECHTOWN."

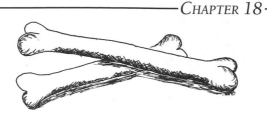

CHAPTER 18

LIGHTLEAF

Rolin shook the lump beside him. "Marlis, wake up!"

"Mph, ahr, wha—," mumbled his wife in sleep-slurred tones. The comforter billowed as she rolled over and snuggled into its warm recesses. "Leave me alon'."

Rolin tugged on her arm. "Don't go back to sleep, lazybones!"

With a huge yawn, the comforter's top half flipped over on itself. "It's cold in here. I hope the children are warm. What is it?"

"I just realized we're in Thalmos!"

"'Falmos'? That's nice. Never heard of it. Wake me in time for breakfast, won't you? Umm. See if your father will fix us some oatcakes, too. There's a dear." The comforter began rising and falling in rhythm with Marlis's soft snoring.

Rolin sighed. How could solid old Beechtown have fallen into wrack and ruin in less than a week? For that matter, where had all the black trees come from? Even they couldn't overrun an entire world in a hand's span of days.

Hours later, dawn squeezed through cracks in the battered door, and the visibles bestirred themselves. Marlis moaned, stretched and threw off the comforter.

"Ready for more acorn mush?" Rolin brightly asked her.

"Ick. You'd better be teasing. I was hoping for oatcakes."

"Shush! Not so loud. You don't want them to hear, do you?"

Marlis's voice rose. "I don't care! They are rude and obnoxious yokels, and their cave stinks. I want to go home *right now*."

Rolin chortled quietly. "We are home—or at least I am."

Marlis touched his smirk-twisted face. "You beast! Don't make such jokes so early in the morning, especially here."

He kissed her on the cheek. "I'm not joking. I'll tell you all about it later. Let's see what the visibles have cooked up for us."

Fortunately, bread and roast skraal—not acorn gruel—were on the menu that morning. After the visibles had wolfed down their portions, they hurried outside to dry the rest of the meat in the sun, leaving their guests to gnaw the scraps off the bones. The two made short work of the leftovers. As the skraal bones danced in the air, it appeared the beast was returning to life!

"How does it feel to be back in Thalmos?" Rolin asked Marlis, wiping his mouth on his sleeve. With invisibility, he was lapsing into sloppy table manners.

She waved a bone at him. "Stop it. It's no use pretending you're back home—unless you want to go mad."

"Who's pretending?" he said. Then he related his vivid dream. "Don't you see? Four of the sign's letters were worn off, and the 'B' had lost its bottom, so it looked like a 'P.' That's where they got the name, 'Peton.'"

"Even if it *was* named 'Beechtown,' that doesn't mean it was *our* Beechtown. For all we know, every world has one."

"Maybe so, but have you forgotten the yegs?"

"What about them?" Marlis countered. "They prove nothing, except that last night's skraal dinner didn't agree with you."

"It was too real for a dream! I was standing right on the riverbank. Remember how raw the riverbed looked downstream from the bridge? When the yegs and gargoyles awaken, the bridge collapses, letting all that backed-up water burst through."

Marlis's bone sailed into the garbage pail. "So the river flooded last spring. That's not unusual. Even the Foamwater floods."

"Peton's river *is* the Foamwater, I tell you!"

Marlis sighed. "I still say it was just a bad dream."

"I wish it were. Think about it. The stone yegs we saw yesterday in Peton looked real, didn't they?"

"Real enough to give you a nightmare," Marlis retorted. She began chewing noisily on another skraal bone.

"That's not what I meant. Don't you remember the Beechtown bridge, the one made of petrified batwolves?"

Marlis stopped chewing. "Surely you don't think—"

"Yes, I do. The 'dream' reminded me of it. Gundul's power has grown so great in Thalmos that its creatures revive at night."

Marlis's bone tapped a nervous rhythm on the table, keeping time with her heart. "Even so, everything in Peton looked so *old*, as if nobody had lived there in centuries."

"I don't understand it, either. Maybe this Thalmos is older than the one we knew. If you'll let me finish, there's more."

Marlis groaned. "Don't tell me. In your dream, the yegs and gargoyles all formed up and spelled out 'Thalmos' in the sky."

"Don't be sarcastic, dear. It's this cave. Ever since Arlan brought us here, I've had a nagging feeling about the place."

The bone stopped its tapping. "As if you'd been here before?"

"Yes! You've felt it, too?"

Marlis touched his hand. "*You're just homesick*, I've been telling myself. After all, I've never been in a cave like this one."

"You have, but it's all cluttered up with the visibles' belongings. Close your eyes and picture it bare, without the door."

"All right, I'll try . . . There. It's empty."

"Now pretend you're walking through the back wall."

"WHAT? No. It can't be. Now I must be the one dreaming. You think this is Grandfather's secret torsil cave?"

"I'm convinced of it. I tried going through the back and it doesn't work any more. The torsil must have died. Bembor took me home through here after the council banished me from Lucambra. That's when we first met, remember?"

Marlis laughed. "How could I forget? It wasn't every day we entertained Thalmosian guests in the heart of our hidden valley. I thought you were the cutest boy I'd ever seen."

"And I'd never met a prettier girl," said Rolin gallantly. "Of course, I didn't know what girls were in those days."

"Oh, go on with you!" Marlis flicked the skraal bone at him, grazing his ear.

"You shoot like a man, but you still throw like a girl," Rolin teased her. His voice softened. "We're a fine pair, aren't we? Two lonely lovers who can't even see each other."

Marlis's chair scraped back and Rolin felt her arms surround him. "I'll be content as long as we're together, visible or not," she said, ruffling his hair. "Come to think of it, if this really is our Thalmos, shouldn't there be some Lucambra torsils here?"

"By Elgathel, there should!" Rolin jumped up, scattering skraal bones in every direction. "Just one is all we need, and I think I know where to find him!"

"Are ye two still in here?" Arlan called, his eyes sweeping the empty cave as he entered.

"At your service!" Rolin said, pointing a skraal bone at himself. "We were just discussing how best to get home."

"And—?" Elena asked with a wary look.

"Rather than rushing off and getting lost," said Rolin, "we'd like to find our bearings first—gain a feel for the land, you might say. If we explore the hills around this cave, we might discover a shortcut back." Marlis squeezed his hand approvingly.

"It's a fine morning outside, and th' hike might do us good," Arlan reflected. "We'd still need to be back before dark, though."

"Naturally." Rolin's fingers drummed invisibly on his plate. Having decided on a plan, he was impatient to leave.

Arlan ducked behind a blanket. "I'll git my bow and arrows, and we'll be off like spooked rabbits."

"Not without a lunch, we won't," Elena called after him. She rummaged around on the shelves, bringing down several bags of dried fruit and hazelnuts. "These should last us for the day," she said. "I've even got some skraal jerky left over from last year." Marlis made retching sounds.

Arlan reemerged with his bow and four arrows. "I don't like leaving without a full quiver, but it's only fer a few hours."

Setting off to the southwest, the six kept to the thick stands of fir and pine mantling the foothills, where the snarks and their strykkie hangers-on hadn't yet taken hold. Rolin led out, his feet finding their own way up flinty bluffs and through canyons choked with scrubby manzanita and chinquapin. He carried a walking stick to help Marlis and the visibles keep track of him.

"Ye're going to git us lost if ye keep ramblin' through th' woods like this," Arlan grumbled. "Ye should let *me* break trail."

"Sorry," Rolin called back. "I'm just looking for a passage through these mountains." How could he explain that his "passage" was actually a *tree* of passage?

At noon, the hikers stopped beside a lush meadow to share their simple meal. Afterwards, Evan and Bronwen chased crickets through the grass. "Don't fergit to watch for grakkles!" Arlan warned them, puffing away on a maple burl pipe.

Marlis nibbled on some sprigs of wild mint she'd found near a stream. "You've mentioned 'grakkles' before. What are they?"

Arlan pointed his pipe stem at the sky. "Winged beasts they are, with beaks longer than a man's body. Some grow big enough to carry off whole trees."

Rolin snorted in disbelief. "What would they want with trees?"

"Fer buildin' their nests with, mostly," Arlan replied, knocking the ashes out of his pipe. "Sometimes they drop logs on eelomars sunning themselves along th' sandbars. Squashes 'em like bugs."

Leaving Arlan to smoke his pipe in solitude, the women gathered herbs while Rolin hunted for mushrooms. He kept one eye on the sky, just in case a log-toting grakkle happened by. In the woods across the meadow, he found a fetching bevy of Shaggy Parasol mushrooms, their scaly caps perched on stately stalks. He was picking one when a husky voice jarred him out of his reverie.

"What have we here? A two-legs, or I'm not a torsil. I thought they'd died out long ago in this world." The voice belonged to a leaning, snaggle-twigged tree sparsely covered with small, sickly leaves. Yet, there was something disturbingly familiar about the torsil's drooping branches and whorled bark.

"Lightleaf?"

"Eh . . . what's that? How do you know my name?"

"It is I, Rolin!" Lightleaf was still alive after all. That clinched it. This *must* be Thalmos. Unable to contain his excitement, Rolin whistled shrilly for Marlis.

"Rolin? Rolin who?" the tree rasped.

"You know very well 'Rolin who.' *King* Rolin, that's who. Don't try to fool me, you crotchety old torsil! You always did have a two-legged sense of humor, and a good one at that."

Lightleaf's limbs trembled. "Fie on you, impostor! I may no longer be as young as I once was, but my heartwood is still as sound as ever. Go back to the black trees, to the father of lies who sent you and trouble me no more!"

"What are you saying? Don't you remember your old friend, Rolin? The one who helped rid Lucambra of the ashtags?"

"That Rolin has been dead these many winters."

"No, he's—no, I'm not!" Rolin protested. "I'm right here in front of you. It's me, it's really me!" Where was Marlis? Surely she could talk some sense into the senile old tree.

At that moment, the grass stirred and Marlis ran into Rolin from behind. "What's the matter?" she asked.

"It's Lightleaf!" Rolin exclaimed. "I've found him!"

"I was never lost," grumped the tree.

Marlis gasped. "This rotting wreck is *Lightleaf?*"

"I beg your pardon," the torsil huffed. "I am in the very prime of my life." (Though trees reckon time by the slow swelling of their girth and the thickening of their bark, they still can be rather touchy about their age.) "Don't tell me I'm addressing the queen of Lucambra, either. She's dead and gone as well."

Rolin asked, "Do you recall what a boy once left on one of your branches many years ago?"

"I do," said Lightleaf warily. "Why do you ask?"

"It was my honey bag, wasn't it?"

The torsil answered as slowly and sadly as the passing of autumn into winter. "Yes. That sack I remember well. Some annoying bees later built a nest around it."

"Now do you believe me?"

"How can I? No two-legs ever lives four hundred summers."

"Four hundred summers!" Marlis burst out. "You've forgotten how to count, dear tree. Rolin and I haven't seen fifty years between us. Our children haven't even won their cloaks yet."

The ground rumbled with Lightleaf's bitter laughter. "It is you who have forgotten how to count, *impostor*. I've added a full four hundred and fifty rings since the day of King Rolin's coronation, a ring for every spring."

CHAPTER 19

TIME TORSILS

Four hundred and fifty springs!" cried Rolin. "That's impossible! We were just picnicking in the mountains when—"

"You disappeared," Lightleaf sighed. "I know. Every tree in the Land of Light has heard the tale of the Last Picnic, when the king and queen vanished, never to be seen again. That's why the People of the Tree stopped having picnics. A shame, really."

"How could everyone find out in such a short time?" Marlis said. "We climbed Thickbark only a few days ago."

"Thickbark, you say?" Lightleaf's branches quivered.

"That's right," Rolin said. "A, ah, *venerable* torsil, like you. He grew in a sheltered mountain valley near a river."

"Grew?"

"Felgor demolished the tree to trap us in Limbo, and he very nearly succeeded," Marlis explained.

"Oh, dear. That old snake? I thought his roots had rotted years ago. I should have known he was still making mischief. Tell me, did this Thickbark say anything before you climbed him?"

"He did, but we couldn't make head or tail of it," recalled Marlis. "The poor tree must have gone soft at the core."

"Some other torsils in the same grove told us to go to 'Father Thickbark,'" Rolin added. "They said he would take us from 'herren to therren,' or some such nonsense."

"Thickbark mentioned 'herren,' too," Marlis said.

"Herren and therren? Are you certain?" asked Lightleaf, all a-tremble. A dead limb broke off his trunk and crashed to the ground, narrowly missing Marlis.

"Quite certain," Rolin replied. "Do you know what he meant?"

"I may. What happened when you climbed Thickbark?"

Rolin related how he and Marlis had escaped Limbo after the torsil's destruction, only to find themselves invisible.

"Invisible? What is that?" the tree asked.

"It means, dear Lightleaf, that no one can see us," Marlis explained. "We can't even see ourselves, much less each other."

"How very odd," murmured the torsil. "I still feel you standing beside me. Is there a cure for this, ummm, *invisibleness?*"

"We don't know of any," said Rolin. "Anyway, that's the least of our problems. We're stranded here. If this world is Thalmos, it's not a very hospitable place in my opinion."

"This *is* Thalmos, and you are far worse off than you can imagine," said Lightleaf solemnly. "While I am delighted to make your acquaintance again, King Rolin and Queen Marlis, I fear you may have been better off dead."

"Why do you say that?" they asked.

"Thickbark was no ordinary tree of passage. He was what you would call a 'there-and-then torsil.' Most unfortunate you happened to climb him, most unfortunate indeed."

"There-and-then," Rolin repeated. "Therren. What exactly does a therren torsil do?"

"Nearly nine centuries old, and I'm teaching a two-legs what any sapling knows," Lightleaf muttered. "To begin with, since our in-and-out worlds are never precisely in time with each other, we torsils often stand between spring and autumn, dawn and dusk."

"Just as Thalmos is a few hours behind Lucambra," said Marlis.

"Quite so. However, a therren torsil is something else again. Such a tree can fling you many summers into the future of another land—or into its past. From 'here-and-when' to 'there-and-then,' in a manner of speaking."

"From herren to therren," Rolin reflected. "*Wherren* must mean 'where-and-when.' How amazing! Thickbark was a time torsil. That would explain why Thalmos has changed so much."

Marlis gripped his arm with the desperate strength of a drowning woman. "Rolin, what are we to do? We're over four hundred years ahead of ourselves—or are we behind?"

"You're in here-and-now," said Lightleaf gravely. "This is wherren you're likely to stay for the rest of your short lives."

"I don't want to live in here-and-now," Marlis shrilled. "I want to live in there-and-then, I mean, where-and-when. Oh, I just want to go back to my own time!"

"Then you'll need to climb another therren torsil," said Lightleaf with a shake of his shabby leaves. "Not just any one, either."

"You're saying we must find a torsil leading not only to Lucambra but also to our own time, is that it?" Rolin asked.

"That is correct. The longer a therren torsil lives, the farther backwards or forwards in the flow of time it will take you. To return to your own there-and-then, you must therefore find a tree of passage of the right age and disposition."

"Disposition?" asked Marlis.

"Why, yes. Most therren torsils are a terribly stuffy lot. They wouldn't warn you if a woodsman were coming to cut you down. That's how stiff-barked they can be. If you don't tell them they're the finest trees in all the land and other such absolute rot, they won't even speak to you."

"Thickbark wasn't at all that way," said Marlis. "I thought he was rather nice about letting us climb him, though he'd never met a two-legs before."

"From what I've heard, Thickbark was a downright decent sort," Lightleaf conceded. "It's a shame he came to such a nasty end." The torsil lapsed into silence. Suspecting his old friend had fallen asleep, Rolin rapped on the tree's trunk.

"Do you know of any therren torsils in these parts?" he asked.

Lightleaf yawned. "Not a one. The last succumbed to the snake trees years ago, as I recall." Marlis groaned.

"How did the ashtags take hold here?" Rolin asked.

"Rumor has it your own people brought the seeds here. 'Greencloaks carried the curse,' the trees have always told me."

"Greencloaks!" Rolin snorted. "That's absurd! No Lucambrian would ever do such a thing."

"Arlan said the 'grennocks' were responsible," Marlis reminded him. "Wait—just listen: Grennocks. Greencloaks. Don't you hear the resemblance?"

"What are you suggesting?" Rolin asked.

"If more than four centuries have passed in Thalmos, couldn't the name 'Greencloaks' have changed to 'grennocks' over time?"

Rolin scratched his chin. "Of course—just as 'Beechtown' became 'Peton.' Why would our people plant ashtags in Thalmos?"

"Rolin! Marlis! Where are you? Time to leave!" Bronwen's and Evan's cries wafted over the field of waving meadow grasses.

"We'd better go," said Marlis. "Lightleaf, it was wonderful to see you again. We'll return later and talk more with you."

"I live to serve my king and queen," Lightleaf replied. "My leaves and limbs are yours, such as they are. I look forward to—"

"We can't leave yet," Rolin interrupted.

"Why not?" Marlis asked.

"We have to find out what's happened to Lucambra!"

"I'm sure it's still there," said Marlis dryly.

"Yes, but don't you want to see our old haunts again?"

Marlis began braiding some grass stems. "Of course, but not in *this* time. We belong 'back then,' or however the torsils put it."

"Even now, it must be nicer than Thalmos," Rolin argued. "Besides, where else will we find a therren torsil to take us home?"

Marlis sighed. "We don't know how much Lucambra has changed. Four hundred and fifty years is an awfully long time."

"Long or short, Lucambra is still our home, and her people are our people. You should know that better than anyone."

"Don't question my loyalty to Lucambra!" Marlis shot back. "I just don't want you getting lost or hurt, that's all. I . . . I couldn't bear to live without you, especially in this desolate place."

Rolin caressed her hand. "Then come with me."

"I won't leave the visibles without an explanation, and we dare not tell them about the torsils. Surely you can understand that."

"Well, I'm not leaving until I've had a look-see around the Hallowfast," Rolin said. "I'll be fine. I'm still invisible, remember? Lightleaf can keep you company while I'm gone, and I'll be back before you know it. I may even bring a friend."

Lightleaf's limbs drooped. "You'll find few friends on the other side. No two-legs has visited me there in many a winter. My tree sense tells me all is not well."

"Oh, bother your 'tree sense,'" said Rolin peevishly.

"Hold on," Marlis broke in. "Do you mean to tell us that there aren't any Lucambrians left?"

"I didn't say that. The place has just been very quiet lately."

Marlis squeezed Rolin's arm. "I don't like the sound of this. Why would our people have stopped seeing Lightleaf? Let's stay put for now. It might be dangerous over there."

"No moreso than here," countered Rolin. "Think of all the nasties we've met: Strykkies and skraals, worggles and eelomars— not to mention the snarks. Little wonder Arlan and his family are the only people left. What could possibly be worse than this?"

"Then may He Who sees the visible and the invisible keep you out of trouble," Marlis sniffed. With that, she marched off through the meadow, scuffling up angry dust clouds as she went.

After calling out another parting promise to return soon, Rolin shinnied up Lightleaf's trunk and caught hold of a limb. "It's been a long while since I last climbed you, dear friend," he remarked, patting the tree affectionately.

"Do be careful!" said Lightleaf. "'Quick to climb, quicker to fall.' My branches are brittle and won't hold your weight the way they did when you were a young whip."

Taking great pains not to damage Lightleaf's living wood, Rolin clambered into the torsil's top. Climbing down again, he quietly departed the land of the potato eaters.

CHAPTER 20

LUCAMBRA'S UNDOING

Ah, this is more like it," said Rolin, surveying the forest surrounding him. Sturdy shore pines braced themselves against the whistling, salt-scented sea winds. Stained a fiery crimson with the setting sun, the Hallowfast jutted above the trees, a granite spike driven into the heart of the cliffs. After four hundred and fifty years, the king had returned to his kingdom.

Making off toward the tower, Rolin discovered the path was nearly overgrown. "No wonder Lightleaf hasn't had any visitors lately," he puffed, battling his way through thickets of salal and sand scrub. "Where is everybody, anyway?" Though the sighing trees must have heard him speaking, they made no reply.

Soon the trail broadened and shrugged off the encroaching underbrush. Rolin had the Hallowfast in sight when a wheezing, wild-eyed figure burst through the bracken and bowled him over. Bony arms and legs pumping furiously and long, gray beard flapping, the man disappeared down the trail in a cloud of dust.

No sooner had Rolin collected his wits than the ferns rustled and parted again. He jumped aside just as a silvery starglass shot out. Bobbing ten feet off the ground, it galloped along with a ghostly *clippety-clop* that left lizard-like tracks on the trail and a burnt-brass smell in the air. A phantom—or an invisible? Goosebumps prickling his arms, Rolin loped after the starglass.

After almost a mile, the glass sidled up to a tree and propped itself across a branch. It was now pointing toward the Hallowfast, which stood a short bowshot away. Though the Lucambrians had built the Tower of the Tree to withstand the fury of the El-marin's winter storms, the centuries had taken their toll.

A mighty warrior grown stooped with age, the sand-scoured tower tilted drunkenly, the broken teeth of fallen battlements lying shattered at its base, its eyeless window-sockets staring blindly. A mournful, neglected air clung to the place.

Beside the tower's door crouched the thin, bearded fugitive, casting fearful glances behind him. Fumbling with a *soros* medallion, he unlocked the door and nipped inside.

Hawww! The starglass broke into a snuffling snigger, a sound that a dying mule might make. Was this a beastly bray of pain—or of rage? The glass advanced upon the tower, stopping just short of the door. "You can't hide in there forever!" rasped the voice, its echoes raking the Hallowfast's ancient stones. "Sooner or later, you must come out and bow to me!"

"Never!" came the reedy reply.

The starglass voice chuckled unpleasantly. "Of course you will. Show yourself—or are you a coward like all your sniveling kind?"

A sallow, terror-pinched face appeared at the tower's rotting ramparts. "Here I am, infernal spirit. What do you want with me?"

"Want with you?" the voice mocked. "I want nothing *with* you, Ansel son of Percel. I've merely come to claim what's mine."

"Nothing here rightfully belongs to you, old ghost! Do you hear me? Nothing! *I* am Lucambra's true king. Haunt this tower if you must, but leave me be. If it's gold or silver you're after, there's none inside—you can be sure of that. I've wasted twenty years of my miserable life scratching through these cursed stones and found nothing but the bones of lords and ladies long gone. I'm sure you'll find them fitting company. I do not."

"You misunderstand me. I seek not riches, but revenge. As the last surviving heir in the fifth generation from Rolin son of Gannon, you shall make my vengeance and my collection complete. It's a pity Rolin himself can't be here to witness your demise."

Rolin strangled a gasp in the birthing. He was looking at his own great-great-great grandson!

Only a stray lock of Ansel's straggly gray hair still showed. "Whatever grudge you may bear against my ancestor, take it up with him, cruel spirit! I've never wronged you. Go away and bedevil someone else."

"I would if I could, dear Ansel," cackled the venomous voice. "Unluckily for you, you're the last Lucambrian. The very last."

"The others—what have you done with them?"

"Don't worry, they're all safe—in here." The floating starglass wobbled. "Years ago, I discovered an ashtag leading to *Limbo*, a place that is the very absence of place. It lies in the eye of the vortex of time. From the wood of that tree, I fashioned this starglass. Would you care to look into it?"

"No! I would not put that infernal thing to my eye for all the wealth in this world or any other."

The silver tube trembled. "As you wish. You shall still join the others, willingly or not. There is room in the Eye of Limbo for every world in my domain, from Amphoron to Zeleth!"

"My people have suffered long enough. Let them go!"

"No amount of suffering will ever satisfy the blood debt Rolin son of Gannon owes me!" the starglass voice bellowed savagely. "Though you wretched *tree rats* rot in Limbo for eternity, you will have only begun to atone for his misdeeds."

Rolin quaked. In all of torsildom, Felgor alone was fond of that slur. The fiend really was invisible!

Ansel's head cautiously re-emerged. "What evil has he done that you would punish us for his acts?"

"What evil?" Felgor hissed. "He demolished my sythan-ar while I was in it, condemning me to this wretched death-in-life existence! Still, he may have done me a favor. Not only am I invisible now, but also invincible. I escaped Limbo with a dragon's egg. *Fangle* is now half-grown and as invisible as I."

Rolin's knees buckled. An invisible dragon. So that was how Felgor had followed him and Marlis to their not-so-private picnic grounds. That also explained the peculiar tracks on the path.

Toying with his prey, Felgor had been pursuing Ansel at a leisurely trot on his spectral serpent.

"Hear me well, soul-stalker!" roared Ansel from the ramparts. "I do not tremble before you, wrapped in Gundul's mists though you may be. Get thee hence and trouble me no more!"

"If you insist," the sorcerer replied in honeyed tones. "First, though, I must read you a few verses."

Ansel edged back from the battlements. "Verses? What verses? Is this more of your sorcery?"

"Oh, no," Felgor said. "These are merely some words engraved on the Eye of Limbo. Since I presume you don't understand the language of Gundul, I'll translate:

> Stare not through me to glimpse the star
> Agleam on satin sea;
> I never show the things that are,
> But only what may be.
>
> Let look be deep and gaze be long,
> Shrink not from what appears,
> For when I tempt to do the wrong,
> I'll play upon your fears.
>
> The things you crave but cannot own,
> When having will bring harm,
> I'll color with deceiving tone,
> The gullible to charm.
>
> When I have wooed the watchers all,
> This world shall share their fate;
> In blackest void they'll ever fall,
> In time, forever late.

Ansel crossed his arms and glared at the starglass. "You've read your precious poem—now go!"

"Aren't you going to ask me what it means?" wheedled Felgor.

"All right, but be quick about it. It's drafty up here."

In answer, the starglass tilted toward the top of the Hallowfast. Black smoke billowed out, quickly enveloping Ansel's gaunt, cringing figure. Then the cloud began to whirl. Ansel clung to the ramparts as the darkness clawed at him, stretching his features and limbs like taffy. Before Rolin's horrified eyes, the twisting, spinning funnel sucked Ansel into its mouth.

"'When I have wooed the watchers all, the land shall share their fate!'" Felgor shrieked. Next, he turned his starglass on the Hallowfast, which dribbled like jelly into the greedy whirlwind's gaping maw. In minutes, nothing was left but a deep, smoking pit. Now Limbo began devouring Lucambra. Trees, lakes and wooded hills—the cyclone swallowed them all, leaving in its wake a gloom deeper than the gathering night.

Even as Rolin raced back up the trail, the howling tornado gobbled up the very ground behind him, like a cleaning woman pulling up an old, dirty rug. The earth was rolling and splitting apart as he staggered through the pine wood. "Lightleaf! Where are you?" he cried, unable to see for swirling dust and leaves. Then he spotted the torsil's tattered top. Heedless of scratchy twigs and bark, he scurried up the tree's gnarled trunk.

"Here now, what's the hurry?" Lightleaf grumbled. "Not so rough! Ow! That was a green limb you just broke. I'm not as supple as I once was, you know."

"Very sorry—can't explain now—tell you all about it later," Rolin apologized breathlessly. After climbing down a few feet, he flung himself into space, landing all too solidly on Thalmosian soil. By the time he had picked himself up, bruised and battered, Lightleaf was already in distress.

Lit by the ghastly red rays of Lucambra's dying sun, the torsil's branches were writhing and thrashing about as if tempest-tossed. Some of the smaller ones broke off to vanish into the vortex on the other side. Then the tree melted and oozed upward like a wax taper set too close to a fierce fire. "Hellllp meeee!" Lightleaf cried. With a slurping sound, the torsil disappeared into Limbo.

TORSILS IN TIME
PART 2

CHAPTER 21

HELMICK SON OF RONNELL

Having made passage through Silverquick, Scanlon found himself hanging precariously from the torsil, which was clinging to the face of a rugged cliff. "Why didn't I bring a rope?" he groaned. Using some scraggly bushes as handholds, he slithered to the base of the cliff, collecting a colorful assortment of bumps and bruises on his way down.

"A pox on all torsils," he muttered, picking himself up. Why was it that trees of passage always seemed to grow in the most awkward of places? He didn't relish the prospect of scaling the cliff ropeless to reach Silverquick after his explorations.

He was at the bottom of a narrow gorge hemmed in by high bluffs. Pale morning light filtered down between them. After tying a bit of red cloth to a willow clump to mark Silverquick's location, he shouldered his lightstaff and set off down a stony path that meandered along the canyon floor. "Gaelathane, grant me Your protection in this world—whatever it is," he prayed.

As the bluffs fell away, the gorge opened onto a dense fir forest carpeted with white-blooming trilliums and decked with crimson sprays of currant flowers. Swallows and swifts looped above the trees on a balmy spring breeze. Scanlon reflected that his excursion might turn out to be a picnic stroll after all!

Minutes later, the trail widened into a rough but well-traveled road, complete with wagon wheel ruts. Scanlon's heart skipped a beat. So people did live here—and where there were wagons, there was bound to be some rope.

Crack! A branch snapped. Quick as a blink, Scanlon slipped behind a birch. No more than twenty yards away, a bearded, green-hooded figure was slinking through the forest. Glancing furtively about, the stranger darted across the road and into the trees. Scanlon started to call out before thinking the better of it. The fellow looked as though he was up to mischief.

Instead, Scanlon trailed the scout from afar, still hoping to find some rope along the way. However, his quarry was quick and cunning, almost losing him in the lush underbrush. Once, the Greencloak doubled back and caught him off guard. Scanlon froze in his tracks as the man's gaze swept through the woods.

Presently, alders and elderberries began appearing among the firs, a sure sign of water. Weary beyond words, Scanlon was about to give up the chase when the green-clad stranger stopped among some alders to peer between their mottled gray trunks. As the sun grew warmer, the man slouched down behind one of the trees, pulled his hood low over his face and nodded off.

Curious to see what had attracted the other scout's interest, Scanlon crept out of the hazel thicket where he had been hiding. He had just reached the alder grove when the stranger shifted positions and his hood fell back. Scanlon flattened against the ground. When the sound of snoring resumed, he risked a quick look at the huddled form.

Helmick! Scanlon all but blurted out the name. Years ago, Helmick son of Ronnell had been one of Councilor Grimmon's most loyal followers. Had been. Like Grimmon, he had succumbed to the sickness. Unlike Grimmon, he had refused the healing power of Gaelathane's blood, thereby condemning himself to an eternity in Gundul's tormenting flames.

Scanlon scratched his head. What sort of world was this where dead men came back to life? Odder still, the sleeping scout looked younger than when Scanlon had last seen him. Might this be Helmick's son or grandson?

Leaving that mystery for the moment, Scanlon backed away from the sleeper and wove his way among the alders until he reached a placid, stream-fed pool. On the opposite shore stood a tidy log cabin, its trim lines darkly mirrored in the water's surface. There was a familiar air about the place, but before Scanlon could put his finger on it, the cabin door swung open and a tall, red-bearded man emerged.

Scanlon ducked behind a huckleberry bush as the man tossed some dirty clothes into the pool and began scrubbing them. When the launderer raised his head to brush the hair out of his eyes, Scanlon gasped. It was Gannon, Rolin's father, and no mistake about it. Like Helmick, he appeared years younger.

Before he could recover from this second shock, Scanlon heard the cabin door creak open again. This time, a slender youth of thirteen or fourteen popped out and made for the creek. Rolin! The boy looked as lively as the day he and Scanlon had first met in Lucambra. Grinning, Gannon made some remark Scanlon couldn't hear. Then he rolled up a wet shirt and threw it at his son, who deftly caught the soggy mess and returned the favor, nearly knocking Gannon into the pool.

Rolin then said something about "oatcakes and honey," whereupon Gannon chuckled and went back to the cabin with his laundry. Rolin sat down beside the pool and began singing softly to himself about "creeks" and "cottonwoods."

Scanlon's face burned with shame. What would Rolin say if he knew his best friend was spying on him? Or was this nothing more than an illusion, the cruel trick of a world where hapless travelers relived the past? He pinched himself. No, he wasn't dreaming. Yet, if this was Rolin-the-lad, where was Rolin-the-king?

All at once, Rolin looked up at him. For a heart-stopping instant, their eyes locked through the scanty huckleberry foliage. Then Scanlon tore his gaze away and slunk back to the alder grove. Consumed with guilt and confusion, he walked right into Helmick, who was sleepily scratching himself.

"Missed your chance there, didn't you?" the scout sneered.

Scanlon's stomach flip-flopped. "Uh, chance for what?"

"Why, to put a dart into the beekeeper's brat, of course. You had the clearest shot at him I've seen yet, and you muffed it. You do know how to use that blowpipe, don't you?"

Icy fingers squeezed Scanlon's throat. He managed a nod.

Helmick broke off a willow twig and idly chewed on it. "Well, no harm done. The boy's a slippery one, but next time he shows his face, you'll do Grimmon proud. You're late, by the way. My relief was supposed to arrive last night. I had to spend the night in a cave farther up the mountain. After two days on watch, all I've gotten for my trouble is a blasted bee sting. Can't imagine why those two keep their hives so close to the house."

Scanlon's mind whirled. Helmick's was no mere spying mission. Worried that the boy Rolin might spoil his plans, Grimmon wanted him out of the way at any cost. Yet, Rolin's first visit to Lucambra had taken place over ten years ago!

". . . I don't recall seeing you at Grimmon's tree before," Helmick was saying, studying Scanlon through slitted eyes. "Are you a new recruit?"

Scanlon thought quickly. "You might say that. I'm from another settlement. It's . . . very far away."

"What's your name?"

"Ah, Corlis son of Farrell." Scanlon hoped Helmick didn't know anyone by that name. He hated lying, but there was no telling what Helmick would do if he realized Bembor's grandson was meddling in Grimmon's affairs.

"Never heard of you. Well, Corlis son of Farrell, if you keep your eyes open and do as Grimmon tells you, you'll make a passable scout." Without so much as a "May your sythan-ar ever flourish," Helmick turned on his heel and left.

Scanlon took a deep breath and tried to stop shaking. Between nerves, the heat and the hiking, his mouth was as dry as dust. Since it wouldn't do to show himself near the pool again, he circled around to rejoin the creek some distance upstream, where he drank deeply of the cold, pure water.

Afterwards, he skipped flat stones across the stream, wondering how he had stumbled upon a Thalmos so identical to the one he'd known years before. Wherever he was, he'd still need a rope to reach Silverquick. Glancing downstream, he had the glimmering of an idea where he might find one.

The king's chief deputy spent the rest of that morning dozing by the creek, covered with his cloak for warmth and concealment. Awakening refreshed, he strolled upstream in search of some lunch. Since he had no fishing line or hooks, and it was still too early in the year for roots or berries, he made do with a handful of watery, brown jelly fungus he found growing on a rotten log near the stream. Though tasteless, the mushrooms helped him to stop thinking about food—but not about home.

Next, he crossed the creek dry-shod on a fallen maple and worked his way downstream through stands of sticky-leafed cottonwoods. Dusk found him perched in a fir near the cabin, where Rolin was sweeping the porch. Gannon was working in the bee yard, wearing a mesh headdress to keep the bees out of his beard. Neither realized the peril that was stalking Rolin, although Scanlon's arrival had bought some precious time; it might be days before another of Grimmon's men drew a bead on the boy.

Something wasn't right in the bee yard. After a moment's reflection, Scanlon realized that the gruesome yeg's head was missing from Nan's hitching post. That meant Rolin and Gannon had yet to skirmish with the batwolves in Farmer Greyson's field.

Night fell. Within the cottage, the old oil lamp sputtered to life, throwing yellow shafts of light through the windows. Still Scanlon waited, until the owls began *hoo-hooing* to one another and the lamp went out. Then he climbed down and crept into the shed where Gannon kept his beekeeping tools.

Any beekeeper worth his honey kept plenty of ropes on hand for climbing bee trees. Much as though Scanlon disliked stealing— and from Lucambra's future king, no less—he had no other choice. It could take weeks to twine a tree-bark rope long and strong enough to suit his purposes.

By the light of his staff, Scanlon could see several thick coils of nettle-fiber rope hanging from the rafters. He selected one toward the back of the shed, where its absence would more likely go unnoticed. Slinging the rope over his shoulder, he sheathed his staff and eased himself out the warped, rickety door.

"Gaelathane be praised for a stout rope!" he breathed.

Lighting the way with his staff, he retraced his steps and crossed the dew-slick maple log. All at once, the staff light went out. The rod usually gave off a clear, steady glow—unless Gaelathane wished otherwise. Trembling, Scanlon pointed the stick outward and slowly moved it in an arc. When he reached a southwesterly heading, it lit up again. However, Silverquick lay to the northwest. Lucambra—and Ironwing—would just have to wait while the staff led elsewhere.

Holding the rod straight out before him, Scanlon tramped into the trackless woods. If he veered too far left or right, the light dimmed until he was back on the proper course. Onward he trudged, all the while fearing that the staff's glow would attract a stray yeg or another snoopy Lucambrian scout.

At length, he glimpsed a gleam through the trees. Following the staff's leading, he came upon a torsil shining with a cool, silvery light, though the night was moonless. Unbidden, long-forgotten words sprang to Scanlon's mind:

For he shall seek the silver tree,
The sentinel beside the sea.

He had found Lightleaf, the Prophecy's "silver tree."

CHAPTER 22

BREAD CAST UPON THE WATER

"Lightleaf?" Scanlon gasped. "Is it really you?"

After a long silence, the tree answered, "It is I. Who are you, two-legged stranger that comes to me so softly in the gloom of night? You do not have a woodcutter's gait."

"It's me, Scanlon," he was about to say, when he realized the torsil had not yet met Scanlon-the-boy, much less Rolin himself.

"A friend," he answered, unable to think of a better reply.

"Welcome, Friend," said Lightleaf gravely. "I have not spoken with one of your kind since the fall of Elgathel. What do you seek here? If it is soft, straight-grained wood, you will find none in me. We trees of passage are a knotty lot."

"Nay, noble torsil. I come in peace at the bidding of the Tree."

"The Tree of trees?" Lightleaf shivered, scattering Lucambrian moonbeams from his new leaves. "What would the Tree want with me, a tired old torsil?"

"That I do not know. For now, please let me rest beside you. I, too, am weary, for I have traveled far and slept little."

"Then you do not wish to visit the Land of Light?" Lightleaf asked in a downcast, rumbly tree voice. "No two-legs has climbed me in years, and I miss the feel of feet and hands."

"Not tonight," yawned Scanlon. "It is late, and I fear I would find a rude reception on the other side. I must sleep. Until the morrow, may you dream of Luralin."

"And you of Gaelessa's glories," replied Lightleaf courteously.

Mounding up some of the torsil's fallen leaves into a pillow, Scanlon curled up next to the trunk, using his cloak as a blanket. He was fast asleep before the light of Lucambra's moon had faded from Lightleaf's foliage.

"Scanlon." My, what a dream was this! The Tree had appeared beside him, its radiance driving away the night shadows.

"Scanlon!" He awoke with a start. Helmick had found him! In one smooth motion, he rolled over, drew his lightstaff and leapt to his feet. Facing him was a tall figure robed in shining white. Scanlon fell on his face before Gaelathane's terrifying splendor.

"Rise, Scanlon son of Emmer," said the King.

Scanlon stood, shielding his eyes from the Creator's dazzling countenance. "What do You wish of me, my Lord?"

Gaelathane's gaze held him captive. "What is in your hand?"

Scanlon still held the rod, which was now glowing ten times more brightly than before. "A lightstaff, O King," he said.

"Give it to Me, My son."

The command was framed so tenderly that Scanlon willingly handed over his staff. "What will You do with it?" he asked.

Gaelathane replied, "Come with Me and I will show you." Scanlon followed the shining figure behind Lightleaf, where the trunk bore a small hole left from a fallen limb.

"Greetings, faithful torsil!" Gaelathane said. Placing His hand on Lightleaf's bark, He whispered a few words out of Scanlon's hearing. The old tree quivered. Then to Scanlon's surprise and consternation, the King of the Trees dropped his most prized possession through the knothole. Still beaming brilliantly, the staff disappeared inside and hit bottom with a hollow *thump*.

Scanlon winced. Now he was in a real pickle. How could he recover his rod without cutting down the tree?

"Be not dismayed," Gaelathane said with a smile. "Your staff will be safe with Lightleaf, I assure you."

"When may I have it back? I can't find my way in the dark without it, and there may be yegs about."

"I will be your Rod and your Staff in the darkness," said the King. "While I am with you, no enemy shall assail you. However, the stick must remain here until one comes who has need of it."

Scanlon shook his head. Who could possibly need that staff more than he, and what good would it do Lightleaf? Unless the tree died prematurely, the knothole would heal over, sealing the staff inside. What an utter waste that would be!

Gaelathane regarded Scanlon with an amused look. "Dear child, have you forgotten? My ways are not your ways, and My plans are not your plans. You must learn to trust Me and not merely rely upon My staffs, as I told you on Luralin."

Scanlon bowed. "I am no longer to be a staff bearer, then."

"I did not say that. 'Cast your bread upon the water, and after many days, you shall find it again.'"

Bread? What did bread have to do with lightstaffs, and why did Gaelathane always speak in riddles? "Are Rolin and Marlis all right?" he asked, dreading the answer.

"They will be, now that you have given Me that which you treasure most. In time to come, you shall see them again."

"You know where they are, then?" Scanlon pressed the King.

However, Gaelathane was gone, His final words echoing in Scanlon's ears, "Trust Me!"

While Lightleaf murmured in restless tree sleep, Scanlon impatiently awaited the dawn. "Lightleaf!" he called at first light. If only he knew what Gaelathane had told the old tree, he might gain more clues as to the king and queen's fate.

The torsil creaked and groaned as the rising sun warmed the sluggish sap in his ancient limbs. "What is it now, two-legs?"

"Can you tell me what Gaelathane said to you last night?"

"Eh? Oh, yes. Good of Him to drop by, wasn't it?"

"It was—but I'd really like to know what passed between you."

"You two-legs are all the same. Always in a hurry. Can't stop to enjoy life. No wonder you usually die before your time."

I may die before getting a straight answer from this tree, Scanlon fumed. "If you'll only be so good as to repeat His words, I won't trouble you further."

"Tempests and termites, but you're a pesky fellow! Very well, if you insist. When I was a sapling, I asked the King to grant me two requests." More creakings, poppings and groanings.

"What were your requests?" Scanlon prodded the torsil.

"I asked for the privilege of serving Him and to receive the spirit of the Tree. Last night, He granted both my petitions."

So that was it. Bursting with the light and spirit of the risen Tree, Scanlon's staff now lay in Lightleaf's heart. "Is that all?"

"He also said He'd send me many friends to usher between this world and the Land of Light." That promise Scanlon knew would come true, for a host of Lucambrians would one day trek to the torsil to enter or leave Thalmos.

Patting Lightleaf's trunk, he said, "May His words come to pass at the proper time." After a last, longing look through the knot-hole, he shouldered his coil of rope and bade Lightleaf farewell.

"You'll visit me again, won't you?" There was a lonely note in the tree's plodding voice.

Scanlon laughed. "Oh, I'll be back. You can be sure of that."

"Until then, may your sythan-ar ever flourish!"

"And may your leaves never wither," returned Scanlon. With that, he set off cross-country to find Silverquick. He was slogging through a boggy brake choked with red-twig dogwood and skunk cabbage when he heard voices from the wooded ridge above him.

"Hmph. Another two-legs," commented a fern-draped maple.

A slender birch said, "What are they all doing out here?"

"Maybe they're woodcutters," suggested the maple.

"Then why aren't they carrying choppers?" said a cedar. "Perhaps it's four-legged bark they're after, not ours."

"They haven't any grabbers," argued the birch.

"Traps. They're called traps," the cedar loftily corrected its neighbor. Then the three trees fell to squabbling.

Another two-legs? Had some woodcutters or fur trappers recently passed by? Leaving the trees to their quarrel, Scanlon pressed onward. He had just reached the ridgetop when he heard voices again—men's voices—and took cover behind a fallen log.

"What exactly are we looking for, Lathred?" said one.

"Not what; it's *who*, you ninny," growled another.

"All right, then, *who*. I thought we were told to watch that renegade half-breed's house." As the two voices grew louder, Scanlon burrowed into the leafy litter behind the log.

"We were," Lathred grunted. "*He* changed our orders. Seems there's another spy on the loose. Helmick says he's a strapping fellow about your height, Tark. Calls himself *Corlis* and made out like he was relieving Helmick. Grimmon's fit to be tied. He's even hotter than the time someone tried to cut down his sythan-ar."

"Haw! If the old goat hadn't nearly nabbed me in the act, I'd a-finished the job," Tark snarled. "When we find this Corlis, what then? Do we bring back his ears or his head for the boss?"

"Grimmon promised a new cloak to anyone who delivers the spy, dead or alive. The job's got to be done quick and quiet-like."

"I could use another cloak," Tark said thoughtfully.

"Don't set your heart on it." Lathred's voice lowered as he and Tark passed Scanlon's log. "I've got fifty darts in my bag with Corlis's name on 'em—and they're all poisoned. That cloak's as good as mine." He barked out a laugh.

Scanlon shuddered. No honorable Lucambrian ever used poisoned blowpipe darts. It was too risky, not to mention unsporting. Anyone caught breaking this unwritten rule could be expelled from his clan and even banished from Lucambra.

Once the two scouts were out of sight, Scanlon mopped the sweat from his brow and murmured a prayer of thanks to Gaelathane. Then he crept out of hiding and trotted up the trail. If Grimmon's men were drawing their dragnet around Rolin's cabin, he would make off in the opposite direction—westward.

That afternoon, he struck up a conversation with a gloomy hemlock. Learning that no two-legs had come that way in many a day, he headed northeast. It was dark when he reached the canyon to find his strip of red cloth still tied to the willows. Hurling

Gannon's rope over a high rock spur, he scaled the cliff and climbed Silverquick. Then he slid down into Lucambra.

"Back so soon?" yawned Ironwing, still stretched out beneath the tree. "I haven't even finished my nap yet. Bless my feathers, how did you get so dirty?"

CHAPTER 23

DARK THREADS AMONG THE LIGHT

L ightleaf, dear friend, don't leave me here!" Rolin wept. "Come back!" Numb with grief, he lay beside the crater where the torsil had stood, pounding the ground with his bare fists until they bled. "Where are You, Gaelathane?" he screamed at the darkening sky. Then he heard a rustling behind him and the tall, wiry grass stems parted.

"Rolin?"

"Marlis?"

"Rolin!" Lunging out as Marlis's feet pattered by, Rolin caught her invisible form about the waist. She melted into his arms.

"I called and called, but you didn't answer!" she sobbed. "Why did you tarry so long in Lucambra, or wherever you went? Now our friends are gone and everything's ruined!"

"I returned as soon as I could. Aren't the visibles with you?"

Marlis wailed, "No, I just told you! They're gone—all of them!"

"Gone? You mean they've left for the cave without us?"

"No! Those *things* snatched them away. Didn't you see?"

"I must have been in Lucambra then. What happened?"

"I was following the others across the meadow to find you when some shadows swooped down on us. They were much bigger than yegs. The next thing I knew, the whole family was taken.

My invisibility must have saved me." She moaned. "Oh, Rolin, they just kept screaming, but there was nothing I could do!"

Rolin groaned and held his head. "I'm so very sorry. If I'd stayed with you, perhaps our friends would still be here." He tenderly embraced his wife. "At least I didn't lose you, my love—thanks be to Gaelathane."

"Yes, but I'll miss the children." Marlis sniffled into Rolin's cloak. "We may as well go back to Lucambra. There's nothing left for us in Thalmos, now that the visibles are . . . no more. I suppose we'll never know what became of them."

Rolin trembled. "There's nothing left of Lucambra now, either," he said dully.

"No Lucambra? What do you mean?"

Then Rolin retold his misadventures in Lucambra future. "It was a clever scheme," he concluded. "At first, Felgor sold us ordinary starglasses through the peddler at the Beechtown market. Then he passed off the Limbo glass. Anyone looking into it long enough would be pulled into the nether world. Once Felgor captured all our people, Lucambra and its torsils were next."

"How dreadful!" murmured Marlis. "Poor old Lightleaf. I'll miss him terribly. He was such a fine, brave torsil." She groaned. "Oh, no! Now that Ansel's gone, we're the last Lucambrians!"

"That's right," Rolin said. "If we want to save Lightleaf, Ansel and all the others, we'd better find a time torsil back to *wherren* we started. In the meantime, let's return to the meadow. Maybe one of the visibles survived by hiding in the grass."

Marlis hiccuped. "I couldn't find the place now. It's too dark."

"Of course you can. The autumn dusk lingers long in these hills. There's still enough light to see the trees around us."

Marlis pinched him. "There's not light enough to see you!"

Rolin chuckled in spite of himself. Looking through Marlis, he realized how dark the meadow had become. Puzzled, he glanced at the spot where Lightleaf had stood, then back. Yes, the hole was brighter than its surroundings.

"There seems to be a light in this pit," he remarked.

"Maybe Lightleaf's remains have caught fire!"

Rolin peered into the crater. Something was softly shining in its depths, all right. "I don't see any smoke or flames," he said. "Do you still have your cloak with you?"

Minutes later, Marlis's cloak was a few inches shorter, and Rolin was tying a loop in one end of the green cloth strip he'd torn from it. Lowering his makeshift rope into the hole, he tried to snare the bright object at the bottom.

Rolin was well aware of his slim chances of success, having fished more than his share of buttons, coins and candles out of cracks and crannies. He was most amazed, then, when the loop caught on something that moved when he tugged on the line.

After drawing up the rope, what should he find but a glowing crystal rod dangling at the end! With a whoop, he jumped up and waved the staff in the air.

"Look! Look what I found, Marlis!"

"How did a lightstaff end up down there?" she gasped.

"I have no idea, but it's ours now." Rolin ran his fingers down the glassy rod. "If I didn't know better, I'd say this was Scanlon's." Mystified but heartened, he and Marlis knelt to thank the King for His miraculous provision.

Afterwards, the two waded into the meadow. By the staff's light, they discovered a patch of beaten-down grass strewn with scraps of the visibles' gleaning sacks, half-gnawed nuts, dried fruit and some tufts of reddish hair.

"Foxes," Rolin groaned. "They beat us to the skraal jerky, too."

"It wasn't foxes I saw; foxes can't fly," Marlis reminded him.

"I know. They're just scavengers and wouldn't harm people, anyway. No, whatever carried off our visibles was very quick. Look here." He held up Arlan's bow, quiver and four arrows.

"Poor fellow," Marlis sighed. "He never had a chance to get off a shot." She sniffed the air. "Rolin, I don't like the smell of this place. Let's leave before those flying things come back!"

"Where would we go? Back to the cave, to eke out our miserable, invisible lives until the worggles smelled us out?" Rolin shook his head, not caring the gesture was wasted on Marlis.

Just then, the sweet strains of a mighty choir swelled in the night sky, and a flurry of filmy snowflakes swirled over the meadow. Rolin batted at the floating flecks, but they flittered out of his reach with wisps of melodious laughter.

"Look, Rolin, they're alive!" cried Marlis.

Sure enough, the "snow" was actually clouds of tiny, white-robed winged beings, all singing joyous praises to Gaelathane and to His Tree. Then Waganupa appeared in a flash of light. Flitting among its blazing branches were more of the winged creatures. Rolin and Marlis gazed spellbound at the scene until the Tree of trees faded from sight and the rapturous music died away.

"Don't go!" Marlis wept. "Please come back!"

From out of the darkness thrummed a voice like waves drumming on the seashore. "Take courage, My children. I am with you. Through you, I shall restore this world and many others besides."

"What of Lucambra? Is it past help?" asked Rolin.

"Nothing is beyond saving in My kingdom, Rolin son of Gannon. As for the Land of Light, your sojourn in the nether world will avert its untimely end."

"Then our accident was part of Your plan?" Marlis blurted out.

"It was not, though I foresaw it. Behold, I am turning all things hurtful in your lives to the good, weaving the dark threads among the light into a living fabric of grace and glory. Though you cannot see the pattern now, one day you shall."

"What would You have us do?" the invisibles asked.

"You must go to your friends."

Rolin looked all around but saw no one. "They're still alive?"

"They are."

"We don't know how to find them!" Marlis protested.

"I will send someone to show you the way. For the visibles to live, another of My creatures must die."

"Who? What creature?" Rolin called out. There was no answer but the wind sighing through the trees.

"That was Gaelathane, wasn't it?" Marlis whispered.

Rolin squeezed her hand. "I wonder what He meant by, 'another of My creatures must die.' I hope He wasn't speaking of us."

Just then, the grasses swished. "Don't move," Rolin hissed as a sleek young buck emerged from the shadows. Ears twitching, it gracefully stepped into the pool of staff light.

"The poor thing," Marlis murmured. "It must be hungry!"

"I don't think so," said Rolin, keeping his eyes on the buck. "There's plenty of meadow grass here. Besides, its ribs aren't showing." The deer's dark, liquid eyes took in the invisibles with the same knowing look as the hare's. Rolin's mind flashed back to the little ball of white beside the river as it patiently waited for Evan to slay it with a stone. Was the deer also to be a decoy?

Take up your weapon, the buck's eyes entreated.

Rolin fitted an arrow to the string of Arlan's bow. He hesitated, unable to bring himself to kill an animal at such close range. Hadn't Gaelathane said He would send someone to show the way? Maybe they were meant to follow the deer, not kill it. He lowered the bow. "Shoo!" he shouted, but the buck stood its ground.

Use it. Those wise and understanding eyes never left Rolin's. He nocked the arrow again and drew back the string. As if to make certain the deadly dart would find its mark, the deer turned its flank to him. *Another of My creatures must die.* But why? Rolin swallowed, his heart pounding painfully.

Now.

Holding the string taut beside his ear, Rolin aimed behind the shoulder. "Please forgive me," he whispered.

Thunngg, sang the string. The arrow flew straight and true. Soundlessly, the stricken animal sank to its knees and the handsome head slumped forward. All knowledge fled the seeing eyes. Rolin shuddered and dropped the bow.

"You mustn't blame yourself," Marlis said. "*He* sent it."

"For what purpose?" cried Rolin. "Its death seems so pointless. I feel like an ogre for killing the poor creature."

"We could always use the meat. Wait—what's that?"

Rolin heard it, too—a muted throbbing, like thunderclaps beating on his ears. Quick as a flash, he thrust the staff into his tunic, dousing its light. *In killing this animal, I've brought death upon us.*

Obeying an urging that could only be Gaelathane's, he flung himself on the lifeless deer and gripped its front legs.

"Quick, Marlis, grab the hind legs and hang on!" he shouted. No sooner did the back legs twitch with her weight than a monstrous shape blotted out the stars and a pair of taloned feet fastened around the deer's middle. Marlis shrieked and Rolin shut his eyes. A horrid stench stung their nostrils.

Whoof! Whoof! Featherless, sail-like wings beat the air, stirring up swirls of dust. The buck shot upward, the invisibles still clinging for dear life to its legs.

Rolin's arms nearly wrenched out of their sockets, while his hands slipped on the buck's blood-slick, bony shanks. He didn't dare move for fear the flying beast would shake off its hangers-on. Likewise, petrifying the creature with his staff would send him and Marlis plummeting to their deaths.

"I can't hold on much longer!" whimpered Marlis.

"You've got to," Rolin grated, grimacing with pain. "Think of the visibles! We're their only hope now."

All at once, the bird-beast slowed, hovered and relaxed its talons. Down the deer dropped and the invisibles with it.

"Oof!" they both grunted, landing with the deer between them on some yielding, crackly sticks. A rush of fetid air fanned Rolin's face as the shadow flew off into the darkness.

Then a boyish voice said, "Father, what just fell into the nest?"

"I ain't sure. Looks like a dead deer to me."

"Push the carcass out or it'll start to stink," croaked a woman.

"It's only injured, not dead," said a girl. "I heard it make a noise." The visibles were still alive, as Gaelathane had promised!

"Don't touch th' thing," Arlan warned. "It's beyond help now. Besides, that young 'un sounds hungry. Better th' deer than us." As he spoke, a dumpy snowman shape lurched closer, gurgling and gargling as it came. Rolin made way for the smelly creature, which bent over the deer's corpse with squeals and snuffles.

"How ugly!" Marlis exclaimed.

The visibles fell silent. Then Elena hissed, "Who said that?"

"I did," Marlis sheepishly replied. "It's Marlis and Rolin."

The children whooped and shouted, "Hooray! The 'visibles are here. We're not going to die after all. We're saved! We're saved!"

"Not unless they can give us wings," said Elena sourly. "Or did you come to watch us be killed and eaten, one by one?"

"Of course not," Marlis snapped. "We're here to rescue you, not sit by and let you be devoured. Nobody's going to die; Gaelathane will protect us, and that's a fact."

Elena broke into shrieks of insane laughter. "Protect us? With what? Fools! Your invisibility can't save you now."

"Hush, all of ye," Arlan ordered with a scowl. "We mustn't draw attention to ourselves. How did ye two git up here so fast?"

"We just 'dropped in,'" Rolin quipped. Then he explained how they had hitched a ride on the dead deer.

Marlis nervously cleared her throat. "Where are we, anyway?"

"You're in a grakkle's nest!" Elena cackled. "If you had any sense, you'd throw yourself over the side before it's too late!

When the wind is still o'er stream and hill,
And the air takes on a sudden chill;
Beware the grakkle!

When the shadows fly and there's a croaking cry,
Then you mustn't move till it passes by;
Beware the grakkle!

With teeth of steel he tears his meal,
And sucks the bones with a grakklish zeal;
Beware the grakkle!

With wings of leather without a feather,
The grakkle flies in any weather;
His beak is long, his talons strong,
The sky and cliff to him belong;
Beware the grakkle!

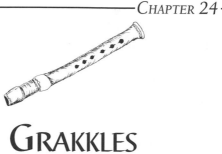

CHAPTER 24

GRAKKLES

Rolin winced at Elena's racking sobs. Grakkles. So that's what they were up against. Balanced precariously on a narrow, rocky shelf, the nest was a jackstraw pile of poles and timbers overlaid with layers of reeds and willow wands. A slathering of sticky mud cemented the whole affair together.

Arlan patted his wife on the back. "Shush, m' dear. We mustn't make so much noise. Don't want to upset the children, do we?"

"Upset the children?" repeated Elena vacantly. "What difference will it make? They already know what awaits them." She slumped down to the bottom of the nest, cradling her head in her arms. Bronwen and Evan started sniffling.

Rolin scooted over to Arlan. "Is there any immediate danger?"

Arlan turned unseeingly toward him. "Not at th' moment," he said with a bleak look. "That hatchling cain't take on all four of us, and its parents are still out finding food. So far, we've survived by playin' dead when they're around. It'll be a different story in th' morning. When th' grown ones see we're still alive, they'll tear us to pieces." He shuddered. "Maybe the deer will keep 'em busy a while longer." As if on cue, the greedy grakkling began feeding noisily on the carcass.

"How many adults are there?"

"Jest two. Ain't that enough?" Arlan gnawed on his moustache. "If ye were thinking of fightin' 'em, fergit it. Nothin' kin kill a grakkle. Nothin'. Arrows and spears jest bounce off their hides. Sometimes they kill each other, but most die o' old age. I'd say our only hope is to climb out of this nest at sunrise."

If the grakkle parents didn't return before then. Shivering with dread, Rolin felt for the staff under his tunic. He'd petrified thousands of yegs with such a rod, but grakkles were larger. Much larger. For the present, he'd keep the staff hidden. He didn't want any awkward questions.

"Ow!" cried Marlis. *Slap!* "These pesky bugs are following me everywhere! How do they know we're here?"

Rolin swatted at the clouds of tiny, biting insects. Apparently, gnats and mosquitoes could smell them out despite their invisibility. He hoped the grakkles wouldn't find them so easily.

"Feels like I'm sittin' on a porcupine," Arlan grumbled. He scraped at the bones, fur and feathers lining the nest—prickly remnants of the grakkles' kills.

Between the annoying insects, the bristly "bed" and fear of what the morrow might bring, no one slept that night. Indeed, it was all Rolin and Arlan could do to restrain a hysterical Elena from leaping out of the nest to her death.

Morning found the six companions huddled miserably against the bone-biting fall chill, leaving the rest of the nest to the grakkling and its grisly meal. In the dawn's unflattering gray light, the nestling looked positively repulsive. Stubby-winged, wrinkled, and sprinkled with downy, white hairs, it resembled an overgrown, plucked turkey. Eyeing the visibles suspiciously, it hunched protectively over the deer's skeletal remains.

Glancing over the side of the nest, Rolin saw with sinking heart how well the grakkles had chosen their home. Below the ledge, a sheer cliff dropped a thousand feet into a snark forest. Without a rope, descent would be impossible. He slipped the lightstaff out of his tunic and held it at the ready. Come what may, he'd give those grakkles the biggest surprise of their grakklish lives!

"What's that shiny stick?" Evan was asking him when a shadow swept over the nest. The grakkles were back.

Elena screamed and fainted, sending everyone but Rolin tumbling to the bottom of the nest in a jumble of arms and legs. Still clutching his staff, Lucambra's king clung to the edge of the nest, where he beheld a bloodcurdling sight.

Having overshot their lair, the screeching grakkles had turned and were flying back at full tilt, savage jaws snapping and a murderous glint in their raging red eyes. With dragon-dwarfing, ninety-foot wingspans, high-crested heads and long, narrow bills set with rows of sharp teeth, they looked capable of swallowing a yeg whole—or of dropping intruders onto the rocks below.

Like Elena, Rolin could scarcely resist the impulse to jump out of the nest right then and there. Putting such cowardly thoughts out of his mind, he leveled his staff at the larger grakkle and cried, *"Mae'r Goeden yn fyw!"*

A bolt of blinding white light caught the he-grakkle with batlike wings fully extended. Mottled red skin turned to gray and the chattering jaws froze shut. Gliding on wings of stone, the creature slammed into the cliff just below the nest, shattering in a shower of petrified claws, teeth, wings and bones.

Just in time, the staff's next beam struck the she-grakkle at the height of her upward wing stroke. She plummeted out of the sky, smashing to stony smithereens on her mate's remains.

The terrified screams from the depths of the nest continued for minutes afterward. Then Bronwen's head cautiously poked up from behind some sticks. She scanned the horizon. "They're gone!" she told the others.

"Are you sure?" asked a wild-eyed Elena.

"Rolin? Rolin! Where are you?" cried Marlis in a panic.

Knees buckling, Rolin slumped against the nest's springy bulwark of mud-laced reeds. "I'm right here," he mumbled.

"What happened to the grakkles?" Bronwen called up to him.

"They're dead," he said, slipping the staff back into his tunic.

Suspicion simmered in Elena's eyes. "Impossible! You must have driven them off. They'll be back."

"No, I killed them."

Arlan nervously searched the sky. "Where are they?"

Rolin pointed. "Down there—at the base of the cliff, that is."

Elena peeked over the edge of the nest. "Did you make them invisible, or are they buried under that rockslide?"

"They *are* the rockslide," Rolin chuckled. Then he was obliged to bring out his staff and explain its remarkable properties. Confronted with the blazing light, the visibles backed away.

"Do ye mean to say that *lightning stick* turned them grakkles to stone?" asked Arlan, tugging on his beard.

"That's right," Rolin replied. "Now they're just a harmless pile of broken statuary, like those ugly carvings in Peton."

Elena eyed the lightstaff. "Won't it do the same to us?"

"Oh, no," Marlis laughed. "Our staffs don't hurt people."

"Why didn't you show us that thing earlier?" Elena demanded.

"Because we found it just before coming up here," Rolin said, revealing how he and Marlis had lost their own rods on entering Thalmos through Thickbark.

"If that don't beat all," said Arlan. "Another land, ye say." His face lit up. "Supposin' we climbed one o' them *passage trees*, could we git into yer world from here?"

"Unfortunately, Lucambra no longer exists," Rolin sighed. Then he described the demise of the Land of Light and his discovery of the staff in Lightleaf's crater.

"There are plenty of other worlds besides Lucambra worth exploring," Marlis said. "The best land of all is Gaelessa, but you can reach it only through Waganupa, the Tree of trees."

Hands on hips, Elena said coldly, "Dreamers! We're not going anywhere. Since there aren't any trees up here, we're still stuck in this nest, unless your toy can turn these reeds to ropes!"

It couldn't, of course. "I'm not a magician, you know," Rolin told her. Needlessly turning his back on the others, he sulkily stared into the distance. If only he could snap his fingers and summon a bevy of sorcs to bear them all to safety! Alas, the griffin race had died out of Thalmos long ago.

The rest of the morning, Arlan searched the rocks above the nest for a route to the top of the cliff. Returning with bloodied fingers and toes, he grunted dispiritedly, "Too many overhangs. We'd never make it."

"Mother, I'm hungry," whined Evan.

Elena threw up her hands. "I've already told you we haven't any food up here. This isn't our cave, you know."

Arlan glanced thoughtfully at the grakkling, which was listlessly picking at the reeking deer skeleton. "We could eat th' grakkle if it came to that. The meat should be plenty tender."

Elena glowered at him. "I'd rather die than eat grakkle."

"If we don't find some vittles soon, ye might," Arlan retorted.

Meanwhile, the grakkling had begun searching the sky for its parents. Not finding them, it toddled after Elena with plaintive, mewling cries. Chewing on the stem of his unlit pipe, Arlan grinned at Elena's futile efforts to avoid the creature.

"It thinks you're its mother!" laughed Evan and Bronwen.

"Well, I'm not!" she retorted, kicking at her tormentor. "Get away from me, you horrid thing!" Heartbroken, the grakkling finally waddled back to its own side.

Rolin pitied the orphaned creature but knew better than to say so. The Thalmosians obviously feared and hated grakkles of any size, no less than Lucambrians despised yegs and all their ilk. By itself, the grakkling posed no danger, although its cries might attract others of its kind.

As the dreary afternoon wore into evening, a haloed half-moon rose. Rolin's skin prickled. What if the shattered grakkle statues returned to life under a full moon, as Peton's yegs and gargoyles had done? He hoped he and his companions weren't anywhere near the nest if that happened.

As if sensing Rolin's fears, Marlis wrapped her invisible arms around him. "Why don't you play your flute?" she suggested. "Some music might help take our minds off our plight."

Rolin brought out the instrument and blew a few notes, pleased to find that his invisible fingers hadn't lost their touch. Then he trilled a sweet melody that echoed back from the cliff and across the dusky hills. Self-conscious, he laid the flute aside.

"Please don't stop," Bronwen begged him.

"I'm afraid I'm hitting more sour notes than true ones."

Bronwen smiled. "Your flute-playing sounds fine to me."

"Yes, do go on," Marlis urged him. As Rolin began again, the visibles nodded in time with the music. Even the grakkling cocked its head and listened as Marlis sang along:

Though here we sit in a grakkle's nest,
Not knowing what to do,
We still believe Your plan is best,
And that You'll see us through.

You've brought us out of Gundul's grip,
Into a broader place;
We know Your hand won't let us slip,
O Lord of time and space.

Though grakkles stalk our nest by night,
And worggles wait by day,
Your Hand is with us in the fight;
We know You'll guard our way.

When all our torsil travels end,
One Torsil will remain,
To take us to our faithful Friend,
The blessed Gaelathane.

"Marlis?" whispered Bronwen. "What's going to happen to us?"

Marlis brushed her fingers through the girl's golden hair. "I don't know, but there is One Who does, and I've been asking Him to rescue us. I believe He will."

"You mean Gaelathane?"

"Yes—the King of the Trees. He is with us now, though you can't see Him. He's promised never to leave or forsake us."

"Does He always answer when you speak to Him?"

"He does, but not always the way we might wish."

"Then I don't need to be afraid, do I?"

"No, child, you don't."

Bronwen snuggled against Marlis's unseen form. While the diamond-bright stars gazed down from their breathless black canopy, the flute warbled on until both player and listeners drifted into a dreamless sleep.

CHAPTER 25

A TRUSTWORTHY TREE

Poke, poke. Something was jabbing Rolin in the back. He flapped his hand behind him. "Shoo! Go away, grakkling, and leave me alone!"

"Rolin—wake up!"

He opened his eyes then shut them against a dazzling white light. *The moon is awfully bright tonight.* The stabbing went on.

"Rolin!"

He rolled over to find nothing but empty air. "Wh—?" Oh, yes. Marlis was still invisible. "What is it? Are the grakkles back?"

"No, you silly goose, it's the Tree! The Tree is here!"

That did it. Rolin was instantly awake. "Where?"

"Over—oh, drat this invisibility. Behind me!"

The Tree's shining shape stood beside the nest, its resplendent trunk rising high into the heavens. "Oh, my!" Rolin said.

"I'll wake the others," whispered Marlis. Moments later, moans and groans sounded from the bottom of the nest.

Arlan was rubbing his eyes. "What's all th' fuss about?" he grunted. His wife and children squatted beside him, also kneading their eyes and squinting in the Tree's radiance.

"Don't you see? Isn't it marvelous?" Marlis bubbled. The Tree's light shone right through her, illuminating the nest and everything in it like the brightest moonwood.

"You woke us all to look at the moon?" grumbled Elena.

"Maybe they don't have a moon in their world," Evan said.

Marlis exhaled noisily. "That's not the moon. It's the Tree of Life, the Tree of trees! Gaelathane sent it. Now we can climb out of this horrible nest and go home."

Arlan scratched his head and yawned. "This must be a dream, because I don't see nothin'. Are ye sure it ain't invisible?"

Marlis groaned. "Of course it's not. Rolin and I can see it!"

"What in the name of Elgathel is the matter with these visibles?" Rolin muttered to himself. "The Tree is standing right in front of their noses!"

"The rest of you can gawk at the moon if you like, but I'm going back to sleep," grumped Elena. "Ow! What are you doing? Let go of me!" Arms flailing, she pranced to the side of the nest.

"Not until you've opened your eyes first," Marlis growled. "*Now* do you see it? This is the same Tree Rolin and I have been telling you about all along."

Elena's lip curled. "That old, dead thing? I've seen sturdier beanpoles. Funny I never noticed it before. You're not suggesting we entrust our lives to such a rotten snag, are you? I doubt it's sound enough to support our weight."

Rolin came to the rescue. "We are—and it is. The Tree's our only hope of reaching the ground, and there's no telling when it will return. Children, you go first, since you're lighter."

Blinking the sleep from their eyes, Bronwen and Evan clambered onto the nest's rim. The mud-caked reeds and willow switches cracked and bent beneath them.

"That's it," Marlis encouraged them. "Now grab one of those limbs and swing into the Tree."

Elena wrung her hands. "Oh, they're going to fall. I just know it. Be careful, children!"

Bronwen rolled her eyes. "Don't worry, Mother, we will."

Evan dug his fingers into the nest and whimpered, "I'm scared! I don't wanna go over there. I wanna stay here."

"You'll be fine," Marlis assured him. "I'll count to three. Then you hop over, all right?" Chewing on a fingernail, Evan nodded.

"Good. One . . . two . . . three!"

Evan stayed put, and neither threats nor cajoling could budge him from his perch. "I'll go first," Bronwen offered. "Then I can help you over." Elena gasped as her daughter leaned out, grasped a branch and swung herself into the Tree.

"There, you see?" Bronwen called back to her brother. "That wasn't so hard. Now it's your turn. Here—hold onto my hand."

Evan bit his lip. With an "I-won't-be-outdone-by-my-big-sister" look, he took Bronwen's hand and propelled himself into her waiting arms. Then he put his ear to the trunk. "I hear music."

"That's just Rolin's flute," sneered Elena, though the flute was stowed away in one of Rolin's pockets next to his lightstaff.

"No, that's the music of Gaelessa," Marlis gently corrected her. "Children, it's your mother and father's turn now. You'd better climb down a little to make room for them." After Bronwen and Evan had descended a few feet, Elena squared her shoulders and swung one leg over the wall of the nest.

The grakkling squawked piteously. Gazing at its "mother" with a forlorn expression, the gawky creature wiggled its useless wing stubs. *Don't leave me here alone*, it seemed to say.

Elena jabbed her thumb in the grakkling's direction. "What about that thing? Aren't you going to kill it before we leave?"

Rolin hesitated. Left to its own devices, the half-grown grakkle would probably starve to death—if bigger grakkles didn't find it first—and it was too small to harm anyone. On the other hand, there was always the chance it would survive to adulthood and terrorize the countryside. One short burst of staff light would end the unfortunate creature's misery.

As Rolin drew his staff, the grakkling waddled toward him. Recalling the gentle look in the hare's and deer's eyes, Rolin vowed never again to take the life of a defenseless wild creature. "We'll

168

leave it be," he told Elena curtly. "My staff is meant only for self-defense, and that poor beast is no threat to us."

Grumbling, "Wait till it grows up," Elena flung herself into the Tree's yielding embrace and wrapped her long arms and legs around the trunk. "Goodness gracious me!" she exclaimed. "What a leap! I didn't think I'd make it."

"How could ye miss?" Arlan mumbled through clenched teeth as he stepped from the nest into the Tree—a matter of three feet.

"Father, isn't this a lovely place?" said Bronwen dreamily. "It's so bright and peaceful, I could stay here forever."

"Don't talk such foolishness, girl!" Elena scolded her. "You're seeing the moon, that's all. Now move along. You don't want another grakkle to catch us up here, do you?"

Just after Rolin and Marlis had also crossed over, a voice softly spoke, "Come up here and I will show you My land."

Marlis squealed with delight. "That would be splendid!" Unlike Rolin, she had never visited Gaelathane's country.

"What about our friends?" Rolin asked the Tree.

"I will watch over them until you return," came the reply.

Rolin called down to the visibles, "The Tree bids us go higher!"

"You can't just leave us here," Elena protested. "What if a grakkle comes by? Tree or not, we'd be devoured for sure!"

"Don't worry; you'll be safe," Marlis told her. "When you reach the bottom, wait for us. We won't be long."

"Safe in *this?*" Elena retorted. "We're more like sitting ducks, I'd say." Then she and her family descended out of earshot.

Rolin gazed up through the ladder of limbs spiraling into the night sky. Even larger than Luralin's original Tree, this one was transparent throughout, making it easier to climb. The invisibles only had to avoid stepping on each other's hands and feet!

Though diamond-hard, the Tree's bright branches were as supple and sweet-scented as a fir's. Each was decked with lacy sprays of exquisite crystal needles that shed sparkly light when touched. Best of all was the singing. Too faint for making out any words, it reminded Rolin of the Tree's appearance in the meadow.

"Isn't this simply amazing?" exclaimed Marlis. "I feel so free!"

"So do I. It's a long way to the top, though." Climbing the Tree was hard work, even when its limbs were so handily arranged.

Marlis drew in her breath sharply. "Did you say we're going all the way to the *top*? Whatever for?"

"The Tree is a torsil, remember?" Rolin called back. "If we're to make passage to Gaelessa, we can't stop partway up."

"I'm too tired to climb that high!" Marlis wailed.

The Tree broke in, "If the journey is too much for you, I will bring My world within your reach. Climb up on that branch just above you and go out to the end."

Rolin noticed a limb that shone more brightly than the others. It swayed alarmingly as first he, then Marlis crawled onto it.

"This doesn't look strong enough to support the both of us," Marlis said with a nervous quiver in her voice.

"Perhaps not," Rolin replied, feeling a bit giddy himself. "Then again, didn't Elena say the same thing about the Tree?"

"There's no call to insult me. Besides, *she* doesn't believe."

The Tree's light flashed. "Do you?"

"You know I do!" Marlis said. "I'm just frightened."

Waganupa sighed. "In times of fear it is best to move ahead."

Rolin felt the branch jiggle as Marlis crept closer. Recalling Arlan's advice at the rope bridge, he told her, "Don't look down—and hurry up, will you? I can't hold on much longer."

"I'm going as fast as I can," she snapped. "Stop shaking the limb! You're making me dizzy."

At the end of the branch where it fanned out into fine twigs, Rolin started slipping off. "Help!" he cried.

"Let go," said the Tree.

"No, I'll fall!"

"I will catch you. Let yourself drop."

Since Rolin was already losing his grip, he relaxed and slid off the limb. A hole opened in the air below him, gushing light and music like water from a spring.

"Wait for me!" Marlis cried. Grabbing Rolin's tunic collar, she tumbled off the limb after him.

CHAPTER 26

GLIMPSES OF GAELESSA

R olin fell through the hole and into the arms of a tall, shining
being with the gentle eyes of the hare and the deer. Turning
his head, Rolin gazed at—not through—Marlis, cradled in
the arms of a similar person.

"Rolin! I can see you!" Marlis cried, waving her arms exuber-
antly at him. "Can you see me?"

"Yes, I can!" What a relief it was to see and to be seen again!

"Who are you and where are we?" Marlis asked her deliverer.

"I am Gamalion. My companion Cristophilus and I will be your
escorts in the Blessed Land during your stay here." Like
Cristophilus, Gamalion resembled a regal young man clad in dazzling white robes. His golden hair cascaded over broad shoulders
that bore graceful, sweeping wings.

Men with wings? How very odd! "What are you?" Rolin asked.

"Like you, we are Gaelathane's servants," Gamalion explained.
"Our chief task is to aid and protect the Children of the Tree—
those who have trusted in the King and in His sacrifice."

Cristophilus added, "In Gaelessa, we are known as 'angels.'"

Suddenly, the sky was filled with angels of every description
singing in full-throated harmony, as if the air itself were ringing
with joy and adoration.

"Now I remember!" Rolin exclaimed. "It was angels we saw when the Tree visited us in the grakkle meadow!"

Cristophilus laughed, a warm, welcoming sort of sound. "Yes, some of us were there that night."

"Why did the Tree bring us here?" Marlis asked. "We haven't died, have we? How would our children manage without us?"

Gamalion shook his head. "That time has not yet come. The King merely wishes to grant you a vision of what lies beyond the bounds of mortal worlds, that you might know the length and breadth and height and depth of His love and His goodness, which surpass all comprehension."

"Take our hands, and you will see some of the wonders the King has prepared for those who love Him," Cristophilus said with a serene smile. Still gazing at each other, a newly visible Rolin and Marlis grasped the hands of their shining companions and soared with them high above the land of Gaelathane.

Marlis kicked her feet. "Wheeee! I'm flying! This is even better than griffin riding."

"There's no fear of falling off, either," Rolin said with a grin.

"Where are you taking us?" asked Marlis as they glided along.

Cristophilus pointed out a brilliant, ruby-red gem set among verdant hills. As the angels swooped lower through the warm, sweet air, the crimson ruby took on the appearance of a sparkling lake. A swarm of gnats hovered over its surface.

Cristophilus explained, "When Waganupa fell, the Everlasting Kingdom convulsed in mourning, opening a breach to receive the Tree's healing lifeblood. Thus the bottomless Lake of Love was born, its waters ever refreshed by the Tree. When the former things have passed away and all worlds are made new, this lake will remain eternal, undimmed in its beauty, unsullied in its purity. Only those who have washed themselves in the blood of the King may partake of its waters."

Now Rolin and Marlis saw that what they had mistaken for a cloud of insects was actually a great company of radiant, angelic beings. All were laughing and singing as they whirled in a ring above the water, their light steps leaving the lake's glassy surface unmarred. Each was clad in garments of shining white, drawn about the waist with a golden belt from which hung a silver cup. From time to time, one or another of the fleet-footed figures would stoop to dip his cup in the lake and drink from it.

In the center of the circle stood a tall, white-haired figure. Beams of light like the spokes of a wheel radiated from Him to touch each of the dancers.

"It's Gaelathane!" Marlis exclaimed. "May we go to Him?"

"Not now," cautioned Gamalion. "A new soul is about to arrive in the Kingdom. We must not interfere."

Just then, an angel bearing a limp figure in his arms appeared before Gaelathane, Who joyfully embraced the bewildered newcomer. Then a burst of light enveloped them both. When the brightness faded, the King stood beside a radiant, transformed creature clad in a white robe and golden belt, silver cup in hand.

Shouts of welcome went up from the circle of men and women, boys and girls. Then the ring made room for the new member and the dance went on.

Rolin turned to Cristophilus. "What just happened?"

"That was an Investiture Ceremony," the angel said.

"Investiture Ceremony? What's that?"

"Investiture means 'to put on.' When a Child of the Tree leaves his material life to enter this one, Gaelathane greets him with the gifts of His eternal love: The Cup of Redemption, the Robe of Righteousness and the Belt of Truth."

Marlis wore a horrified look. "That person just *died?*"

Gamalion smiled. "I believe that is the word you mortals use, yes. We call it, 'Laying aside the physical body.'"

"Why the cup, the gown and the belt?" asked Rolin.

"No one may join the Circle of Celebration without them. The cup is engraved with a name known only to its owner and entitles him to drink freely of the Waters of Life forever."

"The Circle of Celebration on the Waters of Life in the Lake of Love," murmured Marlis. "How perfectly delightful!"

"Will we receive a cup, robe and belt, too?" Rolin asked.

Cristophilus bowed his head. "You shall. When you have finished your appointed work in the King's worlds below, the Tree shall come for you also."

"Come for us?" the visible invisibles asked.

"Of course. When your body is laid aside, you shall climb the Tree into this Blessed Land, where you will be escorted to your own Investiture Ceremony and join the Circle of Celebration."

"Your places in the circle are already reserved, and we eagerly await the day when you shall fill them," said Gamalion.

"What happens if the ring grows too large for the lake to contain it?" Rolin asked.

"Then it extends onto the land, and a new circle forms in the center of the lake," Cristophilus said. He waved his hand toward the shore, where more dancers surrounded the lake. Farther off, another circle wound through the trees and beyond it, yet a third. The concentric rings extended as far as the eye could see, across meadow and mead, through forest and over mountain.

"Won't Gaelessa fill up with all of them?" Marlis asked.

Gamalion's eyes twinkled like twin stars. "No, indeed! Just as the Circles of Celebration have no end, so Gaelathane's land is boundless and limitless. It is wider than eternity, deeper than the Lake of Love and higher than the Tree's never-ending top."

Rolin's face fell. "Then the greater the circles grow, the farther they get from Gaelathane, the Lake of Love and the Tree."

Gamalion spoke to Rolin's companion in strange, melodious words. "You are thinking as one who lives in the worlds of 'up' and 'down,' 'here' and 'there,' 'far' and 'near,'" Cristophilus declared. "In the King's land, the Tree inhabits all places at all times. The larger your circle becomes, the *closer* you are to Gaelathane, the Lake of Love, the Tree and to each other."

Gamalion added, "When time is no more, Gaelathane will gather all His children around the Tree in an everlasting celebration." Rolin shook his head in amazement. What a remarkable world this must be, where it was impossible to escape the loving presence of the King of the Trees!

"Do you wish to see one of the other circles?" the angels asked.

"Oh, yes!" Marlis and Rolin replied. In an eyeblink, they were skimming above a ribbon of celebrants. White faces, red faces, brown faces, yellow faces, black faces blurred by, all bearing the King's stamp of immortal youth, eternal joy and unending love. All sang in the same musical, angelic language:

Codwn ein dwylo i'r gôr a roed,
Er mwyn i bawb gael byw,
Fel caiff holl blant y Torsyl Goed
Ymgrymu i'r un gwiw.

Bendith ar y Brenin! Bendith ar y Goeden!
Bendith ar Frenin y Coed!
Teilwng yw'r Brenin, Crëwr popeth,
Bendith ar Frenin y Coed!

Pan gyll yr haul a'r lloer eu rhin,
Coeden y Coed fydd fyw,
Ei gwaed a leinw'r llyn fel gwin;
Ei nerth tragwyddol yw!

Bendith ar y Brenin! Bendith ar y Goeden!
Bendith ar Frenin y Coed!
Teilwng yw'r Brenin, Crëwr popeth,
Bendith ar Frenin y Coed!

'Does ond Tywysog Tangnefedd fri
All gau y marwol glwy'
At sanctaidd draeth y daeth â ni
Lle pery cariad mwy.

Bendith ar y Brenin! Bendith ar y Goeden!
Bendith ar Frenin y Coed!
Teilwng yw'r Brenin, Crëwr popeth,
Bendith ar Frenin y Coed!

"What are they singing?" asked Marlis.

Gamalion replied, "The Song of the Redeemed, known only to those who have tasted the Waters of Life."

175

"Could you teach us the language of Gaelessa so that we could understand the words?" Rolin asked hopefully.

"Though our language differs but little from the ancient speech you call *Llwcymraeg*, that insight must also await the day of your first draught from the Lake of Love," said Cristophilus. "However, I can give you the sense in your own tongue:

> To Him with thanks we raise our hands,
> Who gave His life for all,
> That men from every torsil land
> Before His feet may fall.
>
> Blessed be the King! Blessed be the Tree!
> Blessed be the King of the Trees!
> Worthy is the King, Creator of all things,
> Blessed be the King of the Trees!
>
> The Tree of trees alone shall shine,
> When sun and moon shall fail;
> Its lifeblood fills the lake like wine;
> Its power will prevail!
>
> Blessed be the King! Blessed be the Tree!
> Blessed be the King of the Trees!
> Worthy is the King, Creator of all things,
> Blessed be the King of the Trees!
>
> For none can save from death's dark door,
> Except the Prince of Peace,
> Who brought us to this blessed shore,
> Where love will never cease.
>
> Blessed be the King! Blessed be the Tree!
> Blessed be the King of the Trees!
> Worthy is the King, Creator of all things,
> Blessed be the King of the Trees!

"Ah, here we are," said Gamalion. "One of these worshippers will especially interest you, Marlis." The angels were hovering over a singer who had paused to admire a bed of lush lady ferns. Her flashing locks of spun gold flowed to the ground, and her eyes were as green as the sea.

"It's my mother!" Marlis gasped. "Mother! Oh, Mother! I'm up here!" She might as well have been talking to a stone. After plucking one of the fern fronds, Nelda rejoined her companions.

"Why won't she look at me?" Marlis cried.

With a sympathetic glance, Gamalion explained, "She cannot hear or see you in your present state."

"Why not? We're visible now, aren't we?"

"Only to Cristophilus and me, and to each other. It must be so for a time. Take heart, child. You and your loved one will soon be reunited forever."

"Can't I talk with her even for a moment?"

The angel shook his head. "What Gaelathane has ordained, we cannot change." As the angels flew on, Marlis continued looking back with anguished eyes.

"Goodbye, dear mother," she wept. "Do not forget me!"

Next, they came upon other worshippers gathered around a cluster of saffron-yellow mushrooms. One of the men in the group called out, "Brother, will you come over here, please?"

Another man with curly brown hair and erect bearing ambled over. "Why, you've found some *lisichkis!*" he exclaimed. "In the Land of Light, we used to gather them under firs and hemlocks in the fall. Don't they have a wonderful apricot fragrance?"

Staring, Marlis gasped, "It's Grimmon, only without his gray hair! What's that traitor doing up here?"

"Don't you remember?" Rolin said. "He drank from my bag of Glymmerin water just before dying of the sickness."

"His former treacheries are remembered in Gaelessa no more," Cristophilus put in. "Such is Gaelathane's infinite forgiveness. His grace and mercy run deeper than mankind's blackest deeds."

"Rolin!" Marlis cried. "Isn't that Gannon speaking with him?"

Rolin glanced down again and his father's familiar features jumped out at him. Gannon looked as handsome and strong as he had in his younger days.

"It *is!* I don't understand. My father hasn't—"

"Have you forgotten?" said Cristophilus gently. "You and Marlis have traveled far into the future. Your father passed over many years ago with the peace of a life well lived."

Rolin wasn't listening. He was staring at two fair-skinned women kneeling beside his father. One was fondly caressing the mushrooms like a mother cuddling her newborn infant. Her hair was as silver as the cup dangling at her waist.

"Aren't these magnificent lisichkis?" she remarked to her neighbor, a green-eyed, willowy beauty whose fine features closely resembled Rolin's.

Rolin blurted out, "It's my mother and grandmother! Hey! Hi! Look up here! I'm—" He stopped and grinned sheepishly at Cristophilus. "I forgot they can't see me."

"One day they will," said the angel, his eyes smiling.

"Then we'll spend all eternity together, won't we?" Marlis said.

"All eternity—and beyond," Gamalion assured her.

"And we'll never grow old?" asked Rolin.

"Never," both angels replied.

"Now that we're here, we won't have to leave, will we?" Rolin anxiously asked, remembering his painful return to Luralin and a world in turmoil after his first visit to Gaelessa.

"I wish it were so," Gamalion said. "However, if you do not leave, you cannot come back as Celebrants, just as spring will not arrive unless winter has come first."

Cristophilus pressed something soft into Rolin's hand. "When you return to your birth-world, share this with your friends. In the meantime, watch for the King and for us, too! We may appear when you least expect it." His voice sounded hollow, distant.

Suddenly, the two angels shrank as Rolin and Marlis flew backward into a long, dark tunnel. Gaelessa's glories rapidly receded into a bright dot. "We're trapped in Limbo again!" Marlis screamed. Then they were standing beside the Tree, snowflakes swirling about their invisible bodies. They were back in Thalmos.

CHAPTER 27

THE WOODSMAN

W hy aren't the 'visibles here yet?" Evan whined, huddling with his family beneath the Tree.

Elena dusted snow out of her hair. "I don't know. Just be patient. The sun should be coming up soon. Not that we'll see it in this blizzard. Oh, to be back in my cave!"

"Them invisibles come and go as they please," Arlan sighed. "Here one minute, gone th' next." He toyed with a piece of petrified grakkle wing. "I expect they'll turn up in a while. They said they'd come back, and they ain't never lied to us."

"Not yet, you mean," muttered Elena darkly. "Now that they've saved their own skins, what's to keep them from deserting us?"

"Rolin and Marlis wouldn't do such a thing!" Bronwen hotly protested. "They'll be back. You'll see."

"She's right. Ye're not bein' fair, dear," Arlan chided his wife. "Th' invisibles risked their necks to rescue us—an' ye kin see fer yerself what Rolin did to them grakkles." For once, Elena couldn't argue with her husband. The creatures' remains lay around her like so much smashed pottery.

"They don't look so fierce now," she remarked, watching Evan try to piece together a grakkle skull. He'd succeeded in assembling what could only be described as a large frog's head.

"I'm thirsty," the boy fretted. He caught some snowflakes on his swollen tongue and swallowed them. The visibles hadn't tasted water since the grakkles had carried them off, and their mouths were parched.

"Ain't no water around here," Arlan said thickly. "Them snarks suck every drop of it out o' th' soil till it's as bone-dry as a grakkle's nest. It's a wonder anything else kin survive in this valley."

Suddenly, Elena's arms flew up and she gave a little shriek. "Oh, I'm sorry," said Rolin. "I didn't mean to startle you. We're back." Fresh from Gaelessa, he had tapped Elena on the shoulder, giving her a nasty shock. The woman glowered at empty space.

"I'm here, too," Marlis piped up. She was standing on the other side of the visibles, her feet dimpling the ankle-deep snow.

"Don't sneak up on us like that again!" Elena scolded them. "You scared me half out of my wits. I thought you were grakkles. 'Where there's one grakkle, there's often more; when you find two, there's bound to be four.'" Just then, the Tree vanished, leaving only a pre-dawn grayness. Elena didn't seem to notice.

"We're hungry!" wailed Bronwen and Evan.

That reminded Rolin of Cristophilus's parting gift, which he'd stuffed in his pocket. It turned out to be a linen sack containing crackerlike squares of a moist bread. After nibbling on a piece, he offered one to Marlis.

"This is very good," she remarked. "It tastes a little like your father's honeyed oatcakes, only sweeter."

Arlan stared at the floating wafers. "What have ye got there?"

"A gift from Gaelathane," Rolin replied. "Want to try some?"

Moments later, all four visibles were munching on Rolin's chewy "angel bread." The children wolfed their portions down without so much as a "thank you."

"These crackers aren't bad for invisibles' food," Elena admitted. "You say you got them from Gaelathane?"

"From one of His servants," Rolin said offhandedly. "He told us to share them with you when we saw you again."

Arlan nodded appreciatively. "That was right decent of 'im."

"May I have some more?" asked Evan. Shaking a wafer into the boy's hand, Rolin noticed the bag still felt full. Was this another of Gaelessa's miracles?

"I'd like one more, too," said Arlan. "If ye've any left, that is."

"So would I," added Elena, her eyes brightening.

"Don't forget me!" Bronwen chirped. Rolin passed out three more large pieces of the angel bread. When he reached for a fourth, he found the bag empty. "That's all," he told the others, turning the sack upside down. Everyone groaned.

"I suppose we'll freeze to death out here," Elena said.

"Not as long as we keep moving," her husband countered. "We'll head out when th' dawn comes." Already the horizon was hazing with snow-pearled light, like sunlight seen through a shell.

Elena snorted. "Where would we go? We must be miles from home with no way through the snarks, let alone all this snow."

"I still have my cloak," Marlis suggested.

"What good is one cloak among the lot of us?" retorted Elena.

By way of answer, cloth ripped and another strip of Marlis's long-suffering garment appeared. Then her tracks made through the snow straight for the brooding snark forest.

"Hold on now; where d' ye think ye're off to?" Arlan hollered. "Don't go in them woods! It's still too dark to find yer way, and—" A sharp cry followed by a heavy thud cut him off.

"Danged invisibles," muttered Arlan. The Thalmosian dropped to his belly and wriggled snakelike through the snow toward the snarks. He hadn't gone far when he ran into Rolin's invisible shin.

"I rescued you once from the strykkies," Rolin told him. "I don't want to do it again! Since she's my wife, I'll go after her. Besides, the flowers won't bother me."

Elena came up behind her husband. "You should listen to him, Arlan. The invisibles can take care of themselves. The minute you stick that warty nose of yours in those snark woods, the strykkies'll fill it so full of darts you'll look like a dog that's tangled with a porcupine—and I left my tweezers at home!"

"Danged women," Arlan growled, reluctantly rejoining his wife. Following Marlis's tracks through the fallen snow, Rolin cautiously entered the dreary forest.

"Marlis!" he called. "Where are you?" There was no reply. Then he noticed a strip of green fabric draped over some roots a few feet away. Was Marlis nearby, or had a skraal carried her off?

Crouching down, he probed the ground around the cloth decoy until his hand met Marlis's invisible torso. Evidently, she had tripped over a gnarled snark root in the dark. Fearing the worst, Rolin bore his unconscious wife back to the visibles, where he laid her body on the snow-covered ground.

"Is she hurt?" they all asked, anxiously crowding around the Marlis-shaped depression in the snow.

"I don't know," Rolin replied. He ran his fingers over his wife's face, finding a sizable lump on her forehead. "Marlis, can you hear me? Wake up! We need you!" *I need you*, he added silently.

The snow stirred and Marlis moaned, "Where am I?"

Rolin firmly held her down. "You mustn't get up yet," he said. "Just rest a bit. Are you bleeding anywhere?"

"I don't think so, but I've got an awful headache."

"Why in the name of Peton did you go off like that?" Elena exclaimed. "You could have been killed! Did you break any bones?"

Evan tugged on his mother's skirt. "Maybe 'visibles don't have bones. Maybe they're like big, mushy caterpillars."

"No, I'm all right—I think," Marlis groggily replied. "I was running through the ash—er, snarks, when I tripped on something. I must have fallen and hit my head." She gripped Rolin's arm. "My decoys won't work here! The trees are set so close together I can't run between them. The darts will hit me instead of the lure!"

"What are you talking about?" Elena demanded. "What lure?"

Arlan explained how Marlis used strips torn from her cloak to draw the strykkies' fire. ". . . but if she cain't git through them trees, neither kin we—leastways, not without flyin'."

"Then there's no way home," Elena wailed. "We're finished!"

Evan patted her hand. "The 'visibles will think of something, Mother. They can do anything."

Marlis laughed weakly. "Not today we can't, and not without Gaelathane. Why don't you ask Him to help us?"

With a weary look, Elena nodded. "What should I say to Him?"

"Just tell Him your feelings and what you need."

"Very well," Elena said crisply. She closed her eyes. "I've never met You," she began. "Our invisibles say You sent them to help us, but I'm not sure I can believe that. If You're real, You already know what a fix we're in. There's a whole passel of snarks and strykkies between us and home. If You could help us, I'd be much obliged." Elena opened her eyes and sheepishly glanced around. "Why, that scraggly snag's gone! Whatever happened to it?"

"Ye done scared it off," Arlan quipped.

"The Tree only stays where it is welcome," spoke another, deeper voice. The visibles whirled to find a bearded, craggy-faced man behind them. Garbed in a homespun tunic, He carried a shiny, double-bitted ax over one shoulder.

Elena drew closer to her husband. "Wh—who are You?"

"A friend," said the stranger with a polite bow.

"That's a mighty sharp-lookin' ax Ye've got there, *friend*," Arlan drawled, warily sizing up the woodcutter.

"It's much sharper than it looks." He tilted the ax to catch some falling snowflakes, and its blade split them cleanly in two.

"Even that ax cain't chop these black trees," Arlan said with a surly scowl. "Tough as granite and hard as iron, they are."

The Woodsman only smiled. "Where are you all going?"

Elena pulled Evan and Bronwen beside her. "What business is it of Yours? We don't hold with outsiders around here."

The Woodsman's shaggy head nodded toward Rolin and Marlis. "I've come to help you and your friends."

Elena sneered, "We don't need Your help, so why don't You go back to wherever You came from and leave—Our f-friends? *What* friends? How did You—?"

"They are your friends, aren't they?" said the woodcutter with a slight smile. He shifted His ax to the other shoulder.

"Why, yes, but they're not—I mean, you can't . . ." Elena's mouth quivered and a wild, hunted look glazed her eyes.

"You're trying to tell Me they're invisible, are you not?"

Arlan stared suspiciously at the stranger. "How kin *Ye* see 'em, when we cain't? Did Ye see their tracks in th' snow?"

"All worlds are continually laid bare before My eyes, including this one," the Woodsman said. He bent down to touch Marlis's invisible head. "How does that feel now?"

"Much better, thank You!" she replied, raising a snow flurry as she got up. Tracing the soft outlines of Marlis's body molded in the snow, Evan said, "She's not like a caterpillar!"

Now the Woodsman straightened, His jerkin sleeves falling back to reveal ropy red scars veining His hands and arms. Arlan and Elena grimaced at the sight.

"Strykkie welts!" Bronwen blurted out. Then she covered her mouth and stared at her feet.

Elena glared at her. "Hush, child! You mustn't speak out of turn to your elders. It's rude."

The Woodsman smiled. "Be at peace. I am pleased you noticed My scars. I shall always bear them as a reminder of My love for you." After patting the children's heads, He turned as if to leave.

Elena caught His arm. "Don't go! I mean—" Flustered, she bit her lip. "Please, Sir, we want to go home, if You know the way."

"I know the way, for I am the way, not only to your home, but to Mine as well: The Kingdom of Love, which lies beyond the Tree you just climbed. Would you like to join My kingdom?"

Arlan glanced askance at the Man. "Ye're a king? Ye don't look like one. Where's Yer crown?"

"Crowns and costly finery do not a sovereign make. There is more to Me than meets your eye, Arlan son of William."

Arlan gasped. "Ye know my name! But how—?"

"Before you became a Keeper of the Chest, I knew you," replied the Woodsman. Arlan stared at Him in blank astonishment.

Elena stuck out her chin defiantly. "If You're a king, who are Your subjects? The trees? The animals? The birds?"

The Woodsman chuckled. "All of those, and anyone else who chooses to follow Me. Will *you* follow Me, Elena?"

As the Keeper's wife lowered her gaze, disappointment clouded the Woodsman's rugged features. Then He lifted His ax high and strode off, a fire blazing in His piercing eyes.

"We'll follow You!" cried the children, nipping at His heels.

"Don't leave without us!" shouted their parents. Exchanging excited hand squeezes, Rolin and Marlis brought up the rear, plowing gouges in the snow.

On reaching the snarks, the Woodsman told His followers, "Wait until I have cleared the way, lest harm befall you." Then He plunged into the trees.

"He's a durn fool to go in there with nothin' more than an ax," Arlan said. "He'll ruin th' blade and His own hide, too, if He's not careful. He hasn't got a fightin' chance."

Whick! Whack! Thick! Thack! Black trees toppled like straws before the Woodsman's whistling ax, which sliced through their stony trunks like a hot knife through beeswax. *Whing! Zing!* sang the strykkies, launching volley after volley of stinging darts at the intruder. He paid them no mind.

Undaunted, He leveled everything before Him, His face shining with a clear light that drove back the snarks' thick gloom. With each mighty swing, He roared, "Let every tree, high or low, be brought down with a single blow!"

Trailing behind, the visibles took care to avoid the strykkie clumps dangling from the fallen snarks. They needn't have feared. Those vicious flowers had already vented all their venom on the Woodsman, frosting his brown tunic with their strings. He shrugged off their fiery darts like a bear robbing a bees' nest.

"He should be dead by now!" Arlan said, shaking his head. "Not even a skraal could survive so many stings." However, survive He did, His glittering ax still whirling through the gibbering trees, while the skraals and worggles slunk away to their caves and dens in the deepest, darkest recesses of the wood.

At length, the travelers could see the far side of the forbidding forest, where lumpy, snow-laden firs marched up the mountainside. Breaking into a snow-slogging run, the six were soon on open ground, laughing and shouting for joy. When they looked for the Woodsman, however, He was gone.

"What happened to Him?" puzzled Elena. "He was just here."

"Gaelathane's like that," Marlis said. "You can never tell when He'll show up—or disappear."

"Gaelathane!" Elena said. "I took Him for a woodcutter."

"That's how He usually appears in Thalmos," Rolin explained. "In other torsil worlds He takes on different guises."

"He's different, all right. What kind of king up and leaves without saying goodbye? It's mighty peculiar, if you ask me. Downright unneighborly, and there's a fact."

"Wherever He went, He didn't leave no tracks behind," said Arlan, searching the snow for footprints. He scratched his beard. "Poor feller. Maybe the strykkies got 'im after all."

"Oh, I don't think so," Rolin laughed. "Nothing can harm *Him!*"

"What made Him help us the way He did?" asked Elena.

Marlis replied, "Love—and because you called on Him."

CHAPTER 28

BURGLED

With frozen feet, the wayfarers wearily tromped homeward. Their footprints filled with white, fat flakes almost as quickly as they made them. Rolin and Marlis hardly noticed their frost-nipped ears and fingers.

"He touched me, He really touched me!" Marlis kept saying.

"I think He's touched the visibles, too," Rolin murmured, his heart aglow. He steadied Bronwen as she stumbled in the snow.

"Thank you," the girl mumbled through blue lips. "I do hope we get home soon. All morning I've been dreaming of our nice, dry cave with a fire in the stove and a pot of hot mint tea."

"M-m-m-me, too," stammered Evan, his teeth chattering.

Elena pointed ahead. "There it is!" She forged through the snow toward the hill and then stopped, frozen in her tracks. Broken nearly in two, the visibles' front door hung crazily ajar on one hinge, creaking as it swung in the snarling winds. Someone had barged into the cave without bothering to knock.

"Help! Murder! Robbery!" howled Elena at the top of her lungs.

"Hush, woman," Arlan growled, stopping the children from entering the cave. He sniffed the air and studied the welter of tracks in the new-fallen snow. "Worggles. They must've jest left, and in a

hurry, too. We was lucky to be away. From th' looks of these clawprints, there were forty or fifty o' the critters."

"Why would they break into your cave?" asked Rolin.

"I ain't rightly sure. Maybe they were lookin' to avenge their dead. Most likely they was after our food. They'll snitch all yer vittles if ye don't keep 'em locked up, 'specially in winter. 'When the master leaves, the worggle thieves.'"

Elena stood by, wringing her hands and weeping. "Whatever are we going to do? Where will we live? Where will we go?"

"We ain't goin' nowhere till we see what them worggles took," Arlan gruffly replied. He led the way inside. Rolin followed, staff in hand. Its light fell upon a dismal scene.

What little the visibles owned was a complete shambles. Table, chairs, stools and benches all were smashed beyond repair. The shelves and their contents had been pulled down. A sticky slurry of jam, honey, dried mulberries and skraal jerky covered the floor, with broken crockery trampled in for good measure.

"Just look at what they've done!" wailed Elena. "Everything's ruined—everything!" She collapsed in tears on a gutted straw mattress, its insides strewn through the wreckage of a jam jar.

Arlan caressed her shaking shoulders. "Don't fret, m' dear. We'll start over somewhere else. We've done it before, an' we kin do it again. This time we'll have th' children to help."

Elena shook off his hand. "I don't want to start over. I like it just fine here!" She broke into a fresh spate of sobbing.

"If it was food they wanted, why spoil it all?" Marlis wondered.

"Worggles are that way," said Bronwen. "What they don't eat or carry away, they foul too badly for anybody else to use."

Grimacing, Arlan brushed aside a shredded blanket partition. He reappeared pushing a huge boulder, which he rolled against the doorway and wedged in place with sticks of furniture. "Always knew this would come in handy," he grunted. "Them worggles'll think twice afore busting into our cave again."

Let them try, thought Rolin grimly. If the creatures so much as poked their pumpkin heads inside again, he'd give them a taste of his lightstaff! Following Elena's example, he crammed rags around the boulder to keep out drafts and blowing snow.

Next, while Marlis and the children scraped the gooey mess off the floor, Rolin stuffed the potbellied stove with a chair's splintered remnants. Then he lit a fire with his flint and steel. Soon the stove was cherry red, and the little hollow under the hill grew warm enough for Marlis to hang up the visibles' dripping outer garments to dry. "Just as cozy as ever!" she said cheerfully.

"It's awfully bare," Elena sniffled. She and her family were huddled around a sputtering candle the looters had overlooked. (Worggles have a taste for wax.) Bronwen's berry-picking basket was also still in one piece, as was Evan's rumpled, sticky sling. Otherwise, most of the family's meager belongings lay in a pitiful pile beside the stove, fit only to be thrown out or burned.

"At least we still have our pillows," Bronwen remarked, stuffing hers with feathers rescued from the dust heap. "Once we sew them up again, they'll be as good as new."

"Sew them up? With what?" said her mother sharply.

Bronwen held up a leather sack. "With these needles I found in Peton. I never took them out of my pocket."

"I've still got my marbles," Evan announced, rolling one across the floor. It threw back the candlelight in crystal spears.

Rolin stoked the fire, sending glowing sparks spitting into the room. "Why do you suppose the worggles tore up your pillows and mattresses? You weren't keeping food in them, were you?"

"Worggles ain't that smart," Arlan wearily replied. "Once they catches the scent of food, they goes into a frenzy, ripping apart everything in sight. Say, speaking o' food, ye don't happen to have more o' them flatcakes, do ye?"

"We ran out this morning," Rolin reminded him. Out of curiosity, he pulled the linen sack from his pocket, finding it full again of the sweet waferbread. "Gaelathane be praised!" he cried, waving the bag. After doling out pieces to Marlis and the visibles, he settled down beside the stove to enjoy his own portion. Basking in the fire's heat, he noticed Marlis hadn't eaten her share.

"Where are you, dear one?" he called out. "Why don't you come over here and finish your meal?"

"I'm scraping jam off the rug. Why don't *you* come over *here* and lend me a hand?" Sighing, Rolin got up and headed toward Marlis's voice, arms held out to keep from running into her.

"Oof!" He sprawled over her kneeling form.

Marlis thumped him on the head. "Why don't you watch where you're going? I asked you to help me, not kick me."

"Sorry! You're invisible, in case you hadn't noticed. Now if you still want me to work with you, please show me your jam spot."

An ugly purple blotch remained where the worggles had tracked jam onto the rug. Adding insult to injury, their claws had cut the carpet to ribbons. "Between the jam and these gashes, I'm afraid your rug's ruined," Marlis told Elena.

Elena shrugged and managed a wan smile. "It was old and tattered, anyhow. I'll make another."

Rolin examined the mangled fabric. "That's odd. Judging from these tracks, I'd say the worggles were searching for something."

Arlan's eyes filled with dread. "Maybe they was." Gripping one edge of the rug, he tore off the stained portion and pulled out the stone block from the floor. Then he hoisted the golden chest out of its niche. "This is what them worggles was looking fer, or I'm not a Keeper," he declared.

Elena breathed a sigh of relief. "Thank goodness they didn't find it! We never would have gotten it back again."

"How could they have known it was here in the first place?" asked Marlis. "It was very cleverly concealed."

"By th' scent," Arlan replied. "Worggles kin smell anything, even if it's buried under six feet o' rock. What they'd want with our chest, I couldn't say. Even worggles cain't eat gold."

———————— ❦ ————————

Sniffing and snooping their way through torsil time, they had sto-len golden crowns, golden scepters and golden trinkets from Thalmosian kings and commoners. "Hollow it must be and of fine gold, studded with gems," their master had told them, scorning their petty pilferings. "Whoever brings me this thing I will grant to drink from the firewell in the Pit, and he shall never die."

Any worggle would give his right claw for just one sip from the firewell, though it would have instantly turned him to ash. This time, having followed the elusive scent of gold into the visibles' cave, the worggles were about to pull up the rug when two terribly bright beings had appeared and chased them away.

CHAPTER 29

NEW HEARTS, NEW RIDDLES

Arlan fondly stroked the gold sphere. "If it was our chest they was after, they'll be back. Worggles never give up. I jest wish I knew why they wanted it."

"Life used to be so simple before the invisibles came," Elena lamented as she trimmed the candle wick. "Now nothing will ever be the same again. I can't even feel safe in my own cave."

"When Gaelathane comes into your life, He often makes many changes," Marlis quietly told her. "They're not always welcome ones, either. We have to trust that He knows what's best for us."

"I never saw no one swing an ax like that, nor any blade cut through snarks the way His did," Arlan said. "It warn't only His ax, either. Them eyes of His were like to split *me* clean in two."

Rolin laughed. "People often feel that way when they first meet Him. He goes straight to work on the heart."

"You can't keep any secrets from Him, either," said Elena. "I was sure He knew everything I'd ever done."

"Or ever thought—good or bad," Bronwen said as she sewed up her pillow.

Arlan borrowed Rolin's knife to whittle a table leg into a short spear. "Elena's right," he drawled softly. "Ye invisibles have brought new ways into our lives, and they're hard to swallow."

"What do you mean?" asked Rolin.

Arlan stopped whittling. "It ain't yer fault. As the Last Family, we've learned to live by our wits. We follow no one's paths but our own. There's an old saying in these parts, 'Them that trust, die.' It's the Way of Peton, and it's kept us alive all these years."

"The Way of Peton?" Marlis asked. "What's that?"

In answer, Bronwen stood and in her high, clear voice recited,

Eat or be eaten;
Beat or be beaten;
Stray from the way
And I'll make you pay!
If you don't flee,
You'll be meat for me!

"That's Peton's way," said Elena grimly. "It devours the simple and unwary. Even the children know that if worggles catch one of us, the others will have no choice but to save themselves."

"How very sad!" said Marlis. "Gaelathane offers you a better way: The Way of Love. In His love for us, He *let* Himself be caught by His enemies so that we could go free. He makes safe, straight paths for us to follow, just as He did through the snarks. That's Gaelathane's Way, and it's the best way."

"Gaelathane's Way, eh?" said Arlan. "Maybe that's why ye and Rolin risked yer lives to rescue me and my family from th' strykkies and the grakkles. Ye an' the other decoys kept us alive."

Elena gave her normally closemouthed mate a hard look. It wasn't like him to ramble. "Decoys? What decoys?"

"Pipe down, woman, and I'll tell ye! We was on th' Peton road when I killed a skraal and cut off a strip of its hide fer Marlis to use as a decoy. Ye might say that skraal died so's we could git through th' strykkies. On our way back from Peton, we needed another decoy fer th' eelomars, but I was fresh out of arrows. When we git to th' bridge, there's a white hare waitin' fer us. It don't hide or run away like most critters do when they see us. It jest sits there, calm and quiet-like until Evan kills it with a rock. Without that rabbit to help us git past th' eelomars, we'd 'a been goners, as sure as I'm a Keeper."

He threw more wood in the stove. "Then there was th' deer. Now, I warn't there to see fer myself, but I kin picture it from what Rolin told us. That buck walked right up to ye invisibles, as tame as tame kin be, jest a-waitin' fer Rolin to kill it. If that critter hadn't showed up, Rolin and Marlis wouldn't have found us, and we'd all four be a heap o' bones at th' bottom of the grakkles' nest." The other visibles shivered at Arlan's pithy description.

Arlan turned to his family. "Don't ye see? Th' invisibles, th' skraal, th' hare and th' deer—they all gave themselves fer us as *decoys*. If that warn't enough, this Gaelathane feller Hisself cuts a road right smack through th' snark woods, takin' all them strykkie stings without battin' an eye."

"Like a *living lure*," breathed Elena, her eyes aflame.

"Well put!" Marlis exclaimed. "Just as the Woodsman took those strykkie darts in our place, He and the Tree took the sting of death for you and me. Just as His ax cleared the way home for us, the axes that wounded the Tree opened the way for us to live forever in Gaelessa, Gaelathane's home. In His kingdom of love there are no snarks or strykkies or grakkles—"

"Or worggles?" Evan cut in.

"Or worggles, or anything else bad—not even death itself."

"Let's go there now!" cried Bronwen. She jumped up and ran to the door. Evan followed her, swinging his sling.

"Come back here, you two!" Rolin laughed. "You'll never find the Tree that way." He gathered them in his invisible arms. "I wish we could all go there together this very night, but we can't."

"Why not?" the children cried.

"Because Gaelathane only allows us into His kingdom when we're ready—not before."

"You mean we have to become 'visibles too?" Evan asked, his lower lip trembling. "I don't think I'd like that very much."

Rolin chuckled. "No, you only must become His children."

"How do we do that?" Bronwen asked with an anxious frown.

"First, you must decide whether you will follow the Way of Gaelathane or Peton's Way, which leads to death. When you ask Gaelathane into your heart, you are choosing His Way—the road to life. Then He makes you His child and a new person on the inside. However, if you're full of hatred, envy or selfishness, you must ask Him to forgive and cleanse you of those things."

Elena groaned, fresh tears flowing from her red-rimmed eyes. "Then I am lost, for who could change a heart as hard as mine?"

"No one can," Marlis agreed. "If you ask Him, though, Gaelathane will give you a new one. All you need do is believe that through the Tree, He died to free you from the guilt and penalty of the wrongs you've done."

Elena bowed her head. "Gaelathane, I believe and I want to follow Your way. Soften this hateful heart of mine; make me a *new person* inside. Please let me live with You forever." Weeping, she found Marlis's hand. "Forgive me, dear friend. I have treated you and Rolin so shabbily!"

"There, there, Elena; all is forgiven," Marlis murmured.

Closing his eyes, Arlan fell to his knees and said, "Gaelathane, don't stop with my wife; I need a new heart, too!"

"Oh, and me, too!" whispered Bronwen.

Evan clasped his hands and said, "I wanna live in Your home."

Tears flowed freely as a sacred hush fell upon the little circle. All at once, the cavern roof faded away, revealing the night sky's vast, velvet dome studded with diamonds. Higher yet shone the figure of a man standing between the heavens and the earth. It was Gaelathane the Ageless One, robed in His eternal radiance.

Speech without words passed between the King of the Trees and the six on their knees in the cave, words of love, words of life, words of hope. As the light brightened, the cowering mortals hid their eyes from its splendor. When they looked up again, Gaelathane stood before them in unveiled glory.

He smiled and held out His scarred hands and arms. "Do not be afraid. It is I, the One Who was dead and now lives, the everlasting King. Welcome to My family, dear Bronwen and Evan, Arlan and Elena! I have long awaited this hour. Ask of Me anything you wish, and I shall give it to you."

Bronwen raised her head. "Please, Sir, we want to live where all the trees are green, not black; where flowers bloom in lovely meadows and the wild creatures won't try to eat us."

"An' where we can play with other children," said Evan.

"I shall grant your requests, not only here but in My home as well," said Gaelathane tenderly. "First, I must ask something of you both. Bronwen, I need your needles and berry basket, and Evan, your marbles and sling."

The two looked at one another. What could the King want with a shabby little wicker basket, some blunt needles, a handful of chipped marbles and a lopsided leather strap? Reluctantly, Evan dropped his sling and marbles into the basket and Bronwen her needle bag. Then she handed the basket to Gaelathane.

"I am honored to be trusted with your most precious possessions," beamed the King. "Your names are no longer 'Bronwen' and 'Evan,' but 'Bronwen the Bold' and 'Evan the Wise.'" He glanced at Arlan and Elena, who were still kneeling in dumbstruck terror. "Have your parents no requests?"

Arlan took a deep breath. "Gaelathane, Sir, Ye know we haven't much left after th' worggles broke into our home. If Ye could jest give us enough to live comfortably—vittles an' warm clothes an' a safe, dry cave—we'd be mighty grateful."

"You shall have those and more besides, dear child. I know of your poverty and all you have endured to feed your family. You can always look to Me for your needs. However, to grant your petition, I must have your dearest possession also."

Arlan was taken aback. "I'd offer Ye my bow and arrows, but they're gone." He felt his pockets. "So's my pipe. It must've fallen out in the grakkles' nest. The worggles took everything else."

"Except your pride," Gaelathane said with a kindly smile.

"Well. Yes," Arlan sighed. "I won't begrudge Ye that much."

"Thank you. Henceforth you shall be called 'Arlan the Lionhearted.'" Gaelathane turned to Elena. "What may I do for you, My blessed daughter?"

Elena blushed. "It's such a foolish thing to ask, but—"

"No need or wish is too trifling for Me to fulfill," said the King warmly. "Indeed, I delight in answering such requests."

"Then I'd like to see the inv—I mean, Rolin and Marlis—as they really are. If it's not too much trouble, that is."

"So you shall, though they must remain unseen for a season. In the meantime, Elena, may I have your candle?"

"We can't light the cave without it!" Elena objected, handing the King her burning taper. It seemed to grow in His grasp.

"However dark your path may be, I will light your way. For now, take courage in being 'Elena the Fearless.' Trust in Me, and you will never be afraid again."

"Can the 'visibles ask for something, too?" said Evan.

"They may. What do *you* wish of Me, My faithful servants?"

"Only to see Lucambra restored," they quickly answered.

"This, too, shall come to pass in its own time," said the King.

"Don't they need to give up something?" the visibles asked, pointing in Rolin and Marlis's general direction.

"King Rolin's hour of sacrifice has passed, is now and is yet to come," Gaelathane told them. "He has lost all that he cherished most, save his wife, whom he cannot see. Queen Marlis has laid at My feet everything she is and all she possesses. She has even yielded up her departed mother's cloak for My sake."

"Why didn't ye say so before, Marlis?" Arlan said. "An' here ye've tore it in pieces to help us! What made ye do sech a thing?"

"It was love," the King told him. "When I have so filled your hearts that there is room for nothing else, then and only then will you know the joy of giving others what you treasure most." Gaelathane looked directly at Rolin. "The sack, please, My son."

Rolin gave the empty bag to Gaelathane, Who breathed upon it and the other objects lying in His hands. Then He prayed:

Bag and basket, wax and sling,
Now swell in service to the King,
And take My servants to the tree,
That opens on their own country.

Glass and steel must work their weal,
With what is torn, the seam to seal;
And flying eye to swiftly smite,
That beak and talon may not bite.

He added, "Arlan, you must lace the bag to the basket with Evan's sling. Your family's future depends upon it."

Arlan's bearded cheeks colored and he growled, "Any child could tie them things together blindfolded!"

"I thought you had given Me your pride, Arlan William's son."

Arlan bowed his head. "I'm sorry, Sir. I'll do as Ye ask."

"Not alone, though. I am blessing your son with the wisdom to help you. Come the dawn, you must all climb into the basket and light the candle. Then you shall see where I will lead you."

Stunned disbelief etched the visibles' faces. Get into Bronwen's berry basket? All six of them? The flimsy wickerwork would hardly hold a plump melon, let alone a person.

"What if we can't all fit inside?" Marlis ventured to ask.

Gaelathane smiled at her. "Have faith in Me; remember My words and do not forget the chest!" With that, He vanished, His glory fading after Him. No one spoke for several minutes. Then everyone started talking at once.

"He was here, wasn't He? He really was here!" the grownups told each other in awe. The children danced for joy.

Then a baffled look came over Elena's face. "Why, I never! The table's back together—and the candle's on it! Look how brightly it's burning, too. You'd think the worggles had never been here."

Evan found his sling lying on Bronwen's newly plump pillow. It had longer thongs and a wider, stronger pouch. No longer chipped and cracked, the marbles clinked crisply in his pocket.

Bronwen's basket and needle pouch turned up next to the stove. The basket was full of nuts—"For planting, not eating," Rolin told her, without mentioning what sort they were—while the polished needles looked spanking new. Bronwen poured the nuts into one pocket and placed the needle pouch in another.

"Here's my bow!" cried Arlan, lifting it off a hook on the wall. He drew a bead on an imaginary worggle. "Well-balanced, too," he grunted. The quiver hanging beside it bristled with bright, well-feathered arrows. Arlan pulled out one of the crystal shafts, marveling, "I've never seen th' like o' these in all my days!"

"That's because they're made from the Tree's shoots," Rolin explained. "Gaelathane must hold you in high esteem!"

Arlan scratched his ear. "Why would He do all this fer us?"

Rolin tried in vain to catch Arlan's eye. "You can't give the King anything without receiving much more in return."

Elena turned toward him. "Speaking of kings, didn't Gaelathane call you two, 'Queen Marlis' and 'King Rolin'?"

Rolin felt his face flush. "Er, yes, He did."

"King and queen of *Peton?*" asked a wide-eyed Bronwen.

"No, of Lucambra," Marlis sadly replied. "Since that land is no more, we are rulers without a country. Even if Lucambra still lived, our subjects would hardly greet an invisible king and queen with open arms." Rolin sensed what his wife had left unsaid: *When will Gaelathane make us visible again?*

That disappointment was soon forgotten with Rolin's discovery that the linen bag was back in his cloak pocket, bulging with more sweet waferbread. After sharing the sack's contents with Marlis and the visibles, he shook the crumbs into Evan's mouth and handed Arlan the empty bag.

When Bronwen gave him her basket, Arlan set to work binding the bag to it with Evan's sling. Meanwhile, Elena was bustling about the cave, singing a song she'd composed on the spot:

> Lord, grant me grace that I might grow,
> And trust You through my trials below,
> That from Your lessons I might learn
> All good to grasp, and evil spurn.
>
> Lord, grant me love that I might live
> In gratitude for all You give,
> To be Your bleeding hands and feet,
> To all Your children whom I meet.

Lord, grant me joy to conquer care,
To help me through dark days' despair,
That other worlds might see in me
The answer to life's mystery.

Lord, grant me peace in place of pain,
To cease my striving and refrain
From leaning on my feeble strength,
To know my loss is gain at length.

Lord, grant me eyes that I might see
Gaelessa's glories in Your Tree;
Open my ears that I might hear
Your sweet voice whisp'ring to me dear.

Lord, grant me life to vanquish death,
That with my final, failing breath
I'd bring You all my brokenness,
To find in You eternal rest.

Marlis squirmed as she and Rolin sat by the stove listening to Elena's sweet voice. "It's awfully hot in here," she muttered. Then her cloak appeared, ragged, threadbare and splotched with mud and dried deer blood. "Shabby old thing," she said as the cloak wadded itself into a ball and flew across the cave.

Elena ran over to pick it up. "Why, Marlis, is this yours? What a lovely shawl. It's just like new."

Marlis gasped. The forest-green cloak was now whole and spotless. Taking the soft, seamless garment from Elena, she declared, "It's *better* than new! I've never seen such a perfectly marvelous cloak. Thank You, dear Gaelathane!"

That was Arlan's cue to show off his handiwork. Rolin's sack was now loosely fastened by its mouth to the bottom of Bronwen's wicker basket. Snickering, Evan showed his red-faced father how to attach the sack properly around the basket's top rim.

"What's this cockeyed contraption fer?" said Arlan.

Bronwen picked up the basket by the bag. "I know! It's a coracle, like the ones Peton's fishermen used to make, and the sack's supposed to be the sail."

Arlan yawned. "If ye're right, all it lacks is a mast and a coat o' pitch t' keep out th' water. Now, what do we need with a toy boat?" It was a question not even Rolin and Marlis could answer.

CHAPTER 30

GAELATHANE MAKES A WAY

The next day, the six Children of the Tree awakened to rank, stuffy air, thanks to the stove's still-smoldering embers. With Rolin's help, Arlan pried the boulder away from the door. Then with bowls, boards and sticks, everyone attacked the wall of snow blocking the entrance. Soon, they had tunneled through to the surface.

"It's wonderful out here!" Elena exclaimed, breathing the cold, crisp air. Shining down from an azure sky, the sun winked and blinked on the pristine, new-fallen powder. Cocky chickadees bravely foraged among stolid, snow-muffled evergreens, while brash crows hovered overhead in hopes of a handout.

"Shoo, crows!" Marlis shouted, waving her arms at them. "We have no food for you. Fly away and leave us be."

"Go away, go away, the two-legs always say!" croaked the black, scraggly birds as they flew off. Rolin was about to yell back a fitting insult before remembering that only he and Marlis could understand the birds' raucous words.

While Bronwen and Evan threw snowballs at one another, Arlan ran a long stick into the powder. "Five foot deep, if it's an inch," he said. "Mark my words, no worggles will be out today."

Rolin briskly rubbed his hands together. "Why not?"

"They dislike the cold," Elena explained. "After the snows come, we rarely see them. That's why we were so surprised when they broke into our cave."

"Then we'd better leave before they return," said Marlis.

"We cain't traipse through this snow without food and proper gear," Arlan argued. "Th' grakkles would pounce on us like hawks on a mouse. I've got a food cache that th' worggles ain't found yet. In a few days, we could be ready to—"

Bronwen interrupted her father to hand him the bag and basket. "Gaelathane told us to get into this today," she said.

"Hush, child," Arlan growled. "Ye must have misunderstood Him. There ain't room in that fer one of us, let alone all six. It's jest a plaything. Ye'd better leave it behind in the cave."

"Bronwen's right," Rolin challenged him. "Gaelathane instructed us all to climb into the basket, and this morning, too."

"I say sech talk is plumb foolishness," Arlan huffed. Tossing the basket into the snow, he stomped back to the cave.

As Elena reluctantly followed him, Marlis told her, "We have a saying in Lucambra: 'When we're willing to obey, Gaelathane will make a way.' Maybe He wants us to do as He's asked, even though we don't understand."

"I'm sorry," Elena tearfully replied. "I love Gaelathane, but my husband is as sensible as snow. This *whilfildigig* is only a toy."

"Whilfildigig?" said Marlis as Elena disappeared into the cave.

"That's what we call things that don't have a name," Bronwen said. Then she and Evan announced, "We're staying out here."

"Very good," said Rolin. "Perhaps you two can help me. Evan, I'll let you steady the basket in the snow. That's right. Bronwen, you may hold the bag to keep it out of the way. Now then, let's have a go at this whilfildigig."

Rolin planted his invisible left foot in the basket, which sank into the snow. Bronwen winced and shut her eyes.

To Rolin's amazement, the basket had grown to fit his foot. With a hop, he placed his right foot inside. Now the basket was larger than a water bucket and no less sturdy.

"Papa! Mama!" called Bronwen and Evan. "Come look! Hurry!" Elena and Arlan popped outside with dark looks. Seeing the basket, they plowed back through the snow.

"Where did you get this?" they demanded.

"It's my basket!" Bronwen squealed. "See how it grew?"

"Impossible!" snorted Arlan. "Baskets don't grow."

Rolin chuckled. "This one did! Climb in. There's room enough and to spare for everyone."

Elena's old suspicions were reviving. "It's a trick!" she warned.

"No, it's not," Marlis laughed. "Just watch. I'm getting in now." The wicker basket abruptly became washtub-size.

Evan and Bronwen clambered in next with their snowballs. "Look at us! We're basketeers!" they cried, gleefully rocking the basket. Then they took their father's arms and helped him inside.

Arlan gulped, shook his head and laughed. "They was right, Elena. There's plenty o' space in here! Say, could ye fetch my bow and arrows? While ye're at it, please bring along the candle. Ye'd better light it first with a coal from the stove."

"Don't forget my pillow!" added Bronwen.

"Or the chest!" said Marlis.

Elena ducked into the cave, grumbling, "Elena, fetch this; Elena, fetch that. I haven't arms enough for it all!" Minutes later, she struggled back to the basket with the bow and quiver, the lit candle, Bronwen's pillow and the golden sphere, which was slung over her shoulder in a tattered pillowcase. When she swung her legs over the side of the basket, it obligingly grew to accommodate her. "Well, I never!" she exclaimed. "All six of us in Bronwen's berry basket. Who would have thought it?"

"Arlan, give me that candle, will you?" Rolin said. Holding the wax stub over his head, he examined the interior of the burgeoning bag. *Foosh!* The candle flame flared up, and the sack stirred and tipped upright.

"Oh!" gasped the visibles, their mouths making little circles.

"Goodness!" said Marlis. Rolin nearly dropped the candle, which was growing bigger by the minute. Its ropelike wick now burned with a bright blue flame.

Filling with the candle's hot air, the sack swelled like an enormous mushroom over the heads of the startled basketeers. The bag continued ballooning, growing taller than the treetops. The basket groaned and shifted in the snow.

Elena tried to jump out, but Rolin held her back. Kicking and clawing, she screamed, "Let go of me! I want out of here!"

Just then, Rolin noticed a long line of lanky figures toiling up the slope toward them. Sunlight flashed on swords and spears.

"Worggles!" Evan cried. "The worggles are coming!"

Rolin counted twenty of the fur-clad creatures slogging through the snow. Shoving the candle into Bronwen's hands, he drew his lightstaff, but it slipped from his grasp and fell to the bottom of the basket. In trying to retrieve it, he bumped Arlan's bow, spoiling his aim. Then Elena the Fearless raised her eyes heavenward and prayed, "Gaelathane, please help us!"

Scarcely had she spoken when the basket shuddered and jerked free of the snow. Caught off guard, the worggles stared up at the strange craft sailing into the sky. By a yeg's hair, their quarry had escaped with the gold *thing*. Enraged, they gnashed their teeth and shook their weapons at the basketeers.

"Can't catch us now, worggles!" shouted Evan, throwing snowballs at them until the balloon was out of range. Still rising, the craft hung like a silvery teardrop above the ground, drifting weightlessly with the shifting winds. In the basket, there was little sense of movement nor scarcely a breath of air.

Elena gazed longingly across the serene snowscape toward the hill with its cozy cave, now receding into the distance. "I'm missing my home already, cramped and dingy though it was," she sighed. "Where do you think we're going, Rolin?"

"Wherever Gaelathane takes us, I suppose," Rolin replied, his arms aching from holding the overgrown candle. The flame had to be centered just right—neither too high nor too low. Too high, and the balloon's fabric might catch fire. Too low, and the air inside the bag would cool, causing the craft to drop. Rolin cast a worried glance westward at the looming Tartellans, whose crumbling crags looked close enough to touch. Streaming down from snowy passes,

stiff crosswinds began buffeting the balloon. Rolin tried not to picture the craft slamming into those frozen peaks, dashing both basket and passengers to pieces.

He was about to ask the others to throw any excess baggage overboard to lighten the balloon when Elena shrilly called out, "Arlan! Come look at this." She was pointing at a dark cloud swiftly approaching the balloon from below. Squinting against the glare of sun on snow, Rolin saw that the "cloud" was actually a swarm of menacing winged shapes.

"Grakkles," Arlan said throatily. Still ravenous after dining on twenty stringy worggles, the creatures were bent on tastier game: A basketful of enticing two-legs.

CHAPTER 31

THE FEATHER BIRDS

Still clutching the candle, Rolin stared in horrified fascination at the oncoming grakkles. The balloon couldn't possibly outpace them. One swipe of their razor-sharp talons would shred the fragile bag, sending the carriage and its precious cargo plunging earthward. He could only thrust the candle higher into the sack's mouth—a futile gesture at best.

"Did you call me, Father?" came Bronwen's sleepy voice from below. After the near brush with the worggles, she had curled up in the bottom of the basket like a cat in an easy chair and had fallen fast asleep on her pillow.

"No, I didn't," replied Arlan, his voice tight with dread.

Bronwen sat up, rubbed her eyes and said, "I'm down here, Father. What did you want?"

"Nothin', daughter," Arlan growled. "Go back to sleep."

Marlis asked, "Did you hear someone calling you, Bronwen?"

"Yes—a man's voice, very deep but soft and gentle."

"The King of the Trees was speaking to you. If you hear His voice again, you must answer, 'Speak, Lord, I am listening.'"

"I'd rather finish my nap," Bronwen yawned. All at once, she raised her head and said, "Speak, Lord, I am listening . . . But it's my only pillow, and I—Oh, all right. If You really want me to."

Hanging her pillow over the side of the wicker carriage, she ripped it open, spilling out clouds of fluffy, white feathers that whirled and swirled around the balloon like flocks of—

"Doves! Where did all those doves come from?" Elena pointed below the basket, where the cascading clumps of feathers had sprouted heads, wings, eyes and tails. Banding together in a milk-white wave, the feather birds scattered the attacking grakkles, which swiftly regrouped and bored in on the balloon again.

Now it was Evan's turn. After cocking his head in a listening pose, he plunged a hand into his pocket and pulled out two marbles. As he held them up to the sunlight, the glass spheres flashed fire, blinding the grakkles. Veering away, the bat-winged beasts exposed their broad, sleek bellies to the terrified basketeers. *And flying eye to swiftly smite, that beak and talon may not bite.*

"Arlan—your bow!" Rolin cried. In a trice, Arlan had the weapon in hand. Letting fly twin shining arrows, he roared, "Fer Gaelathane and th' Tree!"

The light-arrows flew swift and true. Two grakkles froze in mid-flight, their lifeless stone eyes still fixed on the basket. Then they spun toward the waiting rocks below.

Meanwhile, the marbles' light had caused another grakkle to overshoot the mark. In passing, the thing's wing claws tore open the side of the bag. *Whoosh!* As hot air poured out, the balloon hurtled earthward like a stone.

"Rolin!" screamed Marlis. "Do something!"

The candle squirted out of Rolin's grasp. As he grabbed the burning taper, a voice spoke, "Help Bronwen sew up the split."

Rolin hoisted the girl into the balloon's mouth. Then he pulled the lower edges of the rip together while Bronwen dumped some needles out of her leather pouch.

"Thread!" Marlis cried. "Where's the thread?"

Rolin saw to his dismay that Bronwen's needles were all thread-less. What good was a needle without thread? Still the balloon spiraled downward, the wind rushing by ever faster.

As Bronwen jabbed a needle through the wildly flapping fabric, it was torn from her fingers. "Oh, no, I've lost it!" she wailed.

Instead of tumbling into the basket, the needle stitched its way up the slit with a filament finer than a strand of spider's silk. Back and forth the needle wove, mending the tear further with each pass. In less time than it takes to tell, the gap was closed and the needle had returned to rest in Bronwen's hand. *Glass and steel must work their weal, with what is torn, the seam to seal.*

Meanwhile, darting doves were still harassing the remaining grakkles like dogs harrying a mountain lion. The angry grakkles twisted and snapped at their tormentors, but to no avail.

Rolin shoved the candle back under the mended bag, halting the balloon's descent. The basketeers held their breath as their craft drifted away from the brawling birds and grakkles. Maybe they could make good their escape after all! However, the grakkles weren't about to give up the chase. One after another, they broke free of the feather birds to dive on the balloon.

Arlan reached for his bow again. As quickly as he could draw and loose one arrow, his wife pressed another into his hand. Petrified grakkles gyrated into the ground or cartwheeled into rugged mountain cliffs.

"Twelve . . . thirteen . . . fourteen . . ." Arlan counted through gritted teeth. "There's only one left. Another arrow, Elena!"

Elena pawed through the quiver. "It's empty!" she groaned. The last grakkle shook off a feather-bird flock and made straight for the balloon, savagely clacking its jaws.

Still gripping the candle, Rolin grabbed his lightstaff from the bottom of the basket and shot a bolt of light into the grakkle's throat. Its wings askew, the stone beast corkscrewed out of sight. Now only a few drifting feathers remained in the sky, sole mementos of the fearless doves and their fierce aerial battle.

After that, everyone took turns supporting Rolin's invisible arms. They quickly learned that lowering the candle even an inch caused the balloon to sink. Then they might fail to clear the peaks altogether. Slowly, the balloon rose.

Eventually, the craft reached those rarefied realms where the air was thin and very, very cold. It stung the lungs with an icy fire and painted the basketeers' breath on the wicker in layers of frosted lace. The children shivered uncontrollably.

Rolin glanced at the candle, which was steadily burning down. If its flame went out, the balloon would certainly smash into the Tartellans, entombing its passengers forever in ice and snow.

However, Gaelathane had not forgotten His children. The breeze shifted, sweeping the craft toward an ice-choked gorge.

"You'd better brace yourselves!" Rolin shouted. "We may be in for a bumpy ride." The chill winds picked up speed, funneling the balloon into the ice chasm's mouth.

"Oooh!" screamed the basketeers as the crevasse walls' blue-green ice blurred by. The wind howled and moaned around the craft as it careered down the crooked glacial canyon.

Ahead, a huge icefall waited to impale the craft on its bristling crystal daggers. Banshee winds shrieked through the bottleneck. Rolin raised the candle, but the balloon rose only sluggishly.

Just when a collision seemed sure, Marlis seized the lightstaff and aimed it at the jumbled ice. A white-hot beam lanced out, blasting a steaming hole in the ice jam. The balloon squeaked through. In a final act of spite, the winds snuffed out the candle before spitting the craft out the Tartellans' other side.

Beyond, the Green Sea's misty waters stretched to the skyline like a vast, lonely lake. Rolin allowed himself only a quick glance at those mysterious waves. With no way to relight the useless candle stub, he had to find someplace to set down the balloon. Unfortunately, the Tartellans' heavily timbered slopes offered no suitable landing spots. The trees rose up to meet them.

"We're going to crash!" the visibles groaned.

Skimming the treetops, the basket clipped a tall fir. "Get down and hold tight!" Rolin shouted. The balloon sailed on before ricocheting off a pine, which showered everyone with snow and dry, dead needles. Then the forest fell away into a snowless valley, and a wave of warm, moist air greeted the weary travelers.

Sheltered by the Green Sea on one side and the Tartellans on the other, this pleasant vale was Thalmos's last haven from the snarks. Here grew trees found nowhere else in the land. Some resembled cinnamon-barked madrones but with smaller, fragrant leaves. Others recalled evergreen oaks. Even magnolias and rhododendrons bravely bloomed in the lee of the mountains.

Gliding over this lowland forest, the carriage again grazed the tips of the trees, sending its panicked passengers sprawling. The tortured wickerwork creaked and groaned. With a sickening *crunch*, the balloon fetched up against a spruce and crashed through its prickly canopy. At the last moment, the bag snagged on a branch, arresting the basket scant feet off the ground. There it dangled, dizzily swinging back and forth like a clock pendulum.

When the basket stopped swaying, the invisibles were the first to stagger out. Then they helped Evan and Bronwen jump down. Arlan followed, tumbling head-over-heels as he landed. Last of all, after lowering the gold chest in its pillowcase wrapping, Elena climbed out of the carriage and dropped to the ground.

"Where did the *whilfildigig* go?" she asked. The balloon had disappeared as if by magic.

"Maybe it blew away," said Evan, though there was no wind.

It was Marlis who solved the mystery. "It's still in the tree!" she exclaimed, pointing upward with a stick.

"Where?" Arlan demanded. "I don't see nothin'."

"Look right above you. It's stuck on that big limb." Sure enough, the balloon was still lodged high in the spruce, having shrunk back to its original size.

"We'll never git it down from there—and my bow's still in it!" Arlan cried. "What if the grakkles find us here?"

"My sling!" Evan wailed. "I want my sling back!"

Rolin laid a hand on Evan's arm. "I doubt we'll be needing either the sling or the bow," he said. "From now on, Gaelathane will be fighting our battles for us. Anyway, I still have my lightstaff."

"How will we ever get home again?" Bronwen asked, her eyes brimming. Now Evan was weeping, too.

Rolin said, "Don't you remember what Gaelathane told us?

Bag and basket, wax and sling,
Now swell in service to the King,
And take My servants to the tree,
That opens on their own country.

"Then we're looking for a *passage* tree?" said Elena doubtfully.

"Yes—to Lucambra," Rolin replied. Seeing no torsils nearby, his heart sank. Everything depended upon finding the right tree.

"Rolin," Marlis choked out. "It's the wrong time of year for torsil travel. Even if we did find a tree of passage, its branches would be bare. Winter is here, and all the trees are asleep!"

Chapter 32

GREENLEAF

R olin groaned. "I hadn't thought of that." Why would
Gaelathane bring them all the way across the Tartellans on
the verge of winter, only to strand them on the shores of the
Green Sea without food or shelter?

"What did Marlis mean by, 'the wrong time of year'?" asked
Elena nervously. She scanned the sky as if in fear of grakkles.

"Trees of passage can only take you places when they're in leaf,"
Rolin glumly explained. "We'll have to stay here until spring ar-
rives and the torsils awake."

Elena's face tightened. "I knew this whole whilfildigig business
was a bad idea from the beginning. What will we do now with
winter at our doorstep? How will we live without our cave?"

"Some of these trees still have leaves," Evan said, peering into
the forest. "They're very pretty. Maybe they can help us."

"I know, dear boy, but they're the wrong kind of tree," Marlis
said. "What we need is a torsil that's still—"

"I beg-a your pardon," huffed a grumbly voice. "We are-a the
right kind, if I don't mistake your meaning."

Rolin glanced about, seeing only several thick-leaved evergreens
resembling ancient, sprawling laurels. "Who said that?"

"It was Marlis, silly," Elena shot back. "Unless you're hearing
the wind in the trees or the waves on the shore."

"Greenleaf the torsil is-a my name," the voice blithely went on. It belonged to one of the spreading evergreens whose trunk was as big around as the royal table in the Hallowfast's high-vaulted dining hall. "Who are you, two-legs?"

"Rolin son of Gannon, king of Lucambra and tree friend," Rolin replied. "I am pleased to make your acquaintance."

"Pardon me, but I am Marlis daughter of Nelda, *queen* of Lucambra," added his wife pointedly.

"I'm-a very honored to meet you both," said Greenleaf, waving his boughs. "Few two-legs ever come-a this way to see me."

Touching the tree's tortoiseshell bark, Rolin sensed its lively and indomitable spirit. However, the leaves were longer and glossier than any torsil's he had ever seen. He stroked his stubbly face. "You don't look like a torsil."

"Who doesn't look like a torsil?" Elena asked her husband. "I hope he doesn't mean me. Maybe his eyes are going bad."

Arlan shrugged. "Them invisibles live in their own world. It's hard tellin' what goes on between 'em. We shouldn't meddle."

"If you're a tree of passage, why haven't you lost your leaves?" Marlis asked the tree. "I've never met an evergreen torsil."

Greenleaf chuckled dryly. "All-a oaks are-a not alike, are they? Some-a shed their leaves in-a the cold season, while others stay green year 'round, as-a we *wylligen* trees of passage do."

"You never sleep in winter, then?" the invisibles asked.

"Of course, but not as long or as deeply as-a my cousins to the east. I nap a little *herren*, a little *therren*, so as not to miss anything on-a either side. 'Tis a grand life, if I do say so myself."

Rolin's heart leapt. Was Greenleaf a time torsil after all? "My companions and I are on an errand for the King of the Trees. We seek a tree of passage to take us *therren* in the Land of Light."

"Mother, who is Uncle Rolin talking to?" asked Evan.

Elena bit her nails and frowned. "I haven't the foggiest idea."

"Maybe they've met some other invisibles in these woods," said Arlan. "I always thought there must be more of 'em."

His wife tossed her head. "Ones that we can't see *or* hear? Those two have gone daft as a drunken worggle, if you ask me."

The tree's leaves rustled. "The Land of Light is no longer *herren*. If-a my limbs lift you *therren*, you must-a promise to return before *nerren's* darkness swallows all."

Rolin balked at the unfamiliar word. Nerren. 'Nowhere-and-no-when'? The torsil must mean Limbo.

"Who are the other two-legs with you?" Greenleaf asked.

"These are our friends, Arlan, Elena, Bronwen and Evan," Rolin said. "Visibles, may I introduce Greenleaf the Lucambra torsil."

Arlan smirked at Elena and twirled a stubby forefinger around his ear. "This tree has a name, does it?" he sneered.

"Of course," Marlis replied. "People and animals have names. Why shouldn't trees? They're living things, too."

"Well spoken," rumbled Greenleaf. "Though my-a name may be-a rather common for a tree, I am still-a quite proud of it."

Elena sputtered, "Yes, but surely you can't *talk* with them."

"Why not?" Rolin said. "Just because trees don't move doesn't mean they can't talk. Besides, Waganupa speaks to us."

"That's different," Elena argued. "This is just an ordinary *wooden* tree. It's as deaf and mute as a stone, if you ask me."

Bronwen put her ear to the trunk and listened. Her expression soured with disappointment. "If it can talk, why can't *we* hear it?"

"You could if you—oh, snakes and yeg snouts," Marlis fussed. "Please just trust us for now. We'll explain it all later."

"If 'later' ever comes!" snorted Elena. Scorn oozed from every pore in her face and dripped from her tongue.

Thump! Rolin stomped his foot, putting a stop to the quarrel. "Whether you believe us or not, we still must be on the other side of this torsil before sunset. Tree-climbing isn't safe after dark."

"It won't be safe on th' ground then, either," said Arlan. He jerked his thumb toward the encircling woods, where sinister shapes slunk among the shadows. Luminous eyes stared unblinking back at the basketeers. "Wolves, I'll be bound."

"Everybody up the tree and no dawdling," said Rolin briskly. "When you reach the top, climb down again—and do try to stay out of each other's way."

"Oh, we'll stay out of your way, all right," Elena muttered. "As far out of your way as we possibly can!"

While Arlan fended off the wolves with a few well-aimed rocks, the others shinnied into the torsil's crown. Ignoring the yellow eyes boring into his back, Arlan then sized up Greenleaf. "A cockamamie talkin' tree, eh?" he grunted. "Let's see what 'Greenleaf' here has to say about a friendly little jab."

Thunk. The stocky Thalmosian ran Rolin's knife blade deep into the torsil's trunk. Then he used the handle as a springboard to launch himself into the tree—and none too soon. With a lunge, a scrawny wolf snapped at his heels.

Sitting on a branch, Arlan pitched more stones at the snarling beasts. "Thought you'd catch yerselfs some dinner, did ye?" he taunted them. After retrieving the knife, he sneered, "Jest like I thought. Nary a word o' complaint. This tree cain't no more talk than fly." He would soon regret his rashness.

Chapter 33

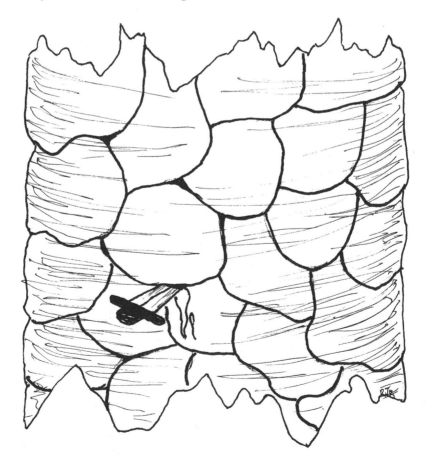

INSULTS AND INJURIES

Rolin was the first to climb down from Greenleaf. On its Lucambrian side, the torsil overlooked a broad ravine where crickets chirped in the pooling twilight. Rich with the sweet, earthy scents of leaf and blossom, the warm evening breeze bespoke a glorious summer. Then another whisper of air announced Marlis's presence. "Glory to Gaelathane, Lucambra is still in one piece, wherren*ever* we are," she quipped.

After helping Bronwen and Evan out of the tree, the invisibles escorted Elena to solid earth. Looking up into the torsil, she asked, "Where's Arlan? I thought he was right behind me."

"I'm sure he'll be along soon," Rolin assured her, also wondering why the Thalmosian was so slow to make passage.

When he finally appeared at the top of the tree, Arlan seemed confused and unsteady. Rolin had forgotten to warn him about the dizziness and tingling that often accompany torsil travel.

All at once, the tree violently whiplashed like a wet dog shaking itself off. "Help!" Arlan cried, wrapping both arms around Greenleaf's shuddering trunk. He began to slip off.

"What in the name of Elgathel has gotten into that tree?" exclaimed Rolin in astonishment. Never before had he seen such behavior in a torsil or any other tree, for that matter.

"Maybe a storm has come up on the other side," Marlis suggested. "I've heard the Green Sea can brew some nasty squalls."

Seeing her husband losing his grip on the torsil, a horror-stricken Elena shouted, "Hang on, Arlan! I'm coming!"

Just as Elena reached Greenleaf, another spasm seized the tree, dislodging its hapless climber. Arlan bounced from one branch to the next before crashing to the ground.

"I thought you said these trees were safe!" cried Elena reproachfully as she rushed to her prostrate husband's side. "Arlan! Arlan! Are you all right?" Arlan's eyes fluttered open and his lips moved soundlessly. His face turned purple.

"What . . . happened?" he groaned.

"You fell out of the tree, silly goose," Elena tearfully told him. "Don't try to talk until you get your wind back."

"Papa! Papa!" cried Evan and Bronwen, running to their father.

"Something's not right here," Rolin muttered to Marlis. Sidling over to Greenleaf, he put his ear to the trunk. What the torsil told him made his blood run cold.

A split second later, Arlan abruptly sat up, his head lolling. Then he catapulted off the ground. Dangling in midair, his tunic bunched around his neck and feet comically flapping, he resembled a loose-limbed puppet. However, one had only to look at the man's bulging, terrified eyes to know it was no joke.

"You bloody fool!" Rolin roared. "You could have gotten us all killed! I never should have trusted a Thalmosian." With every word, Arlan's body shook like a rat in the jaws of a bull terrier.

"Rolin!" Marlis gasped. "Have you lost your senses?"

"Stop it! You let go of my Arlan this instant!" shrilled Elena, beating her clenched fists on Rolin's back.

The children tugged on Rolin's legs. "You put our daddy down right now!" they cried. Then Bronwen kicked him in the shins.

Still hanging helplessly in Rolin's grip, Arlan gurgled, "I cain't breathe! Let me go! I didn't do nothin'!"

"We'll see about that," was Rolin's grim reply. He dragged Arlan to the torsil and thrust his face against Greenleaf's gashed trunk. "Now do you understand what you've done?"

"It's only a little cut," Arlan whimpered. Rolin released him and he collapsed on the ground in a heap.

"That 'little cut,' as you put it, could have cost us our lives," Rolin snarled. "When we told you trees can talk, didn't you stop to think they could also hear and feel? 'Let's see what Greenleaf here has to say about a friendly little jab,' you said. 'This tree cain't no more talk than fly,' you said."

Arlan hung his head. "How did ye know?"

"Greenleaf told me everything, of course."

"I—I'm sorry," he said. "I didn't think I was doin' no harm."

"Well, you did. Plenty of it, too," Rolin darkly replied. "Don't apologize to me, either. Greenleaf's the one you stabbed."

Arlan touched the clear, sticky sap oozing from the knife wound. Then he raised his eyes to the torsil's leafy crown. "I'm sorry," he hoarsely repeated. "I didn't mean to hurt . . . you."

"Greenleaf says not to mention it," Rolin said, his tone softening. "Just don't ever do anything like that again."

Arlan rubbed the scrapes on his back and belly where he had landed on tree limbs. "I won't. I promise. Say, kin we do anything to make th' cut mend faster? Smear a little mud on it, maybe?"

"That's a good idea, but Gaelathane designed tree-flesh to heal on its own without any help from us two-legs," Rolin replied.

"Two-*what?*"

"Two-legs. You know—people."

"Oh." Arlan's brow knitted. "If the wound will mend on its own, why make such a ruckus over it?"

By now, Marlis, Elena, Bronwen and Evan had drawn a subdued little knot around the two men, hanging on their every word. The children were sniffling and wiping their eyes.

Rolin traced two circles in the dust, one marked "L" and the other, "T." "It's all a matter of trust," he said. "After your knife attack, Greenleaf could have refused us passage, exiling us in Thalmos or worse yet, between worlds." Drawing a spiral between the circles, Rolin described how he and Marlis had escaped Limbo with Gaelathane's help, only to find themselves invisible.

"No wonder ye were so upset about Greenleaf," said Arlan. "Ye're sayin' we four could have ended up like ye, if th' tree hadn't let us all th' way through?"

"Or else Greenleaf might have heaved us all out on our faces, as he did you," Rolin said. "Fortunately for us, our friend is fairly tolerant as torsils go."

"Trees of passage are a clannish lot," Marlis explained. "Mistreat one and all the others for miles around will hear of it and have nothing more to do with you. Some trees have been known to shut out *every* two-legs, deservedly or not. A torsil revolt can close off an entire world, often for hundreds of years."

"Can all the trees hear and understand us?" asked Bronwen.

"Indeed they can," said Marlis. "Gaelathane has endowed every living kind with its own special language, from the frogs in the pond to the eagles in their eyries. They are able to understand each other, and us as well—"

"But we can't understand *them*," Bronwen said crossly. "Must we become invisible like you to talk with the trees?"

"Certainly not!" Rolin said. "The gift of understanding comes only through breathing the scent of amenthil flowers. If you plant the nuts Gaelathane gave you and cultivate the trees that grow from them, some day you'll receive the gift, too."

Bronwen's hazel eyes shone. Then her face fell. "That would take years and years. I'll be grown up by then."

Arlan scuffled his feet before offering the air a callused hand. "Cain't say I blame ye fer roughin' me up, Rolin. Seein' how things stand, I s'ppose I had it coming."

"Not necessarily," Rolin said as he shook the other man's hand. "It is I who should apologize for losing my temper."

The other visibles gawked at Arlan and then at each other. "You've changed, Papa!" Bronwen exclaimed.

"What do you mean?" asked Marlis.

Arlan grinned wryly. "I used to have a mean streak longer than a wounded skraal's. The fact is, one reason th' other families around Peton moved away was my cussed orneriness."

"Not to mention my sharp tongue," Elena confessed with an embarrassed laugh. "I'd say Gaelathane has changed us both for the better—and the children, too."

Linking hands with Marlis, Rolin said, "He's changed us all for the better! Now, since we don't know our way around this part of Lucambra, we'd best keep our eyes open." He picked up a stick and waved it so the others could follow him.

Surprise sparked in Elena's eyes. "Wait a minute. You're not making sense again. I thought you said Lucambra was no more."

Rolin coughed apologetically. "That's only partly true. In time to come, Lucambra *may* be no more. It's difficult to explain."

The visibles looked at one another in stark bewilderment. "There they go again, talkin' in riddles," said Arlan, rolling his eyes. Elena scratched her head and frowned.

Then Rolin had to explain the special quirks of time torsils. "That's how we got into your world in the first place," he concluded. "Even we didn't know about those torsils before."

"So Greenleaf is our only way home?" Bronwen asked with an anxious look. "What if he won't let us back through?"

"Don't worry," Marlis said. "He will. Even if he doesn't, we'll just find another Lucambra torsil that can take you and your family *wherren* you wish to go."

"What about grakkles?" Evan asked, peering at the sky.

"You won't find a single one in this world," Rolin told him. *Though there may be yegs, if we've gone too far back in time.*

CHAPTER 34

PERCEL SON OF PELLAGOR

Bidding Greenleaf farewell, the torsil travelers hiked into the rocky hills. Rolin took the lead, keeping a lookout for gorks lurking among the trees or yegs flying overhead. He saw none. Woods and sky were strangely empty.

After a half-mile or so, he came to an overgrown dirt road cut into the hillside. Rolin's sharp eyes picked out fresh footprints in the dust. He was bending over to study the tracks when Arlan blundered into him from behind and knocked him down.

"Will ye look at this! A road. Who d' ye suppose made it?"

"I have no idea," Rolin replied as he got up and spat dirt out of his mouth. The visibles could be so careless sometimes!

Arlan glanced both ways along the brushy track. "I say we go left." He nodded south, where the road wound among pleasant green hills wreathed in a lazy summer haze. Northward, the road climbed higher, snaking up steep slopes and clinging to cliffs.

Elena agreed. "Let's avoid heights if we can. After being stuck in that grakkles' nest, I never want to see another cliff again!"

"Then it's decided," Rolin said, graciously bowing to the visibles' wishes. "You two go on ahead. Marlis and I will follow with the children. We don't want to frighten off any fellow wayfarers."

"We don't know where we're going!" Elena protested.

"Neither do we," said Rolin dryly. "Even if we did, things may have changed for the worse since we last lived here."

Arlan cast a wary glance down the still-deserted road. "I hope they ain't changed too much," he said. Then the six set out for the southlands.

It was a perfect evening for a midsummer eve's stroll. Long-limbed tree-shadows slumbered on the sloping lane. Along its verges, tall spikes of nodding, purple-throated foxglove bells beckoned to bees and other buzzing insects.

"What are those?" asked Bronwen. She pointed to some winking lights weaving over the path in the balmy, deepening dusk.

"We call them 'firflaegen'—'fireflies,' in your tongue," Marlis replied. "They often fly about on warm evenings. Haven't you ever seen one before?"

Bronwen shook her head. "Can they hurt us?"

"No, they're perfectly harmless. Catch one and you'll see."

Evan and Bronwen rushed down the road, swatting at the tiny, blinking beetles. The fireflies evaded them until one flew straight into Bronwen's clutches.

She peered into her cupped hands at the warm, yellowish light, exclaiming at its brightness. Then Evan caught one, too. He opened his hands and cried out as his captive escaped. The creature circled his head before it flew into the forest.

"Come back!" he wailed. Chasing the elusive spot of light, Evan stumbled and fell on the road. "She's gone!" he wept, smearing streaks across his tear-stained face with dirty hands.

"Don't cry; we can catch lots more just like it," said Bronwen soothingly. "Here—you can have this one."

"No! I want mine! She had a pretty face and hands and—"

"Your eyes were just playing tricks on you," said Elena. "It's too dark to see clearly. Anyway, bugs don't have faces."

"This one did! She even smiled and winked at me."

Arlan helped his son up. "Winking bugs. Who ever heard o' sech a thing? Let's move along now." Just then, stones rattled. The visibles froze as a grizzled head bobbed into view. An old man was toiling up the road, toting two dripping buckets. When Arlan cleared his throat, the stranger cried out and dropped both buckets, staggering back with terror in his green eyes.

"Wh-who are you?" he croaked. Rolin put down his walking stick and withdrew with Marlis to the side of the road to avoid getting in the way. He didn't want the old man dying of fright.

"Don't be afraid," said Elena with a disarming smile. "We're not going to hurt you." She helped the trembling stranger pick up his sloshing water buckets.

Arlan introduced himself and his family. "Sorry fer startlin' ye. We're jest travelers on our way to—" He stopped, flustered.

"To the next town," Elena smoothly filled in for him.

The stranger found his voice again. "The next town? The nearest town—if you can call it that—is a month's journey from here."

"Then we're lost!" Elena said with theatrical despair.

Arlan put in, "We used to live a fur piece from here. We was the last to leave. All th' others left years ago."

The old man's face relaxed and he nodded sympathetically. "I'm the last, too—leastways in these parts. Moved down here thirty years back to get away from the—to find someplace quieter. Haven't seen another living soul since. That's why you four gave me such a fright."

"You've lived by yourself all that time?" Bronwen asked.

"That's right. A lonely life it's been, too. I'd be honored if you'd spend the night. My home's as plain as can be, but it's snug and dry. The name's Percel, by the way; Percel son of Pellagor."

Elena's eyes lit up. "It would be a pleasure!" Shouldering the golden chest in its pillowcase, she gave her husband a "don't-say-another-word" look. Arlan meekly fell in behind her as she followed the kindly old Lucambrian back up the road. Evan and Bronwen came next, toting Percel's water buckets. Rolin and Marlis brought up the rear, their stomachs growling.

"Let's hope the old fellow won't mind two more *invisible* mouths to feed," Rolin whispered to his wife. "I'm starving."

"Me, too. I could eat a whole skraal, bones and all!"

At a twisted yew, their guide cut sharply to the right and trotted briskly down the barest hint of a trail until he reached a giant, fern-shrouded fir log. Beside it grew a tall Tree sapling, evidently the hermit's sythan-ar.

Reaching through the tangled ferns, Percel opened a small door in one end of the log. "Welcome to my home!" he said shyly.

Bronwen and Evan gasped, "You live in *there?*"

"Now, children, it's no different than living in a cave," Elena chided them as she wriggled through. With fearful glances, the other visibles followed. Percel entered last, unwittingly closing and latching the door in Rolin's face. Now he and Marlis would have to sleep under the stars, unless the log had a back entrance. The forest suddenly seemed very dark and dreadful.

"How do you suppose the hermit brings in fresh air to breathe?" Rolin wondered aloud. With Marlis in tow, he crawled beside the fir until he reached a large, neat hole bored near the underside of the log. Putting his eye to it, he saw the visibles seated together on a bench carved into one wall of the hollow log. Percel sat across from them on a similar ledge. In the middle stood a crude table fashioned from a stump. Pots, pans and other utensils hung from the walls and ceiling, which gave off the soft, greenish-yellow glow of moonwood.

". . . just about to sit down to supper," Percel was saying. "You're welcome to join me. It's simple fare. If I were expecting company, I'd have roasted a few turtles." Bronwen turned green.

The old man rolled the stump aside, releasing a cloud of pungent steam that sent the visibles into coughing fits. Rolin's eyes smarted. After lifting some burlap bags out of the floor, Percel moved the "table" back into place.

Apologizing for the stench, he explained, "My first winter in this log, I noticed steam rising out of the ground all around it. Turns out there's a hot spring right under our feet. Once I'd chopped through wood to reach dirt, it didn't take much digging to hit water. Then I filled the hole with stones to keep it from caving in. Now I can boil water and cook my meals on the hot rocks and even heat my log during cold spells." He added, "You get used to the smell after a few days."

Percel dumped the sacks' steaming contents onto a platter. There were bundles of fat trout, lamb's-quarter greens, meadow mushrooms and fragrant fiddlehead ferns. Setting the heaping trencher on the table, the hermit announced, "Supper is served!"

Rolin's mouth watered at the toothsome cooking odors. If only his arms were long enough to reach that platter through the hole!

"Trout!" cried the visibles. In Thalmos future, fresh fish was a rare treat, since eelomars love fish—and fishermen, too, when they can get them. Next, the hermit brought out bowls of sweet strawberries and almondy juneberries. Before you could say "trout-and-fiddleheads," Percel and the Thalmosians had devoured practically everything in sight.

The hermit wiped his mouth. "There's nothing finer than a nice mess of fish," he sighed. Though stooped with age, Percel wore the well-muscled look of a much younger man. His work-hardened hands rested on a wide leather belt cinched around his green tunic. A bushy gray beard flowed down his front.

"Evan, why don't you help clear up?" Elena suggested. "Just scrape the plates into that water bucket and dump it *outside*."

Over Percel's protests, Evan scooped up the leftovers and headed down the log. The next thing Rolin knew, the door had opened and Evan was whispering, "Uncle Rolin! Aunt Marlis!" Rolin waved his staff to help the boy find them.

Evan's teeth flashed white in the staff light. "There you are! I brought you something to eat." He set the bucket on the ground.

The king and queen thanked him. "You'd better go back now," said Rolin. "We don't want Percel coming out here after you."

When Evan had left, Marlis and Rolin offered a short prayer of thanks to Gaelathane for the meal. Then they fell to, gobbling up every last morsel and crumb.

After eating, Rolin noticed Evan was still standing at the log-end amidst what appeared to be a swarm of fireflies. All at once, one of the larger lights broke away to flutter in front of the boy's face. When Evan held out his hand, the tiny form alit on it for a breathless moment. Then it darted off, leaving something behind in Evan's palm. Whooping, he dove back through the door.

Rolin knelt at his vent hole in time to spy Evan bursting into Percel's "kitchen," his hair askew and eyes agleam. "I saw her again! She came back and I got to hold her!"

Arlan and Elena glanced askance at each another. "Who came back?" Elena demanded.

"The firefly girl—the same one I saw before!"

Arlan's eyebrows bristled. "Ye mean ye saw another *firefly?*"

"No, he saw what he saw," said Percel softly.

White-lipped, Elena wheeled on the hermit. "Don't tell me you believe in this rubbish, too! What did he see, then? Fairies?"

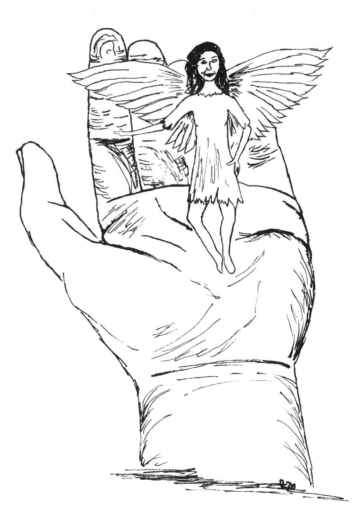

"Some might call them that, but to me they're *gwelies*—'Bed People.' There's nothing hurtful, sly or sneaky about them—unlike some gnomes and wood sprites."

"Bed People!" cried Bronwen, laughing. "What a funny name. Why do you call them that?"

Smiling wryly, Percel explained, "Because I sometimes awaken at night to find them hovering about my bed, as if they were watching over me. Often they bring me gifts from the forest."

"Hmph!" Elena snorted. "I still say it's all poppycock."

Percel asked Evan, "What did she look like, young fellow?"

Evan held his thumb and forefinger some three inches apart. "She was about this high, and she had wings an' hair and tiny hands an' feet. I think she was trying to talk to me."

"A likely story," Arlan grunted.

"More likely than most," Percel said with a thoughtful look. "Did she give you anything? A stone or a leaf or a berry?"

Evan nodded and opened his hand. Inside was a delicate pink blossom. "It smells good, but it gave me a headache," he said.

"Let me see! Let me see!" cried Bronwen, pressing her face into Evan's palm. "How lovely! It does smell sweet." Then she sneezed twice and rubbed her watering eyes.

"What's wrong?" Elena asked sharply.

"My head hurts, that's all." Bronwen steadied herself against the table and pinched the bridge of her nose.

Arlan picked up the blossom by its stem and sniffed it. "A fairy flower, eh?" he said. "Looks ord'nary enough to me. I've never seen the like of it before, though. Here, dear—ye try it."

Elena warily put the flower to her nose. Then her hand flew to her forehead and she collapsed onto the bench. "Oh, dear," she exclaimed. "That scent has set my head to spinning!"

Arlan blinked and rubbed his forehead. Then he sat down heavily. "Does it feel like a nail driven right betwixt yer eyes?" he asked. His wife and daughter nodded.

When her head had cleared, Bronwen scraped some of the glowing, greenish-yellow specks off the ceiling. "These look like tiny fireflies, only brighter," she remarked. "What are they?"

"Moonwood," Percel replied. "You've never seen it before?"

Bronwen shook her head. "It does look a little like moonlight."

"Only greener," said Evan as he picked off more pieces.

"Blast!" Rolin muttered. He'd neglected to tell the visibles that Lucambrians used luminescent fungus-wood to light their homes.

Percel shot Arlan a shrewd look. "Tell me the truth now: Where are you all *really* from?"

Arlan's jaw went slack. "We're Thalmosians," he confessed.

A knowing smile creased Percel's seamed face. "I thought as much. You should have told me so in the first place. I wouldn't have treated you any differently."

"What gave us away?" Elena asked.

"To begin with, your eyes aren't green. Moreover, you told me you were going on 'to the next town.' Lucambrians have never built towns. Our settlements are so small and scattered, you wouldn't recognize one if you stood smack in the middle of it. Just now, when Bronwen let on that she'd never seen moonwood before, I knew something was amiss. Every Lucambrian lad and lass has seen moonwood." Percel paused. "However, it was the flower that clinched it."

"What do you mean?" asked Evan.

"Your gwely gave you an *amenthil* blossom."

Bronwen squealed with glee. "Now I can understand the trees!"

Percel's eyes clouded. "So you do know about the amenthils. Who told you about them, and why did you come to Lucambra?"

The visibles squirmed while Rolin and Marlis held their breath. "It was Gaelathane," Elena stiffly answered. "He sent us here."

CHAPTER 35

RIDDLE ON THE HALF-SHELL

Gaelathane!" Percel cried, jumping up. "Why didn't you say so in the first place? I've been expecting you!"

"You've been expecting us?" repeated the mystified visibles. "How could you have known we were coming?"

"I'll show you." The hermit disappeared behind a curtain dividing the kitchen from the rear of the log. He returned with a curved section of wood resembling the half-shell of a hollow tree.

Bronwen touched the wood. "What is it?"

"An heirloom, you might say," Percel replied in hushed tones. "It has been handed down in my late wife's family for many generations." He paused to wipe a tear from his eye. "If only my son Ansel were here, I would pass it on to him."

"What happened to him?" asked Evan.

Percel sighed. "When I left our home, he refused to join me. Ansel has always dreamed of following in his forebears' footsteps, reviving the fame and glory of the Old Kingdom. For all I know, he's still picking through the Hallowfast's ruins for a bit of gold to claim as his inheritance. I doubt I shall ever see him again."

Elena's brow furrowed. "Inheritance? Do you mean—?"

"Yes. If there weren't so few of us left, Ansel would be king."

"King!" Rolin choked on the word. How could a hermit's son be of royal descent? Then it came to him. Ansel son of *Percel*. The gaunt, pathetic figure Felgor had chased into the Tower of the Tree. The last Lucambrian.

"Were you also a king?" asked the children excitedly.

Percel shook his head sadly. "I'm just a common man. Besides, it's been years since a monarch has sat on Lucambra's throne. After King Rolin and Queen Marlis disappeared, Bembor son of Brenthor ruled as chancellor in their place, refusing to usurp the royal title or crown. His grandson—I don't recall his name—"

Scanlon, Rolin silently mouthed, straining to catch Percel's words. *My dear friend Scanlon. Will I ever see you again?*

". . . was to ascend the throne after Bembor's death, but he also vanished after years of searching in vain for the missing king and queen. After that, the monarchy dissolved, though those in Rolin's line have kept records of their lineage."

"So Rolin and Marlis really *were* king and queen of Lucambra!" cried Bronwen. The elder visibles turned red and put their fingers to their lips. Bronwen shrank against the wall.

Percel gave her a curious look. "You speak as if you knew them personally. Anyway, inscribed on this piece of wood are the words of Gaelathane, Who appeared to Ansel's great-great-grandfather Elwyn in his home tree after he had lost his parents."

Rolin's head swam. *Elwyn*. His playful, red-haired son had been only eight on the day of the fateful picnic. Would Rolin ever live to see his boy grow to manhood?

"Gaelathane warned Elwyn to go into hiding, because the sorcerer Felgor was seeking to destroy him," the hermit went on. "Before He left, the King wrote some words on the wall with His finger. Later, Elwyn cut out that part of the trunk to take with him on his journeys." Percel turned over the wooden relic. On its curving inner side, gleaming letters flashed greenish-gold in the moonwood light. He squinted as he read the fine, flowing script:

When visions fail and faces pale,
When sword and staff cannot avail
Against the deep and nightmare sleep
That snatches simple, trusting sheep;
Lift up thine eyes; in prayer prevail!

While silver snare strikes unawares,
Be not beguiled; Beware! Beware!
For terror stalks beneath the trees,
In search of foolish souls to seize,
And drag into its deadly lair!

When few the faithful in My fold—
The flock for which My blood was sold—
Still stagger on the stricken earth,
And one remains of royal birth,
Then look for strangers bearing gold!

Though foreign be their native land,
And little they may understand
Of Me, and of My mighty works,
Despise them not, and do not shirk
To give them freely from thy hand!

In number six, yet only four
Shall darken the threshold of thy door;
The thing they bring is not for thee,
But in time will unravel the mystery
Of all the departed, gone on before.

Of gold and jewels, no fairer prize
Has ever met mere mortal eyes,
Yet empty now it must remain
—though soon to be the black trees' bane—
When locked, it swiftly will arise . . .

The hermit broke off, gripping the block of wood with white-knuckled hands. "Don't you see?" he cried. "The riddle must be speaking of you four! You're from a foreign land—Thalmos—and you've brought the *thing* here, haven't you?"

Elena clutched the cloth-covered chest to her bosom. "You can't have this. It belongs to the Keeper and to him alone!"

"Don't be afraid," Percel reassured her. "I won't rob you. I only wish to see it, to know for certain you're the ones."

Arlan reluctantly nodded, and Elena set her lumpy pillow-case on the table. Out of habit, the visibles stood, clasped hands and began the old, familiar chant, "The ball has been, the ball will be—" Their voices faltered. The second verse had already come true, for the key to the chest was found. "Until it fulfills its destiny," Elena improvised. Then she unveiled the golden orb.

Percel gasped. "'Of gold and jewels, no fairer prize has ever met mere mortal eyes.'" He turned to Elena. "May I touch it?"

She cracked a strained smile. "I suppose." The children's eyes grew round. No *visible* outsider had ever touched the ball.

Percel reverently ran his fingers across the sphere's gem-studded surface. "It's true, it's all true!" he wept. "I once thought the riddle was just a children's rhyme. Yet here you are, Thalmosians all, with your magnificent golden ball." He paused. "Aren't there supposed to be six of you?"

Elena blanched. "We were six, but the other two had . . . an accident on our way here."

Rolin let out a relieved sigh. Matters were awkward enough without bringing in an invisible king and queen who were supposedly long dead.

"I'm very sorry," said Percel soberly. "The riddle does say that only four will darken my door. Tell me, though, who crafted this exquisite piece of metalwork, and what is its purpose?"

"We only know that th' first Keeper made it," Arlan replied. "That ball's been in our family fer generations, and we was hopin' ye could tell *us* what it's fer."

Elena pointed out the words spiraling around the top of the chest. "The last part of this riddle sounds like yours: 'But now I wait with empty womb for Him to fill this golden room.'"

Percel tested the hinges. "Is there anything inside?"

With a defeated headshake, Arlan said, "When we opened it a few days ago, th' thing was as hollow as a dried-up oak gall."

"Before that, the chest was locked up tighter than an eelomar's teeth," Elena chimed in.

"No matter," said Percel. "Whatever our riddles may mean, Gaelathane will bring their words to pass in the proper time. That reminds me; I've left off the last two stanzas:

By day, direct them on their way,
Nor beg them tarry, nor delay
To point the path where peril looms,
Nor fear they'll falter in the gloom;
I hold their hearts; they cannot stray.

Faint not when dusky days grow grim,
But place undying trust in Him,
Whose promises are true and sure,
To those whose hearts and minds are pure—
While one still lives, the land endures.

The hermit frowned. "If these verses also refer to your family, it appears I'll be sending you all on your way first thing tomorrow. I had hoped to enjoy your company a while longer."

"Oh, but we simply couldn't presume further upon your hospitality," Elena demurred. "Besides, we really must be leaving by daybreak. Rol—I mean *Arlan* says we still have far to travel."

"That's not the worst of it," said Percel gloomily. "If I understand these words aright, you're to go southward on 'the path where peril looms.' Death lies that way."

The visibles traded alarmed glances. "What kind of peril?"

Percel shot them a quizzical look. "The curse of our kind, you might say. It has found me even here."

"Do you mean the snarks?" asked Elena.

"No, I'm afraid this is far worse than anything in your world."

Huge-eyed, the children asked, "Worse than worggles?"

Percel laughed. "I don't know about that. Elwyn's rhyme calls it the 'silver snare,' though how a snare can 'strike' anyone is beyond me. Whatever it is, darkness follows in its wake—then folk start disappearing. By moving south of the Willowahs, I'd hoped to put all that trouble behind me."

"We're south of the Willowah Mountains!" Rolin whispered to Marlis. "Maybe we'll see some sorcs, unless they've all died out."

The hermit rubbed his face. "Just a year ago, a smoky smudge appeared among the trees a few miles south of here. It's waiting for me. I can feel it."

"What's it look like?" Arlan demanded.

Percel combed his fingers through his beard. "I don't know. Nobody does. Those who set out to capture or kill it—if it can be killed—never return. That's why I dread sending you south."

Rolin thought he knew what was causing the "trouble": The Eye of Limbo. Still, how could the starglass travel all about the countryside without someone to carry it, and who save Felgor could touch the tube without eventually being sucked into it? Perhaps the sorcerer possessed more than one of the infernal devices and had scattered them across the land.

The land. What had Percel just read? *While one still lives, the land endures.* Rolin recalled similar words, though not Gaelathane's: *When I have wooed the watchers all, this world shall share their fate . . .*

Rolin shivered. By some unwritten rule of torsildom, when the last Lucambrian tumbled into Limbo, the Land of Light would join him. If events followed their natural course, it was only a matter of time until Percel fell prey to the starglass. Then his son Ansel's life would be forfeit to Felgor.

"Feels a mite stuffy in here," the hermit remarked. "Maybe it's just me. I haven't been well of late. Now where's that vent?" All at once, a moss-green eye filled Rolin's field of vision. Transfixed, he stared back, fearing his invisibility had worn off.

"Too dark to see anything out there," Percel muttered. "Probably those dratted moles have plugged up my vents again. I'll fix them!" Rolin jerked back just as one of the hermit's cedar-bark sandals rammed through the hole.

"This one's clear," Percel grunted. "The hole on the other side must be blocked." The old man clapped Arlan on the back. "But I'm a poor host. You and your family must be weary from your travels. I'll fetch some blankets and you can bed down on these benches." After he had made his guests comfortable, Percel retired to his own room behind the curtain. Soon, the visibles had fallen asleep, the grownups snoring in rhythmic, nasal drones.

In the meantime, Rolin had wrapped Marlis in his cloak, drawing her close beside him under the log's partial shelter. Lulled by the soothing sough of the night air stirring in the treetops, they both drifted off to sleep.

CHAPTER 36

PERCEL'S HOMEGOING

Rolin! Help! The log's on fire!" Groaning, Rolin pulled his cloak over his head, but Marlis yanked it away. A yellow glare lit the slumbering forest. Rubbing the sleep from his eyes, Rolin leapt up to warn Percel and the visibles of their peril, but the log was cold and dark.

Marlis clung to him. "What is it, Rolin? What's happening?"

"I don't know, but I expect we're about to find out." As he spoke, a cloud of golden fireflies burst from Percel's life tree. Wings flashing, the tiny creatures surrounded Rolin and his wife like a swarm of angry bees.

"Why, they're gwelies!" Marlis exclaimed. "Just look at them! How can they see us when nobody else can?"

The two laughed with delight at the dainty figures prancing and spinning about them. Ranging in size from mist-fine to finger-high, they bore the perfectly formed features and limbs that Evan had described. Rolin wrestled with the wind to catch and hold the words the gwelies so softly sang:

Dyma ni, dyma ni'n	We have come, we have come,
Dod ar dranc ein cyfaill cu;	Ere the beating breath is done;
I'w hebrwng y tu hwnt i'r llen	For a friend, for a friend,
At fyd o oes na ddaw i ben.	Bringing life without an end.

Dawnsio wnawn hyd y traeth   Evermore, evermore,
Hyd at dragwyddoldeb maith;   We will dance about the shore;
Oll mewn cylch canwn 'nawr   In a ring, we shall sing
Gân o glod i'r Brenin Mawr.   All our praises to the King.

All at once, the glowing cloud whirled through Rolin's and Marlis's invisible bodies, warming their hearts as it passed. The gwelies surrounded Percel's log, bathing it in blazing splendor.

Then two of the tiny forms shot up, growing into towering, radiant angels garbed in white. Wielding flaming swords, they strode right into the side of the log, reemerging seconds later with a shorter, brilliant being between them.

The three figures stopped a few feet from the invisibles and gazed seeingly down at them. Rolin's neck hairs prickled as he recognized the two taller angels. "Cristophilus and Gamalion!" he exclaimed. "What brings you here?"

"I told you we might appear when you least expected it," said Cristophilus with an angel wink. The third angel, a younger-looking version of the hermit, beamed at Rolin and Marlis with joyous recognition.

Percel's sythan-ar now shone so brightly that even the invisibles' bodies cast faint shadows. Myriads of the miniature "firefly angels" were ascending and descending upon it, filling the air with their rapturous music. Shielding their eyes with pieces of bark, Rolin and Marlis looked on as their two friends floated into the tree. The Percel angel joined them and turned to wave farewell before climbing out of sight.

Clinging to one another, the invisibles trembled like aspen leaves in the wind. "Who was the third angel?" they asked Percel's life tree. The evergreen made no reply as Gaelessa's glory faded from its branches. Then the king and queen collapsed to the ground, where a deep sleep overtook them.

Rolin jerked awake as a shrill, muffled shriek tore through Percel's log. He had been dreaming of fireflies, angels and a beardless hermit—or was it a dream? Forcing his cold-stiffened joints to move, he woke Marlis and staggered over to the log. Elena burst through the door, eyes bulging in her mottled face.

"Invisibles! Where are you?" she croaked. "Come quickly! Something terrible has happened."

Following Elena, Marlis and Rolin sprinted helter-skelter down the moonwood-lit hollow fir. "What's the matter?" Marlis panted.

Elena's lips trembled. "It's P-Percel!"

"What about him?" asked Rolin. "Is he sick?"

Elena pulled aside Percel's tattered curtain. "Worse—" The three ducked inside to find Arlan kneeling beside a makeshift bed, where the old hermit lay pale and still, his sunken eyes staring sightlessly and ashen lips upturned in a familiar smile. Arlan glanced up at his wife and mournfully shook his head.

Rolin grabbed Marlis's hand. "It was *him*, it really was him!"

"Was who?" asked Arlan. He winced as Bronwen and Evan entered the room. Seeing the rigid corpse, they began to whimper.

"Percel!" said Marlis while trying to comfort the children.

Elena dabbed her eyes. "Of course it is—or was."

"No, no!" Marlis protested. "We saw him; he's very much alive!" After hearing what Rolin and Marlis had witnessed, the visibles stared incredulously at Percel's lifeless body.

"He's dead! Can't you see that?" snapped Elena.

"His *body* is dead," Rolin corrected her. "What's left is just a husk, like an eggshell after a baby bird has hatched from it, or a butterfly's empty cocoon. The real Percel is already in Gaelessa."

Arlan's mouth fell open. "Ye're sayin' that when we die, an *angel* comes along to carry th' spirit up there?"

"More or less," Marlis replied. "The angels take you to the Tree of Life or one of its offspring. Each of us will one day climb the Tree to Gaelathane's home, just as Percel did."

"Why did he have to die now?" Bronwen wailed.

Rolin said, "For thirty years, poor Percel has been faithfully waiting for 'strangers bearing gold.' Once we arrived and he'd told us what to do, his job was done. The King called him home."

"If only you could see Percel as he is now, you would rejoice for him," Marlis added. "His smile is lighting up all of Gaelessa."

"We've just been there, too!" said Rolin. Then he told the visibles of his visit with Marlis to that blessed land.

The children flapped their arms like wings. "People up there can fly?" Bronwen exclaimed. "How exciting! Will I fly, too?"

"Of course you will," Marlis laughed. "Just like the angels!"

Rolin closed the hermit's eyes and pulled a coverlet over his shrunken form. "Let this be his final resting place. Gaelathane knows where he lies and will raise up his body on the last day."

After quietly filing out of the room, the torsil travelers helped themselves to some of Percel's nuts, smoked fish and dried fruit to eat on the road. Then they bade a sad farewell to the cozy log house. On her way out, Marlis pried a few chunks of moonwood out of the walls. "We might need some of this where we're going," she told Rolin, dropping the pieces in her bag.

Outside, Percel's sythan-ar was following its planter in death, its needles already drooping and dropping off. Rolin caressed the dying tree before starting up Percel's path with a sack of hazelnuts slung over his shoulder—for visibility as much as for food. Marlis and the visibles tagged along behind.

"What if we meet other people on the road?" asked Bronwen.

"I doubt we will," Rolin grimly replied. "Percel was the last living soul this side of the Willowahs. If we don't hurry, no Lucambrians will be left at all."

CHAPTER 37.

THE DARKEST, IVIED WOOD

Where are you bound, two-legs?" growled a deep voice from the forest. After an hour's travel, the six companions had encountered a shaggy bear shambling out of the woods beside the road.

Fearlessly meeting the bear's suspicious stare, Arlan the Lion-hearted stood his ground. "Southward, Friend Bear."

"Then beware the night-that-stalks-by-day," rumbled the beast. "If you value your lives, go back the way you came and never return!" With that, the bear lumbered into the forest.

"It's a good thing you four received the 'gift' last night," Rolin said. "Who knows what that bear would have done if Marlis or I had spoken to it!"

By midday, the road had dwindled to a miry path that soon surrendered to the encroaching forest. Steeped in shadows thicker than a winter's dripping fog, the silent, windless woods stood close-ranked, moist and muffled.

"Your staff, Rolin," Marlis reminded him. Unsheathed, the staff glowed feebly before going completely dark. Were they headed in the wrong direction? Then a bright stripe of glimmering, shimmering firefly letters spiraled down its lightless length. By rolling the rod clockwise, Rolin could just make out a string of words:

When few remain, though none know why,
Shine me to smite the silver eye,
That lures the soul to endless death,
To realms of blackness without breath.

To find the foe that tries to bind,
Seek out the music of the mind,
And enter darkest, ivied wood—
But look ye not into its hood.

Strike not a savage blow to break
The lidless eyes of the silver snake,
But let me rouse the captives all,
And conquered at His feet they'll fall.

Marlis brushed past him to touch the staff. "What does 'silver eye' mean?" she asked.

Rolin squinted through her invisible fingers at the gleaming writing. "I'm not sure. It sounds like the Eye of Limbo, though."

"So does 'silver snake.' Didn't Elwyn's riddle call it a 'silver snare' or some such thing?"

"Whatever you call it, Felgor's starglass must be hiding somewhere in these woods," Rolin said. "I just hope we find it before it finds us. I don't like the look of this place."

Elena pointed to a spot on the shining spiral. "It says here, 'To find the foe that tries to bind, seek out the music of the mind.' What an odd rhyme!"

"Shush, everyone," said Marlis. "I think I hear something." Then they all heard it: A faint ringing, as of tiny bells tinkling in the wind. Lightstaff at the ready, Rolin led the others toward the sound, tacking first this way, then that. Marlis followed at the rear of the procession, dropping bits of Percel's moonwood behind her to light the way back.

At length they came to a sluggish stream. Beyond its black waters loomed somber, leafy lumps. They had found the "ivied wood." With its thick vines and dark, glossy leaves, the creeping, clinging ivy had strangled every growing thing in that part of the wood.

The suffocating stench of death hung heavily over the forest. "We're going in *there?*" Marlis groaned.

"Only we two," Rolin said. "'When we're willing to obey, Gaelathane will *light* the way.'" He added, "Arlan, you and your family can stay here and wait for us."

"Shouldn't we go along to help you?" asked Elena.

"No, your visibility could endanger us all. Just keep an eye on our food, and don't let that gold chest out of your sight!"

Marlis left her remaining moonwood with the visibles to grant them some small comfort in the gloom. Then she took Rolin's hand, and together they waded through the murky water.

"May Gaelathane go with you!" called the visibles after them.

Once across the stream, the king and queen plunged into the jungle of rampant vines. The smell of rotting ivy recalled those long-ago afternoons when Rolin had played hide-and-seek with his friends among Beechtown's ivy-draped walls and fences.

After a half-hour of following the beguiling chimes, the two came upon a cobblestone path basking in gloriously warm sunshine. Butterflies frolicked in the sunbeams and flitted among clumps of columbines along the trail.

Hearing the music off to their right, Rolin and Marlis were about to take to the path when a mangy raccoon staggered out of the shadows on the opposite side. Its eyes blinking in the bright sunlight, the bewildered, band-tailed creature trotted down the trail toward the jingling chimes. Exchanging firm "be careful" hand squeezes, the invisibles followed.

As the path curved, the enticing music grew louder. The raccoon halted and sat up on its haunches, curiously sniffing the air.

All at once, a swirling puff of smoke engulfed the hapless animal. When the haze had cleared, the raccoon was gone.

Gripping each other's hands until their knuckles cracked, Rolin and Marlis cautiously approached the spot where the raccoon had vanished. There beside the trail lay Felgor's starglass, still as shiny as a new gilder. Watchful, eerie eyes ringed the silver tube—the "lidless eyes of the silver snake."

Rolin was pointing his staff at the starglass when a fetid, fluttering wind stirred up the dust. The Eye of Limbo rose into the air and dropped onto the path at Rolin's feet. A *flying* starglass?

As panic clutched the invisibles' hearts, an ivy-smothered maple near the trail rustled and bent over with an ominous groan. Something heavy was settling in that tree, and Rolin had a very good idea what it was.

Fangle. The name meant "wings of death." So that was how the starglass had traveled the length and breadth of Lucambra! When pickings grew slim in one spot, Felgor's invisible dragon simply moved the Eye of Limbo to a more populous place. Now the tube lay in plain view of any unsuspecting passers-by.

Unable to warn Marlis of this new peril, Rolin drew her off the path. Then he aimed his rod above the maple. The staff spat a stream of light that illumined Fangle's scaly, coiling form and froze his fanged jaws in a surprised snarl.

Crack! Under the weight of the now-visible petrified serpent, the tree came crashing down. "Stay back!" Rolin shouted to Marlis as the starglass swallowed the stone dragon whole—wings, head, tail and all. Silence returned to smother the forest.

"How did you know it was there?" Marlis whispered hoarsely.

Rolin described how the bowed tree had betrayed the invisible beast. "The starglass must only detect movement, since it hasn't reacted to our voices," he added. "Maybe those eyes aren't only for show. We'd better watch what we disturb around here."

"Just think," Marlis said. "If Gaelathane had made us visible, the starglass would have sent us both back to Limbo by now!"

"Visible or invisible, we're still at a stalemate," Rolin reminded his wife. "The 'snake' doesn't know we're here, but we don't know how to kill it without endangering the people inside."

"Doesn't your staff say we're supposed to 'smite' the starglass with it?" Marlis asked.

Rolin pointed a twig at the first stanza's second verse. "It says here to '*shine* me to smite the silver eye.' The last part even tells us not to break 'the lidless eyes of the silver snake.' If we do, it might doom our people to an eternity in Limbo."

"How are we to destroy the thing if we can't break it?"

"Maybe we're not supposed to destroy it. The last two lines say, 'But let me rouse the captives all, and conquered at His feet they'll fall.' If 'me' means the lightstaff, maybe I should shine it on those engraved silver eyes."

"No!" Marlis exclaimed. "We want to rouse the *captives*—the souls inside—not the starglass!"

Rolin eyed the Limbo lure. "How can we do that?"

"What about the glass eyepiece?" Marlis said. "You could shine your staff light through there. If that doesn't shake up our 'captives,' I don't know what will."

"You'd better move back, then," Rolin grunted. "If this staff sets off the starglass, you could be sucked in." He knelt before the tube. Its silver sheath glittered like the coils of a poisonous serpent poised to strike. If only he knew how to charm it! The flange enclosing the eyepiece even resembled a cobra's flaring cowl. Had he read a warning against touching that collar?

Marlis told him, "Rolin, whatever you do, *look ye not into its hood!*" However, he was already roaming the rich, green hills of a wooded starglass world where he was the new king.

"Rolin!"

What had he been doing? The lightstaff. He was supposed to shine it somewhere. Oh, to be king of that inviting land in the eyepiece! All at once, two maple leaves flopped over his eyes.

"Gannon's son, can you hear me?"

Rolin pulled the leaves away, but the enticing vision had vanished, leaving him vexed and empty. What in the name of Elgathel was his wife up to? "I couldn't see anything with those leaves in the way," he grumped.

"That's precisely why I put them there! I'm not about to let Felgor's infernal contraption lure you 'to endless death.' Can you think more clearly now, or shall I bring back the leaves?"

"I'm all right," Rolin said shakily. "Just give me some room." Removing the lightstaff from his tunic, he placed it on the ground pointing toward the eyepiece. Then he hastily stepped back, in case the starglass "went off."

However, the staff went off first, stabbing the glass lens with a blinding torrent of molten light. Black smoke billowed from both ends of the tube. As heat waves danced on the sizzling silver casing, the starglass's glaring eyes widened, melted and fused into gaping pockmarks.

Rising into the sky, the gushing smoke gathered into a spinning cyclone that reared menacingly above the ivy-shrouded trees. Lightning flashed and thunder grumbled as a pair of burning red eyes glared balefully through the whirlwind.

Just when the fiery eyes had fastened on Rolin and Marlis, they wavered, dimmed and faded away. The blackness boiling from the starglass slowed to a trickle. When it stopped, the light rod's ray also ceased to shine.

Rolin took a long, shuddering breath and picked up the staff. Then he nudged the starglass with his foot. Rattling as it rolled, the scorched tube moved a few inches and stopped.

"I'm glad we're still in Lucambra and not stranded in Limbo or some other horrid place," Marlis said, brushing herself off. (A pointless habit for an invisible, she realized.)

Rolin coughed from the smoke and dust. "I'm afraid those captives are trapped inside for good now. It looks as if the starglass is too badly damaged to get them out."

All of a sudden, a white mist began pouring from the Eye of Limbo, noiselessly spreading over the path and into the forest. Decayed wood and tangled ivy melted away at its touch, making way for lush green grass to spring up. The fog swirled and thickened, deadening all sight and sound.

"Rolin, are you still here?" cried Marlis. She groped through the milky mist to find his hand. "Oh, look at the starglass!" The tarnished tube was emitting a soft, warm glow, as if the staff light had at last reached the other end. Now a rushing sound filled the silence, like the twittering of birds greeting the dawn. The murmuring grew to a babbling and the babbling rose to a roar. A wild, unbridled joy welled up in the invisibles' hearts.

As the sun broke through the lifting mist, the roar lapsed into a dismayed rumble. Though Rolin saw no one, he sensed a living presence all around him.

Marlis clung to his arm. "Do you hear that? Whatever is making those sounds, it's giving me goosebumps."

"If I'm not mistaken, we've got company," Rolin replied with the ghost of a chuckle. "The starglass just released its captives."

"Then they're invisible, just like us. How marvelous! That means we're not alone any more."

"It also means we're king and queen of more subjects than we know what to do with—and we can't even see them!" As if in response to Rolin's words, a collective moan of fear and dismay arose from the invisible host.

"Am I dead?" some cried.

"I can't see myself!" others lamented.

"What's happened to my children?" wailed the mothers.

"Mother! Father! Where are you?" the children called.

Then all the voices joined in a plaintive cry: "Gaelathane, don't leave us like this. Please save us!"

"Be not afraid. I am here." The King appeared in a burst of light, His voice carrying above the tumult. A hush fell over that great company of unseen souls as Gaelathane gazed sternly at the blackened starglass. "Begone!" He commanded, and the tube burst into flames and burned to ash. With joyful cries, Rolin and Marlis fell at their Master's wounded feet.

CHAPTER 38

FINE ROBES, CLEAN AND WHITE

"King Rolin and Queen Marlis, you must now intercede for your people," Gaelathane told them. "Since you have shared in the sufferings of My sheep, you know best how to pray for them—and for yourselves."

Rolin bowed his head. "Dear Father, we long to be visible again, to see ourselves as You see us and no longer fumble blindly for our loved ones' hands. Robe us in Your holiness, so that we may not be ashamed to be called Your children."

"Mae'r Goeden yn fyw!" said Marlis. "Mae'r Goeden yn fyw!" repeated other invisibles around them. "Mae'r Goeden yn fyw!" roared the multitude. Then Waganupa appeared, its radiance sweetly washing over and through the worshippers.

Gaelathane laughed for joy. "Your petition is granted. With My goodness you shall be clothed!" At these words, a sheer layer of the Tree's shining, transparent bark peeled away from the trunk.

"This is My body, given for you," sighed the Tree. Floating over the invisible host, the gossamer sheet settled earthward.

At the first touch of the crystal canopy, every man, woman, boy, girl and beast sprang into full visibility. Laughter and shrieks of embarrassment rippled through the throng as each beheld himself and his neighbor in the glaring light of truth.

"What a grimy face you've got, my queen," Rolin chortled. "Your hair's an absolute fright, too! I shouldn't wonder if something has been living in it."

Marlis's hand flew to her head, smoothing down her unkempt mop. "You're a fine one to talk, scruffy-beard," she retorted. "You need a shave and a haircut, and that's only the beginning!"

As the Tree's filmy "skin" kept dropping, it draped itself over each visible body as a soft, supple white robe that healed all wounds and smoothed away all flaws. Now the perfect picture of royalty, Rolin and Marlis embraced with tears of joy.

"Glory to Gaelathane in the highest!" thundered His white-clad children. "Glory and praise to the One Tree! Glory to Him Who died and came to life and lives forevermore!" Visible tears fell from visible eyes, watering the earth. Then the crowd surged forward to climb the Tree like ants swarming up a table leg.

In answer to Rolin's questioning look, Gaelathane explained, "My children are returning to their former lives. Unlike other torsils, the Tree transcends *all* time and space. Beyond its boughs, climbers may relive any day that has ever dawned in any world I have ever created—or will create."

"How will they know which branch to take?" asked Marlis.

"I lead each to his proper limb, as I did you and Rolin. The higher one climbs, the more recent the time. At the very top, however, Gaelessa is timeless."

Just then, four familiar faces appeared in the milling crowd. "Oh, hello! We're over here!" Marlis called out with a wave.

Staring at her blankly, the white-robed visibles shrugged and turned away, but Rolin and Marlis blocked their path. "How could you pass us by without a word?" Marlis demanded.

Elena gawked at her. "I'm sorry, but you must have mistaken us—" Her eyes grew round as saucers. "You—you're . . ."

"Indeed I am; it's me, Marlis!"

Now it was Arlan's turn to goggle. "Ye're Marlis? Forgive me, but we thought—that is, we never dreamed—I mean, that ye . . ."

"That you were so . . . so . . . ." Bronwen stammered.

"Pretty!" Evan blurted out for all of them.

252

Marlis laughed merrily. "Thank you! There is no need to apologize, though. How could you have recognized someone you had never seen before? I am sorry for playing such a mean trick on you. Elena, now you know how Rolin and I really look."

"Rolin? This is *Rolin?*" they all gasped. Rolin grinned at them.

"Now that you're visible, what should we call you?" asked Bronwen bashfully. "His and her Highness?"

Marlis smiled. "Oh, no, just Rolin and Marlis. We haven't changed a bit—at least not on the inside, where it counts."

"Then why are we wearin' these, uh, dresses?" Arlan mumbled.

"You are robed in My righteousness," Gaelathane broke in. Amazed, the Thalmosians fell on their knees before Him.

"Rise, Arlan the Lionhearted, Elena the Fearless, Bronwen the Bold and Evan the Wise! You have remained true to Me through your many trials, though your faith has been sorely tested. When all torsil worlds are no more, the kindness you have shown My two servants here will still be remembered in Gaelessa."

Gesturing toward the Tree, Gaelathane continued, "Though My Lucambrian children are free, I have yet to restore Thalmos. In order to cleanse that land, I must ask you all to return to the place where the evils first began. Will you go?"

"We will!" the six chorused.

"Then do you recall, Rolin, My saying that your 'hour of sacrifice has passed, is now and is yet to come'?"

Rolin thought back to that night in the cave when the visibles had given Gaelathane their most precious possessions. Only Rolin had been spared some personal sacrifice—for a season. What could the King possibly want of him now?

"The staff," said Gaelathane softly. "Will you trust Me with it?"

Recalling his former words to Arlan, "You can't give the King anything without receiving much more in return," Rolin handed over the rod. Marlis hugged him, admiration shining in her eyes.

Gaelathane warmly smiled His thanks. Then He squeezed and molded the staff in His hands. Light streamed between His fingers like juice squirting from a cider press. When He was done, a perfectly round ball sat on His palm, shining with Gaelessa's splendor. He gave the reshaped rod back to Rolin.

"What is it?" everyone asked.

"It is what it is," Gaelathane replied. "I have merely changed its form, the better to suit My purposes."

"What should I do with it now?" asked Rolin. In its new form, his staff was gloriously useless, either as a stave or as a weapon.

"You shall have need of it where I am sending you." With that, Gaelathane escorted the six companions to the Tree, where He lifted His hands to bless them. "Do not fear; I shall never leave you or forsake you. Wherever you may go, I am already preparing the way before you. Trust in Me, and remember these words:

> The first you meet upon the road
> Will test your faith in Me;
> He'll have with him a heavy load,
> To blind all those who see.
>
> Four words will put the bird to flight,
> Whence other five have flown;
> To spread a plague and bitter blight,
> Where never seed was sown.
>
> Do not delay until they sprout,
> For then they shall abide;
> Ere searching eyes can put to rout
> Their pestilence and pride.
>
> Return to where the scourge began;
> Do battle in the square;
> The blazing ball will purge the land
> According to your prayer.

"Why must You always speak to us in riddles?" Rolin asked.

Gaelathane's eyes glowed like fiery coals. "The day shall come when I will speak to you plainly. For now, I cloak My plans in obscure rhymes to confound My enemies. As for you, Rolin son of

Gannon, one world is enough for any king to govern!" Rolin blushed, remembering his secret wish to rule the starglass land.

While the Thalmosians climbed into the Tree, Gaelathane told Marlis and Rolin, "As Felgor left you with a curse, so I shall leave you with a blessing: 'As *I* am, so you also shall be.' Some day, all My children shall inherit immortal bodies."

"May that day come soon," murmured Marlis.

"My words shall come to pass much sooner than you imagine," said the King. "That is why you must trust Me, even when it appears your plans have gone awry. *Your times are in My hands.* Now up you go!" When Rolin and Marlis looked down from the Tree a moment later, Gaelathane had vanished.

CHAPTER 39

THE PEDDLER FLIES THE COOP

This is *Thalmos?*" grunted Arlan. "I don't see no snarks." Garbed again in their own shabby clothes, the travelers stood between the Tree and a broad, rutted byway. Abruptly, Waganupa faded from sight, leaving the sun to swim undimmed in a sea-blue sky.

"That's because we're in Thalmos past," said Rolin, having recognized the Foamwater swirling by the river road. He was on familiar ground again—and visible.

Several hundred yards away, a puff of dust smudged the roadway. Recalling Gaelathane's warning, "The first you meet upon the road will test your faith in Me," Rolin packed off the women and children behind some bushes. Then he and Arlan settled down on a cottonwood log to await their fellow traveler.

Presently, a battered caravan pulled by two forlorn-looking donkeys hove into view. Nodding over the reins was a balding, wizened little man, half-asleep with the warm sun and the cart's gentle swaying. As the donkeys came abreast, Rolin jumped up and seized their harnesses.

"Shove off, ye scurvy vagabond!" sputtered the indignant driver, now fully awake. He swallowed convulsively, the prominent bones in his long vulture's neck bobbing up and down. "If ye're aimin' to rob me, I'm just an old peddler with hardly a farthing to me name. Now git on wi' ye!"

"We mean you no harm, good sir," said Rolin. "We only wish to know, uh, how far it is to the next town." As the peddler's weather-beaten face suspiciously peered down at him, Rolin was keenly aware of his visibility.

The dark-eyed driver jabbed a thumb behind him. "There's a town not five miles that-a-way. The fall market just finished to-day." He lifted his reins again, but Rolin still held the harnesses fast. Arlan shot his friend a baffled look, as if to say, "He's just a harmless old man. Why don't you let him go?"

"I *told* ye, I haven't got any money!" the peddler said sharply. "Leave me be, ruffians!"

"We will, as soon as you tell us what's in your wagon," said Rolin, stalling. Surely this pathetic old peddler had nothing to do with the future troubles of Thalmos and Lucambra!

The peddler's pinched face relaxed. "Ain't nothin' back there but me wares and a crust of bread for me supper."

"What kind of wares?"

"*Starglasses*, I call 'em. Ye can have one for ten gilders, and it's a fair price at that. Make up yer mind now; what'll it be? Will ye buy, or will I be done wi' ye?"

The old man's words and his hypnotic, singsong voice jogged Rolin's memory. "You!" he cried. "You're the starglass peddler!"

The driver's eyes narrowed. "Aye—what of it?"

Throwing back his cloak hood, Rolin held up the shining staff-ball. "I am Rolin, king of Lucambra. Your accursed starglasses will enslave my people no more!"

Seeing the sphere, the peddler shrieked and covered his eyes. Then he lashed the reins in a desperate attempt at escape. Since Rolin still gripped the donkeys' bridles, the driver dropped the reins and threw up his clawlike hands. "A king?" he quavered. "Have pity on a poor old wretch, my lord; I meant no harm!"

Rolin wavered. Could the starglass peddler have been duped into selling his alluring wares? He was about to release the bridles when he caught a crafty gleam in the old man's eyes. "Give it to me!" he sternly demanded, snapping his fingers.

The whining peddler groveled on his seat. "Don't hurt me, kind sir. I've nought but a few starglasses, and ye can have those for free if ye'll let me go. I don't know what else ye could want."

"You know quite well what I want, you old thief. The Eye of Limbo! Hand it over now, or so help me, I'll tear this caravan apart piece by piece to find it!"

At this, the driver threw back his head and brayed like one of his donkeys. "Ye're too late! *Too late!* The glass is gone, and so are my pets!" Then he chanted:

Five black pearls for five black ravens;
Fly them to their hidden havens!
There to swell in sunny regions,
Opening gates to Gundul's legions.

"Ye'll never find them now!" he cried and flung himself backward through a small door behind the seat. Rolin plunged through the opening after him. Inside, the windowless stall was darker than Limbo. Stumbling over starglasses and bumping into shelves, Rolin found his way into a gloomy chamber that was dimly lit by an open ceiling hatch. Five wooden pegs jutted from the back wall. There was no sign of the peddler.

After pulling himself through the trap door onto the roof, Rolin called down to Arlan, "Did you see which way he went?"

The Thalmosian gave him a vacant look. "Who, the peddler? Nothin' came out o' that wagon except a ratty old buzzard."

A *buzzard?* What would the peddler want with one of those foul birds? Rolin jumped down to check beneath the cart. Still nothing. Searching inside again, he found no trace of the driver or of his silver starglass. Then he remembered Gaelathane's parting rhyme: "Four words will put the bird to flight . . ."

So that was it. Rolin's four words—"the Eye of Limbo"—had spooked the peddler. Realizing the game was up, he'd made good his getaway by changing into a carrion bird—a sorcerer's trick, no doubt. With a disappointed sigh, Rolin slumped down beside Arlan and stared morosely at the scrawny donkeys.

Marlis came running up with Arlan's family. "What happened? Where's the caravan driver?" she asked breathlessly.

"Flew away," was Rolin's terse reply.

"Th' weasely varmint made hisself invisible?" Arlan asked.

"Not invisible, but something just as clever. He gave us the slip by turning into a bird and flying off."

Arlan slapped his knee. "Ye don't say! If that don't beat all."

"Now let's make sure the old scoundrel doesn't come back to roost," said Rolin. After unhitching the donkeys, he and Arlan rolled the cart to the roadside.

"What are you doing?" asked Bronwen and Evan.

"This," Rolin grated. Putting his shoulder to the yoke, he pushed the caravan off the road. With a clitter and a clatter, the cart drunkenly careened down the steep embankment, strewing shattered starglasses in its wake. One wobbling wheel flew off before the stall tumbled end-over-end into the river.

"Why did you do that?" cried Elena, flailing her arms at Rolin. "It would have made us such a splendid little travel carriage!"

"I wouldn't have ridden anywhere in that infernal cart for all the gold in Thalmos!" Rolin growled. "The peddler's wares were— would have been—our people's downfall. Unfortunately, we just missed the Eye of Limbo by a few hours."

"Do you mean it's been sold already?" Marlis gasped.

"I'm afraid so. Or perhaps I should say it was *traded*." Rolin picked up five smooth river rocks. "Some years back, Arvin son of Gaflin found five black pearls under the dragon's mountain. This morning at the market, he bartered them for the Eye of Limbo. The peddler even made up a ditty about them: 'Five black pearls for five black ravens; fly them to their hidden havens. There to swell in sunny regions, opening gates to Gundul's legions.'"

Elena frowned. "Real pearls wouldn't 'swell,' would they?"

"Probably not," Rolin agreed. "However, what else could they be, and how could they open 'gates to Gundul's legions'?"

"What did they look like?" Bronwen asked.

"As I recall, they were shiny, round and jet black—just like the rarest and most perfect of pearls," Rolin said.

"What looks like a pearl, but isn't?" Marlis mused.

"Marbles?" suggested Evan, holding up one of his own.

"Lumps of coal?" Bronwen offered.

Marlis clapped her hands. "I have it! Ashtags, er, *snarks!*"

Elena gave her a bewildered frown. "Snarks don't look anything like pearls, at least not where we come from."

"No, but their seeds do," Marlis reminded her. "They're a shiny black when dried, and about the same size as pearls."

"She's right!" Arlan exclaimed. "Don't ye remember th' seeds them snarks shot at us when we was coming home from Peton?"

"What would ravens want with snark seeds?" Elena asked. "They're too hard and nasty-smelling to eat."

Rolin knees went weak. "Those seeds weren't meant for raven food; the *ravens* were for the *seeds!* Before I 'put the bird to flight' just now, the ravens—the 'other five'—had 'flown' while the stall was still in Beechtown! Each bird must have carried a single seed to spread a 'plague and bitter blight where never seed was sown.' Gaelathane meant the ravens will sow snark seeds where they have never grown, and we're too late to stop them!"

Marlis's mouth dropped open. "So a grennock *was* responsible for bringing the first snarks to Thalmos! How dreadful!"

The visibles stared at her. "You know the grennocks?" They glanced nervously about, as if expecting fanged and clawed creatures to emerge slavering from the forest.

"We—*we're* the grennocks!" Marlis sobbed, burying her face in her hands. "We're to blame for all that ruin in Thalmos future."

Rolin wrapped a comforting arm around her. "You can't blame yourself for Arvin's actions," he said. Then he told the visibles of the connection between "Greencloaks" and "grennocks."

Elena marched up to Marlis and smothered her in a crushing embrace. "Just you never mind about that, m' dear," she said. "Arvin didn't know what his 'black pearls' would do. Anyway, Gaelathane sent you to put matters right—and so you shall."

"It don't matter how them seeds got here," Arlan agreed. "What we got to figger out is how to undo what's bin done."

Rolin arranged his five stones in a circle on the road. "I don't see any way of stamping out those snarks before they spread," he said. "The peddler must have trained his ravens to fly the seeds to some remote 'hidden havens' far beyond our reach. Even if we split up, I doubt we'd ever find and destroy all five."

Marlis sniffled, "After those seeds sprout, the snarks will act as 'gates to Gundul's legions,' letting in all sorts of nasty creatures."

"Like the worggles and the grakkles," Bronwen said.

"I'll find 'em," piped up Evan. "I've got good eyes!"

Rolin tousled the boy's hair. "I'm sure you do. However, I'm afraid the peddler's pets have flown the coop, and we can't bring them back. If only we had some sorcs to help us!"

Marlis brightened. "Who says we have to bring them back? Gaelathane said nothing about finding the ravens or the seeds." Then she repeated the final two stanzas of Gaelathane's riddle:

> Do not delay until they sprout,
> For then they shall abide;
> Ere searching eyes can put to rout
> Their pestilence and pride.
>
> Return to where the scourge began;
> Do battle in the square;
> The blazing ball will purge the land
> According to your prayer.

"It is clear we must 'return to where the scourge began'—to the Beechtown square," she went on. "Also, we mustn't 'delay,' lest the seeds sprout. That's how I see it, anyway."

"What will we do once we get to the square?" asked Elena.

Arlan shrugged. "I reckon we'll 'do battle.'"

Rolin glanced at Marlis. Her wide eyes mirrored his own fear: How were they to prepare for battle with an unknown enemy?

CHAPTER 40

THE BALL WITHIN THE BALL

Seating Marlis on one of the peddler's patient donkeys and Elena on the other, Rolin led the way toward Beechtown. When the children stopped to pick some late-blooming asters by the roadside, Marlis chatted with a family of song sparrows, who cheerily trilled, "Fall is here and winter's on the way! We must be finding food; there's no time to play!"

Chipmunks and squirrels also appeared, scolding the weary travelers from overhanging limbs: "Two-legs! Long-legs! Can't run on their front legs!" Once, a red fox darted in front of the donkeys, yelping, "Bless my tail, a two-legs on a four-legs! The missus will never believe *this!*"

When the sun had climbed higher in the sky, the hungry hikers stopped to picnic by the river among some cottonwoods. Afterwards, while the donkeys grazed on sweet river grass, Rolin, Marlis, Elena and the children went wading in the Foamwater.

However, nothing could convince Arlan to join them. "Ye never know when an eelomar will come out of his hole," he said, and that was that. Even when the waders returned to shore with all their toes intact, Arlan still refused to set foot in the river.

After another hour on the road, the six came in sight of the Beechtown bridge. "This 'un looks just like Peton's, only it goes all th' way across!" Arlan exclaimed.

Rolin grinned. "You still don't know where you are, do you? This *is* Peton, four hundred and fifty years before your time. 'Peton' is actually 'Beechtown'!"

Arlan turned a shade paler and sagged against the bridge's parapet, only to recoil as if bitten. "Watch out!" he shouted at some men on a passing barge. "Git out o' the water!"

Mystified, the bargemen stared at him. Then they shook their fists and jeered at him in their boisterous river jargon.

When Rolin tried to pull his friend away from the side, the Thalmosian fought back, crying, "Leave me alone! Them men— they've got to git out o' the water before—"

"Before what?" said Rolin. "We have no eelomars here, or grakkles or worggles, either. Our rivers are perfectly safe for boating and swimming. You're visiting a different 'Peton' now."

As Rolin's words sank in, Arlan's face went slack and he sheepishly slunk back to Elena's side, muttering, "Ain't no sech thing as a 'safe river.'" He continued staring down at the brown, swirling waters while Marlis described the Battle of Beechtown.

Hoping to avoid meeting himself in the square, where he was helping his father sell potatoes and honey that afternoon, Rolin took Marlis and the visibles on a tour of Beechtown's narrow cobblestone streets and quaint brick houses. Accustomed as they were to the seasonal ebb and flow of outlandish visitors, the good townspeople hardly gave the strangers a second glance.

Their last stop was the village square, empty of booths and stalls now that the market had ended. Rolin pointed out the peddler's customary post, a patch of broken cobbles and hardpacked dirt. There was no sign of ravens, black or otherwise.

"So this is where it all started," murmured Elena. She and the children scoured the cobbles for snark seeds the ravens might have dropped. They found none.

Meanwhile, poised on a steep side street some sixty yards away, a wagon piled high with potatoes lurched and rumbled toward the square. As the cart gathered speed, heads popped out of windows and raised the alarm, "Runaway wagon!"

Just in time, Rolin spotted the peril bearing down on them. "Look out!" he cried. Pushing Marlis and the visibles out of harm's way, he leapt clear himself at the last second. The cart clattered by with only inches to spare and plowed into a bakery across the square. The donkeys scattered.

As everyone stood gaping at the wreckage, a rumpled man clad in a farmer's leather jerkin and breeches ran up, clutching an armload of potatoes. "The name's Jenkins," he said, doffing his cap. "That was my wagon. Are you folks all right?"

When Rolin assured him they were, he babbled, "I don't understand how this could have happened. I *know* I left bricks under all four wheels! Dear me, someone could have been hurt. I don't even want to think about it. First, my mule gets sick. By the time I can borrow another, I've missed the market altogether. Now no one will buy my spuds, bruised as they are." Still apologizing, Farmer Jenkins scurried around the square, collecting his battered potatoes with Bronwen and Evan's help.

While Marlis, Arlan and Elena rounded up the donkeys, Rolin and ten gilders talked the farmer into delivering some of his salvaged tubers to Gannon for spring planting. The wagon smashup also proved to be a windfall in disguise for the baker; for weeks afterward, his shop turned out dozens of potato rolls!

Later, Rolin strolled up the street to the spot where the cart had broken loose. There he found four bricks lined up neatly by the curb. Had someone intentionally moved them, and if so, why? Surely no one in Beechtown bore him or his companions any ill will. Mulling over this mystery, he returned to the square.

By then, evening's shadows were creeping across the cobbles. Mongrel dogs roamed about, sniffing out castoff morsels of food. Marlis and the visibles huddled around a hearth used by merchants to cook their meals. The dying fire's sullen coals afforded scant relief from the cool winds whipping across the square. Ominous black clouds boiled over the Tartellans.

All eyes turned toward Rolin as he approached, jolting him after his weeks of ghostlike invisibility. "What now?" Arlan asked, chewing on a crusty roll that had escaped the Great Bakery Disaster. A dog hungrily licked up the crumbs.

In answer, Rolin scratched out some words in bold, black letters on the stones, using a piece of charcoal from the fire:

Elwyn's Riddle—
. . . Yet empty now it must remain
—though soon to be the black trees' bane—
When locked, it swiftly will arise . . .

The Gold Chest—
. . . For me to doom each viper's den,
You must return to where and when;
And set me on the selfsame site,
Where five black ravens once took flight . . .

. . . But now I wait with empty womb,
For Him to fill this golden room;
The ball within the ball will nest;
When once I'm closed, He'll do the rest.

Gaelathane's Latest Revelation—
Do not delay until they sprout,
For then they shall abide;
Ere searching eyes can put to rout
Their pestilence and pride.

Return to where the scourge began;
Do battle in the square;
The blazing ball will purge the land
According to your prayer.

"These are the remaining unfulfilled verses of Gaelathane's riddles," he explained. "Any suggestions?"

"I'm hungry enough to 'do battle' with that cur over there for its bone," said Elena. She tossed a rock at the dog.

Bronwen wrapped her thin arms around herself and whimpered, "I'm freezing!" Evan was too busy batting a stone with a stick to feel the chill air.

Marlis reminded Rolin, "It's getting dark, and without your staff, we won't have any light. Since we can't spend the night in the square, maybe we should find an empty barge or boat."

"We still have the ball, and my father has extra beds," Rolin said. Unfolding Marlis's cloak, he released the crystal sphere's blinding radiance into the waning light of eventide. "This makes a fine lantern, but otherwise, I can't see any purpose for it."

Elena glanced from the staff-ball to the golden chest sitting in her lap. Then she opened the lid and all the color drained from her face. "I know what it's for," she murmured and looked at Rolin. "May I?" Rolin handed her the ball, which she dropped into the chest's hollow lower half. *Kerplunk.*

"It fits!" crowed Evan and Bronwen.

"As snug as a nut in the shell," Arlan marveled.

As Elena shut the domed top, she chanted, "'But now I wait with empty womb, for Him to fill this golden room; the ball within the ball will nest; when once I'm closed, He'll do the rest.'"

For the first time since Garth the River-Rover had fashioned it, the jewel-studded sphere sprang to life. The rubies glowed with red fire, while the diamond flared in many-faceted splendor. The Keeper and his family held their breath. The chest stayed put.

"What's wrong? Why won't it work?" cried Elena. "We've closed the lid, just as the riddle says. What more can we do?"

Rolin tapped the chest. "Maybe something's missing, Elena."

"'When locked, it swiftly will arise,'" quoted Marlis. Arlan was inserting the key in the lock when the chest flew from his grasp and stopped in midair, wobbling ever so slightly.

Evan clapped his hands. "It's flying! It's flying!"

"Not for long," sneered a voice from the chest.

Elena took a step backward. "It can *talk*?"

Rolin knew better. Grabbing the golden ball with both hands, he tugged against an unseen force. "Felgor!" he roared. "I command you in the name of Gaelathane and the One Tree—begone!"

"And if I don't leave?" the voice mocked.

"I'll—" Suddenly, the tug-of-war ceased and Rolin wrested the chest from Felgor's clutches. A grinning Arlan had pinned the sorcerer's invisible arms to his sides.

"Let me go! Let me go!" cried Felgor, struggling to free himself.

"So—it *was* you who tried to run us over with that wagon!" Rolin growled. "I should have known."

"It would have been a fitting end after you destroyed the starglass wagon," Felgor spat. "How did you know it was I?"

"Who else would want to kill us? Besides, if you hadn't noticed, invisible sorcerers are rare in Beechtown."

"You already knew I was invisible? How?"

"Simple," Rolin said. "I was at the Hallowfast when your starglass sucked up poor Ansel like a harmless fly—and all Lucambra with him. I barely escaped with my own life."

"You were there? Impossible! I was alone."

"You and Fangle only *thought* you were alone."

Felgor stopped struggling. "You were invisible, too?"

"Of course. Wasn't that your plan in destroying Thickbark?"

"Yes, but how did you become visible again?"

"Gaelathane restored Marlis and me to visibility, along with all the captives in your starglass, which He unmade, by the way."

Felgor let out a piercing shriek. "You're lying! *Lying!* Nothing in this world or any other can destroy the Eye of Limbo."

Rolin shrugged. "Whether you believe me or not, it's true."

"Even if you did unmake my starglass *therren*, you cannot touch it *herren!*" Felgor blustered. "I can still claim souls for Limbo in the present. Today is all that matters!"

"Quite right, and today you've met your match in the King," Rolin informed him. "Your invisibility can't save you now."

"Nor can your visibility save you! Even if you knew how to use your precious chest, it's too late to find my black pearls. Thalmos will be mine, in time. I've won!"

"We'll see about that," said Rolin grimly. "If I could, I'd send you straight back to Limbo, where you belong."

Felgor sniggered. "I'd still escape the way I did the first time!"

"How is that?"

"Through my starglass, of course. When you exiled me to *nerren*, I found a hole in the vortex leading out through the Eye of Limbo and emerged here smack in the middle of one of your disgusting market days—completely invisible. Send me back, and I'll return to haunt you. You'll never know *wherren* I'll be!"

Lightning glinted off a knife in Arlan's fist. With Felgor still clamped in a burly arm, the Thalmosian slashed one finger across his throat. Then he raised his eyebrows questioningly at Rolin.

"No, Arlan, let's do this Gaelathane's way, without bloodshed."

"Oho, still ordering Thalmosians about, I see," Felgor taunted. "Don't you potato-eating simpletons realize that this traitor and his wife are *grennocks*? Before you know it, they'll make you their slaves. Then where will you be? If I were you, I would—"

Felgor's sentence ended in a gurgle as Arlan wrapped his beefy hands around the sorcerer's invisible neck. "We do know who they are—and who ye are, liar," he growled. "I oughter wring yer scrawny gullet like a chicken's!"

"That's enough," Rolin said. "We'll not stoop to taking our own revenge. Let Gaelathane do with the fiend as He sees fit. Besides, Felgor's invisibility is punishment enough as it is."

After recovering his breath, the sorcerer tried a different tack. "Let me go. I won't harm you. I only want to leave here alive!"

"Leave alive?" Rolin said. "You're safe with us. I've no intention of killing you. Depart now if you wish and never return. However, you must leave the golden orb in our keeping."

"Fool! You do not know its power. If you lock that chest, it will be the end of Thalmos and us, too! You must believe me."

Rolin laughed. "In that case, we shall all perish together." He firmly twisted the key in the lock. *Click.*

"Nooooo!" With a cruel kick at his captor's shins and an inhuman burst of strength, Felgor broke free of Arlan's grasp.

Before Rolin could react, the locked chest was torn from his hands and flew through the air across the square. All at once, it paused, its diamond pulsing with an unearthly radiance.

"Stop! Come back!" cried Felgor. Hovering weightlessly about four feet off the ground, the glowing golden sphere swiftly glided back to the torsil travelers, coming to a stop in front of Arlan.

"It knows its Keeper," Rolin wryly observed.

"Look, it's upside down!" cried Evan. Sure enough, the enormous diamond now pointed straight down, still spouting a brilliant stream of liquid light. Though duller than the diamond, the five rubies surrounding it resembled the petals of a purple violet.

"Very pretty—and so very useless!" Felgor sneered.

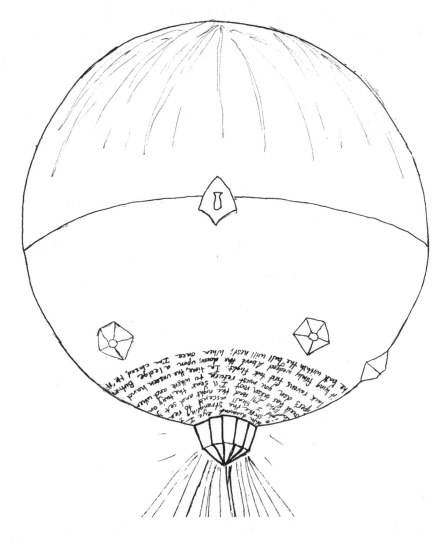

Bronwen touched the floating chest, which spun this way and that as if seeking something with its ruby eyes. "Maybe this is all the higher it goes," she remarked.

"Didn't Gaelathane say, 'The blazing ball will purge the land, according to your prayer,' or something like that?" said Elena.

Marlis's head bobbed. "Of course; we haven't prayed yet!"

"Shall we?" said Rolin, and they all joined hands around the floating sphere. "King of all torsil worlds," he began, "we have fulfilled Your commands, but now we know not what to do. Our enemy mocks us, saying we are too late to save Thalmos. Perhaps he is right. Since we don't know the purpose of the golden ball, we ask You to direct it however You will. Purge this land of the snarks according to Your promise, that Thalmosians in every age may glorify and worship the name of Gaelathane. The Tree lives!"

"The Tree lives!" echoed the others.

"The Tree lives!" Felgor mimicked. "What rot! Admit it: Your gold ball is just a shiny bauble that doesn't do anything at all."

"Look—it's stopped spinning!" cried Evan.

The chest had come to rest with a ruby pointing in Felgor's general direction. Quick as a blink, a blood-red ray spurted from the gem, illumining a man's shrunken form. In that crimson instant, Felgor was exposed for the hateful, helpless wretch he really was. Pierced through and through with the ruby light, the scarecrow figure dissolved into a gray mist that drifted away.

Even as that beam died out, the diamond light intensified, blistering the cobblestones beneath it. Soundlessly, the ball shot into the heavens. The six torsil travelers watched dumbstruck as a new star rose into the unutterable blackness. Then it paused. *Blink . . . blink . . . . . blink*, the red jewels flashed as the revolving sphere slowly came to a stop. The diamond light dimmed.

"It's going to fall on us!" screamed Bronwen.

"No—wait," Rolin cautioned. Then five dazzling scarlet rays lanced out, each striking a different spot in Thalmos: A stinking swamp; a high mountain gorge; the shore of a remote lake; the corner of a fallow corn field and a parched patch of uninhabited desert. Five puffs of coal-black smoke curled above the earth. Then the red shafts winked out and the brilliant orb blossomed like an exploding star before blazing across the horizon.

Heartbeats later, Bronwen's sweet voice broke the holy hush:

With diamond eye I'll pierce the sky,
To strike the strangling trees on high;
On rays of light I shall ascend,
To realms of wonder without end.

With ruby light I'll rend the night,
And set your fiercest foes to flight;
Where greedy seed has taken root,
I'll sear the twig and scorch the shoot.

Rolin said softly, "I believe our black pearl problem has been solved. Let's go home."

———————— ⚬ ————————

That very night, Arvin son of Gaflin sat in the top of Graylimb the fir, gripping the Eye of Limbo. One minute he had been climbing the Tree, and the next, he was back home with the starglass. He trembled. What should he do with it? There was only one thing to do. Summoning all his strength, he flung the starglass high into the darkness. Long seconds later, he heard it shatter on the rocks below, and his heart soared beyond the star-sequined sky.

CHAPTER 41

OATCAKES AND HONEY

Home. For Rolin, that would always be the humble log house where he had spent his boyhood amidst the buzzing of his father's honeybees and the cinnamon-scented rustling of creekside cottonwoods. Home—the promise of a friendly face, a warm fire, hot food and a soft bed—drew him like bees to clover.

The trek to the cabin proved dark and dangerous. Just as the travelers reached the Beechtown bridge, the storm clouds burst overhead. Rolin cried out as the bridge's petrified yegs snapped and snarled at him as if under Peton's spell, but it was only a trick of the lightning glaring on the wet stones.

Once past the bridge, the stolid donkeys mired down in the muck of the rain-soaked road. Grumbling, their riders dismounted and walked alongside. Slipping and sliding for mile after muddy mile, the six companions finally found the uphill track leading to Gannon's house. The rain lashed down in earnest now, soaking man and beast and turning the trail into a quagmire. The donkeys often lost their footing in the torrents of brown water washing down the path. Then the thunderstorm broke in its full fury.

Forked lightning flayed the sky, casting snaky shadows across the path and charging the air with a sharp tang. Lightning-blasted trees exploded on all sides. Everyone's hair stood on end, while an eerie blue fire crackled among the rocks. Thunder rumbled and tumbled down the valley as if bent on bowling the intruders off the path. The donkeys' eyes grew huge with fright.

Mud-spattered from head to toe, the torsil travelers and their beasts dragged up to the old log cabin. Cold, drenched and dark, the shuttered cottage hunkered down against the deluge, water sluicing off its gutterless shake roof in sheets.

"This way!" cried Rolin. He led the others to the rain-slick porch, where they found Nan the mule munching contentedly on some wisps of lowland hay. To all appearances, little had changed since Rolin's last visit.

"You're baaaack!" Nan brayed, nuzzling her nose against Rolin's neck. "Did you bring me some sugar lumps?"

Rolin laughed and patted her head. "Yes, I'm back, you silly old mule, but I haven't any sugar for you this time. Instead, I brought along a couple of donkeys to keep you out of mischief."

"Then who's to keep my son out of mischief?" boomed a familiar voice from the door. It was Gannon. He embraced Marlis and Rolin but stopped short on seeing the rest of the bedraggled company dripping on his doorstep. "If I might ask," he said, "who are these fine folk you've brought with you?"

Rolin introduced the four Thalmosians, who all bowed in a show of respect that made a great impression on the beekeeper.

"You are welcome in my home," Gannon said with a smile. Turning to Rolin, he asked, "What brings you back so soon to my corner of the woods, and on such a miserable night? I thought you'd left for home this after—" He broke off, staring at Rolin's tear-streaked face. "Is something the matter?"

"I . . . I just thought I'd never see you again," said Rolin huskily. He fiercely hugged his red-bearded father.

Gannon shot him a quizzical look. "Never see me again? You should know better than that; I haven't any plans to move away."

Rolin chuckled. His father's dogged devotion to this rugged tract of mountainside was legendary. Neither fires, floods, bears, batwolves nor even Glenna, his sharp-tongued sister could budge Gannon from his homestead.

"I won't keep you standing out here in your wet clothes," the beekeeper said. "You all look like drowned rats! Come in and wash up. Then you can dry yourselves by the stove and share an early breakfast with me. Rolin and Marlis, I'd love to hear the latest news from Lucambra, if you've got time."

Rolin coughed to keep from laughing. Lucambra's latest news hadn't happened yet. Whether Gannon would believe his and Marlis's tale was another matter.

After a hearty oatcakes-and-honey breakfast followed by long naps all around, Rolin and Marlis settled on the sun-soaked porch with Gannon. Bronwen and Evan were climbing trees, a forbidden pastime in Thalmos future, where climbers often fell prey to grakkles. Finding Cottonwood Creek free of eelomars, Arlan and Elena were cooling their feet in the pool beside the cabin.

While Marlis and Rolin munched on candied beechnuts, Gannon leaned back in his chair and propped his feet on the porch railing. "Tell me, boy, where have you been, and how did you manage to grow such a thick beard in only a few hours?"

Beginning with their ill-fated picnic expedition to the Valley of Wherren and Therren, Rolin and Marlis recounted their recent adventures. They didn't mention becoming invisible, however.

Gannon's eyes bugged out. "You're telling me that torsil trees can move you backward or forward in time?"

"To a specific time and place, and only if you climb a *therren* torsil," Marlis said. "However, the Tree of trees can take you to *any* place and time. That's how we all ended up here."

Gannon fell backward in his chair with a *thump*. After picking himself up, he grunted, "These friends of yours are from four hundred and fifty years in the future?"

"Give or take a few years," Rolin said with a grin.

"How will they get home—or am I to put them up here?"

Rolin scratched his head. Gaelathane hadn't said anything about sending the visibles back to their own time and place. "I'm not sure, but I know they don't belong *herren*."

Gannon's eyes misted over. "What about you two? Are you saying you don't belong here, either? Nan and I would be awfully lonely without you. I'm afraid my bees aren't the best company."

Marlis laughed. "We'll be knocking at your door before you know it—especially if you keep your oatcake griddle hot!"

Just then, Arlan and Elena gave a shout as a white light bathed the cabin. The Tree had appeared across the creek. Gannon gaped and Rolin and Marlis squeezed hands, an "invisible" habit that would remain with them all their days.

Sensing it was time to leave, the visibles scurried over the stream to gather beside the Tree. Rolin, Marlis and Gannon quickly joined them. "Please come with us, Uncle Rolin and Aunt Marlis!" the children begged. "We can't leave without you."

Weeping, the king and queen could only promise they would all meet again in Gaelessa one day, if not in Thalmos future. "Friends in Him are friends forever!" Marlis reminded them. After hugging the children, she shrugged off her cloak and draped it over Elena's shoulders, "to remember me by."

"I won't forget you as long as I live!" cried Elena as she threw her arms around Marlis. The two embraced for a long while, tears streaming down their cheeks.

Arlan tried to return Rolin's knife to him. "Please keep it!" said Rolin, swallowing a lump in his throat. Then Gannon loaded down the Thalmosians with dried apples, oatmeal muffins, goat cheese and honeycomb from his larder.

After more affectionate hugs all around, Rolin instructed Bronwen to plant her amenthil nuts "where the sun is strong and the soil is sweet." Then Arlan the Lionhearted, Elena the Fearless, Bronwen the Bold and Evan the Wise began climbing the Tree into their own time and place.

"Goodbye, dear friends!" cried Rolin and Marlis. "Until we meet again, go with Gaelathane and He will go with you!"

"Goodbye, dear invisibles!" called back the climbers. "May the blessings of field and forest be yours in abundance!"

"May your cave ever be filled with joy and laughter!" Marlis whispered through her tears as the visibles disappeared among

Waganupa's shining branches. Then she wiped her eyes, put on a brave smile and said, "My husband, the Tree is still here. You know what that means, don't you?"

"I do. It's our turn now." Rolin embraced Gannon. "Goodbye, Father. Please take good care of those donkeys for us."

"That I shall," Gannon replied, smiling weakly. "Nan will be glad of the company. Come back when you can stay longer!"

"We will!" promised Marlis. Then Lucambra's king and queen ascended the Tree into a bright but not-so-distant future.

EPILOGUE

Once Rolin and Marlis had resumed their rightful places as Lucambra's rulers, they quietly set a permanent griffin guard over the Valley of Wherren and Therren to prevent further misadventures. With Scanlon, they visited the torsil dell once a year on the anniversary of their picnic. They rarely climbed any of the torsils there.

Graylimb the fir survived a mild case of heart rot to live another hundred and ten years, enjoying the companionship of Arvin's and Sylvie's children and grandchildren. Lightleaf also lived to a ripe old age, never realizing the part he had played in saving Rolin and Marlis—and Lucambra itself.

Arvin lived to see his great-grandchildren and in his later years became renowned as a toymaker. His favorite creation was a long, wooden tube filled with bits of colored glass and glitter, which he called a "stargazer."

Fitted with an eyepiece, Arvin's gazing tubes displayed colorful, starburst patterns when turned or shaken, thanks to a clever arrangement of mirrors. The devices even caught on in Thalmos, where they were known as "kildigigs," a form of "whilfildigig." Future Thalmosians would change the name to "kaleidoscope."

278

For months, Scanlon mourned the loss of the lightstaff he had dropped into Lightleaf's trunk. Then one evening, he arrived home to discover a shining sphere sitting on his bed. "Cast your bread upon the water, and after many days, you shall find it again," Gaelathane had told him, and so it turned out.

Looking into the staff-turned-spasel, Scanlon and Rolin saw a Thalmos future free of snarks and worggles—not to mention eelomars and grakkles. Even better, a bustling, prosperous Beechtown stood where ruined Peton had languished.

On another occasion, the spasel revealed a grown-up Bronwen and Evan talking in a grove of trees—amenthils sprung from the nuts Bronwen had planted. Nearby was a tidy cottage. Though spasels convey only images, Rolin thought he heard the two telling him, "Gaelathane has answered our prayer! We now live 'where all the trees are green, not black; where flowers bloom in lovely meadows and the wild creatures won't try to eat us.'"

The window on Thalmos future revealed no further scenes of the visibles. I'm told, however, that soon after they moved back into their cave, the gold chest turned up beside the stove. Selling the piece for a handsome sum, they were able to live quite comfortably the rest of their lives. Gaelathane had given them abundantly more than they could ask or imagine, as is His nature.

I'm also told that during December's grayest days, when the snow lies thick and heavy upon the frozen earth, future Thalmosians still deck their homes with firs and pines, trimming them with wax tapers and colored strings in memory of Elena's candle and Evan's sling. Red and gold baubles recall the ruby-encrusted golden chest. A silver star is placed atop the evergreen in honor of the one that briefly shone high above Beechtown. (The King often announces His greatest miracles with a star.) Finally, a shimmering wrap of spun glass represents the Tree's gossamer covering that restored visibility to Rolin and Marlis. Many families also exchange presents, leaving them in stockings hanging on the wall as a reminder of the quiver where Arlan found Gaelathane's gift of shining Tree-arrows.

Sadly, the King's gifts of love and forgiveness are still unclaimed in many torsil worlds. One day, perhaps you or I will carry the Name to the inhabitants of some new land. If we should meet on the other side of a torsil tree—or even in Gaelessa itself—I shall be glad to make your acquaintance.

These words are written that you might know Him Who is Torsil of torsils, the Lord of time and eternity, and that believing in His name you may have the life that endures forever. *Mae'r Goeden yn fyw!* The Tree lives!

As Timothy closed the book, a scrap of parchment slipped out and fluttered to the floor. Some words were scribbled on it—apparently a message from the writer.

"Ironwing, please place this manuscript in my yeg-wing satchel and fly it to the torsil dell. Do be careful with it! King Rolin and Queen Marlis are already there, awaiting its arrival. They're having one of their 'anniversary picnics.' (Try to behave like a civilized sorc if they offer you fresh meat, won't you?) After I have brought my report on these matters before Whitewing, I shall join you. May Gaelathane speed your journey. Windsong."

Timothy smiled to himself. Now he knew who had written the manuscript. Some day he would have a go at climbing the time torsil where he had found the satchel, which Ironwing must have accidentally dropped while flying into the torsil dell. Even if there were no reward for returning the papers to their rightful owner, he'd still give anything to ride a real griffin, meet King Rolin and Queen Marlis and learn to talk with the trees.

He slid the book back into its leather case, which he hid beneath his bed. Then he raced out the front door.

Outside, he noticed a vulture perched in a willow tree beside the cottage. The bird had been hanging around ever since Timothy had found the satchel. Could this be the same one he'd seen in the torsil? Ruffling its wings, the bald, soot-black bird glared at him with an insolent eye.

"Shoo! Go away, you nasty thing!" Timothy shouted. When the bird wouldn't budge, he threw a rock at it. The vulture croaked and flew off with many a murderous look backward.

Timothy brushed off his hands and stepped into his father's workshop, where Garth was busily sanding a wagon wheel spoke. Putting on an innocent grin, he said, "Father, about that gold chest you made for the mayor . . ."

Glossary & Pronunciation Guide

a'menthil. Tree of understanding.

An'sel son of Percel. Rolin's great-great-great grandson.

Ar'lan son of William. Thalmosian whom Rolin saves from the strykkies.

Ar'vin son of Gaflin. Purchaser of Felgor's special starglass.

ash'tag. Torsil of Gundul; "black tree."

Bag'lot son of Baldwyn. The brash bully of Beechtown.

batwolf. Creature with body of a wolf, wings and head of a bat.

Beechtown. Nearest town to King Rolin's birthplace.

Bembor son of Brenthor. High chancellor of Lucambra.

Bron'wen daughter of Elena. Arlan and Elena's eldest child.

Brynn'mor Mts. (pr. Brin'-more). Lucambrian coastal range.

cor'acle (pr. kor'-uh-kul). Round wicker boats once used on the Foamwater.

Cottonwood Creek. Stream near Rolin's former home in Thalmos.

Cristoph'ilus (pr. Kris-taw'-fil-us). One of Gaelathane's angelic servants.

eel´omars. River serpents living in Thalmos.

El´gathel. Former king of Lucambra; Rolin's grandfather.

El´wyn son of Rolin. Percel's great-grandfather. (Rolin's only son.)

Ele´na daughter of Selena. Arlan's wife.

Evan son of Arlan. Arlan and Elena's youngest child.

Eye of Limbo. Felgor's special starglass.

Fan´gle. Felgor's invisible dragon.

Fel´gor. Sorcerer (formerly "Finegold").

firflae´gen (pr. fir-flay´-gen). Lucambrian word for fireflies.

Foamwater. Beechtown's river (Thalmos).

Forlorn Fens. Peat bogs occupying Lucambra's northern reaches.

Gael´athane (pr. Gale´-uh-thane). King of the Trees. (In the Lucambrian: *Gêlathên*.)

Gaeles´sa (pr. Gale-ess´-uh). Gaelathane's home. (In the Lucambrian: *Gêlessa*.)

Gaf´lin son of Hargyll. Father of Arvin.

gallump´ing. Worggles' way of walking to avoid strykkie fire.

Gama´lion (pr. Guh-may´-lee-on). An angelic servant.

Gannon son of Hemmett. Rolin's father.

gar´goyle. Grotesque stone carving meant to frighten off yegs.

Garth. Father of Timothy.

gil´der. Thalmosian coin, equivalent to a penny.

Glenna daughter of Girta. Rolin's aunt (Father's sister).

Glym´merin (pr. Glim´-mer-in). River flowing from Luralin.

gorks. Felgor's foot soldiers (pl. also gorku; adj. gorkin).

grak´kles. Featherless winged creatures (larger than yegs).

grak´kling. Baby grakkle.

Graylimb. Arvin's home tree (a fir).

Green Sea. Thalmosian body of water.

Greencloak. Thalmosian name for Lucambrian scout.

Greenleaf. Time torsil between Thalmos and Lucambra.

grif´fling. Young griffin.

Gun´dul. Underworld; a place of darkness and death.

gwe´lies. Percel's name for small angels, meaning "Bed People."

Gwynneth daughter of Marlis. Rolin and Marlis's eldest daughter.

Hal´lowfast. Tower of the Tree (near the Sea of El-Marin).

Hel´mick son of Ronnell. Lucambrian whom Scanlon meets in Thalmos past.

her´ren (pr. hair´-ren). Time torsil term meaning, "here-and-then."

Ironwing. Griffin character (Scanlon's mount).

Janna daughter of Adelka. Rolin's mother (deceased).

Lathred, Tark. Lucambrian scouts sent to capture Scanlon.

Le´pia daughter of Melli´a. Arvin's mother.

Lightleaf. Torsil between Thalmos and Lucambra.

Limbo. Netherworld between torsil worlds.

lisich´ki (pr. lee-seech´-key). Type of goblet-shaped, edible wild mushroom.

Llwcymraeg. The language of Lucambra.

Lucam´bra (pr. Loo-kam´-bruh). "Land of Light." (In the Lucambrian: *Llwcymru*.)

Lur´alin (pr. Lure´-uh-linn). Lucambrians' original (island) home.

Mae'r Goeden yn fyw! Lucambrian phrase meaning, "The Tree lives!"

Mar´lis daughter of Nelda. Scanlon's sister, Rolin's wife and queen of Lucambra.

Meghan daughter of Marlis. Rolin and Marlis's younger daughter.

moonwood. Luminescent wood infected with lunicep mushrooms.

Mosswine. River near Gaflin's home.

Mountains of the Moon. Easternmost and second highest Lucambrian mountain range.

Mt. Golgun´thor. Felgor's mountain. Also known as the dragon's mountain.

Myce´na daughter of Nelda. Scanlon's sister, once carried off by batwolves.

ner´ren. Time torsil term meaning, "nowhere-and-no-when."

Nora. Timothy's mother.

Opio and Gemmio, sons of Nolan. Lucambrian brothers; advisors to King Rolin.

Pe´ton. Ruined town below Arlan and Elena's cave.

People of the Tree. Lucambrians.

Percel son of Pellagor. Solitary old man living in Lucambra future.

pogan´ka (pr. po-gawn´-kuh). Type of poisonous wild mushroom.

Rolin son of Gannon. King of Lucambra.

Scanlon son of Emmer. Rolin's chief deputy and Bembor's grandson.

Sea of El´-marin. Lucambrian sea; location of Isle of Luralin.

Silverquick. Time torsil between Thalmos and Lucambra.

skraal (pr. scrawl). Large, bear-like creature; inhabits snark woods.

snarks. Thalmosian word for ashtags.

sor´cathel. Pavilion at the top of the Hallowfast.

sor´os. Medallion used as symbol of royalty (plural—sorosa).

sorc. Ancient name for griffin (plural—sorcs or sorca).

spas´el (pr. spass´-uhl). Torsil sap ball (plural—spasla).

Spirelight. Rolin and Marlis's Lucambrian sythan-ar.

stryk´kies. Death lilies (found among ashtags).

sy´than-ar (pr. sigh´-thun-ar). Lucambrian word for "life tree."

Sylvie daughter of Le´pia. Arvin's older sister.

tara-torsils. Trees of intra-world passage.

Tartel´lans. Mountains above Beechtown.

Thal´mos (pr. Thall´-mose). Rolin's home world.

ther´ren (pr. there´-ren). Time torsil term meaning, "there-and-then."

Thickbark. Time torsil from Lucambra.

Timothy son of Garth (Thalmos). Finder of manuscript, *Torsils in Time.*

tor´sils. Trees of passage.

torsil dell. Valley where time torsils grow.

Valley of Wher´ren and Ther´ren. Tree name for torsil dell.

Waganu´pa (pr. Wog-un-oop´-a). Tree of Life that once grew on island of Luralin.

wher´ren (pr. where´-ren). Time torsil term meaning, "where-and-when."

whilfil´digig. Thalmosian word for "doodad."

Whitewing. King of the griffins.

Wil´lowahs. Mountains where griffins live.

willy-willy. Type of bird fond of strykkie nectar.

Windsong. Royal scribe and Rolin's personal mount.

worg´gles. Thalmosian name for gorks.

wyl´ligen. Evergreen tree of passage.

yeg. Batwolf (plural—yegs or yeggoroth; adj.—yeggish).